A FOX IN THE FOLD

A FOX IN THE FOLD

Candace Robb

SEVERN HOUSE

First world edition published in Great Britain and the USA in 2022
by Severn House, an imprint of Canongate Books Ltd,
14 High Street, Edinburgh EH1 1TE.

Trade paperback edition first published in Great Britain and the USA in 2023
by Severn House, an imprint of Canongate Books Ltd.

severnhouse.com

British Library Cataloguing-in-Publication Data
A CIP catalogue record for this title is available from the British Library.

ISBN-13: 978-1-78029-137-6 (cased)
ISBN-13: 978-1-4483-0977-1 (trade paper)
ISBN-13: 978-1-4483-0960-3 (e-book)

All Severn House titles are printed on acid-free paper.

Typeset by Palimpsest Boo
Falkirk, Stirlingshire, Scot
Printed and bound in Grea
TJ Books, Padstow, Cornv

For Christie
with immense gratitude

ACKNOWLEDGMENTS

Enormous thanks to my friends Louise Hampson, PhD, and Mary Morse, PhD, for reading with care and thought my belated (as in last minute) delivery of a draft manuscript. Both were facing their own book deadlines yet took the time to check for flow, clarity, and historical accuracy. I am in your debt. Huge thanks to my agent Jennifer Weltz, whose keen eye for character consistency and radar for missed opportunities in the story never fails me. I am so fortunate.

Thanks also to Anne Louise Avery, whose brilliant retelling of the medieval tales of Reynard the Fox (Bodleian Library Publishing 2020) indirectly inspired the title and a character, though the personality of my fox is as Reynard is perceived by his victims, cunning and cruel. Apologies to Old Fox, the character in Anne Louise's wonderful twitter tales – I intend no slander of your kin. (@AnneLouiseAvery)

Many thanks and much admiration to the team at Severn House for taking my manuscripts and turning them into beautiful books.

As ever I am grateful to my husband Charlie for his beautiful maps, and all his loving support. Especially near deadlines it can't be easy sharing a house with me.

Last but never least, my thanks to my readers for falling in love with my unruly characters and welcoming them into your homes.

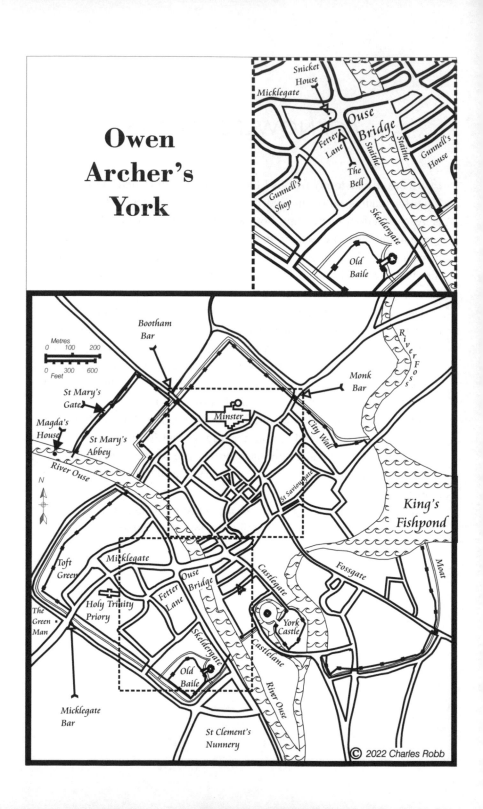

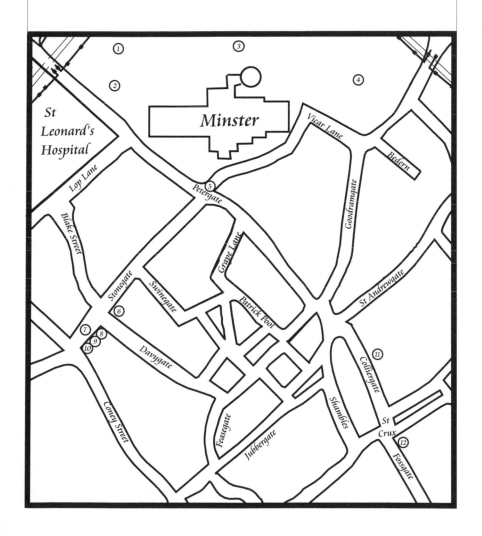

1. Archbishop's Palace
2. Mason's Lodge
3. Palace Chapel
4. Jehannes's House
5. Minster Gate
6. St Helen's Church
7. St Helen's Churchyard
8. Lucie and Owen's House
9. Lucie's Apothecary
10. York Tavern
11. Bolton House
12. Stillington House

St Leonard's Hospital

Minster

Vicar Lane

Bedern

Lop Lane

Petergate

Goodramgate

Blake Street

Grape Lane

St Andrewgate

Stonegate

Swinegate

Patrick Pool

Davygate

Colliergate

Coney Street

Feasegate

Shambles

St Crux

Jubbergate

Fossgate

'. . . *our bad neighbour makes us early stirrers,*
Which is both healthful and good husbandry:
Besides, they are our outward consciences,
And preachers to us all, admonishing
That we should dress us fairly for our end.
Thus may we gather honey from the weed,
And make a moral of the devil himself.'

William Shakespeare, *Henry V* 4:1

ONE

A Son's Temper,
an Unexpected Reunion

York, October 1376

From her seat in the shade of the linden, Lucie Wilton observed the young man bending to his work on the stone wall, golden in the autumn sunlight. The stack already rose several layers above the ditch her husband had dug to outline the foundation of the new garden wall, providing her a clearer sense of how she might shape the garden round the extended building and the new arc of the walkway leading from the gate to the York Tavern yard. The enlarged apothecary would provide much-needed space for her work, but digging up two of the oldest beds of essential herbs had felt a desecration of her first husband's masterwork, an apothecary garden of more variety than might be found even in the wealthiest monasteries. She reminded herself that even before the wall the garden had changed, expanding to more than twice the size it had been in Nicholas's lifetime. Her father had gifted her the house next to the shop, with its own large garden, where she and Owen, her present husband, might raise their family. Even so, she felt a tug of remorse.

Seeking to buoy her mood, she walked along the winding garden path, letting the morning sun warm her, smelling the rich scent of the earth after last night's rain, looking up at the colors of the changing leaves, listening to the bees seeking out the last hardy blossoms, and trying not to spy on her ten-year-old daughter Gwenllian as she flirted with the young laborer.

Gwen watched Rhys tuck the chisel into a fold in the stone, take a deep breath, and, with the care of someone working a delicate carving, tap it with his hammer. A shard flew toward her, just missing her cheek.

'I pray you retreat to a safe distance, my lady,' said Rhys in his soft voice. 'I would never forgive myself if a stray shard marred your beauty.'

She stepped back with a giggle and a blush. Gwen hated how easily the color rose – Rhys would think her such a child. But he was smiling, not laughing. A beautiful smile. If it were not for the long scar on the right side of his face, he might be almost as handsome as her father. Da's was not so disfiguring – he said that was thanks to the salve her mother made him, softening the scar and keeping it from tightening and puckering his face. Rhys's scar lifted the right side of his mouth and lowered the outer corner of his right eye so that he looked as if he were ever wincing in pain. And the line stayed a nasty red. It looked as if someone had slashed him from temple to chin with a sword, though he claimed it was nothing so exciting. She had overheard her father talking to the joiner who had hired Rhys to help with the apothecary addition. Will said by the looks of it Rhys had been injured shortly before he had arrived in York looking for work. Months ago now.

Settling on a bench, near but far enough away so that she would not alarm him, Gwen asked if he would like to hear the story of how her father lost the sight in his left eye.

'I have wondered. He was a soldier, I think?' He moved his hand over a side of the stone, turned it toward him, placed the chisel, and tapped.

'Captain of archers for the Duke of Lancaster.' She cleared her throat and began the tale of her father's terrible injury. How one night, when he was on guard at the tents where the noble prisoners were sleeping, he caught a Breton jongleur whose life he had saved cutting the throats of the French nobles held for high ransom. A woman helping the jongleur came up behind and – as her father turned round – the knife meant for his neck sliced his eye instead.

Rhys had stopped working to listen. 'What happened to the two traitors?'

'Da killed them.' Gwen took a deep breath, pushing aside the image that always arose with the tale, of her father with a hand over his eye, the blood seeping through his fingers.

'The pain. How does a man bear it?' Rhys touched his own wound. 'At least I did not lose my eye.'

'No. But Dame Magda says Da has a third eye. It helps him see things more clearly than others do.'

'Is that like the Sight? Can he see the future?'

'No. It's more like he understands what is happening.'

Nodding, Rhys turned back to his work. He chose a stone from the pile, using both hands to hold it and move it slightly back and forth and side to side, all the while standing with eyes closed. She knew from asking him before that he was weighing the stone, sensing its balance, where it was heavy, and imagining where it would best fit. Now, with a little nod, he opened his eyes and carried it to the wall he was building, setting it not where she had expected, but a few stones away from that.

He'd told her he had always loved stone. When he held one he knew its heart, saw the 'true shape of it.' She liked how he spoke about stone, much like her father about archery, or her mother about how to tend the plants in the garden and how she mixed the physicks in her apothecary. When she'd asked her mother how she knew that is what spoke to her, she had smiled with surprise, asking where Gwen had learned that phrase.

'I heard someone talking about it. So how did you know?'

'As a child I found peace in the gardens at Freythorpe, and at the priory I enjoyed helping in the garden. Dame Doltrice encouraged me to come whenever I had time, kindly saying I was a help, though I doubt it. I interrupted her with questions. When I married Nicholas Wilton I asked him to teach me all he knew. And he did.'

Gwen's father said that all young men learned archery when he was a lad, just as many did now, and he had developed a liking for it. She was glad of that. Had he not been so good he might not have been captain of archers for the old Duke of Lancaster, then come to York when his lord died. If he had not come to York and met her mother, Gwen would have different parents. And she adored her parents. She was proud to be Gwenllian Archer.

'The captain was in a hurry this morning,' said Rhys. 'Was there trouble in the city?' He had paused to drink water.

'No. Dom Jehannes wished to see him. He's the Archdeacon of York. Almost as important as the archbishop. They are good friends, Father and Dom Jehannes. I think he sought Father's counsel.' She felt quite grown up, explaining all that.

'I am glad that is all it was.'

Her turn for a question. 'What were you arguing about with the man in the market the other day?' she asked.

'Arguing?' He frowned, shaking his head.

She knew that look, with the glance away and down. Her father did that when she asked about something he had not wanted her to hear, something he feared would make her uneasy. But it was only fair that Rhys answer her question in turn, so Gwen waited.

He lifted another stone, gently tossing it hand to hand, his eyes moving as he weighed how to answer her question. So he had secrets. Of course he did. All adults did. He gave a little nod.

'I remember. The man standing by the far stall. I thought he meant to cheat me. He looked away as if he thought we were finished, but he'd yet to hand me the coins in change. When I asked him for what he owed me he took it badly. Some folk cannot abide being caught in error. But we parted amiably.'

She had seen no exchange of coins, or goods. To her eyes, Rhys had rushed up to the man and spoken as if he knew him and was surprised to see him there. The man had laughed. Not a nice laugh. And then Rhys had looked worried, but grew angry as the other crossed his arms and smiled. But she let Rhys think she was satisfied. She did not know how he would take more questioning and she liked talking to him. Still, she liked him a little less for it. He had been different since talking to that man. Looking over his shoulder, as if expecting trouble.

Rhys glanced behind her and straightened. 'Jasper.'

Gwen turned round to see whether her brother would look her way. She yearned for his forgiveness, which was unfair because she had done what he had asked – kept his secret. His and Alisoun's. He believed she had told father. How could he think she would betray them? Why would she? It hurt. And his anger hurt even more. Jasper was everything she hoped one day to be, wise in the ways of healing, a true partner with their mother in the apothecary.

But Jasper kept his eyes on Rhys as he said, 'Forgive me for robbing you of your companion, but Gwen has chores to do.'

One of them being to sweep the workroom before Jasper opened the shop, which she had forgotten to do this morning. Giving Rhys a little wave she hurried after Jasper.

*   *   *

Autumn was in the air, a chilly undercurrent in the breeze. Owen welcomed the excuse to step out into it and away from his troubles. But he could not escape them. Captain of archers; spy, steward, and captain of guards for an archbishop; spy for a prince, now a princeling and his dam; captain of the bailiffs of the great city of York – Owen was, or had been, all of these and more, yet nothing in his experience challenged him as much as fatherhood. He stood in awe of all fathers before him, around him, and in times to come.

He had of late tripped over his own best intentions, struggling to make sense of a rift between his son Jasper and his daughter Gwen. The young man – for he was almost twenty now, no longer a boy – had burdened his sister, a child of half his age, to keep a secret, and she had done so; yet because Owen had guessed what was afoot, Jasper wrongly accused his sister of betraying him, punishing her with stony silence. His attempts to convince his son of her innocence were of no avail. It was so unlike Jasper that Owen wondered whether he was expressing anger over something unrelated. He'd always been a perceptive young man with a kind heart. Surely he knew that his sister looked up to him, sought to be like him, and would never betray him.

As a father, Owen could ignore neither his son's stubborn cruelty nor the secret itself. The romance between Jasper and Alisoun had simmered for years; that their attraction had at last been set to boil was no surprise – if that is what had happened. If so, what should he do? Encourage them to plight their troth? Insist upon it? He was not so old he forgot his own sexual encounters at his son's age. But as a father he could not condone Jasper's secretiveness about what had happened in the early morning up in his room above the apothecary, the morning both he and, apparently, Gwen witnessed Alisoun slipping out at the first cock crow. Nor would he tolerate Jasper's refusal to believe his sister's loyalty. She had not told Owen of the incident; he had seen Alisoun from his bedroom window and guessed where she had been. When he had asked his son, he had exploded in anger at his sister. What to do? How could fatherhood be so difficult for a seasoned soldier?

He was crossing Petergate when someone cried out, 'Archer!'

His friend and colleague, Bailiff George Hempe. He gestured for him to join him and kept walking toward the minster gate.

'You are an annoying man,' Hempe wheezed as he caught up.

'You would be wise to show more respect to your captain, bailiff.'

Hempe gave a loud guffaw and slapped Owen on the back. 'But I think you might wish to turn round. Sir Ralph Hastings needs you. He said to come at once.'

Both Owen, as captain of the city bailiffs, and Hempe answered to the mayor, not the sheriff. But as the mayor answered to the sheriff, it was likely he would support the summons. 'I am not aware of any trouble in the city this morning,' Owen said as they crossed into the minster close.

'Might we speak away from other folk?'

Hempe's serious tone caught Owen's attention. He drew his friend over to the side.

'What is it?'

'A body found in a field along the king's road. Not far outside Micklegate Bar, according to the sheriff. He believes the dead man might have been heading to the city.'

'Beyond the gates? We guard the city, not the shire.'

'I posed the same argument, but Sir Ralph insisted. He said that the murderer might have taken his victim's place coming into the city.'

Owen saw the problem. 'Tell Sir Ralph he might expect me in an hour.'

'He was on his way to Micklegate Bar when I left him. He means to be ready to ride out to where they found the body as soon as you join him. He'll be testy if you keep him waiting so long.'

The sheriff presumed much.

Hempe was about to add something when two men passed them, loudly talking of the murder just outside Micklegate Bar. He cocked his head toward them. 'As you heard, folk are already talking.'

Never a good thing. Telling the guard at the gate to send word to Archdeacon Jehannes that he had been delayed, Owen changed direction, heading toward the other side of the city.

A group of men had congregated outside Trinity Priory's great door. The sheriff was dressed to ride out, his tunic, leggings, wool hat, high boots, all costly. A well-muscled man belying his age – he had recently celebrated the marriage of a granddaughter, and the hair curling out from his hat was streaked with white.

'*Benedicite*, Captain Archer. I am glad to see you. Thank you, Hempe.'

'Sir Ralph—' Hempe began, but the sheriff waved him off.

'I depend upon you to find out who has arrived in York the past several days.'

'Let's talk later today,' said Owen.

Hempe nodded as he turned away.

Sir Ralph told the men seeing to the horses to bring Owen the black mount.

'A fine horse,' said Owen as one of them walked it over to him.

'From my stables,' said the sheriff. 'It was the least I could do to make amends for the abrupt summons. I do wish the carter who reported the attack had raised the hue and cry at once. He claims to have come as soon as he was able, but my men tell me the man in the field looks to be several days dead.'

Owen listened as he adjusted the saddle and introduced himself to the horse. 'You have a witness to the killing? That is helpful. But why do you come to me? What has this to do with York?'

'The carter believes the thieves will think they can sell the stolen goods in the city – a cart of fine stone meant for St Clement's Priory.'

Good building stones were always welcome in York, that was true. 'So it is the carter's man who was murdered, and his cart stolen?'

'The cart for certain, and likely the dead man. The coroner advised us to leave the corpse as we found it until you arrived.' Sir Ralph patted his horse. 'Shall we depart?'

'Let us see what we might learn.' Owen led his horse to Micklegate Bar.

Once through the gate they mounted.

'It is not far,' said Sir Ralph. 'And the day is fair.'

They talked of mutual acquaintances as they rode, the sheriff bringing it round to the powerful Percy and Neville families.

'Your name comes up whenever I am in their company, inquiring as to your situation since the death of Prince Edward. It is said that Princess Joan wishes to retain you in service to her son the prince. They are curious about what you might decide.'

Prince Edward had died in June, a death long dreaded not only by his family but by a majority of the baronage. A dread deepened after the fact by the king's increasing debility and the prospect of a boy ascending the throne. Prince Richard was but a year older than Owen's daughter Gwen. Shortly after Prince Edward's death, King Edward had made a point of declaring Prince Richard his heir, insisting that the nobles pay him obeisance as the future king. Yet all worried that Richard's uncles would fight amongst themselves to gain power as regent; his mother worried most of all. Within a few weeks of her husband's death, Princess Joan had sent a messenger to York imploring Owen to continue as he had been, with regular missives regarding the temper in York and the surrounding areas, and any news of the powerful families. He had assured her that he would do what he could, but, as he had told both her and her husband a year earlier, his duties in York prevented him from long trips around the shire gathering information. Much could be learned in the city of York, more from visitors, but beyond that he could do little. She had expressed gratitude for whatever he might manage.

'They might have asked me at any time,' Owen told Sir Ralph. 'I am retained by Prince Richard's household.'

'I am glad to hear it.'

'Why is that?'

'As captain of the city your connection to the royal court benefits York, gives the barons pause about causing trouble – including our new archbishop.'

'Archbishop Neville concerns you?'

'He is a Neville – contentious, ambitious, and impious.'

Owen chuckled. 'You have locked horns with him?'

'He is far too slippery for that. He calls you "the Warlord", did you know? Sometimes "the Pirate".'

That was the first Owen had heard of it, though it did not surprise him. 'In what context has my name arisen?'

'We spoke of order in the city. When I praised you, he scoffed. Said you behaved as if it were your city. Hence "the Warlord".'

'And "the Pirate"?'

Sir Ralph cleared his throat.

'My scarred face.'

'Yes. Forgive me for mentioning it.'

'I am accustomed to it.'

The sheriff grew quiet, gazing round at the fields, up into the trees as they entered a wooded area, his men on the alert for the unwelcome. They were riding out farther than Owen had expected, and a suspicion that had been but a kernel grew into a certainty as Sir Ralph's men turned off the road into a field without hesitation – they knew the area well. The track of a cart was visible in a muddy space beneath a tree; the depth of the ruts suggested a heavy load.

'This is a distance from the city,' Owen said. 'The carter led your men out here?'

'One of my men alerted me of the body in the field.' A subtle shift in Sir Ralph's posture suggested unease.

'What had he been doing out here?'

'I neglected to ask.' Meaning he did not yet wish to say. 'But when the carter came with his tale, I thought of it at once.'

'Did he offer to lead you here?'

'He was unsure whether he could find the place again.'

Yet the sheriff's men had. 'So what did he want of you?'

'To find the cart, his men, and their attackers.'

'How many men in his party?'

'A pair of laborers. He thought both of them missing.'

Owen reined in his horse. 'You had best tell me the rest.'

'There is little else. They had moved off the road for the night. It was already dark when they were set upon by thieves. He believes there were three. His men told him to flee, they would fight them off, then follow on to Clementhorpe. But they never arrived.'

'So he went straight to Clementhorpe? To the priory?'

'No, not to the priory. He was vague about where he found shelter.'

'Most would seek help at the nearest house. Or at least hide in an outbuilding, then return to discover what had happened.'

'So I would have thought, but he did not. Nor did the family there see him or the other missing man, though they were the ones who found the body,' said the sheriff, quickly adding, 'according to my men.'

Owen ignored the oddity in that statement. 'Why is this carter not with us?'

'He said he feared for his life.'

'Your men were not armed?'

'They were.' A shrug. 'Merchants think only of their comforts.'

'Is he a York man?'

'No. From the south. Near Winchester.'

'A carter coming all this way to deliver stones?'

'So he says.'

They rode on across a field, up and over a steep slope, and finally Owen spotted two men pacing round a blanket-covered mound. Clearly country laborers, not a sheriff's armed men.

'So far off the road. How do you know this man was involved in the carter's incident? Might he be a laborer from the area?' Owen turned in his saddle to watch Sir Ralph as he answered.

A hesitation. Sir Ralph began to shape a no, caught himself, and said, 'The family did not recognize the man. And considering the carter's story . . .'

Dismounting, Owen walked round the covered body and lifted a corner of the blanket, stepping back as flies rose from the corpse. From its condition the body had been there at least several days, as Sir Ralph had said. 'Two evenings past we had a drenching rain,' Owen noted. 'More rain last night. Unfortunate.' He crouched at the corpse's head. At first glance it might have been an accident, a man thrown from his horse, scavengers coming along and stripping the body of anything valuable. But the cart had not been brought so far – at least not with the heavy load. He bowed his head and crossed himself.

Sir Ralph handed Owen a kerchief. 'To cover your mouth and nose,' he said.

With thanks, Owen donned it and moved closer. The man lay on his front. An older man, his skin beginning to sag, yet still strong by the look of him. Old scars crisscrossed his back as well as his muscular thighs and calves. Calloused feet, his hands rough, thick-fingered, tanned.

'He was found naked?'

'As you see him.'

Odd.

'Does he look like a carter's man?' Sir Ralph asked.

'Perhaps recently, but his strength and the types of scars make me think once a soldier,' said Owen.

'So he might be one of the attackers.'

'Or an old soldier willing to do the work of a laborer.' Owen crouched closer, gestured to slashes and bruises on the man's limbs, shoulder, blood caked on the visible side of his mouth. 'He died fighting.'

'That supports the carter's story. Are you ready for my men to turn him over?'

Owen nodded, and Sir Ralph ordered his men to roll the body onto the blanket. As he watched he felt a shower of needle pricks over his ruined eye and glanced round to see if it was a portent of danger. But he saw nothing.

Perhaps the clear evidence that this was no accident? The man had been stabbed three times, throat, chest, stomach. Wounds that would have bled a lot. Even the heavy rain would not have completely washed away such a torrent. It seemed likely he had been carried here as he bled to death. Find the cart, find bloodstains, he guessed.

Bald. Long scars puckered his forehead and the right side of his face to the neck. Far worse than the young stone worker, Rhys. Or Owen. Birds had gotten to the eyes. The scars told him little, except that they were old scars, both on his body and his face. The red mark on the right hipbone might be something a wife or mother would recognize.

'I have seen what there is to see,' said Owen. 'He can be removed now. Did anyone follow the cart tracks looking closely for signs of struggle on the ground? There would have been much blood.' They would not find much, not after the hard rains. But perhaps bloodstains beneath a tree.

'Not yet. I thought you might advise them.'

Not at all like previous sheriffs. Sir Ralph seemed engaged, yet aware of his limitations. 'Of course,' said Owen. 'Would you like a few of my men to assist them?'

'As this is outside the city, I would prefer to keep the bailiffs and your men out of it until I speak with the mayor.'

'I understand. Not only outside the city, but on your land.' Owen met the sheriff's startled gaze. 'How else would you have learned of this, so far off the road, so far beyond the cart tracks, so far from York? And the men guarding – why would farm laborers take the time out of their day for you?'

'I am sheriff of the shire,' said Sir Ralph, but he had a sheepish grin as he nodded. 'You have proved to me I requested the right man. I would count it a great favor if you would take charge of finding out what happened. If the mayor agrees, might I count on you? You will be paid.'

'It may be too late to learn much, if anything.'

'I understand. You will agree?'

'If Hornby approves it.' Owen could not predict the decision of the mayor and council. 'But if you like, I will guide your men in the next step.'

'I would be grateful.'

'What is the name of the carter? Where is he?'

'He is lodging next door to you, at the York Tavern. Name's Gerald Trent.'

'The York?' He would have entered the city at Micklegate Bar and found many taverns and inns of varying quality. How had he chosen the York? 'When did he come to you?'

'Late yesterday.'

He recalled a travel-worn man in the tavern the previous evening inquiring about a private room. Bess Merchet, who owned the tavern with her husband Tom, had chuckled to Owen and his companion Crispin Poole that the man balked at the room up two sets of steps, the second set quite narrow and steep. But he had accepted it. Begrudgingly. 'When had you heard from your tenants about the dead man?'

'Early yesterday.'

'So your men had already been out here?'

'Yes. It was a long day for them, sending for the coroner, awaiting him. That is why today I had the farmer's sons watch over the body.'

Sons. Owen walked over to them, introduced himself. One was a few years older than his son Jasper, the other older. They straightened, seemingly surprised to be addressed. He asked whether they had seen anyone in the area a few nights past, or since. They exchanged glances, the older giving a slight nod.

'I thought I heard something the night of the storm. But when I went out the next day all I found was blood. One of the sheep did go missing, so I thought I'd heard a poacher at his work.'

'Can you lead us to where you saw that?'

'I can. It's not far. But there's more. Yesterday there was a man walking through one of our fields. When we called out to him, he ran.'

'What did he look like?'

'Small man. Could not see much, but he was not dressed as a poacher, or someone working the fields nearby.'

It was not far to the place where he had seen the blood, beneath a tree, much closer to the road. Along the cart tracks. It fit. Thanking the young men, Owen let them go back to their work.

'But the corpse,' said Sir Ralph.

'Your men can carry it back to the city,' said Owen. 'Trent can come to the castle to see if it's one of his. I will send two of my own men to search the road.' He took the sheriff's men aside to show them how to fashion a carrier slung from both horses to convey the body to the castle.

As they rode back toward the city, Sir Ralph apologized for summoning him on false pretenses.

'It might yet prove to be of import to the city,' said Owen. 'If Hornby agrees and nothing in the city prevents my working on this, will you pay for my own men to assist?'

'You and whoever you deem necessary for the investigation. That is only fair.' Sir Ralph cleared his throat. 'The way you studied the body – almost as if you thought you might know him.'

'No.' But he had felt the needle pricks.

'One of my men mentioned that you have a young man working with stone in your garden. Didn't recognize him.'

Few secrets in the city, especially when one lived next to a tavern. 'Rhys. He's working on the paths and walls in my garden. Recommended by the builder who is adding onto the apothecary. He'd come to York seeking work, experienced with stonework – walls, foundations. He'd done fine work on the foundation for us, so I offered him the extra task.'

'Where is he lodged?'

'With us. His landlord needed the rooms he had let. He is a good sort. Not your murderer.' He permitted a sharpness in the response.

'Forgive me, Captain. I did not mean – I do not usually listen to my men's prattle. But this sign of violence in my fields . . .'

'I understand.'

They rode on in silence, both lost in their own concerns.

As they neared Clementhorpe, Owen asked if he'd sent someone to St Clement's to alert them to the trouble.

'I did not.'

'It might prove useful to speak with the prioress.'

TWO
Catalyst, and Nemesis

Outside the York city walls on the south bank of the Ouse, St Clement's Priory, a Benedictine convent of modest size, was surrounded by orchards of gnarled apples, pears, medlars, their colors fading, not yet bright with autumn's sun. A place of peace. But Prioress Isobel was anything but peaceful when she stepped into her parlor to greet Owen and the sheriff.

'*Benedicite*, Sir Ralph. Captain Archer. This is a morning for unexpected visitors.'

'We will not keep you, Mother Isobel,' said Sir Ralph. 'We thought you would be made easier knowing that Captain Archer is looking into the theft of your cart of stones.'

'Our cart—' She glanced from the sheriff to Owen. 'I trust you were unaware that His Grace was coming, that had you been you would have thought to warn us. But then why should you think he would appear without warning?'

'I am not sure what you mean. It was a cart of stones,' said the sheriff, 'no more.'

'You say His Grace has come,' said Owen. 'A noble? A royal?'

'You did not know? I speak of the Bishop of Winchester. Here. This morning. Escorting two sisters from Wherwell Abbey.'

'I heard nothing of such a visitation by Bishop Wykeham,' said Sir Ralph.

Nor had Owen. 'His Grace is connected to the stolen cart?'

'He means to take Dame Marian from us. And in exchange give us stones for our orchard wall,' a sniff, 'and his protégée in exchange. She who is deemed inadequate for the grand Wherwell but fine for us, so small, so insignificant.' The last words came out more of a hiss than speech.

'Is the bishop here now?' Owen asked.

'No. He is lodging with Dom Jehannes, the Archdeacon of York.'

Doubtless the reason the archdeacon wished to see him this morning.

'But the sisters will lodge here,' the prioress continued. She glanced at both of them, then belatedly asked, 'Would you care for some refreshment? You look as if you have been riding a while.'

'A cup of wine would be welcome,' said Sir Ralph.

Isobel gestured toward the servant standing near the door, who hurried out.

As they sipped their wine, Sir Ralph explained that the attack had occurred on his property, a man – either one of the carter's men or one of the attackers – died of his injuries, but he did not go into detail, and Mother Isobel did not ask. Her complaint was in the unexpected arrival of the sisters, who must be lodged, and the insulting imbalance of Wykeham's proposed trade – an unwanted subcantrice and a cart of stones in exchange for the most excellent Dame Marian, who had proved an inspiring, knowledgeable, and organized cantrice, transforming the priory's feeble-voiced sisters into a choir that drew worshippers – and their purses – to the chapel on Sundays and feast days.

'A cartload of stones seems a paltry compensation,' said Sir Ralph. 'What does His Grace expect you to do with it?'

'Those coming by cart are from a site not far from here, ornamental, to be used, His Grace suggested, as an archway near the chapel. More are arriving by barge to repair the orchard wall.' Mother Isobel sniffed. 'It seems our confessor has been His Grace's confidant.'

'No doubt he meant well,' said Sir Ralph.

'Or hoped to be invited to Winchester.' The prioress brushed invisible lint from her sleeve.

Owen was more interested in Wykeham's motivation in traveling so far with what the prioress described as a modest retinue – two priests, two servants, the sisters, and their servants. 'He travelled with so few?'

The prioress nodded. 'Garbed as a humble priest. Had I not met him on his previous visit to York years ago I might have – well, one does not know what to say of such behavior. His Grace was quite clear we were to say nothing to anyone about his presence.'

No wonder Owen had felt the familiar needle pricks beneath his eye patch. On his last visitation, Bishop Wykeham had brought death to York. The corpse of a midwife dear to Lucie and many in York was found in the ashes of a fire in the bishop's town house on Petergate. The woman had been murdered. Owen's gut told him that once again Wykeham was the catalyst for death in the city.

God grant the dead man and the theft be the extent of the trouble this time.

As they parted inside Micklegate Bar, Owen asked, 'Do you want to talk to Gerald Trent when I bring him to view the body?'

The sheriff waved away the suggestion. 'I have other matters to attend.'

'Of course.'

'But I am eager for your report. Tomorrow morning? By then I hope to know whether the mayor wishes you to proceed with the inquiry.'

With Wykeham involved, Owen had no doubt this was now his investigation. 'I will come to the castle early on the morrow to tell you all I've discovered. Toward that end I am heading straight for Dom Jehannes's house.'

'Would you wish me to accompany you?'

'It is kind of you to offer, Sir Ralph, but I think it better I speak with His Grace alone. If you would tell my men to search the city for rumors of strangers or sightings of a cart of stones, and bring any news to my home.'

'It is the least I can do. I am grateful, Captain. I do not like the feel of this.'

'Nor do I.'

Brother Michaelo's eyes swept Owen from head to toe. 'Long journey out to see the corpse?'

'Much farther than I expected. It might have been worse. But the sheriff provided good mounts from his stable.' Owen glanced past him. 'Wykeham is here?'

A raised brow. 'When did you learn of his presence?'

'At St Clement's Priory. Sir Ralph and I stopped to warn Mother Isobel of the cart's disappearance. She told me he was lodging here.'

'Ah, the cart of stones that never arrived.' Michaelo nodded. 'The dead man is one of the carter's missing men?'

'Likely. The carter reported the theft. After he spent a night at the York Tavern. But the sheriff already knew of the murder.'

'A murder. Ah. How did Sir Ralph learn of it?'

'He owns the land. Might I come within and speak with His Grace?'

A slow grin. 'If that is your pleasure.'

Owen ignored that. 'Do not go far. If he agrees, I will want you to act as my scribe.'

'Scribe,' Michaelo muttered as he escorted Owen past two priests sitting by the fire and showed him into Jehannes's parlor. 'His Grace should soon be here. Jehannes took him to see the work on the minster. You know his delight in all matters pertaining to building works. Despite the incident some years past.'

Before the fire and the woman's death, a falling roof tile had barely missed the bishop as he inspected the construction of the minster's lady chapel.

'I presume the bishop was in a foul temper when he arrived, and Jehannes sought to sweeten his mood by showing him the progress on the lady chapel?' said Owen.

'Indeed.'

'What does he want?'

'That is not yet clear. As you doubtless know, his travel companions included two sisters from Wherwell Abbey who seek the aid of Mother Isobel in convincing Dame Marian to return to Wherwell. It seems their new abbess is dissatisfied with Wykeham's protégée and he . . . wishes to make amends.' A sniff. 'I find it difficult to believe, but he sounded sincere. Even so, why he came himself, and why he wished to lodge with Jehannes – nothing he said explained that to my satisfaction.' The monk lifted his elegant head as if listening to something outside the door. 'I believe they have returned. I will send Perkin with wine. And stand ready to play scribe.' He bowed out.

With an absurd sense of preparing to meet his doom, Owen settled into one of two chairs arranged near the window of Jehannes's parlor, thanking the manservant who entered with wine, bread, and cheese. Perkin, the new cook. An older man, he seemed familiar, but was gone before Owen could ask whether they might have met before. Relaxing his head against the high back of the chair, he noticed a weariness, of body but also of heart. Jasper and Gwenllian.

Why would his son refuse to believe the younger sister who adored him? A memory arose, his sister Gwen, the trickster of the family, blamed for something that had in truth been an accident. A branch damaged by a storm so recently that the leaves had not yet lost luster. Owen had climbed out just far enough to snap it, tumbling down into the grass and badly spraining a leg. He had blamed her for an hour or two, until his father showed him the uneven break in the branch and the dry edges of the leaves. Shame had kept him from admitting he had been wrong to blame Gwen. But when she apologized to him for not having seen that the branch was dying, he relented. That she would take the responsibility solely because she meant with her jests to provoke laughter, not pain – no, he refused to lay the burden on her and accepted his own culpability. Would Jasper see? Was there any way Owen might help?

He pushed away those thoughts. At least they had cleared the dread. He poured himself some wine and was appreciating the first sip when someone knocked on the door, opening it without waiting for him to respond.

William Wykeham, Bishop of Winchester and sometime Lord Chancellor of England, entered the room.

'Thank you for coming, Captain.'

He settled in the other chair before Owen could rise in deference. He wore a plain wool houpelande and leggings, brown, unadorned but for green embroidery on the sleeves. Never a large man, he was thinner than Owen had seen him in the past. There was a pinched quality to his mouth, the lines around his eyes were more prominent, and what little hair remained was gray. A neat beard followed his jawline, like Owen's. That was new.

'I understand you are now captain of the city,' said Wykeham. 'Did John Thoresby arrange for that before he died?'

'No. The mayor and council approached me.'

'Princess Joan did not oppose the idea?'

'On the contrary, Her Grace approved of it as a way to assure the king's peace in York.'

'Do you feel tugged in two directions?'

A frequent question. 'I do not.'

'Most fortunate. You were occupied earlier today. I understand it was the sheriff, Sir Ralph Hastings, who summoned you. About a murder on the road north to the city.'

Nodding, Owen asked whether Brother Michaelo might join them. 'He works closely with me in both my roles, as secretary and scribe. It would be useful for him to make note of all that we discuss regarding my morning. You will understand why when I begin.'

'The late archbishop's secretary now serves you?'

'Among others.'

'As I recall, he was a fallen monk. A poisoner.'

'Redeemed through service to a good man.'

A thin smile. 'You refer to the late archbishop as a good man now, but I recall the two of you often sparring.'

'One can as easily disagree with a good man as a bad. We came to respect each other. He stood as godfather to my children.'

'I do recall him speaking of that. And this Brother Michaelo. You trust him?'

'Over time he has proved himself trustworthy, yes. I now find him an excellent assistant.'

'He is discreet?'

'Remarkably so.'

Wykeham gestured toward the door. 'Call him.'

Brother Michaelo waited on a bench in the corridor, on his lap the items he would need. As he rose, he nodded toward the kitchen. 'Alfred awaits you when you are finished here. He has news.' With no more ado he swept into Jehannes's parlor, taking a seat near Owen, facing the bishop, and quietly arranged his things on a small table.

Owen launched into an account of the morning's discoveries, and what he had learned about Trent from Sir Ralph.

Wykeham grew increasingly pale as Owen spoke. 'That my gesture should be tarnished by violence.' He pressed his forehead, whispered a short prayer for the dead. 'I am glad you are in charge of the investigation. I know you as a fair man.'

He had not always thought so. Owen wondered what had changed his opinion. 'Might I ask how you come to know Gerald Trent?' Owen asked. 'Does he often serve as your carter?'

'He does. A long while. Years.'

'But he hires his own help?'

'Yes.'

'Forgive me, but I have more questions.'

Wykeham poured himself a cup of wine, sat back, motioning for him to proceed.

'His home is near Winchester?'

'It is.'

'Is it not unusual for a carter to journey so far from his business? Why not find someone closer to York. Or to the quarry?'

'For the ornamental stones from the quarry south of York, I thought the same, and asked him to suggest someone. But he offered to do it himself. Apparently he had a delivery between Winchester and the quarry. He would take the opportunity to explore the possibility of expanding his business to the north. As the larger part of the delivery is coming by barge it was no more convenient to arrange for someone nearer.'

'He has a partner up here?'

'I did not ask. It was enough that he agreed to my schedule.'

'As to that schedule, have the stones arrived as well, the ones coming by barge?'

'Not yet, no. I presume Trent is seeing to it.'

'How did you know of the crumbling wall?'

'Clergy passing through York stopped at St Clement's to view the milk of the Blessed Mother. They mentioned the poor workmanship on the orchard wall near the church, so unworthy a home for the holy relic. I wrote to the priory's confessor and he provided more detail.'

'Why not make a donation for the work?'

'Why indeed?' Wykeham's gaze moved beyond Owen to the window. 'It was all part of my attempt to appease Cecily, Abbess of Wherwell. I wished to speak to Dame Marian myself, and offer a suitable gift to the Prioress of St Clement's. All had gone terribly wrong.'

'Was Dame Marian receptive?' Owen knew her well.

'I cannot tell what is in her mind. But what is clear is that the prioress thought the proposed exchange an insult.'

'Nothing has yet been decided?'

'No. We will speak again.'

'Concerning Trent, have you had any previous trouble with him?'

'I would not patronize him if he were not competent,' the bishop said sharply, more in character with the Wykeham of yore. Then he shook his head. 'No, that is not entirely true. According to my chamberlain there were irregularities. Complaints from the masons that Trent demanded additional funds or delayed delivery.'

'You confronted him about this?'

'I did. He made excuses, a shortage of certain types of stone, too-demanding masons, builders who did not understand the logistics, on and on. I told him we would be watching him. No more incidents. I believe his offer to complete this mission was his attempt to make amends. Much as I was.' He massaged his temples, his expression one of dismay. 'I regret engaging him.'

Yet at first he had declared him competent. 'You will be summoning him before you?'

'I will. Doubtless he will blame it all on his hired men, and beg to lodge here, at the archdeacon's expense. I will not have it.'

Brother Michaelo mumbled something unintelligible as his stylus scratched away on the wax tablets.

'And I trust you will be questioning him?' Wykeham added.

'I plan to do that next,' said Owen. 'It seems he is lodging near my home.'

'An odd coincidence.'

'That was my thought.'

Wykeham sighed. 'You will keep me informed about what you discover?'

'Of course.'

'We must talk further, about this and another, urgent, matter. I will detain you no longer today, but I give you this to read at your leisure.' He slipped a sealed letter from his sleeve, holding it out to Owen. 'I will ask my generous host when it might be convenient to invite you and your wife the apothecary to dine with us.'

'My wife?'

'Many at court speak highly of her, and the letter writer suggested it would facilitate matters were she included in our conversation.'

Mystery of mysteries. Owen accepted the letter with unease.

In the kitchen, Alfred was drinking ale while talking to Perkin. The cook quickly moved away as Owen and Michaelo approached.

'A skittish sort,' Owen said softly, for Michaelo's ears.

'He is.'

Tossing back the rest of his ale and collecting a leather pouch containing something that clattered, Alfred joined Owen and Michaelo. He held out the pouch.

'We found this tucked into a cart filled with stones abandoned on Toft Green. Caught several would-be thieves. They took few stones as each one is an armful. Old Salt was the one who found this. She tried to keep it from our Stephen. A strong old woman, but Stephen always wins.'

One-legged and toothless, Old Salt was one of the poor who begged for alms at St Mary's and slept near the minster. She rarely stole unless the object was worth enough coin to change her life. Owen was most curious what she had hoped to keep from Stephen, his strongest man.

The pouch was heavy for its size. Within were tools rolled up in sheepskin. Owen unrolled enough to discover a fine chisel, clean and sharp. It had a good balance in the hand. 'Old Salt has an eye for value. His Grace might wish to see these.'

By the time Owen had spread the tools out on the table, Michaelo returned with Wykeham. The bishop examined them with interest. He, too, tested the balance, lifting each one, murmuring to himself. Owen caught words such as 'fine lines' and 'delicate curves'. At last Wykeham stepped back, shaking his head.

'Trent had no need for a stone carver's tools. He was delivering material to repair a wall, not for statuary.'

'Can you think of a reason why these would be left in the cart, Your Grace?' Owen asked.

'None. I will be interested to hear how Trent explains this. Who discovered them?'

Owen introduced Alfred. 'My lieutenant.'

'Good work,' said Wykeham, and, with a nod, he withdrew.

'Is Old Salt injured?' asked Michaelo. He had taken it as his mission to attend the poor who lived in the shacks on the south end of the minster.

'She looks frail, but the strength of her grip surprised Stephen,' said Alfred. 'I did notice her rubbing her arm when she hastened away.'

'I will go to her,' said Michaelo. 'She is usually to be found at the alms gate outside the abbey walls at this time.'

'Would she tell you whether the tools were in plain view or she saw someone stash them there?' asked Owen.

'She might.'

'Send word to me if you learn anything. I will be at the York Tavern, and then home.' It had been a long morning.

As Owen and Alfred moved through the minster yard, they paused to show the master mason and some of his men the pack of tools. Much admiration, but no one recognized it.

'Costly,' said the master mason. 'Whoever lost these tools will search for them.'

Of that, Owen had no doubt. As they moved on, he asked Alfred about the condition of the stones.

'Any blood on them? Or the cart?'

'I saw none. The stone is very fine. Much like that here, on the minster.'

A costly gift to the priory.

THREE

Secrets & Riddles

Standing at the garden gate, Alisoun watched Dame Lucie clipping the last of the roses on this crisp autumn morning, her movements graceful, efficient, practiced. How many hours of her life had she devoted to the herb garden, her first husband's masterwork? She stole moments from her busy apothecary to tend it, worrying about it when she had no time to spare. One spring when she left it for weeks, Alisoun and Jasper had scrambled to maintain it, guide the new growth, protect it from a late frost, terrified that they might disappoint her. Alisoun had found it a burden. Jasper had noticed, assuring her that when they wed he would not expect her to share his work in the garden, nor would his mother. If necessary, they could surely hire a gardener. He'd apologized for not thinking of that at the time.

It was one of the many things they had sat up late into the night talking about – on that night visit now causing a rift between Jasper and his sister Gwen. And despite the long conversation, she still had so many questions. Would they wed? She had never been less certain than she was now. She did not question her love for Jasper, but did he love her? And, if he did, was his love strong enough to resist the siren-call of the monastery? Would she always feel she was competing with the memory of Brother Wulfstan, his mentor and comforter, a man whose death had beatified him in Jasper's mind and heart? And what of her own yearnings? What of her apprenticeship with the healer Magda Digby? She had never wanted anything more than this precious time with Dame Magda, not even Jasper – or in a different way. And there was the pull of undertaking a pilgrimage of the heart and soul, as Magda's great-grandson Einar was doing, though not to find her true calling but to fulfill it, going where she was needed.

And there was Einar himself. She had come upon him after escorting her teacher's daughter, Dame Asa, up to the moors, spent several days with him. One night in a shepherds' hut – nothing had prepared her for her body's response to his touch . . . All the other questions about her future with Jasper paled against that. For she had not yet told him.

Dame Lucie's greeting brought her back to herself. She was sitting on her heels looking on Alisoun with puzzlement. 'You need never await an invitation, not here.'

Alisoun realized that she had stood outside the gate so long that her feet and hands were cold. She lifted the latch and entered the garden, saying nothing until she was close enough to speak in a voice not easily overheard. 'I hoped we might talk. Away from Jasper and the children.'

If the request surprised Lucie, she did not show it. 'Come. I now have a bench in the far corner. My quiet place. All know that when I sit there, I do not wish to be disturbed.'

Alisoun followed Lucie Wilton's lead, winding down the paths of the autumn garden, a pleasing mix of last bursts of color and stolid shrubs that were evergreen, rosemary and lavender still leaving a scent as her skirt brushed against them. Beneath the pleasant smells she caught a hint of leaf mold, but the dreariness of the autumnal decay was not yet dominant. She admired Lucie Wilton – a knowledgeable apothecary, a fair employer when she had cared for the children, a wise woman with remarkable patience, a fierce loving mother, and a tender (and most fortunate) wife. Alisoun trusted her with her heart. She might have guessed that the 'quiet

place' was beside the graves of her first husband and child, conse-
crated as a great favor by the previous archbishop. Once they were
seated side by side, Lucie shook out a blanket and draped it over
both their laps. Alisoun appreciated the comfort.

'I am aware of the rift between Jasper and Gwenllian, and I know
I am partly responsible,' she began. 'Had I not spent the night up
above the shop this would not have happened.'

'Your behavior did not cause Jasper's reaction,' said Lucie. 'I
have never known him to refuse to believe his father. He insists that
his sister betrayed him. I would hear your thoughts on why he might
behave so.'

'Before we speak of that, I want you to know that we did not
lie together that night. We held each other, but no more than that.'

'Oh. I—' Dame Lucie touched her heart. 'To have resisted such
temptation . . . Is he talking of the monastery again?'

Alisoun was so surprised by the question she gave a little laugh.
'No. Oh, no, not at all. He was willing that night. I am the problem.
I fear that I might disappoint him, and once it is done, he will feel
committed, betrothed, all but wed to me. Like you I am aware that he
yet feels the lure of the monastery, of taking vows and following in
Brother Wulfstan's footsteps. I think he is torn between following your
example, your happy marriage, and that. Taking vows.'

'Is that your only fear? What of the life you have made with
Magda?'

'Dame Magda would not hold marriage against me. She was wed
at least thrice.'

'She would be glad for you, yes. But you would no longer live
with her.'

Confused by the wave of sorrow, Alisoun bowed her head. 'No.'
Her breath caught. 'All would change.'

Dame Lucie took her hands. Alisoun looked into eyes warm with
affection and understanding, melting the block in her heart.

'I do not deserve you,' she whispered as the tears flowed and she
was pulled into a comforting embrace. She let herself be enfolded
in warmth for a few moments before gently moving away. 'There
is more. I said I might disappoint him . . .'

Lucie pressed Alisoun's hands. 'I would hear more, but you
should know that I will share anything regarding our children with
my husband. That is how it is with us. If this is something that you

do not wish Owen to know, or if you believe Jasper should hear it first . . .' She leveled her gaze at Alisoun.

It was one thing to share this with a woman she regarded as a friend and advisor, quite another to share it with the captain, a man who had first awakened her awareness of men as objects of desire. She felt herself blush. 'I will say no more for now.'

'All I ask is that you make the choice about whether to bind yourself to my son from your heart, not your head,' said Lucie.

As Owen walked through the streets toward home, Alfred recounted how he and Stephen discovered the cart, and the pouch of tools. He ended his account by cursing the curs who got away.

'We learned so much in the course of one morning, but we want more,' said Owen. 'Greedy is what we are.' He slapped Alfred on the back. 'Excellent work, both you and Stephen. God be thanked you're still by my side.'

His companion grinned. 'Mayor Hornby treated me with courtesy on the street today, referring to me as your second. Asked if I would be so kind as to deliver a message. Never gave me a nod in the past.'

Owen glanced at his longtime comrade, seeing him as the mayor did, dressed modestly but well, hair tidy, nails clean. He'd noticed the transformation since Alfred's marriage, but only vaguely. Now he took a moment to appreciate the change Dame Winifrith had wrought. It went beyond Alfred's appearance to his stance, and, most of all, his spirit. The morose man, all sunken in on himself, was now a man with responsibilities he relished, and most definitely in love with both his wife and the children she brought to the marriage. And now they had a baby on the way. 'Old Bede's daughter has made you a man of consequence, Alfred. Hornby sees it. Wykeham as well, I believe. Was his message for me?'

'He extended his thanks for helping Sir Ralph and said he was discussing the matter with the council.'

'Good. I am glad of that. And that he understands your worth.'

They had reached the apothecary. Bobbing his head in unaccustomed shyness, Alfred declared himself off to collect Stephen and the cart he was guarding and take them to the castle. They would then take a few other men and search along the road south for signs of the cart having been taken into the fields once more after the murder. If one man had been fatally injured, there might have been more.

Thinking to discuss his approach to Trent with Lucie, Owen stepped into the shop, but Jasper was alone.

'Mother is in the garden.'

'She will be in soon,' said Owen in passing. 'Looks like rain.'

Outside the workroom, Rhys was assembling the final row of stones for the wall separating the workshop space from the garden.

'Almost finished,' said Owen. 'We will miss you.'

Rhys glanced at the pouch in Owen's hands. 'Dame Lucie asked if I might strengthen an old section of the garden wall. So I will be here for a few more days.' He looked again at the pouch, his eyes troubled, then away.

'Speaking of Dame Lucie, is she still out here?'

'In the far corner of the garden with Mistress Alisoun.'

Of course, there they were, the two women bent close. Lucie seemed to be comforting Alisoun. Judging it best not to interrupt, Owen headed next door.

Tom Merchet was polishing tankards at the counter. 'I hear you've been out on the king's road with the sheriff.' Tom's wife Bess was ever alert to the talk flowing round her at the tavern.

'I have.' Owen glanced round. The York was not crowded, a rowdy table up toward the door, workmen, a few other small groups, and a solitary drinker, the one he had noticed the previous evening. He dropped his voice. 'The man in my usual corner – Trent?'

'Yes. Murderer or next victim?'

'Not likely the first.'

Tom held the pewter tankard up to the light, squinting, polishing a spot. 'You'll be wanting Bess then. And there she is.'

From the kitchen threshold Bess gestured to Owen, leading him through and out into the stable yard. Head down, arms crossed, she listened to his account of her lodger's adventures.

'I almost refused him the room last night, but he was soaked through. And he paid in coin from what looked to be a generous pouch.'

So he had not personally been robbed.

'To have him here might be of use to me. Has anyone come asking for him today?'

Bess shook her head, the ribbons on her white cap dancing. 'You will know if I see anyone about. But who are you expecting?'

'The fate of his hired men is unknown. It's possible one or both are injured. If not, they might come seeking Trent's assistance. Or their pay. As to the attackers, I know nothing.' He touched the pouch of tools tied to his belt. 'One of them might be a stone carver. They left fine tools in the cart.'

'I will be watching. I saw Trent had tucked himself in your corner. You should have quiet there. I will bring ale.'

Bess led the way back to the tavern room, where Trent now sat up as if watching for their return.

'This is my neighbor, Owen Archer, Captain of the city. The sheriff has engaged him to find those who attacked you and your men. He has just come from His Grace the Bishop of Winchester and would speak with you.'

As Owen nodded to him the man seemed to remember himself, rising to give him a small bow. 'Gerald Trent, Captain.' He was a short, tidy man with a hint of a belly. 'I pray you join me. I told Sir Ralph all I know.' He spoke in a soft voice, his eyes focused on Owen's patch and scar. Intimidated. Good. 'His Grace has arrived safely in the city?'

'He has.'

'I should go to him. But how to explain—'

'He will summon you when he is ready.'

'Ah.' The man drew a linen cloth from his sleeve to pat his sweaty forehead. 'I pray the barge carrying the additional stones arrives before we speak.'

'You will be contacted here?'

'I must check the staithes each day.'

Owen settled on a bench at an angle from Trent so that he was not completely blind to anyone arriving at the door, yet could watch the man's expressions. Bess placed a tankard of ale before him and withdrew.

'I have seen the place the attack likely happened. A corpse has been found nearby. By his condition, he's been dead for several days. Where have you been all that time?'

'Several days?' The man kept his eyes on his tankard. 'Has it been that long?' He finally glanced up. 'Was the dead man one of my workers?'

Owen ignored the question. That was for Trent to tell him at the castle. 'Where did you shelter during the storm two nights past?'

'Storm.' Trent seemed unable to keep his gaze from his tankard. 'I suppose that was the night I found shelter in a barn.'

'Whose barn?'

'Cannot say. I am from the south.'

'Describe it to me.'

'It was dark.'

And so it went for a time, until Owen reached over and clutched Trent by the arm, drawing him across the table so that their eyes were inches apart. Around them, all was hushed, as if their fellow drinkers held their collective breath.

'We'll see what a night or two in a cell in the castle does for your memory. Most men find it clears away all confusion.'

'No! No need, Captain. I was here. In the city. An inn near the river.'

'Name of the inn?'

'I – I don't recall. Filthy, it was, full of rough folk. I did not feel safe.'

'Name of the innkeeper?'

'How would I know?'

'Come, Gerald, you are a carter patronized by the wealthy Bishop of Winchester. Surely you made your complaint to the innkeeper of the filthy, unsafe lodging. If not his name, describe him for me.'

'But you see I did not make my complaint as I have little coin. The attack—'

'Little coin? Mistress Merchet says otherwise.'

'Ah. I . . .' He squirmed beneath Owen's grasp. 'God's grace. If you will unhand me, I will tell you.'

Owen released the miserable liar and signaled Tom for another round. Gradually the room around them returned to life.

Fussing with his tunic, Trent made a show of recovering his dignity while Tom refilled their tankards.

'I am listening,' said Owen.

A sip of ale, a moment brushing an invisible speck off his sleeve. 'One likes to think that danger will bring out one's courage. In truth, I had wandered off from my men to relieve myself before sleep. When I returned I heard the trouble. One of my men waved me away. He need not. I was already turning away. I plucked my traveling pack from my horse and ran.'

'You didn't ride?'

'I never ride in the dark. Never. I know what you're going to say, I might have led him. And that I might have, but it would be slow and I felt the need to run.'

'Go on.'

'I found a place by a creek, not really a cave, but under roots. I stayed there until it was light enough that I thought I might find my way back to the camp. No sign of the cart, the carthorse, my fine mount, or my men. You say you found a body?'

'I will take you to him. Go on. You found the camp, but none of your things . . .'

'I did see blood on the ground. All I could think was to find my way to York. I stayed one night at the Bell. By the bridge. As I said, filled with rowdy, unsavory men. But the storm drove me to stay.'

'When you arrived here last night you were soaked through. Where did you spend the day?'

'I left the city again, hoping to find my men on the road. But nothing. And then the rain came.'

'Why here? The York Tavern?'

'The innkeeper at the Bell said that if I wished for a law-abiding clientele, the York Tavern was the place, and good riddance. I would be drinking with bailiffs, coroners, and the captain of the city.'

Owen finished his ale and rose. 'We can continue this conversation on the way to the castle.'

'The castle? But I . . . Do I have no say in this?'

'I am not locking you up. I want to know whether the dead man is one of yours.'

'Yes, I see. Who else might do it?' A sigh. He downed what was left in his tankard and rose, a little shakily.

As Owen felt the eyes of all in the tavern on him and his companion, he thought it best to say loudly, 'It is good of you to agree to accompany me, Master Gerald. Let us hope it is no one you know.'

Once outside, Trent had the good grace to thank Owen for that.

'I would as lief not be stared at in the public room.'

'I doubt you will avoid that. Word of a body found on the road to the city has already spread. It will not be long before people know you were attacked, and the murderers possibly in the city. People will hope you might enlighten them, at least tell a good tale.

And I will be asked over and again what has happened, whether folk are—'

As if on cue, a couple hailed Owen. 'Captain Archer, I hear a man was murdered on the sheriff's land just without the gate,' said the man.

'Are we in danger?' asked the woman.

'The incident occurred days ago and there has been no trouble in the city,' said Owen. 'But you may be sure we are keeping close watch.'

Blessing his efforts, the couple hurried on.

'You have the respect of the people of York,' said Trent. His tone indicated puzzlement.

'I am captain of the city by invitation,' Owen said.

'Unexpected.'

'You had a different opinion of me before we met? From whom?'

Trent inhaled sharply and cleared his throat. 'It was your appearance . . . Forgive me. My wife says I trip over my tongue because I do not pause to note what I am about to say.'

In this case she was wrong – to an extent. What he had originally meant was not what he said. He had reached for the first thing that came to mind to cover himself.

'What does your wife think of the journey you undertook for His Grace?'

'She is the reason I am here. A penance of sorts.'

Owen learned little more as they hurried along, but what he had heard put some meat to the man's bones. It was at the castle, as the man gazed down on the corpse, that Owen began to think the shower of needle pricks might have had nothing to do with Wykeham.

'One of your men?'

'He was, yes. Beck. I am amazed that anyone could cut him down. Strong as an ox, a temper far too easy to spark into violence.'

'There are signs he fought.'

'I do not doubt it.'

'What of the other?'

Trent glanced round, as if to check that he could not be overheard. 'Strong as well, and quick. Cleverer than this one, so more dangerous.'

He feared them.

'You chose them for protection?'

'Little good that would have done. But I did not choose them.'

'Who did?'

'They presented themselves the day of departure. Said the men I had hired found work that paid as well but did not take them away for so long.'

Owen felt the shower of needle pricks. 'And you agreed? Embarking on a long journey with strangers?'

'No. I am not that reckless. Or perhaps I am. I had employed them before, offered to me by the Bishop of Salisbury when I needed to replace a pair who were injured in a tavern brawl. Not a pair I would have chosen for this, but I could not spare the time to replace them.'

'You often work for the Bishop of Salisbury?'

'Only that one time. I have not heard from him since.'

'Do you have any idea who attacked you?'

'None.' He had been backing away from the ripe corpse, which was understandable, and now glanced round to discover the cart of stones. He gestured toward it. 'We carried building stones. I am at a loss to think how anyone would decide to rob travelers of a cart of stone – heavy, lumbering.' He tsked and shook his head.

'Perhaps it was not the cart, but the attendants,' said Owen.

'That I would believe.'

'Describe Beck's companion to me. What is his name?'

Again he looked round as if worried who might hear, then moved closer to say in a quiet voice, 'Raymond. Average height, slender but strong, fading red hair, thinning. A sly look about him – arched brows, dark eyes. He has the coloring of a fair-haired man but for the eyes. Calloused hands. Like yours, in fact. As were Beck's.'

'Have they always been laborers? The scars on Beck's body made me think he'd been a soldier.'

'I am certain both were soldiers. Archers, I imagine. Both carried bows and quivers of arrows and were fine marksmen. They caught a fair amount of game to eat along the way.'

The needle pricks. Did Owen know them? 'You did not ask whether they'd been archers?'

'The less I knew, the better – that was my feeling.'

Owen led him over to the cart, asked if he noticed anything missing.

'All their belongings. And a fair number of stones.' He ran his hand along the waxed cloth that covered the goods. 'I would say a half-dozen are missing.'

Drawing out the pouch of tools, Owen asked whether Trent had seen it before.

'No. But I did not search their packs.'

Owen parted from Trent in the yard of the York Tavern, heading for home. Hunger drew him into the kitchen, where he found Jasper and Rhys talking amiably over a spicy stew and plenteous bread and cheese.

'Customers have seen you all about the city and beyond today, Da,' was Jasper's greeting. 'A corpse, an abandoned cart of stones, a stranger who did not seem at ease walking with you, and a rumor of Bishop Wykeham.'

Owen laughed. 'You forgot the sheriff.' He took a seat at the table. 'Tell me about your days while I fill my stomach.' He helped himself to stew, ale, and the remainder of the loaf of bread. It was not often he could match the appetites of young men, but today he was ravenous.

Jasper talked about his old friend's farewell dinner that had been set for Saturday but was now happening on the morrow because of complications in their travel arrangements. Simon was leaving for Antwerp, where he would join his uncle's trading company; his betrothed awaited him there. 'But with you caught up in all this, I need to help Mother in the shop.'

Owen doubted Lucie would deny him the chance to celebrate his long friendship. 'And what did your mother say?'

'That I might tend the shop alone after my dinner today and give her time in the garden in exchange for being away tomorrow.'

'Seems a fair offer,' said Owen.

'More than fair,' said Rhys. 'Has your friend met his betrothed?'

'A few years ago,' said Jasper. 'He says he is the most fortunate man. She is beautiful and well-spoken, modest and devout.'

'A nun?'

Jasper laughed.

'So will you go?' Owen asked.

'I will decide in the morning. Rhys will be leaving tomorrow, did you hear?'

'Oh?' Owen noticed Rhys eyeing the pouch of tools again. 'I

have not forgotten what we spoke of – my finding more work for you in the city.'

'I am grateful for the offer, Captain. But I heard of work in Beverley, something that might lead to an apprenticeship.'

'Wise to pursue that,' said Owen.

Rhys touched the pouch. 'I've not seen you with that before.'

'Found in the abandoned cart.' Owen opened the pouch, watching Rhys as he drew out one of the tools.

Rhys touched it, his hand trembling. 'Finely made.' A tight voice. 'A carver's tool for decorating stone.'

'Odd for a delivery meant to repair an orchard wall,' Owen said softly. 'The carter had never seen it before.' He drew out another tool.

Rhys brushed it with his fingers, a reverent gesture. 'Very fine.'

'Have you seen these before, Rhys?'

The young man's face reddened, almost matching his scar. 'No. How would I have?' He avoided Owen's gaze. 'I just know stone carving tools.'

'His brother is a carver,' said Jasper.

Rhys shot him an angry look.

'Of course,' said Owen, interested.

'I suppose one of the carter's men might have hoped to find work at the minster,' said Jasper.

As Rhys was still mostly a cipher to Owen, he chose to say no more about the cart in his presence, nothing of why that was unlikely, that none of the three who were attacked were such artisans. 'We know little about what happened,' he said.

In truth, he did not know who had driven the cart into the city. It might have been the attackers, or possibly Trent's Raymond.

Rhys rose, saying he needed to complete the work on the wall.

'So who is the man lodging at the York?' asked Jasper when they were alone.

'The carter. Gerald Trent. Lodging there since last night.'

'How did he choose it?'

'He did not feel safe at the first inn he tried, so the taverner suggested the York because the captain of the city lives nearby.'

Jasper grinned. 'And no one dares cause trouble in Bess Merchet's tavern.'

Owen laughed with him.

'Is it the carter's man who died?'

'One of them. He doesn't know what's become of the other, or who attacked them. He thinks they were the target. If you hear of a stranger named Raymond, fading red hair, dark eyes, possibly an archer's shoulders, let me know.'

'Not a man to be noticed in a crowded city.' Jasper pushed back from the table. 'But I will pay attention. And now to work.' He paused in the doorway to the kitchen. 'You didn't believe Rhys. You think he's seen the tools before.'

'You noticed?'

Jasper shrugged. 'You're my dad.'

'What do you know of his brother?'

'David? I don't know where he is, but Rhys says God gifted him the skill to bring life to stone. He said he's good with stone, like his father, but they cannot do what David can. Do you think he might have something to do with this?'

'I would not consider it if Rhys had not seemed drawn to the pouch of tools the moment he saw it. I'm glad you mentioned the brother. Will you miss him?'

'No. I'd rather not have a stranger over the shop.'

'Have you found anything missing?'

'It's not that I think he's stealing, I just . . . that room . . . We had talked about how we would paint it after the builders enlarge it . . .' He shrugged.

He and Alisoun. 'He intrudes on your dreams.'

'I don't know what I mean. It doesn't matter,' Jasper muttered as he headed for the door. 'I should be in the shop.' He hurried out.

Owen wished he could get to the root of his son's unhappiness. Had he and Alisoun argued? Was that why Lucie had been comforting her earlier?

Finishing his meal, he was cheered by the sound of the children's rowdy play in the garden and wandered out to where Kate was watching them. Emma reached her chubby arms up to him and he swung her about, her throaty laughter lifting his spirits. A good long chase with Hugh and Gwen ended with them all tumbling onto the lawn beneath the apple trees. Emma came rushing to dive onto the three, completing the pile.

When Kate collected Emma to tuck her in for her afternoon nap, Gwen and Hugh wandered away to resume their own game.

'If you were not already exhausted . . .' Lucie laughed as she joined him.

'I was worse before laughing with them.'

'Come talk to me while I work.'

He followed her to the garden shed.

'If you would carry the baskets of straw. And the bucket of ripe soil behind the shed,' she said. 'I'm working on the delicate herbs by the apple trees.'

She followed him there with a basket piled with gloves, a rake, pruning shears, a small knife, and a short-handled shovel.

Owen settled on a bench near the bed Lucie was covering for the winter and told her of his morning, ending with his recent exchange with Jasper. 'I wish I knew what was troubling him.'

'You might be right that not all is well with him and Alisoun. I don't know. If that is it, I pray they resolve it quickly.' She bent again to her work.

Leaning back to look up into the tree above him, Owen remembered the letter in his scrip. Drawing it out, he noticed the seal. Virgin with child.

'Dame Alice writes to us,' he said.

'Alice Perrers? When did that arrive?'

'Wykeham gave it to me. Asked me to read it before we talk again.'

Lucie brushed off her skirts and joined him on the bench. King Edward's longtime mistress had befriended her two springs earlier and offered helpful advice regarding the royal family. 'News of the king? Would you read it aloud?'

Since the death of Prince Edward in June, the word was that the king's health, already fragile, had deteriorated. The letter confirmed that, along with news of Princess Joan's mourning, her difficulties with her youngest son, now heir to the throne and far too aware of that, and other royal family news. Alice said little of John of Gaunt, Duke of Lancaster, beyond that his father the king was grateful for his willingness to take on the added burden of his late brother's duties. More to the point was a brief comment at the end of the letter that she prayed Owen would grant an ear to the friend who carried it. *It is in your power to be of assistance, though I would never ask you to betray your conscience. I say only that he speaks the truth in describing his immediate peril. I believe his hope lies in nurturing a path of peace that will serve him when tempers calm.*

'What is in your power?' Lucie wondered aloud when Owen had finished.

'Something to do with his purpose in coming all the way to York himself? I had hoped it had nothing to do with me.'

'And the immediate peril?'

'I've no idea. I will go to him as soon as I might tomorrow.'

'Good.'

'I do not understand why he seeks out me and Jehannes.'

'Perhaps he has alienated all his powerful allies,' said Lucie.

'I don't like the sound of that.'

FOUR

Troubled Hearts

The children had gone to bed, Rhys and Jasper had retired to their rooms over the apothecary, Kate was tidying the kitchen. Owen and Lucie relaxed on the long window seat looking out into the garden, enjoying the evening air chilled by rain and smelling of turned earth and the smoke of cooking fires. Owen stroked Lucie's hair as she leaned back against him. She held up the parchment to catch the light from a lamp behind them so they might reread Alice Perrers's letter.

'I admire the care with which Dame Alice writes,' said Lucie, 'though I understand it is not meant to impress but rather protect her children and herself, ever aware that she is watched. Judged. How can people believe that she chose such a life, mistress of the king, their children illegitimate, her position precarious at best?'

'Those who see only the pearls, the gowns, the properties. Until one has been amongst the royal family and their court, the life seems one of immense pleasure. They have no sense of the shifting sands. At any moment it all might be snatched away.'

She folded the letter and set it aside. 'Heavy thoughts on a sweet evening.'

'And to no purpose,' said Owen. 'Until I meet with Wykeham I cannot guess the purpose of her closing words.' He inhaled deeply. 'What is it about an evening rain that feels so comforting?'

'The day's tasks are finished,' said Lucie. 'And if there is nothing clamoring for your attention, such as a querulous child, you need do nothing but enjoy the coolness.'

'And allow it to settle you toward sleep.'

For a while, they sat listening to the rain on the leaves.

'Gwen will miss Rhys,' said Lucie, breaking the silence.

Owen thought of the young man. 'Did you know he meant to leave so soon?'

'What is there to keep him?'

'We had talked about my finding him other work.'

'That was kind. Perhaps he thought you too busy?'

'And I am, now. You must be right. He admired the stone carving tools. The way he touched them, the reverence – I felt he had seen them before. But he denied it.'

'Something he dreamed of for himself?'

'Jasper says his brother David is a gifted stone carver. Maybe they reminded him of his brother's tools.'

'A strange thing to be in that cart. When did the cart appear at Toft Green?'

Owen kissed the top of her head. 'Not yesterday evening, but it was there by early morning according to those Stephen questioned.'

'So where was it for several days?' Lucie wondered aloud.

'That is why I have Alfred and Stephen searching.' He told her of Alfred's pride in the mayor's newfound respect for him.

'I am happy for them. Winifrith says the children already adore him, and he's kind to her father.' She sighed and stretched.

It was not her first such sigh. 'What troubles you?'

'Giving advice about the heart is impossible.'

'Alisoun? I saw you two in the garden.'

'I could provide little comfort for what ails her. I almost wish it were as easy for Jasper and Alisoun to know they want to be together as it was for us.'

'Easy? I remember a long while of you keeping me at arm's length. Until that night . . .'

'You cannot know how hard I struggled against my feelings for you! It took immense effort to resist them. But that night, finding you out in the garden stripped to the waist, sweat casting a sheen on the muscles of your back and chest . . .' There was a smile in her voice.

'And you coming out in only your shift, your hair tumbling around your shoulders.' He groaned into her hair as he moved a hand down her shoulder to her breast. 'Jasper and Alisoun are resisting each other?'

'Mmm. She is resisting.'

'Wise. They are not yet betrothed.'

'No. But they are old enough to be.' She turned to look up at him. 'Shall we go up to bed?'

Laughing, he let her lead him up the steps.

'What bliss is this?' he whispered after the lovemaking. 'No interrupting knocks on the door, calls from the nursery . . .'

Lucie gave a wicked laugh from deep in her throat as she slipped a leg over him. And so they began again.

Later, the covers thrown back, they shared a cup of wine and continued the interrupted conversation.

'They did not lie together the night she stayed with him?' he asked.

'No. God forgive me, but a part of me was disappointed to hear it. I had hoped—'

'That passion would end Jasper's thoughts of entering the monastery?'

'What mother so yearns for her son to sin?'

'To be happy.' Owen kissed her forehead. 'We both want that.'

'And if taking religious vows was his path to happiness?' she asked.

'Then so be it. Jasper has his own mind.'

'Keenly proved of late.'

'Painfully,' Owen said. 'But you say it is Alisoun who resists?'

'She is just as conflicted,' said Lucie. 'Which has me doubting they will ever be together. She believes his frustration caused Jasper's uncommon anger.'

Owen considered the possibility. Even if Jasper were meant for the Church, he was a young man with a healthy appetite – he had often witnessed how eagerly his son rushed to assist young women in the shop. 'I can see how that might be true. You don't think he hopes to force her to a decision?' He held up a hand as Lucie began to protest. 'No, I know, that's not our son. But to express his frustrated desire by making his sister so unhappy. I cannot ignore that. God's blood, being a father can be a torment.'

Lucie gave a soft laugh, handing him the cup.

He drank, thinking of the prickly Alisoun. He often wondered if she was right for Jasper. But he did seem to love her. 'She hesitates because of her work with Magda?'

'That is much of it. But there is more. She began to say something about disappointing Jasper. When I told her that whatever it was, he should hear it from her first, before you and I knew of it, she grew quiet.'

'Little frightens her. But there was the time Sir John Holland tried to seduce her,' said Owen. 'Or perhaps she fears what I feared – that you would find me lacking.'

Again the naughty laugh. 'Surely you did not fear that.'

'I did.'

'Difficult to believe, my love.' Her laughter turned to sighing. 'I pray that whatever it is, telling him does not make him even more disagreeable. Poor Gwen.' She leaned her head on his shoulder. 'I wish I could think of something to cheer her. But I fear it may not be in our power to soothe her. I think only Jasper can undo this.'

'I agree. Shall I fetch some wine?'

'No. I think I can sleep now.'

Moments after Owen had shuttered the lantern kept by the door, he thought he heard voices down below. Stepping out onto the landing, he pricked his ears. Not in the house, out in the garden. Male and female.

'What is it?' Lucie whispered, joining him.

'Alisoun and Jasper. In the garden.'

Lucie crept down a few steps, paused, listening, and climbed back. 'Tomorrow may be difficult. Let us get some sleep if we can.'

In the night, Alisoun had told the guard at Bootham Bar that she could not sleep for worry about Anna Thornton, who was about to give birth. It was true she was concerned for Anna, and she would go to her in a little while, but she was not the cause of Alisoun's sleeplessness. Lucie Wilton's advice haunted her. For more than a year she had rushed past the shadow of an event that would almost certainly change Jasper's idea of her, each moment of delay in telling him about it making it more unlikely that he would take it well.

She had not even confided in her teacher, for she had known what Magda would say – tell him. What madness had kept her silent? In the beginning, she had been confused about how she felt and feared that to speak of it in such state might make it worse. Yet she saw in that argument the very reason for telling him. He deserved to know, deserved a chance to express his feelings, and together they might have . . . might have what? There. That was the fear. They might have decided to end their courtship.

Magda had heard her cry out in the night from suffocating dreams, and doubtless guessed that Alisoun agonized over a painful secret. But it was not her way to force a confidence. At any other time Alisoun would have described the dreams, eager for her teacher's insight. But she could not. And Magda had behaved as if nothing were between them, which was maddening at times. And instructive. Her problem was entirely of her own making.

After parting with Lucie in the garden that morning, she had gone about her duties with only half her attention, pondering how she might best approach Jasper. At the end of the day she'd fled home to confide in Magda at last and seek her advice. They had walked along the river into the forest of Galtres, her teacher listening, asking questions, helping her pour out her tangled thoughts. The experience was far harder than she had anticipated. By the time she had talked herself hoarse, Magda had brought them to a rest beneath a willow and settled on a fallen log.

She took Alisoun's hand in hers, looking into her eyes. 'So long thou hast held close this secret.'

'Too long.'

'Thy delay will make it all the more painful for Jasper. That thou didst not trust him to understand.'

'I know.'

'Magda has many questions. But this is for thee to resolve.'

'A test?'

Her teacher's smile was tinged with sadness. 'Speak from thine heart to Jasper. It is for him to receive it however he may. Thou canst no more control his heart than thou canst thine own.'

'And then?'

'Though it may be painful, accepting whatever comes is the path to the fastest healing. For both.'

'You know he won't forgive me.'

'Magda knows nothing of the future. But she has witnessed many wounded hearts.'

'Can I forgive myself?'

'Every act has consequences. Dost thou regret what thou didst, or how long it has taken thee to tell him?'

The strength in her teacher's firm, warm grasp encouraged her to consider the question with care. She did not like the answer. 'I regret how long it took me to speak of it. To you and to Jasper.'

'And now thou must face the consequences. Thou wilt survive the ordeal.'

'I will be whole.'

Magda looked deep into Alisoun's eyes and pressed her hands. 'Thou *art* whole. There is no question of that.'

Returning in a companionable silence, a soft rain spurring them to a faster pace, Alisoun had felt lighter, freer, and crawled beneath her bedclothes eager for the oblivion of sleep. But the specter of telling all to Jasper arose to torment her, shredding her short-lived peace. She'd fetched a sleep potion, but feeling Magda's eyes on her she set it aside. Time and again her teacher warned against escaping the inevitable. Each missed opportunity worsened the pain, and delayed healing, sometimes irrevocably. She had already delayed too long. The time to tell Jasper about her days with another up on the moors had been at Martinmas the past year, on her return. That chance was lost. She would wait no longer.

Reaching the apothecary, she woke Jasper by tossing pebbles against the shutters of his bedchamber on the first floor. In a moment he had come below to open the shop door, a finger to his lips, and led her through the building and out into the garden.

'Why not upstairs?' she asked, uneasy about their voices carrying into his parents' house from the garden. And though the rain had stopped, it was chilly now, all the surfaces damp.

'Have you forgotten what happened the last time?'

'Of course.' She was so caught up in her own worries she had not thought of that.

He took her hands. 'What brings you out so late? Were you with Dame Anna?'

'I will go to her in a little while. I need to tell you about last autumn, up on the moors.' She took a deep breath, looped her arm through his, and led him in a slow walk along the garden path away from the house. 'Magda's great-grandson was up there.'

'Einar?'

'No one in Asa's village knew he was there. When I turned home, I happened upon him sitting by a beck. He had just come up onto the moors from York and was gathering his strength, praying for guidance about which way to go.' Magda had sent him away to be alone, find his calling, after working among the folk during an outbreak of pestilence in the previous summer. 'We spoke of Magda, the mystery surrounding her. I learned how she came to the settlement where she met his great-grandfather. A strange tale.'

'You come in the middle of the night to tell me about something that happened a year ago?' Jasper stopped and turned to face her. 'You did not mention seeing Einar when you returned.'

'No. I should have.' She reached for his hands. 'But I was confused. How could I tell you when I didn't understand?'

'There is more to this than Einar telling you an odd story about Magda Digby.'

The tightness in his voice almost made her stop. She forced herself to continue.

'Yes. And if you care for me as you say you do, you will allow me the courtesy of hearing my story.'

He withdrew his hands and took a step back. 'You lay with him, didn't you?'

Was she that obvious? 'Yes. But that is only part of my tale.'

'How could you?' he hissed.

'I am not excusing myself. At the time I felt so close to him, we have a deep connection through Magda . . .' She heard how foolish she sounded. Because she was not speaking from her heart as Magda had advised. But how could she tell Jasper that Einar's nearness had made her heart race, that his touch had sent waves of heat through her unlike anything she had ever experienced? 'In the moment I thought it was love. But later it felt more like an enchantment.'

'You would not lie with me, but you did with him.' Jasper's voice was sharp with hurt.

She could not blame him. 'It is why I hesitated that night. I wanted you to know this first. I should have told you a year ago. I'm sorry I didn't. I don't love him, Jasper. Not as I love you.'

'Am I to thank you for telling me that you gave yourself to him even though you don't love him? And then waited so long to tell me? Let me keep dreaming of being with you for another year when all along . . . I can't, Alisoun.'

She caught his arm as he turned from her. 'Many a time you have told me of the debate you have with yourself, whether you are called to be an apothecary and husband, or if God calls you instead to take monastic vows. I have listened with all patience, trying never to let you see my pain because I know you would never be happy were you to force yourself to turn away from a true calling. But it tore at my heart. Were you to choose the Church you would cut me off from you for good. What happened with Einar is not like that.'

'Of course it is.'

'No. I am telling you it means nothing about what is between us. I don't love him. I love you.'

'Yet it took you a year to tell me you had slept with him.' He moved an arm's length from her, bowing his head.

She let go his arm and waited.

'You choose me now,' he said after a long pause. 'But if his search brings him back to Magda, how do you know you'll not regret your decision?'

'What if you choose me, we wed, I am with child, and you decide you made the wrong decision, that God is calling you to the abbey?'

'You think I would abandon you and our child?'

'You seem to think *I* would.'

'It's not the same.' His tone was angry, pushing her away.

'No? Why? Because you would claim a higher calling? A holier path?'

'You would disdain such a choice?'

'How can you ask that when I have waited patiently for you to choose between me or the Church? In all this time I have not pushed, I have not taunted or tried to tempt you away. If you left me – I've thought about this so often, the pain, the loneliness, knowing you would not be there, I would not see you . . .' Her voice broke and she stopped to breathe. 'But I would pray to find forgiveness in my heart,' she whispered.

'Forgiveness?' His voice dripped with disdain. 'What would there be to forgive? I would be answering God's call.'

'Are you so hard-hearted? You wouldn't care how I felt?'

'If God calls me—'

'But you must know how hard that would be for me. And even so I would pray to understand. Will you not do the same?'

A sharp snort. 'You are nobler of heart than I am. Is that what you want me to say? Was it noble to lie to me for a year?'

'I wasn't—' She stopped. Calmed herself. 'I ask only that you listen, and that we move forward with no secrets between us.'

'I have listened. Now I need to sleep.' He retreated so suddenly it took her a moment to move herself to follow, and by the time she reached the door to the workshop he had shut it.

Slumping down to the ground, she pressed her hands to her mouth to muffle the scream of frustration.

Bess Merchet woke to a voice somewhere in the bedchambers. Earlier she had heard voices in Lucie's garden, stepped close to check that there was no trouble. Alisoun and Jasper, their voices tense. As long as they were not intruders, she had no cause to bother. But now the voice was near at hand, male, sounding frightened. And was there another? A low murmur? Were they up above? She stepped out of her chamber, listening. Silence now but for a snore below. Perhaps it had been in the yard. Crossing to the window she opened the shutter and looked out, but the moon did not light the shadows. In case they were there she shooed them off as she would stray cats. When she stepped back to close the shutters a cloaked figure slipped from Lucie Wilton's garden and out toward St Helen's cemetery. Female, she thought. Alisoun. Perhaps she had been confused.

FIVE

A Body in the Beck, a Bishop's Troubles

Morning dawned grey and chill, with intermittent squalls. Autumn settling in. Stepping through the space in the new foundation for an expanded workshop, Owen almost tripped over Rhys's hammer and chisel. Kate had mentioned seeing the young man already at work out there when the lad from the

York Tavern delivered a cask of ale first thing. Now he was nowhere to be seen. He tucked the tools in a dry spot.

Owen found him in the workroom, searching the shelves near the doorway into the shop. Recalling the dropped tools, Owen asked whether he had injured himself.

Startled, Rhys apologized for the intrusion.

'Hardly an intrusion when you are working here and lodging with us.'

An uneasy smile. 'You have all been so kind.'

'Let me see your injury. I have tended many on the battlefield and among my men.'

Rhys touched the still raw scar running down the side of his face. 'I thought to find some of the salve your daughter mentioned, that keeps your scar from pulling. I mean to pay.'

Owen guessed a random comment to be the likely source of the stonecutter's unease. Gwen's bluntness could sting. 'I am glad she thought to suggest it, though I apologize for her candor.' Reaching for the jar of ointment he kept by the garden door, he measured out a penny's worth. 'This should last a long while. You will depart today?'

'I will walk round the garden wall to see whether I missed any places that need repair. If I finish in time, I plan to start out today. I am grateful for all you have done for me.'

Once the young man went out to the garden, Owen peered into the shop, curious who had been talking to Lucie all the while. She was handing a package to Gerald Trent. He noticed Owen.

'Good day to you, Captain. The Merchets suggested I come here for . . .' He colored. 'It is a long while since I traveled so far.' He thanked Lucie, bobbed his head at Owen, and limped out.

'Saddle sores and blistered feet from walking in wet boots,' said Lucie.

'I could swear he had no limp yesterday.'

'He certainly does now. Perhaps he had a difficult night and today feels it more.'

Quite possible. 'Talkative.'

'He began with much complaint, I countered with questions. I hoped to learn something in exchange for the tedium.'

'And did you?'

'He was keen to talk about Rhys's work. It appears he's watched him and finds him admirably careful. Commended his stonework.'

'I hope he passed that on to Rhys.' Perhaps the young man had overheard?

'I suggested it, but as you saw he hurried off.'

'Anything else?'

'He seemed impressed by your connection to Prince Richard and Princess Joan, knew of our journey to see the late prince before he died. But he evaded my attempts to learn more.'

Why would that matter to a carter? And where had he heard of it? 'That might be helpful.' He glanced round. 'Where is Jasper?'

'The farewell feast for Simon.'

'Ah. I'd forgotten. I've not seen him this morning. The argument in the garden with Alisoun . . . How did he seem after last night?'

'He is worse than before if that's what you're wondering. Whatever she told him, he did not take it well.'

'And now he's spending the day with someone happily in love?'

'An arranged marriage. The couple have met, but briefly.'

'Is his friend happy about it?'

'It's Simon. What do you think?'

A young man with a gift for seeing the good in everything. 'If only Jasper might learn his skill.'

'I would not wish that for him,' said Lucie. 'Simon has lived a comfortable life, with a happy family, wealth, health. Jasper has that now, but before he came to us he experienced loss, and disappointments. He is aware that things can easily change. Simon is not.'

'You're right. Simon will expect his good fortune to continue. He's unprepared for life. But our son's present temper—'

Lucie touched Owen's wrist as a customer entered the shop.

'Captain Archer! What news of the murderer?' the woman asked.

'That is precisely what I must be away to discover.' He bowed to her and exited by the shop door, lifting his hood as a shield as the sky opened.

In his chamber at the castle, Sir Ralph welcomed Owen and Brother Michaelo with bread and cheese, watered wine, and a roaring fire, the latter much appreciated after walking through intermittent squalls on the way. It pleased him that Michaelo would keep a record of the investigation, and he expressed his admiration for how quickly Owen had learned so much about the event. Indeed, they dispatched their business so quickly that Owen feared his clothes would still be damp when he rose from the comfort of the fireside chair.

But Sir Ralph poured more wine and settled back with his cup. 'There is a new development. The men brought in a body found lying in a beck just beyond my property. Neck broken, and it looks as if he might have been stabbed. The animals had been at him, so it is difficult to tell. I hesitate to suggest, but do you think the carter should be brought here again to see if this is his other man?'

'Thinning red hair, an archer's body, calloused hands, about my age?' Owen asked.

'Ah. No. Younger than you, dark hair, plenty of it. Not him, then. Yet – though he's mentioned only the two, wouldn't he travel with a manservant?'

'I think he would have mentioned him. But I will talk to him again. You are fairly certain it's a stab wound?'

'See for yourself. It looked so to me.'

Alfred awaited them outside the sheriff's chamber.

'Here to escort us to the body?'

'It is not a pretty sight.'

They had it in a sheltered corner of the castle yard rather than indoors. That would not do for the night, but Owen appreciated the fresh air. Alfred pulled away the blanket to show them wounds on the chest that could indeed be stab wounds, since widened by whatever fed on the corpse. The condition of the neck was unmistakable. He asked Alfred about the search for bloody stones offloaded along the way. Or anything else too blood-soaked to risk being seen by the guard at Micklegate.

'Nothing yet.'

This morning Bishop Wykeham's garb still echoed the modesty with which he had made the journey north. Not merely the exigencies of travel, then. Michaelo had said the bishop maintained a solemn countenance and listened far more than he spoke. He greeted Owen with an untoward cordiality, but no smile.

'Brother Michaelo is welcome to act as scribe today,' Wykeham said as he led the way to Jehannes's parlor.

Within, a table was set with wine, bread, cheese, apples, nuts.

Two high-backed chairs flanked it, facing the garden window. A brazier warmed the room. A small table and stool for a scribe was placed to one side of the chair that Wykeham apparently remembered Owen would choose – always to the left so that his good eye was on the side facing the bishop.

'You were confident I would call today,' Owen said as he stood by his seat.

'I pray you, sit when you please,' said Wykeham. He nodded when Owen settled. 'I did suppose that Dame Alice's seal would catch your attention.' The hint of a smile.

As Brother Michaelo set down his wax tablets, a servant moved out of the shadows to pour wine for all three, pass around the food. He then departed, closing the door behind him.

After commenting on the weather – 'I had forgotten how early the rains come this far north' – Wykeham settled back in his chair. 'Dame Alice Perrers encourages me to trust you, Archer. She said you are owned by no man, not even the late prince. Or Thoresby.'

Owen digested that with the cheese, chased it down with wine. Fine wine. Jehannes was not a stingy man when it came to guests, even those he had not invited.

'Is she right? Can I trust you?' Wykeham's gaze was locked on Owen's good eye.

'I hope I might be trusted to do the right thing,' said Owen. 'But one might not always agree with me about what that is.'

'Cleverly cautious.' Wykeham nodded to himself as he sipped his wine, his eyes wandering to the window. Several vicars hurried past, heads bent against a sudden downpour. 'Dame Marian of St Clement's Priory speaks highly of you.'

'I am glad to hear it.'

'As you know, I come to York as a favor to the new abbess of Wherwell, Dame Cecily, who wishes Dame Marian to return and resume her training with Dame Eloise, the aging cantrice. Marian would become cantrice upon her teacher's retirement, which is imminent. My ward has proved unequal to the position. But her training would be an asset to such a modest priory as St Clement's.'

Owen knew all this. 'Have you had word from Dame Marian?'

'She has not yet declared her intent. But as St Clement's is a poor community, I am confident that she will choose to return to the estimable Wherwell. I saw few signs of prosperity.'

'Lord Neville's wife would be disappointed to hear that. She has become a generous patron.'

'Lady Maude?' Wykeham considered that news as he set his cup aside. 'I was unaware.'

'This matter of the cantrice seems a small thing to bring you to York. Why not send representatives to see to it?'

Wykeham cleared his throat and studied his excessively clean hands. 'Should Dame Marian return to Wherwell, I hoped you might commend me to her guardian, Sir Thomas Percy, and intercede on my behalf regarding another issue.'

Now they arrived at the true purpose. Yet Owen still did not understand. 'Sir Thomas? I met him on the occasion of his niece's coming to York, but I've had no communication with him since.'

'You rescued his ward, kept her safe, introduced her to the prioress of St Clement's.'

'The latter was facilitated by Lady Maude. She was in residence there before the enthronement ceremony for Lord Neville's brother.'

'Of course. They are now the power here.' He glanced at Michaelo, who had stopped scratching on the tablet. 'You are discreet?'

'I am enumerating only the information that will be of use to Captain Archer, Your Grace,' said Michaelo.

'Good.' Wykeham returned to Owen. 'You demur about your influence with Sir Thomas, but I have heard him praise you.'

'Then you are in communication with him. So why—'

'He is Lancaster's man. As is Ergham, Bishop of Salisbury and Lancaster's chancellor.'

'I know nothing of Ergham.'

'He is a close friend of Dame Cecily Lavington, the new Abbess of Wherwell.'

The circle closed. 'Ah.' Owen considered all the bishop had said – and not said – as he helped himself to more wine, settled in his chair. 'You and the Duke of Lancaster have clashed again?'

'Sadly, yes. Since the death of Prince Edward, as Lancaster has assumed the king's duties while his father mourns, he has methodically undone the work of the recent Parliament. Rendering him unpopular with the citizens of London, the clergy, and the members of Parliament. In such a moment rumors fly. The particularly heinous one that has time and again been ascribed to me, of the duke being a changeling and no royal son, is resurrected.'

'He still believes you to be the author of that slander?'

'It is convenient for him to do so. One needs a scapegoat. As a wealthy member of the clergy, I am an excellent candidate. But I understand his anger. We – by that I mean the government in Westminster – failed him three years ago, when his army, battered by French assaults, with many dead or captured, arrived in Bordeaux to find the city in tatters. Famine and pestilence. His men starved. We did not know. And when at last we learned of his plight, his need for money and men, Parliament refused to help. Even when the king ordered them to send funds, nothing was done. Is it any wonder Lancaster returned furious with the Parliament?'

'But why you as the scapegoat?'

'Habit? In a strange way I have come to see it a fitting reprimand. My arrogance blinded me. I have tried to talk to him, but he refuses to speak with me.'

'And so this penitential journey?'

'A part of the reason, yes.'

'Forgive me, but I cannot see what this has to do with Thomas Percy.'

'He is one of Lancaster's close advisers. The royal family is gathering next month to confer on the state of the realm. I have been warned that Lancaster will work to convince King Edward to humble me by stripping me of my temporalities in order to render me impotent outside of my spiritual duties.' More softly Wykeham added, 'And helpless against my enemies.'

A cruel spite. 'How do you know this? Dame Alice?'

'And a cleric I will not name. Both are in the confidence of the king, who grieves for his old friend, yet understands that his family walks a delicate path through parlous times, with a dying king whose heir is but a child. He dare not attempt to protect me in this moment. I did not read her letter, but I imagine Dame Alice expressed doubt that any actions might prevent what is coming.'

Such fear in his eyes. 'Dame Alice led you astray in sending you to me. I have no influence with the Duke of Lancaster. I have met him, spoken with him, dined with him, but I am not in any sense part of his affinity. Nor would Prince Richard's mother wish me to be.'

'You think she would disapprove your interceding for me.'

'More to the point, I have not the means to do so. I cannot think of any reason the duke or Sir Thomas would pay heed to such a request from me.'

Wykeham poured more wine, sat back, studying Owen. 'I cannot decide whether you seek to deceive me or you are singularly unaware of your influence.'

The calculation in the bishop's eyes gave Owen pause. 'What influence?'

'The parents of the heir to the throne personally chose you to protect their son. The Duke of Lancaster looked to his elder brother as a model prince, warrior, lord. His men know this, and know your position in Prince Richard's household. You are respected.'

Owen moved to argue, but stopped, seeing some truth in the bishop's words. The respect might not be quite so strong as stated, but it made sense. And served as a warning for him. With such respect came enmity, the enmity of all those who would choose to believe he might be bought by their own enemies, or those of their lord. Did Wykeham depend on Owen not seeing that? It was good he did not trust the man.

'Years ago I chose to serve the Archbishop of York rather than the Duke of Lancaster,' said Owen. 'The duke has a long memory. He is courteous to me because I represented his beloved brother, and now his son, nothing more.'

'A sign that he understands what he lost. But I did not ask you here to argue. Would you speak with Dame Marian and Sir Thomas?'

'I do not even know where I might find Percy.'

'Nor do I,' said Wykeham, 'and that worries me. But Dame Marian is near. She might know. And if you would encourage her return to Wherwell, I would be forever in your debt.'

That held no weight with Owen. He knew all too well that lords had short memories regarding their debts. 'Have you considered confiding in her about your troubles?'

The bishop paused as he reached for the wine, casting a quizzical look at Owen. 'I do not see the purpose. She would have no wish to help me. It cannot be presented as a favor to me, no, no, that would not do.'

'She is a woman who has witnessed the dance of power – indeed her own situation is the result, as it was the power of her aunt, Lady Maud, that influenced the prioress of St Clements to argue for her right to return to the order.'

'And my influence that doubtless led her to choose to remain here.'

'At the time, yes. But she would understand.' Owen felt certain of that.

'And if she still chooses to stay here?'

'Then she has made her choice. Does it occur to you that God might have led her here? A cruel journey, yet I've no doubt she grew in wisdom.'

With a shake of his head, Wykeham rose.

Owen quickly followed. 'It would help my investigation to know why you traveled so modestly. Other than it being a penance. You said that was only part of it. Did you hope to conceal your whereabouts?'

'I meant that the purpose of my journey was partly to return with Dame Marian and partly to ask you to intercede for me with Lancaster. As to whether my quiet arrival was to elude spies, the answer is yes. I should think our discussion makes it clear why.'

'Lancaster's spies will not be fooled. Nor Neville's.'

'But perhaps confused.' Wykeham began to hold out his hand for Owen to kiss his ring, then withdrew it. 'We will speak again on the morrow. Dom Jehannes invites you and your wife to dine with us. Meanwhile, I hope you will consider how you might convince Dame Marian that her place is at Wherwell. And ask her where to find her uncle.'

The man was not listening. Owen merely bowed his head and took his leave, asking Michaelo to accompany him.

Outside, clouds still blocked the autumn sunlight, but the rain had stopped and Owen lifted his face to the sharp breeze, drinking in the air. The brazier in Jehannes's study had quickly dried his clothes, and then it had felt oppressive. Or was that the company? He had yearned to open the glazed window. He headed out toward Stonegate.

'I was impressed by your lack of deference to His Grace,' said Michaelo. 'And so was he, I think. He needs clear thinkers.'

'He might find any number of them among the clergy, of which we have plenty in York. Why not reach out to them? He must know that by now they are all aware of his presence.'

'You are right. When he asked Dom Jehannes to say nothing of his presence in York, our friend pointed out that so many already

know. Even should the sisters of St Clement's keep his confidence,
the servants will spread the word. And the incident with the cart
– surely Gerald Trent has not held his silence. In the end he admitted
that he'd underestimated the difficulty of secrecy.'

'Yet he does not seek the counsel of the abbots and canons of
the city?'

'Most assuredly not.'

'Queer,' Owen muttered.

They were headed for the York Tavern to collect Gerald Trent
and take him to see the new body in the castle yard, then Michaelo
would deliver him to Wykeham. Reaching St Helen's Square, they
went straight to the York Tavern, where Tom Merchet directed them
up to the top chamber.

'He was out, but came through moments ago cursing the weather.
Will there be trouble?'

'If he refuses to come along willingly, I might be carrying him
over my shoulder,' said Owen. 'Shall I gag him?'

A grin. 'Might be a treat. But no need to do so.'

Trent made a choking noise in response to the knock. Clearly
standing close to the door.

'It's Captain Archer.'

A sigh. The door opened a crack. 'I told you all I know.' He tried
to shut the door.

But Owen held it there with little effort, then slowly pushed it
wider, catching Trent as he began to topple and setting him on his
feet by the pair of boots near the bed. 'You'll need these. You're
coming with me to look at a body found at the border of the same
property as your man Beck.'

'And you think it is Raymond?' He looked pasty. Unwell. His
eyes shadowed.

'You said Raymond had thinning hair, fair?'

'I did.'

'This one has a full head of hair.'

'Then you've no need of me.'

'You are wrong about that.' Owen crossed his arms. 'Boots.'

Trent glanced behind Owen. 'A monk?'

'Brother Michaelo. My secretary.'

'A city captain with a secretary.'

'Captain Archer is part of Prince Richard's household,' said

Michaelo. 'A post requiring frequent correspondence. And after the castle I shall escort you to Bishop Wykeham.'

'His Grace has summoned me? Should that not be the priority?'

'I am a busy man, Master Gerald,' Owen said quietly. 'Come along now.'

'And if I refuse?'

'The only question is whether you walk or I carry you.'

'How dare you—?'

'His Grace is already disturbed by your handling of this incident, and the caliber of men you hired. Perhaps you do not depend on his patronage?'

'His Grace.' Trent sat heavily on the bed, frowning down at his stockinged feet, then bent to lift one of his boots.

The corpse was no lovelier than earlier in the day.

'God help me,' Trent groaned, covering his nose and mouth as he turned aside.

Owen pulled him back, holding his head so that the man looked at the corpse. 'Do you know this man?'

Michaelo stood opposite, studying Trent's expression. He gave Owen a subtle nod.

So he knew him from somewhere. 'Did you travel with more than the pair you've mentioned?' Owen asked.

'No. Only the two.'

'Have you seen this man before? Not to know, but in passing?'

'I do not believe so. How might anyone know for certain, with so much damage.' He turned away, retching.

Owen let him go. For now.

With Brother Michaelo escorting Trent to Jehannes's home, Owen took his time crossing the city, stopping in the minster stoneyard. This time he was fortunate to find another one of the master masons.

'If you would look at this pouch of tools for fine stone carving,' said Owen.

'I have been curious to see them.'

The mason cleared a place on his worktable and lay down a clean piece of hide.

Opening the pouch of tools, Owen spread them out, explaining where they had been found, and described the second corpse as best he could, someone who might be connected to the cart of stones stolen, then abandoned.

The mason touched each item, nodding. 'Fine tools. Well cared for.' He lifted one, squinted at some lines scratched into the handle, then passed it to a young man standing beside him. 'Recognize that mark?' To Owen the mason said, 'Young eyes.'

The young man shook his head. 'No, master. I've not seen that mark before.'

'I can tell you these are the tools of one doing fine stone carving,' said the master mason. 'Figures. Faces. Not strictly cutting tools. Costly. Someone will be missing them. You think they belonged to the dead man?'

'I do wonder. Might you come have a look at him before he's buried?'

The man made a face. 'You ask much. And as I do not recognize the mark, and none of our carvers are missing . . .' But he nodded. 'When I'm finished for the day. He's at the castle?'

'I am grateful.'

'You'll owe me some of Merchet's fine ale for this.'

'A fair price.'

SIX

An Angry Young Man, the Cemetery

Lost in worry about Anna Thornton's condition, Alisoun did not see Jasper and his friends until one of them – Simon – called out to her. Or, rather, called to Jasper that his ladylove approached. Laughter bubbled up as she engaged in the ensuing exchange with the young men who bragged that they were heading to a tavern to drink the day away before Simon embarked on a long journey to meet his betrothed. 'Come along,' they called. The glare with which Jasper glanced her way made plain that the hours had not softened his anger. She waved them off, feeling sad for Simon, burdened by the presence of a friend who would stew in his anger all the day.

With that look he'd intended to hurt her, but she felt it as a shock of cold water. She had opened her heart to him and he had slammed the door on her without any sign that he wanted to understand. He'd not asked her how she felt, whether she understood why it happened, he'd condemned her without hesitation. How easily he turned off what she had thought was love and kicked her away. Remembering her tears of the previous night, how she had struggled to set aside her pain and give Anna Thornton all of her attention, she felt foolish. Jasper was not the person she had thought him. Nor was it Alisoun he had thought he loved, but an idea of her that was all wrong.

Well then. God be thanked he revealed himself. She was well rid of him.

Still, in the pit of her stomach she wondered how this would have gone had she told him a year ago. But what was done was done.

As she approached her destination, the Wilton apothecary, she was glad there was no chance of seeing him. No telling what she would say if he suddenly appeared before her. She focused on reviewing the list of physicks she had already tried with Anna Thornton. With them in mind, she moved forward just as Captain Archer stepped from the shop door.

'*Benedicite*, Alisoun. How is Dame Anna?'

'No better. I hope Dame Lucie can give me something to calm her without weakening her for the birthing.'

'It is close now?'

'Tonight or tomorrow, I think.'

'She is fortunate to be in your care.'

He was kind to say so when she was partly – now wholly? – responsible for the upheaval in his household. She felt she must warn him. 'Jasper and I had a falling out in the evening. He seems angrier than ever today.'

'I heard. You will not find him here to glower at you while you consult with my wife.'

'I know. I passed him with his friends. A scowling spirit amongst the merriment. Poor Simon.'

'No doubt he will be worse yet when he returns. I pray Anna Thornton will soon be safe delivered of a healthy child.' He nodded to her and moved on.

In the doorway of the apothecary she exchanged pleasantries with a departing customer before greeting Dame Lucie. 'Forgive me, but I am uneasy about being away from Dame Anna too long.' She explained her concern, listing all she had tried.

Assuring her she understood, Lucie described various mixtures, the strengths and weaknesses of each. After discussing them at length, Alisoun chose one. While Lucie measured out the powder, Alisoun said, 'I told Jasper what I felt he must know.'

'From his mood today it did not go well,' Lucie said softly, keeping her focus on her task.

'No. He judges me harshly. As I do myself. But I had hoped that, schooled by the gentle Brother Wulfstan, he would be more forgiving, at least hear all that I wished to tell him.'

'Dear Wulfstan taught him forgiveness, I am sure,' said Lucie. 'But our hearts do not always heed the lessons we most need.' As she offered Alisoun the package, she held her hand for a moment, looking into her eyes. 'I am his mother, but I am also your friend. Can I be of help?'

'This is help enough. Thank you. Whatever you say to him, do not mention Einar.'

'Magda's great-grandson?' A sad smile. 'I will heed your warning. Now go. May God watch over you and Anna.'

The smile . . . Alisoun yearned to stay, to pour out her heart to Lucie. But she must return to Anna. 'Might we talk more about this at another time?'

'I welcome it,' said Lucie. 'Quiet your mind now. You are needed.'

Lucie was measuring out a physick for a customer when the workshop door slammed, followed by a clatter and a thud. She excused herself.

Jasper sat slumped against a worktable, weakly resisting Rhys's attempts to right him. His eyes were closed, his face red and bloated with drink.

'Where would you like me to move him?' Rhys asked.

'Bless you. We need to get him up to his bed.'

Between the two of them they maneuvered Jasper upright, but he could not catch his balance.

'No matter.' Rhys hoisted Jasper over his shoulder and climbed up the stairs.

Once they had eased him onto the bed, Lucie removed his shoes and tucked him in, something she'd not done in a long while, and kissed his hot forehead.

He opened his eyes. 'Ma?'

'I must see to the shop. I will check on you later. The best thing for you is to sleep.'

'I will fetch him water,' Rhys offered. 'He will want it when he wakes.'

Thanking him, Lucie returned to the shop, where Maud Miller waited, a keen glint in her eyes.

'I never thought to see young Jasper in such state,' she said.

'A farewell gathering for a friend embarking on a long journey,' said Lucie, keeping her eyes on her work, reminding herself that Maud was not the only witness. Jasper had somehow made his way home from the other side of the river. Tongues would be wagging throughout the city. It might be best to confine him to the workshop for a few days until the gossip died down.

Jasper opened his eyes, expecting his mother. But it was *him*, looming over the bed, smirking. 'What are you doing here?' That's what he meant to say, but it came out all slurred together.

'I brought water.'

'Go 'way.'

'I will set it here, beside you.' He turned away.

'Traitor.'

He looked back, frowning.

Pretending still? Jasper's head was muddled, but he spewed out all he was feeling. Why not? Teach him to come here to brag. He laughed, cursed, spat . . .

Awake again. Light different. Alone now. Thirsty. So thirsty. Jasper reached for the water beside him, then stopped. Did Einar bring it? Might be poisoned. He turned away, though the thirst was so strong. His stomach heaved. Pulling himself to the edge of the bed, he vomited. God help him. Had he already drunk the poisoned water? Was he dying?

Again he woke with a heaving stomach. Someone was there, offering water. He was so thirsty. What did it matter if he drank it? He was already poisoned. He gulped it down. Fell back against the pillows.

* * *

In the Bell, the tavern across the Ouse Bridge where Trent had first
lodged, Owen spoke with the taverner, Dunn.

'Little man, big purse. I remember him. Clothes soiled and torn,
I thought him a beggar. But he set me straight flashing silver coin.
When he complained about the noise, I told him old Jonas Snicket
across the way was taking lodgers. Don't know if he ever talked to
him. Next morning he complained he had not slept all night, felt
unsafe. I gave him directions to the York Tavern. "The captain of
the city lives nearby, drinks there most nights," I told him. Glad to
be rid of him. Sorry to send the lout your way.'

'Happens it's good he's nearby.' But the other recommendation.
There might be others looking for lodging. 'Have you told any other
customers about Snicket?'

'Now and then. Have you seen his house? Falling down around
him. Landlord's asked me to help out.'

'Any others of late?'

'One or two.'

'Anyone seem interested in Trent?'

The innkeeper squinted at Owen. 'So he had some trouble, eh?
Men following him now?' He shrugged at Owen's lack of response.
'Can't say that I— No.' He slapped the counter. 'There was a pair
in here drinking. Looked as if they'd been in a fight. One of them
bandaged, the other limping. They watched him for a while, then
left. Didn't see them again.'

'Strangers to the city?'

'No one I'd served before.'

'Can you describe them?'

'Hats pulled down over their hair, plain faces, no scars, no
beauty, I'll tell you that. One missing several teeth, the older one.
My age, I'd say – I've seen more than forty winters and feel them
in my bones. He was the limping one. The younger had what
looked like a bandage round his arm. Right one, I think. Plainly
dressed. Not rags. No one special.'

Owen thanked him and headed across to Jonas Snicket's house.
It sat behind a shop that had once been Snicket's. Now a sailmaker's
shop. Across the yard, the house looked as if it were tipping its hat
to him as he approached, the first story sagging to the left.

His knock was met by the sound of shuffling feet approaching. The
door opened with a painful creak, a wizened manservant peering out.

'Is it Captain Archer?' Before Owen could answer, the servant had turned to call out, 'Master Jonas, Captain Archer is at the door.'

In a moment an even older man rudely shoved the manservant out of the way. 'What does the captain of the city want with me?'

'I understand you take in lodgers.'

'No lodgers. You waste your time.' Snicket pushed shut the door.

'Pity the man who gives that old thief his coin for a room and board,' said a deep voice behind Owen.

He turned.

A bronze-haired giant nodded to him with a grin. 'Laurence Gunnell, sailmaker. You will never get a civil word out of that man. Tell you who might help you, though. Mistress Alisoun, the healer. She has a way with him.'

'He is ill?'

'Old man with a weak heart. Walks to church now and then, leaning on his faithful servant, Pete. He's not much younger but strong from years of work. Pete sends for Mistress Alisoun when his master takes a tumble or he cannot wake him.'

A fortunate connection. 'Anyone lodging with him now?'

'I've seen no strangers coming and going, but I will keep an eye out. I'm not here at night, though, so I might not see.'

After Lucie shut the shop she went up to check on Jasper, found him sleeping. She detected the scent of vomit, but neither the sheets nor the floor were soiled. Rhys stood in the doorway across the landing.

'Has he been sick?'

'Twice,' said Rhys. 'I cleaned it. Kate gave me cloths and a pail of water.'

'I am sorry—'

'No. I was glad to be of help. He reminds me of my brother. Never could drink more than one ale.'

'I have never seen him like this.'

'He mistook me for someone he accuses of bedding Mistress Alisoun. I learned some new curses.'

Bedding Alisoun? Is that what they had argued about? And then he had attended a celebration of his friend's coming marriage. 'Would you prefer to move next door for the night? We have room.'

'Do not trouble yourself. He will doubtless sleep through the

night. And it might be good to have someone to help him if he falls
from the bed.'

'Did he come through the garden gate? From the York Tavern
yard?'

'He did. I turned round, saw someone dash from the gate. Could
not see who. Jasper was staggering forward but tilting so he would
have soon fallen on his face. I helped him inside.'

'He fought you?'

'Not at first.'

One of Jasper's friends must have helped him home. Thanking
Rhys, she peeked in to see that Jasper still slept, then slipped off
to the house.

Owen forgot his own concerns as he listened to Lucie's account of
Jasper's homecoming.

'I hope he can tell us in the morning who helped him home. I
wish to thank him – and find out how much Jasper said in public.
If he maligned Alisoun—' She broke off, but Owen saw the worry
in her eyes. 'I understand he is hurt and angry. But I pray that he
did not start gossip that will spread through the city, damaging her
in the eyes of all. She is a skilled midwife and healer. But if people
shun her . . .' She shook her head.

Owen echoed her prayer. 'A man's devils come forth in drink. I
hoped I'd taught him that.'

'I should not have given him permission to leave me alone in
the shop. I knew what a temper he was in.'

Tilting her chin up, Owen looked into Lucie's blue-gray eyes,
seeing the pain. 'You could not have predicted this. I certainly did
not. We will work through this. Rhys might have misunderstood.'

'Something happened, it is clear,' said Lucie. 'His first love. First
heartbreak.' Her eyes widened. 'Einar. This afternoon Alisoun
warned me not to mention him to Jasper.'

'Magda's great-grandson? But he went away.'

'Perhaps he returned to consult with Magda and . . . Poor Jasper.
I had never imagined Einar as a rival. In truth, I thought he and
Alisoun might resent each other's importance to Magda, great-
grandson and apprentice seeming to each a possible rival.' Lucie
paused. 'But Einar does have a way with him, and a presence.'

'That he is Magda's kin might make it all the harder for Jasper.

He may not believe he can compare, that Einar has more to offer her than he does.'

'I am sad for our son,' said Lucie, 'but he cannot continue to punish others for his pain – first Gwen, now Alisoun.'

'I will talk to him,' Owen offered, though he could not think how to begin.

'It might be best coming from you. I am not only his mother but his master in his trade, and I sometimes work closely with Alisoun.'

As Owen might need to do if Gunnell was right about her connection to Snicket. He hoped it would not come to that, but the exchanges, both with Snicket and Gunnell, had left him doubting both men.

Gwen had crouched on the bench outside the garden window listening to her parents. She'd seen Jasper's arrival and wanted to hear what they said about it. He'd been drunk like some she had seen staggering out of the York Tavern next door. Her brother. She did not understand why. When she learned he was out to celebrate his friend's betrothal she had envied him, imagining a wondrous array of food, minstrels, dancing. To have drunk so much in so short a time – he had not been gone so very long. Had he joined in the celebration at all? Perhaps young men did not feast and dance at such times. Though clearly they drank. And now to hear her parents' concern about Jasper spreading gossip about Alisoun. She did not entirely understand what she had done and why he might use it to ruin her. It made her feel fortunate he'd merely ignored her.

Why was he so hateful of late? She might understand why he was mean to her, believing she had betrayed him, but she did not understand his being hateful to Alisoun. Something about Einar. She'd liked him. He'd reminded her of Dame Magda, what she might have been like when younger, not yet so wise, but already someone who paid close attention, and cared. Maybe Alisoun had told Jasper she loved Einar? Or had she chided him about being mean to his annoying little sister? Was she responsible for this, too? But that wouldn't involve Einar.

In bed now she could not sleep for all she had heard earlier. Tossing and turning, she tried to think how to make amends. For now, she should warn Alisoun.

She was startled from her worry by a loud voice, followed by a quieter one. Outside, she thought. She slipped from bed, turning her head to judge the direction. The voices came from the lane in front of the house. She moved a stool to the window and looked out. In the moonlight she saw two men in the cemetery, arms gesturing in angry argument. Only the lantern over the door of the York Tavern was lit. It must be very late. The street was quiet except for the two men. She must have fallen asleep after all.

The loud one shouted, 'You will do it.' The other spoke softly, motioning for the man to calm. She wondered whether they had stumbled from the tavern at closing and wandered out among the graves to continue their argument. Or they might have dared each other to so disturb the dead and now waited to see which would be first to turn tail and run. If one did, the other would soon follow, surely. The loud one said something in a threatening tone, but he was quieter now and she could not make out his words. The other seemed to reach out for him, and then suddenly the louder one jerked as if someone had yanked on his shoulder. Had they awakened a corpse by arguing over the graves? The man slumped onto his knees, then fell sideways. The quieter one made a sound as he reached down toward his fallen companion, then looked up toward the shop window. In the moonlight she thought she saw a line across his pale cheek. Rhys? Was Rhys glancing up at Jasper's bedroom window, fearful they'd wakened him? Wasn't he worried his friend had wakened the dead person on whose grave they stood, and they meant to pull him down, trapping him in a grave while still alive? But Rhys seemed more concerned about who might be watching from the house or shop. Now he was looking her way and she hid, fearing the dead might come if he pointed her out. She crawled into bed, squeezing closed her eyes, shivering with fear.

Next door, Jasper, too, ducked as the man looked up to his window. He had no doubt the man searched for him.

He knelt on the floor, pressing his forehead to the planks, praying for forgiveness, vowing never again to surrender his will to drunkenness.

By the time he rose, the men had gone. He wept.

SEVEN
The Morning After, the Stonecutter

I t was Gwen's task in early morning to take Hugh out to the privy while Kate dressed Emma. This morning the scene in the cemetery haunted her and she feared what she might find, though it was clear the dead had not come for her. Yet. In no mood for her little brother's usual antics, she yanked him out the door with her, hurrying down the pathway.

'Go first, while I peek in to say good morning to Jasper.' She shooed him on and doubled back, heading for the apothecary. Beneath the linden she stopped as Rhys rose from behind the foundation he was working on, a heavy stone in his arms. Had that been him last night? Had he stabbed the man he'd argued with? She had not noticed him moving toward the man before he fell, but he might have struck so fast she did not catch it.

She tilted her head, studying him. 'Why are you hugging that stone to you?'

He turned a little away from her. 'I believe your brother might welcome help preparing the shop this morning.'

Moving closer, she noticed blood on Rhys's shirt. And on one hand. 'Have you cut yourself?'

'What?' He looked down. Groaned. Took a few steps away and dropped the stone. 'My hands are so toughened by my work I cannot always feel when a sharpened tool slices me.' He grimaced.

Was it his blood? Or the man's from last night? 'Jasper can clean and bandage that. Come with me.' At the door to the workshop she took a deep breath, remembering her brother's state the day before. Maybe she should offer to clean and bandage Rhys's hand. It would give her the chance to examine the cut. If there was a cut.

Two lamps burned in the workroom, indicating that her brother was up and about somewhere. 'Jasper?'

'Here.' His voice came from the shop.

He was sitting on a stool at the counter, holding a small bowl of liquid, foul-smelling.

'Feeling better?' Rhys asked.

Jasper blinked at them, as if he could not see clearly. But the shop door was open and they stood within the circle of light from the lamp on the counter. Even on the brightest days they needed at least one, or often a pair of lamps for the close work of measuring physicks. 'What do you want, Gwen?'

'Rhys is injured,' she said. 'I offered to clean and bandage it.'

'I'll do that,' said Jasper, taking his time standing up.

'No need,' said Rhys. 'If you point me to the bandages I can help myself.'

'Come,' said Jasper. 'Sweep outside the shop, Gwen.'

She thought it best not to argue over who bandaged Rhys. Fetching the broom from the workroom, she stepped out into the lane. The work took longer than usual because Alice Baker came past tsking about Gwen being forced to do her brother's work while he recovered from a day of drinking. She was shooed away by Tom Merchet, who winked at Gwen and went about his business tidying the tavern yard with a rake.

When she finished sweeping, she leaned the broom in the doorway and took the few steps into the walled cemetery, stopping on the top step. From there she looked up to her window and tried to remember how far into the cemetery the two men had stood in the night. Crossing herself and praying for protection from any uneasy spirits, she placed one foot down onto the grassy edge, then the other. Slowly, pausing with each step to listen and feel for movement beneath her, Gwen inched toward what she thought might be the spot. She had never before dared step into this place of eternal sleep. The ground was far more disturbed than she had expected, full of partial footprints and animal tracks. It might be impossible to tell where the two men had been. But then she spied a trail of something dark. Blood? She tried to go further, but her heart began beating faster and faster until she could not breathe. Turning, she stumbled back to the wall, pressing her hands to her heart to try to slow it.

Jasper stood at the top of the steps watching her. 'What are you doing?'

'I – I saw something last night.'

'In the cemetery?'

She nodded, biting her lip.

'What were you—' He stopped. 'You are shaking.'

She hugged herself to try to stop shivering. 'Will the dead punish me for walking on their bones?'

He gathered her up and set her down in the lane, holding her until she was steady on her feet. 'You were brave to go there.' His voice was soft, kind, like the old Jasper.

If he had been mean she might not have cried. 'I wanted to see,' she blubbered.

Jasper crouched to meet her eyes. 'And did you see anything?'

'Maybe some blood.'

'Blood? No wonder you were frightened. I will check. Wait for me in the shop.' He kissed her cheek and rose.

She touched the spot he'd kissed and smiled through her tears. 'You aren't afraid?'

'Have you watched a burial?'

'Course I have.'

'Did the dead rise up to strike down any of the mourners? Or the priest? Or gravediggers?'

'No.' She drew out the word, then took a deep breath. 'If I watch, I can guide you.'

He hugged her. His breath smelled of the foul herbs he'd been drinking. 'Wait here on the steps and call out to me.' He went into the cemetery, heading toward the spot where she had stopped.

'Here?' he called to her.

She climbed up the steps. 'I think so. Do you see the dark spots?'

He was already crouching, pressing a hand to the ground, holding it up to his mouth, tasting. He nodded to himself and had begun to walk when he crouched again, picked something up, glanced back toward the upper story of the apothecary, then stuck something up his sleeve. Rising, he circled again, searching the ground, then at last walked a line toward the lane beyond the York Tavern, stepping down into Coney Street and coming round to her, his eyes moving here and there, still searching for evidence.

'What did you find out there?' she asked.

'A trail of what tastes like blood. We will show Da. Whoever it was went toward Coney Street.' He took her arm, gently, patting her on the back. 'Come into the shop and tell me everything.'

He'd said nothing about what he tucked up his sleeve. Maybe a sample of the blood? He was being so sweet to her, she did not want to spoil that by asking him about what he had taken. 'Where is Rhys?' She did not want him to hear her account.

'He put on clean clothes and took his stained shirt to Kate, along with mine from yesterday. I was about to follow him – I need some food – but I saw you and came out here instead.'

In the shop she told him everything – what she had witnessed in the night, what she thought had happened.

'Rhys?' He frowned down at the basket of bandages. 'His cut was deep. I know some of his tools are that sharp. But it was a lot of blood on his shirt, and I didn't look to see if any of it was more dried than the rest.' He shook his head. 'Da will sort that out. I will tell him to look at the stain before Kate works on it.'

Gwen was sniffing the bowl of herbs. 'I saw you yesterday.'

'Oh.' He winced. 'I am sorry you saw me like that. And about how I have treated you.' He leaned down to kiss her cheek. 'Can you forgive me?'

'I would never betray you,' she whispered, feeling the tears rising again.

'When I think clearly, I know that.' He pressed his hands to his face, then raked them through his fine hair. 'There is no excuse for how I've behaved. And yesterday. I paid no heed to how much I drank. I remember nothing of the afternoon. Not even how I made my way home.'

'One of your friends brought you to the gate. Rhys helped you inside.'

He looked confused. 'And up to my bed? That was Rhys?' He muttered something.

'What did you say?'

'I was praying for the courage to ask what you've heard about my behavior.'

'You want it all?'

He nodded.

She told him what she had heard their parents say.

He listened with bowed head, his ears turning a bright red. When she finished he groaned. 'How can they forgive me? And Alisoun. God help me, I betrayed her?' His voice broke.

She would never fall in love. It made people so unhappy. Changed them.

Owen stood beneath the linden talking with Francis Hull, one of the nightwatchmen, when Jasper and Gwen stepped out of the workshop. Hand in hand. What miracle was this? He was so caught up in the joy of seeing brother and sister reconciled that he had to ask Hull to repeat what he'd said.

'Would you prefer not to speak of this in front of the children?' Hull asked.

'They will hear about it in the house,' said Owen. 'Whether we mean for them to or not.'

Hull, a father himself, grinned and nodded. 'I was saying that I followed the trail of blood to a spot on the riverbank. I guess whoever it was washed it off in the flood. Or mud, depending on the tide.'

'You found nothing to suggest where the injured person had gone after that?'

'Nothing. But I might have seen the injured man earlier. A pair weaving their way from this direction on Coney Street, one helping the other who seemed about to fall over. I see such things all the time, crawling from taverns and alehouses, and thought no more of them. Until I saw the bloody handprint on a wall.'

'Would you know them again?'

'Doubt I would. I can say they were not old men, not beggarly in their appearance, and now I'm guessing one of them is injured. I might even go so far as to say probably the right shoulder from how he held himself. And there might have been a third man following close behind. Might not have been with them.'

'Did you hear their voices?'

'No. One of them was muttering, but I could not even tell you which one.'

'This is far more than I had before. Will you take me?'

Gwen stepped forward as Owen and Hull began to depart. 'Jasper has something to show you.'

'And Gwen saw something in the night that might be connected to what you're talking about,' said Jasper.

'Wait for me in the kitchen,' said Owen, continuing out of the gate.

*   *   *

A bloody trail in the cemetery – Jasper had collected a stone with a sample of the blood, the two – possibly three – men on Coney Street, and now a name for the corpse in the beck, courtesy of the master mason. David Wells. That was Rhys's family name. The dead man was his brother the stone carver? Owen had much to think about as he crossed the minster yard to Jehannes's house. He hated that his young daughter had witnessed something that so frightened her, but he was gladdened by Jasper's kindness toward her. Some good had come from a troubling incident. But who was the man arguing with Rhys in the cemetery – if it was the young stonecutter she had seen – and what had happened? He suspected she was right, as Rhys had suddenly disappeared after offering to take his soiled shirt and Jasper's to Kate for washing. He'd not come to the house to break his fast. Why would he run from them? Even if he had not been in the cemetery the previous night, his sudden departure – with his tools and his pack – was still troubling. Did he know they had identified his brother's body? Had he known his brother was involved in the attack?

Gwen's description bothered Owen. What if Rhys had not stabbed his companion, but someone else had come upon them? Or shot at them from an upper-floor window or a roof? Trent had mentioned his men being fine marksmen. Might Rhys have something to do with the attack on Trent and his men? Did he know the other attackers with his brother? As he reached Jehannes's door, Owen shook himself to quiet the rushing thoughts. He must be clear-headed when talking to Wykeham.

'You shake your head. Am I to understand you would have preferred that I refused to open the door?' Brother Michaelo asked with a sniff.

Only he could make Owen laugh at the moment. 'I was arguing with myself.'

'Were you indeed?'

'Is Trent still here?'

'No. Their meeting was brief, and, I believe, unsettling for the carter. He rushed out with ears ablaze.'

'Unfortunately for me, I would like to have a word with His Grace.'

Michaelo stepped back and motioned for Owen to enter.

'My dear friend.' Archdeacon Jehannes came forward to greet Owen. 'Will you and Lucie be dining with us today?'

Owen had forgotten. 'Forgive me.'

Jehannes patted his arm. 'Another day. You've much on your mind.'

'You are kind. I came to speak with—'

'His Grace. I heard. He is in my parlor – perhaps I should say his parlor.' Coming closer, Jehannes whispered, 'I pray you, do what you can to hurry him away. I am forced to dictate to Michaelo in my bedchamber.' He smiled, but his eyes pleaded.

'I am not sure I have such power, but I will do all I can – short of offering him shelter in my home.'

They shared a laugh.

In the parlor, Wykeham sat by the garden window, one of his priests at the small table Michaelo had used.

'Archer. Have you news?'

'I have, Your Grace. The name and some information about the man found in the beck.'

'Sit, I pray you.'

The servant who had answered Owen's knock now placed a chair close to the bishop and, once Owen was seated, brought a cup of wine.

'I had only just heard about the man. You move quickly, Captain. I am pleased. So what have you learned?'

'Yesterday, one of the master masons working on the minster looked at the body at my request and recognized the young man. Not long before your carter and his men were attacked, the young man had appeared at the minster stoneyard seeking work. He reminded the mason that they had met several years earlier – his father had introduced them. It had been on the site of one of your building works outside Winchester. You had asked to consult with the mason on a structural concern in the nave of the old church being repaired. Later the mason heard of the father's death in a fall at the building site.' Master masons communicated through many channels, sharing information, trading skilled workers. 'The surname was Wells, and the dead man's name David.'

Wykeham tried the name on his tongue. 'David Wells.' He shook his head. 'I recall no one by that name, but then it would be my masons who hired him. You say his father died of a fall at a church being restored?' He looked to the priest who had sat silently, head bowed. 'Dom Sebastian, is the name familiar?'

The man looked up, nodding. 'I have been thinking. There was that case, the widow and her son accusing you of negligence in seeing to the safety of your workers. That the men you hired to oversee them were malicious.'

Wykeham nodded. 'Old St Floribert's. I came to think the project cursed. Was she the woman who made a spectacle of herself in the square?'

The priest nodded, his pale eyes averted.

Owen was curious. 'Cursed project?'

'Delay after delay, until the work planned for summer extended into autumn and had to be abandoned when ice storms made it impossible to continue,' said Wykeham.

'Is that why the man fell?'

Wykeham looked to Dom Sebastian.

'That is *when* he did,' said the priest, 'but there is disagreement about the *why*. The family, and some of Wells's fellows, claimed the mason's men forced him to climb when they knew it to be dangerous. But my mason swore that his men had called off the workers for the day and Wells chose to go against their order and climbed up to retrieve one of his tools.'

'What do you think?'

'Our opinion is unimportant,' said Wykeham.

'What became of them?' Owen asked.

'I believe they were resettled on one of His Grace's manors,' said Dom Sebastian.

'Which one?' asked Owen, thinking of his own, deeded to him by Wykeham a few years earlier.

'I could not say, Captain,' said the priest. 'But I assure you it was fairly done.'

'In other words, you've heard no more complaints,' said Owen.

Wykeham smiled, but his eyes were troubled. 'What are you thinking, Archer?'

'It may be nothing, yet the connection is suggestive, is it not?'

Taking up his cup, Wykeham sipped his wine as he made a show of considering the matter. 'Perhaps.'

The delicate carving tools . . . Wells's sons had taken after their father in being good with stone, David having a special gift. It seemed more and more likely the tools were his, and that was why Rhys had kept glancing at the pack. 'What caused the delays?'

'Deliveries were late, incomplete,' said Wykeham. 'It happens with all such projects, but this one seemed to be constantly behind. Yet the workers expected to be paid for sitting about and waiting.'

Deliveries . . . 'Was Trent one of the carters on the project?'

Once more, Wykeham looked to Sebastian. The priest's eyes had widened.

'I believe he might have been. We use him for that type of work, a smaller church. And he has been one to cause delays. Forgive me, but I did not travel with any records.'

'Do you know the names of the mason's men overseeing the work? The men blamed for ordering the father to climb the icy wall?'

The priest shook his head.

'I begin to see . . .' Wykeham pressed one of his temples, his expression pained. 'Trent said he had not chosen the men, Beck and Raymond, but they volunteered when the pair he'd chosen took other jobs. They are the ones responsible for the death of David's father?'

'At this moment it is only a seed,' said Owen. 'But it might explain David's apparent involvement. He might have found work in the city. I need to find out where.'

'Who are the other men? Trent said three attacked.'

'We are searching for them.' Owen chose not to mention the incident in the cemetery. He wanted to find Rhys first. 'I've been told that the mason who worked for you on St Floribert's is now working at Rievaulx. If you would write to him, Your Grace, ask him for the names.'

'I will. But it will take time for him to be found, and to respond.'

'It is worth a try.'

Owen did not choose to share what else the mason had said.

I can tell you that one of the carters who works for the Bishop of Winchester was later recommended to me, but I had been warned against him – Gerald Trent, the one who was attacked on the road to York.

'Who warned you? And why?'

'A fellow mason who had used him for a job. He quotes a price far lower than what he will bill, and he never delivers on time,

citing issues. Plenty of carters like that. It's how they make their
money. But we come to know the reliable ones and spread the word.'

Yet Wykeham, who prided himself on his building works, employed him. Owen studied the bishop, puzzling over that. A lack of judgment that might go quite a way in explaining his troubles.

'Are you worried that the Wells widow and son were sent to the manor I ceded to you?' Wykeham asked as Owen continued to ponder.

'Llŷnfield? I had wondered.' Though Owen made regular trips to the manor, he had not yet met all the tenants. 'My steward says little about the tenants.'

'You changed the name. What is the significance?'

'Llŷn was my home in Wales. There is a stretch of the property that reminds me of the one broad field near my home.'

To Owen's surprise, the bishop smiled. A sincere smile.

'I am glad of that, Archer. The land should be loved.'

He had a heart, it seemed.

'If I might,' said Dom Sebastian, 'there were two Wells sons. This David, and one I did not meet. I don't know the other son's name. But perhaps he was involved in the attack?'

Still not ready to implicate Rhys, Owen said, 'That might be helpful. If you recall anything more—'

'I will be certain to inform Brother Michaelo.'

Owen thanked them both.

Wykeham rose. 'Does your wife await us in the hall?'

The forgotten invitation. 'Not today,' said Owen. 'She was needed in the apothecary.'

'A pity. Perhaps tomorrow. I will confer with Dom Jehannes.'

Neither Alfred nor Stephen had any luck finding more witnesses to the incident in the cemetery. They had gone round the square questioning neighbors. In the evening they would talk to the night watch, who were all abed at present.

Thinking about his conversation with Laurence Gunnell, the sailmaker whose shop sat in front of Jonas Snicket's house, Owen stopped in the apothecary to see whether Alisoun had come by.

Jasper colored to the roots of his hair and shook his head. 'I've not seen her. Ma's been in the garden.'

Owen was surprised. He had imagined she would give Jasper

time before facing those who had heard of his drunkenness. 'Have people been difficult today?'

'Alice Baker's been by to sneer. But everyone else has done their best to pretend they've heard nothing.'

'Perhaps Alice has failed to spread the word.'

On a typical day that would have won a snort from Jasper, but he seemed distracted – his bruised honor? Owen pressed his son's shoulder. 'It will pass.'

'But Alisoun,' Jasper said. 'I don't know what I might have said to my friends. Or out in the street.'

'Do you know you said anything?'

'No, but . . .'

'Perhaps your friends kept you quiet.'

Jasper grunted.

Out in the garden, Lucie was lugging an overflowing basket. Owen plucked it from her hands.

'Have you seen Alisoun today?'

'No. I imagine she is with Anna Thornton. A long labor. Poor woman. How is His Grace?'

'Wykeham surprised me. Made no fuss over my forgetting we were to dine with him today.'

'We? You hadn't told me.'

'I'd forgotten. Apparently Dame Alice suggested you might be of help.'

'In what way?'

'I believe with your insight into what is left unsaid around the table.'

'A compliment, to be sure. But this does not sound like Bishop Wykeham.'

'He is not quite the man I knew before. In the past I would not expect him to show such poor judgment in choosing Gerald Trent for this mission.' He told her about the mason being warned against using the carter, and how he might be connected to a death that could explain the attack on the cart. 'Not that he could have anticipated the man's kin, or friends, to come so far for vengeance, but he himself admits the man is problematic.'

'We felt the same about the clerks he chose to accompany him on his last visit to York,' she said.

She was right. 'As ever, I am grateful for your memory. But he's changed in other ways. Softened. He liked that I renamed the manor. "The land should be loved." He said that with a smile.'

'Now I am curious. I look forward to dining with him. This latest body, the young man who might be the son. Those were his carving tools?'

'It seems likely. Rhys knew what the tools were for because his brother is a skilled carver. Apparently David Wells had a brother.'

'Wells? But that's Rhys's family name.'

'Yes. I had little cause to connect the two until I learned the name. And now with Rhys's altercation in the cemetery last night, the blood Gwen said was on his shirt this morning, and his disappearance . . .'

'Is there any question they are brothers? Do you think he knows of his brother's death?'

'He might have guessed when he saw the pack. Or knew of the plan to attack. I don't like to think he might have been a part of it.'

'Magda would tell you to trust yourself in this.'

The healer believed his half blinding had strengthened what she called clear-seeing in Owen. He nodded.

'But why was he here if not to take part in the plan?' she asked.

'Another reason to find him.'

'You don't believe he's gone to Beverley for work?'

'No.' Owen lifted the basket. 'Where do you want this?'

'The workshop.'

They moved together toward it.

'I hate that Gwen witnessed such a thing,' said Lucie. 'And I'd no idea she feared the dead would rise from St Helen's churchyard to punish her for walking on their graves.'

'Nor I. But her fear might be what finally turned Jasper round.'

Lucie stopped at the new stone steps leading down into the small sunken garden near the expanded foundation and turned to Owen. 'What a joy to see them hand in hand this morning. I worry now that I thrust him forward in the shop too soon. Did you speak with him?'

'Most are being diplomatic.'

'Or have not yet heard about it.'

'Alice Baker stopped by to taunt him.'

Lucie had borne the brunt of the woman's ire for years, for recognizing her tendency to abuse physicks and refusing to sell her more than she should take in a day. The woman had done her best to stir up trouble for Lucie ever since, an effort with little success, for too many townspeople had suffered similar tantrums from the woman.

'Then all the city knows by now,' she said.

'Most likely.'

Inside the workshop, Lucie bent down to some cloth wadded up and dropped near the door. Picking it up, she shook it out. Rhys's bloody shirt.

'Copious bleeding,' she said softly, as if to herself.

'I'll take that.' Owen found Jasper alone in the shop. 'How serious was Rhys's wound?'

'He'd sliced his hand.'

Owen shook out the shirt. 'Would it have bled this much?'

'No.' He rubbed his eyes. 'I should have noticed that this morning. I'm sorry, Da.'

'He might have thought you had noticed and that's why he fled.'

'If I'd told you—'

'I doubt we could have stopped him.' Owen wadded up the shirt as the shop door opened and slipped back to the workroom.

With a weary grunt, Crispin Poole settled next to Owen. He nodded toward Gerald Trent, who sat at the next table trying not to watch them – and failing. The gesture caused the man to frown down into his tankard, face flushed.

'Is he the carter who suffered the attack?' Poole asked under his breath.

'He is.' Owen took equal care to modulate his voice. He nodded to Hempe as he joined them.

The three friends often sat at this table in the far corner of the York Tavern, drinking ale and talking about their days. Poole was the coroner of the forest of Galtres upstream from the city. Both he and Hempe were successful merchants who enjoyed assisting Owen in his work. It lent spice to their days, according to their wives.

'Tell us about the young man we're to watch out for,' said Hempe.

Owen described Rhys and explained what might have caused his sudden departure.

'Poor Gwen, seeing such a thing,' said Poole. He had two young daughters, one only months old.

'His brother is the second corpse? You think Rhys might have been involved in the attack?' Hempe asked softly. 'Christ, I wish we had a fiddler tonight so we might talk freely.'

'I have a mind to clear the table nearest us,' Owen said quietly. 'Knowing how much we know can loosen a man's tongue.'

He raised his voice and launched into the tale of the corpse in the beck, and his connection to a story out of the South, a mason working on St Floribert's fallen to his death after being ordered to climb an icy wall. No names, just the outline. All the while he watched Trent, who turned slightly away. But when he lifted his tankard he could not hide his trembling. Owen finished with the question, 'So I put it to you, would you consider it mere coincidence that this man is found murdered on the road to York after an incident with a carter involved in that project, as well as one or both of the men who ordered his father to climb to his death?'

With that, Trent rose and stumbled out of the tavern.

'You brought up the bile in him,' said Poole, 'that is clear. But whether he'll now talk . . .'

Bess Merchet came to refill their tankards. 'Ned and another young man are following Master Gerald,' she said.

Owen thanked her for the report. All was working as planned.

'You'll be watching him and searching for this Raymond, and the lad who was working on your wall?' asked Poole.

'And I'd have you put the word out to the king's men in Galtres to keep their eyes open for either of them,' said Owen. 'As well as an injured man and his partner. Though I am guessing they're still in the city.'

'Young Rhys would not be helping Raymond,' said Hempe. 'Chasing him?'

'I think it more likely he might be helping the injured one and his partner, if they're the ones who attacked the cart. I wish I knew their connection to David Wells.'

'And his brother right there in your home. Bold young man.'

'Our men will be watching here and on their rounds,' said Hempe.

'What about your house and shop?' Poole asked. 'If Rhys is connected, the men now know that you are leading the investigation. They might try to stop you.'

'That's always a risk. But so far I've seen no sign of that.'

'The cemetery incident did not worry you?' asked Poole. 'Do you think they were watching for Trent?'

'I tell you what worries me,' said Owen. 'How Gwen described the way the man jerked, then toppled. As if he'd been hit by an arrow.'

'At night?' Hempe shook his head.

'In order to see as much as she did, they must have been standing in some light,' said Owen. 'Maybe from the lantern in the tavern yard.'

'Someone up on a roof,' said Poole. 'I don't like the thought of that.'

'Nor do I,' said Owen. He told them what Trent had said about his traveling companions being skilled marksmen.

'Have you had the men asking people who live around St Helen's churchyard about hearing anything up on their roofs?' asked Hempe.

'About whether they heard or saw anything,' said Owen.

'I'll send a few around in the morning, asking about the rooftops,' said Hempe. 'I hate to think of the damage an archer might do in the city.'

Owen knew only too well how dangerous an archer might be.

EIGHT

A Stranger in the Garden

Someone shook Owen awake.

'Da! Da!' Gwen stood over him, her face flushed with sleep. Behind her, a gap in the shutters showed the silvery light of dawn.

'What is it? Are you hurt? Hugh? Emma?'

Lucie bent over him to take Gwen's hand. 'You are so cold.'

'I went down the steps for water and saw him in the garden. A man. Curled up on the bench beneath the linden.'

'Is it Rhys?' asked Lucie. 'Did he wander back last night and not want to disturb Jasper?'

'Ma, I would have said. This is a stranger.'

Owen sat up, realizing in time that he was naked. 'Go back to your room, my love. I will see to it and then bring your water. Do not follow me.'

She nodded and scurried out.

Lucie plucked up her gown from the stool beside the bed as she stood. 'Poor child. Another fright.'

'Don't get up with me,' said Owen. 'Stay here. In case.'

'But—'

'I pray you.' Leggings, a linen shirt. Picking up his shoes he opened the door.

'Your patch.' Lucie tossed it to him.

'I might use the scar to frighten him away.' But he took it.

At the bottom of the steps, Owen looked out the garden window. It was as Gwen had described, but he could not see enough of the man to identify him. He stepped into his shoes, covered his scarred eye, and went into the kitchen. Kate, kneeling to stoke the fire, sleepily asked him if he would like some ale.

'Not yet. Have you looked without?'

'No. What is it?'

'Stay in here.' He tucked a knife into his belt, then eased the door open, stepping out into a misty morning.

The man opened an eye as Owen approached, then scuttled upright, catching himself as he was about to fall off the bench. He cradled his left arm, the sleeve soiled with what looked like dried blood. Jonas Snicket's elderly manservant.

'Forgive me, Captain, but I did not know where else to go and I'm that worried about my master.' His teeth rattled with his shivering.

'You are injured.'

'They said they'd do worse the next time they saw me.'

'Come within. I will see to your arm while you tell me your tale.'

'Bless you, Captain. Forgive me for waking you.'

Owen escorted him to the house.

In the doorway, Kate nodded. 'That is three ales then,' she said, standing aside to allow the man through.

His clothing looked as if it had been tidy, if a bit threadbare, before the injury and the night outside. He bobbed his head to Kate as he passed her, stopping just within the door to greet Lucie by name.

'Mistress Wilton.'

'Pete, isn't it?'

'Bless you, Mistress, it is.'

Motioning him to come sit by the fire, she asked Owen to bring the basket holding salves and powders that she kept on the bench near the door.

'This is Pete, Jonas Snicket's serving man. He comes to the apothecary for his master's physicks. A weak heart.' Over the man's head she made a face that said Pete was honest. 'Is it your master? Is he ill?' she asked as Kate offered him a bowl of ale.

'Bless you, no, Mistress, it is not his heart this time.' He took a long drink.

Lucie gently pushed up his sleeve, but the dried blood had molded it to his upper arm. 'I will need to remove your shirt. Are you in much pain?'

His shivering was easing. 'Not so much as I cannot bear it.' He emptied the bowl of ale and began to struggle with the shirt.

'Let me help.' Owen crouched down to him. 'And while we work, we can talk. You said you were worried for your master. Were you injured protecting him?'

'I was, and he cast me out for my pains. He is mad is what he is, moon mad. He thinks himself cunning, addled old fool. And I fear by this morning he may be dead.'

Lucie pressed a warm, wet cloth to the upper arm so the sleeve would come away from the skin. Once Owen had pulled the shirt over the man's head, she set to cleaning the arm. Clearly a knife wound, a slash, not so deep as to be dangerous if cleaned and bandaged soon enough. Pray it was soon enough. The flesh looked angry, but the man had no fever. His earlier shivering seemed the result of a chill from sleeping outside on an October evening with no jacket.

'Who slashed you with the knife?' Owen asked.

'One of the strangers who came to the door late last night. We'd been abed when the banging started. The master barked at me to go tell the drunken louts from the Bell they had the wrong door. But they weren't drunks. And I did not like the looks of them. One held his left arm close, a bloody bandage on that shoulder. They said the taverner at the Bell had told them Master Jonas might

provide lodging. At first the master said he wanted no trouble, he
had no rooms to let, and I told the two to go. But the one pushed
past me and flashed coin at the master, said they would pay a good
price for a clean, quiet room and no gossip. Master Jonas is greedy.
Ordered me to show them to the room up in the loft – was his until
he could no longer climb the ladder. I refused. Told the men the
poor sisters in Castlegate could see to the one's injury, or the friars
on the river. The master barked at me to do his bidding. I started
for the door. Thought to go to the Bell, wake Dunn the taverner,
and find out what he sent our way. The one said no worry, they
could find their way up the ladder. One of the men leaned down to
the master where he sat in that chair he never leaves now and said
he would be able to hire a younger, more obedient servant with all
the money they would pay. Then the one came after me. Slashed
me. The master laughed. Laughed at me bleeding.' He bowed his
head.

'How did you get away?' asked Owen.

'Took off running, the one coming after me, and I ducked down
an alley. Lost him. His limp slowed him, and I know all the ginnels
and alleyways, don't I?'

Owen and Lucie exchanged a look. Pete did not look like a man
who could outrun a person desperate to silence him. He'd not smelled
of drink when out in the garden, but perhaps it did not take much.
Still, the account brought to mind the pair the Bell taverner had
noticed.

'You say the one limped and the other seemed to have been
injured in the shoulder or upper arm?'

'That I did. You've heard of them?'

'Our men have been searching for them.'

'Then it's good I came straight here, isn't it?'

Too convenient? Something did not feel right.

Hugh broke Gwen's cover, running toward her as she pressed her
ear to the door and cawing, 'What?' Noisy rook. In a moment the
kitchen door opened and Kate shook her head at them.

'I will bring your food out here,' she said. 'You can sit on the
window seat and eat. Would you like that?' She ruffled Hugh's hair.
'Now stay. I will fetch Emma.'

*   *   *

Owen asked Pete to describe the men as best he could.

'Wore hats that covered most of their hair, short cloaks. The one with the knife was rounder, older, with a sharp voice. Not so old as me, but the wounded one was younger. Not so young as your Jasper. Beardless, both of 'em. Not from the North. Different, but not foreign, I don't think.'

Owen nodded, took Lucie aside. 'What do you think?'

'His wound is not deep,' she said. 'He will be fine. I've no doubt he was frightened, but then I've never seen him at ease. He comes to me only when Jonas Snicket is ill.' She studied his face. 'You do not believe him.'

'Something happened, to be sure. He would not report such an attack had it not happened. I would quickly find him out. I cannot explain it, but it feels too easy. Do you need help bandaging him?'

'No. But eat something before you leave.'

A knock on the door. Kate opened it.

'Alisoun,' Lucie whispered to Owen and hurried to the door.

'Come, sit, Alisoun. Is Dame Anna delivered of her child?'

Sinking down onto the bench inside the door, Alisoun looked bleary-eyed. 'She is. But it was a difficult birth, a day and a night. I sent for Magda when I found that the baby's head had not turned. Two of us would work more quickly. Dame Anna and her sweet son are fed and resting. She will take a while to regain her strength, but the boy seems healthy.'

'She was fortunate to have you in attendance,' said Lucie. 'Are you hungry?'

'I broke my fast with Magda.' She glanced toward Pete. 'Has Jonas Snicket taken a turn?'

Owen joined them while Lucie was describing what had happened.

Alisoun shook her head. 'I have no doubt at one time or another he offered to take in lodgers for a bit of coin, but his landlord has forbidden it. Whoever the men were, they would be foolish to stay with him. The landlord keeps a sharp eye on the house. Would you like me to talk to Master Jonas? He trusts me, and I would like to help. He might be injured.'

Glancing over at Pete, Owen hesitated to accept. 'I cannot ask you to take such a risk.'

'Now that I know of it, I will not rest easy until I have seen him,' said Alisoun. 'He's not a bad man at heart.'

'Would he open the door to Owen?' Lucie asked.

'It is possible. But it's usually Pete who answers the door. Jonas moves about very little. I think it best I come along.'

Something in the way she said it made Owen ask, 'This has happened before?'

'Similar. Jonas believes himself to be cleverer than his fellows and he's ever scheming to take advantage. He trips over his own imagined cleverness, and when it comes tumbling down about him he often blames Pete. Throws him out, locks the doors, and then his weak heart betrays him. I have worked out a way to climb in without attracting notice on the street. By now he counts on me to come.'

'But this time the men injured Pete,' said Lucie. 'If they are still with him, you would be walking into danger.'

'I know I take a risk. But I feel responsible. He counts on my coming in time. Do you see?'

'He is an old fool,' Lucie said softly.

'If the men are gone, the door might be unlocked,' said Owen. 'I do not need him to open it for me.'

'And if it is locked?'

'Tell me your secret way.'

'Forgive me, Captain, but you are not as nimble or as light as I am. And with his bad heart we must not delay. Come.'

While Owen went for his cloak, Alisoun asked, 'How is Jasper today?'

Lucie moaned. 'I've not yet seen him this morning. He moved slowly yesterday. He came home very drunk, confused Rhys with Einar, and what he said – I pray he was not overheard in the tavern.'

'His friend Carl lives near the Thorntons. He came this morning to warn me of what Jasper had said. Fortunately they drank in a private room, and he'd said nothing about it on the way but that he was finished with me. Coming home, Carl kept a hand over his mouth.'

'I am so sorry,' Lucie said.

'You have no control over him,' said Alisoun. 'He is grown.'

'He was better yesterday,' said Owen, rejoining them. 'All is well between him and Gwen. But I will speak with him when we've seen about Jonas.'

'Let me give you some of his heart medicine. In case you cannot find it,' said Lucie, hurrying out of the kitchen.

Owen and Alisoun followed her, waiting outside the workshop door.

'What will you say to Jasper?' she asked.

'I don't know. If he were one of my men, I would humiliate him in front of his fellows and then toss him out in disgrace. Though if it was his first time so drunk . . . What would you have me do?'

Her brown-eyed gaze steady, lacking emotion, she said, 'I am not asking you to do anything. I delayed telling him something he had a right to know months ago. He is right to be angry.'

'But this behavior . . .'

'I pray you, be gentle with him. If he has made amends with Gwen, I am happy.'

They were quiet awhile, until Pete shuffled out the door, wearing a blanket like a cloak. 'Are you going to see the master, Mistress Alisoun?'

'In a moment,' she said. 'Dame Lucie is preparing more of his medicine, in case I cannot find his.'

'Let me go,' said Pete. 'I don't like to see you hurt.'

'The captain will make certain nothing happens to me.'

'The old fool might need me.'

'No,' Owen said.

'You cannot keep me here against my will,' said Pete. 'I've done nothing wrong.'

'It is for your own good,' said Alisoun.

But it was soon plain to Owen that the man was determined, and when Lucie appeared with the medicine he nodded to both of them. 'Time to go.'

On the way, Alisoun had suggested that if no one answered the door she would sneak in, surprising the intruders – if they were still there. Owen could wait for them at the door, entering if he heard anything that concerned him. 'It is a poor house,' she had pointed out, 'neither waxed parchment nor glass in the windows. You will hear everything.'

He had agreed.

Now, stepping up to the door, one hand on the hilt of the knife in her basket, she knocked. Hearing neither a voice nor movement within, she pushed at the door. Something prevented her from opening it. Nodding to where Owen crouched in the shadow of

Laurence Gunnell's shop, she turned down the alleyway and paused, listening. No one coming, no sound from within. Placing her basket on the ground she tied a rope to the handle, tucked the other end into her girdle, and climbed up the drainpipe to a windowsill. Taking a breath, she slowly pushed aside the loose shutter, again stopping to listen before easing down onto the table set beneath the window inside. Another pause. Still no sign of discovery. After freeing her skirts and retrieving her basket, she closed the shutter and crept out of the room, keeping an eye peeled for the intruders. The solar was empty. Messy, as if someone had been searching for something. A few steps down the ladder to the main part of the house, she paused, bending over to peer out. Seeing no sign of movement, she descended. On the bed tucked off to one side were rumpled bedclothes, but no Jonas. In the dimness it took her a moment to see that it was he who lay against the outside door, curled into a ball beneath a blood-stained blanket.

His hands and feet were cold and dried blood matted the sparse hair at the back of his head, but she felt a faint, uneven heartbeat. Gently easing him onto his back she could see that his face was bruised and one of his hands swollen. Pushing up his sleeve she found more signs of beating. Poor man. With care she moved him aside and opened the door.

The captain rushed in. 'You are unhurt?'

'I am. He is in there, battered, alive, but I am worried. If you could find me some water.'

'I will fetch it,' Pete cried, hastening out from behind the captain.

In short order the bed was stripped, fresh blankets and a pillow provided from a large chest, and Jonas was lying with a pillow behind his head after a move that had him whimpering and his heartbeat fluttering.

Pete had brought a cup of water so murky that Alisoun would normally reject it, but time was of the essence. She added Jonas's heart tincture and coaxed him to drink a little.

'It is Mistress Alisoun. I am with Captain Archer and your loyal Pete,' she said, embarrassed for her companions to hear the emotion in her voice as she leaned close to hear his weak voice.

'Just you . . .' a breath, '. . . and the captain.'

'Did he say aught?' asked Pete, bending over her.

Alisoun turned to the servant. 'I need you to fetch fresh water and some wine from the Bell. Stay outside until the captain lets you in.'

'He is in good hands,' the captain assured him. 'We will not keep you waiting long.'

'Best not. I'll have the water and wine.' Pete gave a half-hearted laugh and shuffled off.

Alisoun lifted the cup to Jonas's lips for another sip of the physick. When he had swallowed and lay back to rest on the pillow, she said, 'Tell Captain Archer what happened.'

He did his best to nod without raising his head.

When they first arrived, Owen had left Jonas to Alisoun's competent ministrations while he searched for signs of lurkers. He found no one, but the house was in such disorder that he'd asked Pete about it.

'I may not be the best housekeeper, Captain, but those men tossed everything about. No wonder the master's heart gave out.'

Now Owen settled beside Jonas Snicket and asked him what they were searching for. He had to lean close to hear the man's whisper over the rising sound of voices out in the yard.

Snicket's eyes, clouded with age, filled with tears. 'Coins . . .' He took a breath. 'Silver. Gold. How?'

'How did they find it?'

A nod, then a coughing fit had Jonas wrapping his arms round him, as if to hold himself together.

Owen waited until Alisoun gave the man more of the tincture, then asked, 'The men who came last night took it? You know this?'

'Showed me,' he whispered with eyes closed.

'How many people knew of the hiding place?'

'I trusted . . .' A long moment in which he fought for breath. 'Betrayed . . .' His voice faded to nothing.

Alisoun put a hand on Owen's arm, a light tug indicating he should let the man rest. Straightening, he followed her toward the door.

'I do not think he will be with us long,' she said. 'Could you quiet the people out there? Let him die in peace?'

Dying. 'Do you think he's telling the truth?' Owen asked.

'I do not think he would have used what little strength he has to lie to you.'

'Did you know he had money in the house?'

'He bragged of it. I will tell you what I know after Pete brings the water and wine.'

Owen stepped out, motioning for Pete to go in, then turned to face a crowd gathering round Colby, Jonas's landlord, who shrilly proclaimed that he would toss Snicket out onto the street for being a menace.

'The only menace in this tale is whoever beat your tenant to the point of death,' Owen said. 'Was it you?'

While Colby choked on his indignation, Owen spoke in a quiet voice that required the man to make the effort to listen. He made no threats, but rather informed the man how he should proceed if he wished to keep his name out of gossip about the incident. 'And that includes all of you,' he said, taking in the rest. 'Master Jonas's manservant says that one of the intruders who badly beat Master Jonas is injured in his shoulder or upper arm. The other one is older, with a limp. Has anyone seen them?'

Shaking heads, curious glances round the crowd. One woman stepped forward, speaking of a cry in the night, several voices. Owen asked her where she lived. He would speak with her more. 'Anyone else?' With shakes of their heads, the others scurried off, leaving Colby the landlord.

'I have a right to choose my tenants.'

'Is Jonas Snicket in arrears on his rent?'

'No.'

'Then what is your complaint? Do you think he asked for this trouble?'

'He complains to anyone who will listen that he was a wealthy man before his family deserted him. But neighbors said he was so stingy they almost starved, and his wife took the children away to find a better life. So where is all his wealth?'

'Is that why you want him gone? So you can tear up the walls and floorboards searching for treasure?'

'What? I never said that.'

'If I hear you've tossed him out—' Owen glared at him.

The man shrunk into himself and hurried away, muttering about abuse.

When Colby was gone, Laurence Gunnell came out from his shop, his face creased with concern. 'I heard you say "to the point of death". Is the old man dying?'

'I think so.'

Gunnell crossed himself. 'I am sorry. He was a mean old dog, but I hope to have half his fire when I'm that age.'

Nodding to him, Owen went back into the house. Jonas lay still, his old servant kneeling beside him, weeping and praying. Gone. Murdered. By the same men who murdered Beck?

While they waited for the coroner, Owen helped Pete tidy the house. Let him have a clean place to sleep until Colby evicted him.

Once the coroner had seen Jonas and questioned Alisoun, Owen, and Pete, he said they were free to go about their day.

As Owen took up Alisoun's basket, the coroner said, 'You will be searching for the men who beat him?'

'I will.'

'Has this anything to do with the Bishop of Winchester?'

'Why do you ask?'

'Third body in what, three or four days, two of them from the attack on his carter . . .'

'Where did you learn of Bishop Wykeham's presence in the city?'

'The sheriff.'

'Do most people know?'

'I would say so. By now. People remember the murder of the young midwife when he last visited York. So? Does this have to do with him?'

'Too soon to say.'

'And if you knew, you would not tell me.'

'Why do you say that?'

'You're a sly one, Archer. Keep your information close but for your friends Poole and Hempe. I suppose it's wise in your work. But it makes people wonder.'

Meaning he wondered. Owen thanked him for attending so quickly and took his leave.

Out in the yard, Owen took a good look at Alisoun. Despite some grime on hem and cobwebs in her hair from the house of old men who saw no reason to fuss much, she presented a respectable front.

But he sensed grief and deep weariness in her eyes and the tenor of her voice.

Nodding to him, she started moving away from the house.

'I am sorry I was not with you when Jonas died,' Owen said as he fell into step beside her.

'Magda taught me to open my heart when I sit with the dying, holding them, reassuring them. This morning was not the first time I have felt life slip away in a patient. But . . .' She took a deep breath. 'Jonas was so alone, his spirit so thin, as if he died long ago.' She met Owen's eye and forced a smile. 'It is my sleeplessness speaking.'

Perhaps. Though he wondered how much of Jonas Snicket's curtness had been an attempt to cover a disappointment in life, and whether with Magda's training Alisoun could sense that. Added to her vigil of two nights and a day assisting at a difficult birth, and her argument with Jasper, he marveled at her vigorous stride.

'When was the last time you slept?'

'Two days ago,' she said as she bobbed her head at a passerby who called out a greeting.

'To ensure that you go straightaway home, I will escort you to Bootham Bar.'

'You mean to protect me from the gossips who might have heard Jasper's insults.'

Despite being tired she was sharp.

'That is part of it,' he admitted.

'I am protected by Magda's dragon,' she said, 'didn't you know?'

Owen glanced over at her, remembering a strange moment when he had thought he saw Magda's dragon reach down to Einar, the healer's great-grandson, in a protective posture. A few blinks and the vision had passed, but for that moment . . . Alisoun's eyes were soft, as if seeing something in memory. 'I am glad of that,' he said. 'But I will escort you anyway.'

'Even after I betrayed your son?'

'What you did for Jonas, your care for those who seek your help, that is what I am honoring.'

'Thank you.' Her smile was tinged with sadness. 'Then I welcome your company.'

He proffered his arm and she threaded hers through his and matched his stride, which he shortened for her sake. Far more comfortable together than was their wont. He remembered his impression when watching her attend Jonas Snicket – in the past year she had truly come into her own authority as a healer. She no longer behaved like an apprentice – hesitant, murmuring Magda's advice under her breath.

'Colby mentioned a wife and children,' he said. 'Do you know anything of them?'

'He had many stories of his family. In some his wife and an ever-changing number of children simply walked away, in others he had a son who had gone a-soldiering and never returned. Once he mentioned a daughter who died of the pestilence, as had his wife.'

'No idea what might have been the true story?'

'I think the saddest one. It did not suit him to have lost his family to pestilence and war.'

'So he might have a living son?'

Alisoun chuckled. 'You do not mean to spend time chasing after what might exist only in my head, do you?'

'No.' He knew he had grasped at the tale of a son going off to be a soldier as something familiar. He had done so – conscripted, not his choice. And he knew the pain of feeling he'd left it too late to return to the home of his birth. Nor had he been able to imagine what sort of life he could make in Wales. Trained from youth as an archer, he'd felt at the time he was good for little else. When the old duke, Henry of Grosmont, chose him for one of his spies, he had schooled Owen in reading, writing, dressing, speaking, behaving as a lesser noble. Which had brought him to the attention of Archbishop Thoresby on the old duke's death, and hence to York. Jonas's son's tale would doubtless be different, but likely just as unpredictable. If he even existed.

'I just pray that the son so long lost to him was not one of the men who beat and robbed him,' said Alisoun. 'A son might have known where to look.'

Owen mulled over her idea as she paused to give the good news of the birth of Anna's child to a woman who asked, crouching down to greet the woman's daughter, who giggled at Alisoun's teasing.

When they walked on he asked how she had thought of that – Jonas's son being one of the intruders.

'My mind often works that way, imagining the worst that could happen to someone I've come to care for.'

'How often are you right?'

'Almost never, I am glad to report.' A little laugh.

'Until Jonas said he'd been robbed, I wondered how the pair dared attack his house, knowing I'd been there to see whether the old man had lodged the men who attacked Gerald Trent and the others. I made no secret of my purpose.'

'Whoever it was knew of the money, and where to find it,' said Alisoun. 'That would mean they are likely people of York.'

'Who might Jonas have forgotten he'd told?'

'Any number of people. When the weakness came upon him, he grew forgetful. I do not envy you your job, Captain.'

In the walk from Jonas's home to Bootham Bar, nary a person taunted Alisoun. It seemed Jasper's friend had spoken the truth about her being safe from his foul mouth. A blessing. Owen, however, fielded a few jolly comments about his son's drunken walk across the city.

'I wish I had the time to ask Magda's advice about my son,' he said as they reached the city gate.

'You are a good father, Captain. He was not copying anything you did.'

Not now, not since he'd come to York. But Owen could not say it was true of him when a soldier.

NINE

A Carving, a Kindness, an Arrow

As he crossed the minster yard, Owen heard someone calling to him. He turned to see a muscular man of middle age dressed in the dusty tunic and leggings of an artisan.

'Marcus Bolton, Captain. You've no cause to know me, but I heard about the man you found in the beck, and that he might be David Wells. So I took myself to the castle and – God help me, what a stench, I pity the guards – from what I could tell it is the young man who was working for me.'

A bit of luck. 'Go on. How did you come to hire him?'

'He came to the city wanting work in the stoneyard at the minster. When they had no need for him, they suggested he see me. He hoped, with his fine tools, that working for a stonemason might lead to his being hired at the minster. He proved a good worker, though I employed him on humble houses, nothing so fine I needed a skilled carver. And he was that.' Bolton pulled a small stone from his scrip and placed it in Owen's hand.

Deep-set eyes glared at him from a sea of wrinkles, the mouth pursed in disapproval, hair wildly curled about the head.

'A ceiling boss to give nightmares to the unsuspecting soul during a sermon,' said Owen.

The man was laughing. 'A gorgon, that's what she is. But you see the skill. I hoped to keep him on long enough to have time to persuade someone to take him on at the minster. Think what he might have done.'

'A waste of a life,' said Owen. 'I would like to show you a pack of tools. They might have been his. I could bring it to you if you tell me where.'

Bolton began to answer, forming one word before changing it. 'You will be busy with all this, so why don't I come to you?'

Col, that's the word Owen saw him form. And then changed his mind. It might be nothing, but Owen would send someone to observe the man's house in Colliergate. 'Sooner is much better than later,' he said.

'I will come as soon as I may. Is it true David was here only to attack the carter he blamed for his father's death?'

'Who told you that?'

'Harold, one of the minster masons. I cannot understand. I've never been so wrong about a worker. I believed him in earnest when he talked of carving decorated stones for the great York Minster being his dream.'

'A man can journey far for one cause and discover another, closer to his heart,' said Owen. 'Did he have any visitors while he worked for you?'

'He did. The young man John the Joiner took on to work on Dame Lucie's apothecary. Rhys. He came to see David a few times. They would argue, Rhys would go off angry. Seemed to me they knew each other well. Like brothers, I thought.'

No wonder. 'Has he been back since David disappeared?'

'Haven't seen him.'

Had Rhys been part of the plan? But why had he not taken part in the attack? The scar, the arguments . . . Related?

Owen realized he still held the gorgon and handed it to Bolton. 'I thank you for the information.'

'You are welcome to the stone,' said Bolton. 'I'll come to see the tools in the next day or so.'

'Another death?' Michaelo looked grieved. 'You will wish to speak with His Grace?'

'Is he here?'

'In the garden.' The monk touched Owen's arm. 'If there is anything I can do—'

'Send word the moment you sense danger. Anything out of the ordinary.'

'A chilling request.'

'Three deaths, none of them anticipated.' Owen nodded to him and headed for the garden.

Wykeham rose at his approach. 'Such a grim face. More trouble?' He listened with bowed head to the tale of Jonas Snicket. 'A sad ending. But what has this to do with your investigation of the attack on Trent and his men?'

'The city was quiet for a long while before that event, Your Grace. Then the attack, a body, the abandoned cart, another body, and this latest.' He did not mention the incident in the cemetery, though it must be connected. 'I cannot help but suspect the men involved in your problem are leaving a trail of trouble behind them.'

'I see. I pray you, keep me informed. And I still wish to dine with you and Dame Lucie. Dom Jehannes welcomes you whenever you might find time in your busy days.'

Courteous, accepting his judgment? Owen did not understand this Wykeham. And he should, for the sake of the city. 'If my wife feels easy leaving the shop for a few hours, and Dom Jehannes believes his cook able to accommodate us, we will join you tomorrow. Do you know if he is at home?'

'He retreated to his parlor with a comely young man who came seeking counsel. They might have adjourned by now. I look forward to a long conversation on the morrow.' He walked with Owen to the door – more unusual behavior – adding, 'You should know that the sheriff had sent a messenger to ask what I wished to do with the cart of stones. I had them delivered to St Clement's. They may find them useful.'

'I am glad to hear it.'

In the hall, Owen asked Brother Michaelo whether he thought Jehannes would be comfortable with Wykeham's invitation for dinner the following day.

'He will be glad of it, relieved of the responsibility of entertaining His Grace. I will inform him when his visitor departs.'

'The young man is still with him?'

Michaelo raised a brow. 'His Grace noticed him?'

'He knew only that he sought our friend's counsel, and that he was comely.'

Nodding, Michaelo promised to arrange the dinner with the cook. Something in his expression puzzled Owen. He felt he left with more questions than when he'd arrived.

On his way home, Owen stopped at the house of Gemma Rydale, mother of their maidservant Kate as well as Tildy, now married to the steward of Lucie's family manor, and Rob and Rose, twins who had proved excellent spies for him in the past. Lucie often teased that they could not survive without the Rydale brood, and wondered how many of the younger siblings they might engage in future. Today he had need of the twins.

'You will find them doing penance in the kitchen yard, Captain, raking leaves and tidying the herb patch.'

'Might I employ them for some tracking?'

'Bless you, Captain. You will be doing me a kindness giving them work.'

He found Rose kneeling at a small, tidy bed of herbs, plucking fallen leaves from the lavender and rosemary. Rob shook a rake at a mongrel dog trading barks with him. As children, the pair had been almost identical in appearance, until they moved – Rose was all speed and surprising grace, Rob more measured and heavy, though he could be quick when the situation required it. But now, at seventeen, one would not know they were twins except for their mannerisms when speaking, especially their colorful vocabularies. Rose had a delicate beauty, with pale brown hair tumbling round her shoulders and enormous green eyes in a heart-shaped face, full lips that were more often turned up in a smile than not. Her looks deceived, and she delighted in using that to her benefit. Rob's hair, in contrast, had darkened and thickened, standing up about his square face. His form was solid, muscular, his expression bland, as if he had not a thought in his head, and he spoke so quietly that folk must come close to hear him. Few dared.

Owen crouched down beside Rose. 'He's taken to barking now?'

'Captain!' She sat back on her heels, grinning at him. 'Two curs trading insults.'

'You two have quarreled?'

'Of late he's all noise and no wit. The lad's in love, and he caught her riding a rival.'

Echoes of his own son's woes. 'I was hoping I might hire the pair of you to search for some miscreants. But if you'd rather work alone . . .'

'Just what's needed!' Springing onto her feet, she sprinted over to her twin and took him by the shoulder, shaking him. 'Shut your jaw and come hear what the captain needs of us.'

With the twins out in the city, hunting for signs of Rhys, Raymond, and the vaguely described pair who had robbed Jonas, who might or might not be the same as the surviving pair from the attack on the cart, Owen headed home. He found Lucie alone in the apothecary.

'No Jasper?'

'He asked leave to go to the minster and pray,' she said. 'He is filled with remorse and wishes for atonement. Magda's in the kitchen. She wanted to hear about Jonas Snicket. How is he?'

'Word has not gotten round the city yet?'

'I've heard nothing.'

'Beaten so badly his heart pulled him down. He died while we were there.' Owen managed to tell her most of the tale before a customer interrupted. 'Jasper needs to watch the shop tomorrow. We're dining with Jehannes and the bishop.'

'Are we?' Lucie raised a brow. 'I doubt Jasper will complain of it. He's been away for a while this morning. But will you have the time?'

'What he wishes to discuss in your presence may prove helpful.'

'I hope so. Go now, dine with Magda. Kate will serve me when Jasper returns.'

In the kitchen, Magda held Emma on her lap, teaching her a complicated string game. Peals of laughter as his youngest tangled herself, then found her way out. Owen laughed with her.

'She is quick-fingered,' said Magda with a fond smile.

'Don't I know that!' Kate laughed from her spot stirring a stew. She wiped her hands on a cloth and stepped over to relieve Magda of the four-year-old. 'If you will fetch the ale, Captain, I will bring the food to the hall,' she said.

Scooping up a jug and two bowls, Owen followed Magda out of the kitchen. They settled round a corner of the table that afforded both of them a view of the garden. Kate arrived with roasted fowl, pottage, and cheese, Emma with a basket of bread. Owen and Magda fussed over Emma's success in delivering the food without mishap. Giggling, she tugged at Kate's hand, leading her back to the kitchen. As they reached the door she cried, 'We're going to pick apples!'

Magda laughed and clapped her hands. Owen thanked Kate as she disappeared through the door.

'Have you seen the others?'

'Gwen and Hugh are pulling weeds in the garden beds.' Magda poured ale for both of them as she spoke, handing one to Owen and urging him to drink up. 'Thou hast witnessed a death today. This and a full stomach will calm thee. Tell Magda what is tumbling round in thy head when thou art full.'

Seeing the wisdom in her advice, Owen fell to the food with more enthusiasm than he had expected. While he ate, Magda told him what she knew of his concerns so that he would not need to repeat himself. She also surprised him with an account of a conversation with Gwen.

'Thine eldest proposes Magda take her into Galtres to learn to gather roots, berries, nuts, and wild herbs, while her dam teaches her the properties of all in the garden and gives her chores there and in the apothecary. She means to be either a healer or an apothecary. Didst thou know?'

He recalled her questioning about how he had known what he wished to do. She had asked Lucie about her vocation as well. 'Do you think she is sincere?'

'As a child can be. She may try many other paths before finding her own. For now, she is keen.'

A pleasant bit of news on a trying day. Sitting back, he proceeded to give Magda an account of all that had happened since Wykeham arrived in York. By the time he was finished, he'd downed another full bowl of ale in wetting his throat. All the while Magda listened without comment.

Now she touched his hand. 'So much weighing on thee, Bird-eye. Do not mourn Jonas too long. His heart died with his wife. He was lost without her calm counsel, and her head for business.'

He asked her about the various versions of his family.

'Son went off to be a soldier, swearing Jonas would never see him again, wife and daughter dead of pestilence.' She shifted in her chair to look more closely at him. 'As to the Winchester crow, he, too, is lost. His king is dying, and the king's sons do not share their father's love for him. He feels choked by enemies, and he may well be right to feel so. His power diminishes. What did he love before he gave his life to his king?'

'Building.' Owen described to her a room at Windsor Castle in which Wykeham had built a model of how he wished to change the castle. 'He talked of going there when he was wakeful, finding calm in the planning.'

Her eyes smiled. 'That is good. Speak to him of that. Say thou art curious whether he yet has such a chamber to which he might retreat. Thou couldst inspire him anew.' Owen must have flinched at the suggestion. Magda chuckled. 'There is no harm in showing kindness to one who is a sometime enemy. Much good might come of it. For both.'

As ever, he saw the wisdom in her words. 'I would welcome something to distract me from my own dark suspicions. I see plotters and murderers everywhere.'

'It is the nature of thy work, Bird-eye. And why thou art good at it. Magda is sorry for young Rhys. When he is found, listen with care. Do not be quick to condemn him.'

He bit his tongue on his arguments. Doubtless she was right in this. 'And Jasper. How might I help him?'

'In his time of trial.' She turned to gaze out the window.

'When did Einar last visit?'

'More than a year ago.' She nodded. 'Alisoun clutched it to her heart a long while, as if hoping it might soften with time.'

'A year?'

'Yes.'

'If she had told him as soon as she returned . . .' he began, but stopped when she turned back to him with a frown.

'He would not have felt so betrayed? She lay with Einar. That is all he truly hears now. That she has no wish to live with Einar matters little at present. In time her delay will carry more sting.'

Owen nodded. At present the pain came from what happened with Einar. Alisoun's hesitation might make Jasper wonder whether she was not sure what she felt. But the deed was done. *He* saw the implications, but his son might not yet be clear-headed enough to consider them.

'How can I help him?'

'He must find his own way, Bird-eye. It is a hard lesson for a father.'

'His anger with Gwen, getting drunk at Simon's farewell party, should I not intervene?'

'A most difficult passage for a young man,' said Magda. 'But attempts to help, no matter how gentle and caring, will be met with resistance. And more temper.'

They spoke a while longer, but she held to her simple advice – allow Jasper to find his way. She promised to watch for Rhys, the pair who had attacked Jonas, and for Raymond.

'Hast thou spoken to Angel-voice at the priory? Will she return with the Winchester crow?'

'I have not. Dame Marian would have no insight into the attack on Trent and his men.'

'But she might provide a sense of the Winchester crow's standing in the realm. Perhaps advice from her kin.'

He considered that, but could not see the immediate benefit.

'Thou couldst then tell the crow that thou hast spoken with her.'

'You think it important that I be kind to him,' he said. 'Why?'

'Magda senses a desperate man.'

'As do I,' said Lucie. Owen had not noticed her enter the room. She bent to kiss his cheek.

'Jasper has returned?'

'He has.'

Magda pressed Owen's hand. 'Ride out to Clementhorpe. The sun is shining, the air is crisp, and the brief journey might clear thy head.'

Owen knelt before the altar in the priory chapel, praying for the soul of Jonas Snicket, whose ending weighed on his heart during the solitary journey to St Clement's – bitter, lost, railing against the world, being brought down so cruelly through someone's betrayal. Whose? He bowed his head, pushing aside the question. *Blessed Mother Mary, I pray you intercede on behalf of the soul of Jonas Snicket. May your son, God Almighty, grant him grace.*

A rustle of prayer beads behind him announced the arrival of Dame Marian. He crossed himself and rose.

'Forgive me for interrupting your devotions,' she said.

'A moment of peace. I am ready to resume my work.'

She bowed and led him out of the chapel toward the orchard.

'So this is not just a friendly visit?' Her pale eyes twinkled.

'That, too.'

He took a moment to appreciate how changed she was from the frightened waif Brother Michaelo had brought to his door on a snowy morning a few years earlier. It was more than the Benedictine habit she now wore. Her eyes spoke of contentment, and her presence radiated a calm, as if the world might be trusted to walk in grace.

They said nothing for a while, a companionable silence. A dappled light and the spicy scent of late apples invited a stroll along the paths. Feeling the peace of the priory enveloping him, Owen was grateful to Magda for guiding him here.

'You come to speak of Bishop Wykeham's request?' she asked.

'Of the circumstances that led him to such an undertaking. Has your family spoken of it?'

'Oh yes. I have heard much of his woes from my aunts. It seems the bishop's nemesis, the Duke of Lancaster, acts on behalf of his father the king, but with his own prejudices. For the sake of my Percy kin, especially Uncle Thomas, I am advised to do nothing that might be construed as a favor to Wykeham.'

Sir Thomas Percy again. 'Have they provided details of Lancaster's intentions regarding Wykeham?'

'He is to be stripped of his temporalities, reducing his income and properties to those attached to his bishopric.'

Quite a loss. Not one that would leave Wykeham destitute, but, as he'd said, stripped him of the means to sustain influence in the realm, a frightening prospect for a man with many powerful enemies. 'Once the king's favorite, now to be brought so low. And all for a false rumor.'

'I doubt that is the sole cause,' said Marian. 'According to my uncle and aunts, the duke is so like his father and eldest brother in temperament and sense of duty, and looks so like both of them, that it is impossible for anyone who knows him to believe he is a changeling. But perhaps in his own heart he doubts? Being the son of such a king, and the brother of such a warrior as Prince Edward might prove a heavy burden. He might feel lesser in comparison. Poor man.'

He thought of Magda's guidance – kindness. It seemed that Dame Marian was the model of kindness. 'All that being possible, I still fail to understand Lancaster's purpose in such an extreme action against the Bishop of Winchester.'

'Nor do my aunts. The clerics will see it as a threat. Wonder which one of them might be next. And His Grace King Edward, should he recover his strength, will he not be offended? This man he held in such esteem?'

Owen recalled Thoresby's falling out with the king over Alice Perrers because he disapproved of the romantic liaison, feeling that her presence was a constant insult to Queen Philippa, whom he revered. 'For all we know the king might approve. Royal favor is never secure. Perhaps the duke means it as a warning to tread with care, not to assume the throne is weak because of the king's failing health.'

'I do not like to think they would so use a man who has faithfully served his king and his God.' She paused and lifted her face to gaze up at the overhanging branches as wind danced in the leaves around them, sending some twirling from their branches and spiraling down to the ground. 'I have been content here. And yet beneath that contentment is ever a hum of worry that my place is with Dame Eloise in her final days. Now my kin would have me choose them over my dear teacher.'

'I am sorry.'

'I wonder – is God testing me? Taking the advice of my aunts and uncle and staying here has much appeal. But Dame Eloise taught me most of what I know of sacred music, loved me, encouraged me, and now I might comfort her in her final days, ease her worries. If it were not that in returning to her I might endanger my kin, my duty would be clear to me.' She bowed her head, the graceful dip of a swan. He saw a tear travel down her cheek.

'How might I help?'

She touched his arm. 'You have listened. It has helped to speak of it with a friend who has no need to urge me to either choice. Bless you for coming. Tell me about Gwen, Hugh, and Emma. Are they singing?'

Owen laughed. 'Oh yes. And they argue about which one of them you will praise on your next visit.'

'Should I decide to return to Wherwell, I will miss them.'

'Take their laughter with you in your heart.'

'Bless you, Captain, I will.'

By the time Owen left her, he sensed that she had made a decision.

When he reached the priory yard, the cart of stones sat just within the gate. Beside it, Prioress Isobel stood with hands on hips, studying the stones someone had taken off the cart and placed on a low wall.

She glanced up at his approach. 'Captain Archer, will you look at the stones His Grace gifted us for the orchard wall?'

'*Benedicite*, Mother Isobel.' He bobbed his head to her and moved closer to run his hand over them. 'So fine. Are they all like this?'

'They are. Far too fine for an orchard wall. But perhaps we might take his advice, use these for an archway beside the chapel . . .' Her eyes brightened.

Wykeham's scheme had worked?

'A gift fit for St Clement's after all,' Owen said.

'Perhaps.' She motioned to a tall sister striding toward them. 'Dame Perpetua will have the gardeners unload this in the stables.'

Owen offered to help the sister move the cart away from the gate, but Dame Perpetua would not hear of it.

'I will see to it.'

Expressing his gratitude for giving Dame Marian leave to speak with him, Owen took his leave before Mother Isobel grew curious about the conversation. He noticed his horse had been offered water, and smelled apples on her breath.

'Your groom was kind,' he said.

'That was Dame Perpetua,' said Mother Isobel, giving her companion a fond smile.

The visit had shifted Owen's mood, and he hummed as he rode back toward the city, looking round, noticing how the autumn sun picked out the gold and red leaves carpeting the ground beneath partially bared trees.

Until he felt a shiver up his spine and his ruined eye began to throb. Closing his good for a moment, he sought the direction from which came the threat. Just as he'd established it was to his left, the sense passed. Ambling off the road in that direction he found nothing. But it had been there, he was sure of it.

From the stables near Micklegate Bar he sought out the riverside home of the woman who had heard the cry in the night. She welcomed him into her modest house next door to Snicket's, shooing a small boy and a kitten away from a bench by the fire.

'I have some ale,' she said.

'A mouthful would be most welcome. Thank you.' Owen settled on the bench.

She handed him a small cup as she perched beside him. 'You've come about what I heard, the night that poor man was robbed.' She glanced round, lowered her voice. 'I believe it was Master Jonas I heard. I would have thought nothing of it – he oft wept and cried out in his sleep. He told me his wife came to him, but as they were kissing she would turn into a creature out of hell and choke him.' She crossed herself.

'But this night?'

'After his cry I heard laughter. Oh, Captain, such evil, wicked laughter. And I'd a mind I was hearing the she-devil in his dreams. In the morning I chided myself. *You foolish Margery, you can't hear another's dreams.* And I remembered a man's angry voice after the laughter. And another. When I heard old Jonas had been attacked, I thought to speak up.'

'It was the laughter that caused you to think of a she-devil?'

'Have you ever heard an owl's hunting cry? The one that sounds like a cackle? That's the sound. I've always thought it how the devil would laugh.'

His ruined eye throbbed. He once knew someone with such a

laugh. Many of Owen's archers thought him the devil himself, though he was one of them. 'What part of the night?'

'I'd been asleep a long while, but it was still dark as pitch. And I fell back to sleep until the lad woke me at dawn.'

Drinking down the ale, Owen thanked her for her help.

'It was important?'

'Every piece is, Dame Margery. Bless you.'

Deep in dark memories of the man with such a laugh, a thorn amongst his archers, he was startled back to the present by Rob and Rose rushing up to him on Ouse Bridge, clearly excited. Over the bridge and into Coney Street they hurried him, leading him down a narrow alley where they stopped just before the buildings gave way to the mud flats on the riverbank.

From beneath his tunic, Rob drew out an arrow snapped in half, and Rose went to stand in the corner where they had found it, lifting a rag and presenting it to him. The remains of a shirt stiff with blood.

'How you noticed these here, where the light never reaches . . .'

'We are closer to the ground than you are, Captain,' Rose said with a laugh.

That they were.

'Is it helpful?' Rob asked.

Owen moved out onto the mud flat to examine the broken arrow in better light. Blood-stained as well. The arrowhead was not the simple sort used for hunting small game, but an archer's point. He examined the other half. The fletching was set at an uncommon slant. He had last seen this among his men when he was captain of the duke's archers. A small group led by his most skilled but least trusted archer, he of the evil laugh, who claimed the odd slant made an arrow faster. Owen never could see the difference. The arrow had been dropped recently, else the remains would have been scavenged for the arrowhead, which was still useful.

'Might be,' said Owen. 'You've already earned a day's pay.'

'It's still early!' Rose declared as the two hurried off.

The arrow was the kind used in battle, not hunting or practicing at the butts, its use in the city prohibited, punished by a large fine and confiscation of all archery equipment. He wrapped the broken arrow in the remnants of the shirt and stuck them in his scrip. He needed to talk to Trent, find out if the laugh and the arrowhead were Raymond's.

TEN

An Attack, a Confession, a Child's Bold Question

'Trent is not here,' said Bess. Owen had found her in the tavern kitchen, discussing a potage with the cook, a rat of a man who created remarkably fine food. She had taken Owen aside in the small space between kitchen and tavern room she referred to as her parlor. 'And yes, we have at long last found a cook we will do whatever it takes to keep. Within reason. So praise the food loudly, my friend.'

'I will. How long has Trent been out?' It was coming on dusk. He'd counted on the man being in the tavern, staring into a tankard of ale, at this hour.

'He left not long after midday. Ate dinner, then asked about merchants traveling south. Seems the bishop did not appear to want him in his traveling party.'

'Wykeham told him that?'

'Not directly, but Trent said it was clear. A pity. He had humbled himself before the bishop, confided in him that his wife had pushed him to make this journey despite his unease about the men accompanying him. Seems she'd heard him brag to a prominent merchant about cheating his clients, even the mighty Wykeham, and stuffing his coffers. She told him the journey would be his penance, and God might bless them with a child once he made reparations.'

'He told you this?'

'Men far from home often confide in me. Once it was in the hopes of taking me to bed.' She laughed.

'I think it likely that is still their hope.'

She wrinkled her nose at him. 'You are kind.' But just in case, she felt round her beribboned cap, tucking in stray locks.

'Did you know of a party with whom he might make the journey?'

'I've not heard of any, so I sent him to Crispin Poole. He keeps an eye out for opportunities to send his factor with other merchants. And you will be sure to hear where he went next.' She smiled.

'You are a good friend.' He kissed her cheek. 'I will be back in a little while to meet Poole and Hempe. I hope to see Trent here as well.'

After the sense of someone watching on the road, he felt the need to see Lucie and the children, be assured that they were safe.

In the workshop, Lucie was showing Gwen how to heat wax in which to mix a poultice. Kissing her on the neck, Owen stepped past her to peek at Jasper, who was helping an elderly couple hard of hearing, using his entire body to communicate his questions. As Owen backed away, he found himself in Lucie's arms.

'You are worried for us, my love?' she whispered in his ear.

He turned in her arms. 'As ever when there is trouble in the city.'

'Did you go to the priory?'

'I did. Mother Isobel is pleased with Wykeham's gift, and Dame Marian might return with him. So perhaps he will soon depart.'

'I sense there is more.'

'It may prove to be nothing. I must speak with Trent.' He kissed her and went seeking Hugh and Emma. Not finding them in the garden, he checked the kitchen. His worries eased to see Emma racing round the room with a string of yarn, chased by the cat, and Hugh hunched over wax tablets, complaining whenever his little sister or the cat careened into him. Kate hummed as she spun yarn near the window. When she glanced up, he motioned that he did not want to disturb them. Smiling, she returned to her task.

He headed back to the York.

Still no Trent, but Hempe and Poole sat at their usual table in the corner. Owen joined them, asking Poole whether the carter had called on him.

'He did. I sent him to Stillington on Fossgate. He's likely to travel south soon, but I warned the carter that most merchants would be traveling to London, not Winchester. I hope I did not send trouble Stillington's way. Carters. I remember how we hated them on campaigns in France, always blaming someone else for their spoiled meat and moldy bread. By the way, my wife noticed your man Alfred standing in the shadows outside. She tells me she invited him into the kitchen for an ale, but he refused.'

'I am glad to hear it.'

Something in Owen's voice made both men lean in.

'More trouble?' Poole asked.

'I heard they delivered the cart of stones to the priory,' said Hempe. 'Did the sisters find something in there?'

'The stones are of good quality,' said Owen. 'The prioress now looks on Bishop Wykeham with favor.'

'So what worries you?' asked Hempe. 'The carter's other man? Or the two surviving attackers?'

Owen was filling them in on what he'd learned about the attack on Jonas, the sense of someone following him on his ride back to the city, the broken arrow and bloody shirt, when the voices around them hushed and heads turned toward a figure just inside the door talking to Tom Merchet. The moment Owen saw that it was Gwen he was on his feet and pushing past the crowded tables. She would not be here in the evening unless something had happened at home.

'You're to hurry home with her,' said Tom, frowning. 'No one is ill?'

'Not in our household,' said Gwen with the dignity of a child given an important task. 'I'm to say no more until we're well away.'

Nodding to Tom, Owen took his daughter's hand and left the tavern, Hempe and Poole following on their heels.

Once outside the circle of light from the lantern at the entrance, Gwen said, 'Alfred is hurt. But the man they carried is worse.'

'What man?' Owen asked.

'They called him Trent. An arrow's sticking from his chest and he's covered in blood, Da.'

Alfred stood in the doorway, backlit by light spilling from the kitchen beyond, his right arm cradling his left. 'They were upon us before I could stop them,' he said.

'You've no cause to explain yourself. Come inside. Let me see to your arm.'

Gwen hurried past them. As Owen moved forward with Alfred, he could hear her announcing a successful summoning. The scene that met his eyes on reaching the threshold was of a hive of activity, Jasper carrying water, rags draped over one arm, two unfamiliar men anxiously watching while clutching bowls of ale. Trent lay on a pallet by the fire, eyes closed, breathing raggedly, cushions keeping him on his right side so the arrow would not touch the pallet. Lucie was cutting away his blood-soaked shirt. She glanced up, thanked Gwen, and told her to go up to take over with Hugh and Emma so that Kate could help in the kitchen.

'His breathing has steadied a little with some brandywine,' she told Owen. 'His heartbeat was fluttery, but it is steadying. I thought him in a faint, but he was able to mutter something about reparations, God's will.' While she spoke she washed Trent's chest, then spooned a numbing tonic into his mouth, watching that he swallowed. So he was conscious, but barely. At last she rose. 'When you have removed the arrow, I will clean and pack the wound.'

The arrow had entered on Trent's left side, just below the ribs, the arrowhead sticking out the front. Damaging, but not necessarily fatal as long as it was well cleaned. And he should be able to remove the arrow without causing him to bleed to death.

'Once I've finished here I'll see to your arm, Alfred.'

'It's not much. Should I let Stillington's men go home?'

Owen went over to thank them, ascertained that they'd come too late to identify any of the attackers, then sent them off.

Hempe and Poole offered to hold Trent down.

'I'll take his legs,' said Poole. 'One hand and a knee should hold him.'

Hempe took up position at Trent's shoulders.

'Jasper, some more of the brandywine in a spoon,' said Owen.

When Jasper had managed to coax Trent to swallow by massaging his throat, Owen was ready. Getting a grip on the fletched end he snapped it, checked for splinters, then slowly pulled the arrow out the front. Trent jerked and cried out.

Jasper had gone white. Owen nodded to him. 'Go outside, gulp some air.' His son hurried out.

Poole and Hempe retreated to the fire.

Lucie came forward, wiping the blood, motioning for Kate to assist. The household knew the routine for such an injury.

Owen led Alfred to a high-backed chair by the fire near Hempe and Poole, and crouched down, asking him about the weapons used while he peeled away the bloody shirt to see to the wound.

'The one nicked me with a knife, but they kept it to kicking and beating with Trent, that I could tell,' he said. 'The one with the bandaged shoulder used his boots, the other his fists. Strong as an ox, the older one with the fists. I stabbed him in the side. He was ready for more, but both ran off when the archer hit Trent.'

An archer. Owen would return to that. 'Your wound is too long for me to clean with the shirt on. Can you lift your arms so I can pull it off, or is that too painful?'

Clenching his jaw, Alfred raised his arms. As Owen drew off the shirt he asked about the archer.

'I can't swear to it, but I think he's the same one as called to Trent from the alley, said he might like to see who was behind him. Three men arguing. As Trent reached the alley, the three came rushing forward. The one who'd called Trent over ran toward the rear gardens, and the younger of the three, I could swear it was Rhys, chased after him when one of his mates said, "David's murderer." The other two fell on Trent, as I said, beating and kicking.'

'And you believe the one they called David's murderer was the one who started it?'

'That's who Rhys chased, I think. And I supposed he climbed to the roof and shot Trent.'

Raymond? And he'd had his bow and arrows hidden up there?

'I'm sorry I didn't give chase. Thought Trent more important,' said Alfred.

'Where did this happen?'

'Fossgate. Trent had called on Thomas Stillington and was headed back. The one waited for him a few houses down. Going soft now I'm a husband and father,' Alfred muttered.

'You're still my best man.'

'You're good to say that.'

'The one you think was Rhys, did you see him after he chased his brother's murderer?'

'No.'

'Some brandywine?'

Alfred grinned. 'Brandywine. A rare pleasure for the likes of me.'

As Jasper handed Owen a cup he whispered, 'When we are finished here, I need to tell you something.'

'Should not be long.'

Alfred made short work of the brandywine after the first approving sip. 'That'll set me right.'

Owen looked to Poole. 'Walk him home?'

'Gladly.'

'Tell Dame Winifrith we can launder your shirt if she's not accustomed to washing out blood,' Kate told Alfred as she opened the door for them.

'My wife has been cleaning up for her father all her life,' said Alfred. 'This will be nothing.' Old Bede had a talent for arguments that led to brawls. It had taken him some time to notice that, as he aged, he lost more than he won.

Hempe headed for the door. 'I'll set men to search, then put guards on your house tonight.'

'Ned, another walker, and a marksman for the roof,' said Owen. 'And call on Marcus Bolton on Colliergate. He employed David Wells, the one who died in the attack. The two survivors might have gone to him. I should have checked earlier.'

Once the five were gone, Owen turned to Lucie, kneeling beside her as she packed Trent's wound front and back with a poultice. Jasper had thread and needle ready for the stitching.

'Setting a watch through the night,' she said softly to Owen. 'Who are you expecting?'

'I don't know. I wasn't expecting Rhys to betray our trust.'

She patted her forehead with her sleeve. 'No.'

Dipping a clean cloth in the bowl of lavender water that sat near her, Owen dabbed at her forehead, taking care not to get in her way.

'Bless you,' she murmured. 'I will stitch it at both ends. But first, some poppy in the brandywine.' She cleaned her hands and picked up a small bowl with a little spout, coaxed open Trent's mouth, poured in a minuscule amount, then massaged his throat, whispering for him to swallow.

Owen breathed out when he saw the action in his throat. 'He still lives.'

'Did you doubt it?'

In the field such an injury meant almost certain death, but they had moved quickly. 'I will take him to St Mary's infirmary in the morning.' The abbey was near, and the infirmarian Brother Henry could be trusted.

'Will Abbot William agree to take him in?' she asked.

'Trent is Wykeham's man.'

'But Wykeham is out of favor. You know the abbot, he ever looks to please the king.'

'I will take him straight to the infirmary.'

Though she kept her focus on her work, beginning to stitch, Lucie smiled.

Once the stitching was finished, Owen suggested Jasper wait for him in the garden. First he wanted to examine the arrow. His first glance had disturbed him – it looked like one of Alisoun's arrows, the fletching, the type of point for hunting small game. On closer examination he saw that he was right. How had the archer acquired it?

After the warmth of the kitchen, the evening chill was welcoming as he stepped out the door. All the same, Owen carried a small cup of brandywine to warm him. He'd taken some to Lucie as she'd settled by the fire to watch over Trent, and she'd insisted he share it with Jasper.

'I am glad he is ready to unburden himself,' she said. 'I think his behavior at Simon's farewell has unsettled him.'

Jasper waited on the bench beneath the linden. He shook his head when Owen offered him the cup as he took a seat beside him.

'Am I about to learn why the arrow I removed from Gerald Trent's body is one of Alisoun's?'

'Alisoun's? But—' A sharp exhale. 'God help me. I am so ashamed.'

Not words a father welcomes. 'Tell me.'

'The night after Simon's farewell. You know my state. Rhys helped me. But I thought he was Einar, enjoying seeing me brought so low. It angered me and . . .' He took a breath.

A sharp breeze caught the leaves in the garden, stirring autumn scents of fading blossoms and green decay.

'In the night I dreamed you were at a farewell feast for one of your archers, the finest of them all, you kept saying, toasting him. And he looked like Rhys, who I thought was Einar. When I woke I was angry. All the years at the butts on St George's Field and never had you called me the finest of them all. I must have strung my bow. I don't remember doing it. But when I heard voices down below, in the cemetery, it was in my hand, with an arrow. When I saw Rhys . . .'

God's blood.

'I shot, Da, and the man fell back. In the moonlight I saw it. I can't explain the arrow Rob and Rose found. Or how the one I shot

was used by the archer today. If it's the same one. But I don't see
how else he would have one of hers.'

'Did you run down to them?'

'No. Rhys looked up at my window and I dropped to the floor.
I might have killed him, Da. And he wasn't the one I wanted to
hurt. I wanted Einar.'

'You want to hurt Einar,' Owen said softly, 'and you chose not
one of your arrows with blunt points for practice at the butts but one
of Alisoun's hunting arrows.'

'I know I've no cause to attack him. I have no claim to Alisoun
and even if I did . . . I am not a murderer, Da.' His voice broke and
he stifled a sob.

'Drink,' Owen growled, thrusting the cup of brandywine into his
son's hand.

'Da . . .'

'No argument. So that's what you were doing in the cemetery
the next morning when you found the bloodstains? Searching for
your arrow?'

'It wasn't there.'

No. Owen was thinking there had been two archers that night,
one on the roof and one below him – Jasper. Perhaps the second
archer had retrieved Jasper's arrow while his son hid from Rhys.
'Why did you have some of hers?'

'She was teaching me how to track small game. Gave me a few
arrows.'

Owen swallowed the curses on his tongue. 'Does Gwen know?'

'No. I've spoken of this only to Dom Jehannes. I sought his
counsel.'

He'd already guessed that Jasper had been the 'comely young
man' closed up with the archdeacon. 'Did Jehannes send you to
me?'

'I would have told you anyway. You need to know. I am sorry I
did not tell you sooner. I was so ashamed.'

'Yes, I needed to know.' Owen did not trust himself to say more
just yet. What Jasper did was a betrayal of the trust he'd placed in
him. To use a bow when drunk, to aim out of a window in the dark
of night, to intend to harm someone out of jealousy, and then to
say nothing when it was clearly part of Owen's investigation – had
this been one of his archers, he would have given his anger free

rein. But this was his son. Until now a responsible young man, pious, kind. What was Owen to do?

'I heard you send for a marksman. I want to stand the watch tonight, Da. After that, I will destroy my bow.'

Owen could not see his son's face in the dark garden, but he heard the pain and humiliation in his voice. The penance he offered was an acknowledgment of the seriousness of his act. But was it the right thing? *All the years at the butts on St George's Field and never had you called me the finest of them all.* Jasper needed to understand how he differed from the men Owen spoke about, men tested in battle. Standing watch was one way. But the archer was skilled. Could Owen put his son in danger?

'Excelling at the butts is one thing, but how a man shoots when the enemy is charging, or after a long watch – that is quite another,' said Owen.

'Give me a chance to learn. And begin to earn your trust again.' The pain in his voice cut to the heart.

'The finest archer in my company was the devil's own. I knew it the moment I met him. I made good use of him in battle, but never allowed him to move up in the ranks. So he hated me. The night the jongleur and his leman slipped into the camp and I caught them, the night I lost my eye, the devil was on watch.'

'He betrayed you,' Jasper whispered.

'Me, the old duke, the king, and all the realm. But he did it in the hope I would die.'

'Why are you telling me this?'

'Because using your arrow – what he thought was yours – to shoot the man I was protecting is what he would do. Reynard. I believe he is the one you would be up against. He is older now, but Trent told me both men were skilled marksmen who kept them fed on the journey. He may no longer be in the duke's service, but he hit the man in the cemetery at night. Still a skilled marksman.'

'And you think he's the one who shot Trent?'

'Yes.'

'If I'd not told you how he came to have Alisoun's arrow, you wouldn't know?'

'I'd thought of him earlier. Something someone said about a laugh, and a feeling I had when riding from the priory today. This makes it plain.'

'I should have told you earlier.'

'Yes.'

'He was tracking you today?'

'I believe so. Do you still want to stand watch?'

'More than ever. I won't be alone. There will be another marksman on the watch, right? I need to do this, Da.'

'Let me think.' Owen got up to pace in the twilight garden, his feet stirring up dried leaves. He disciplined himself to consider Jasper's skill as a marksman, as if he were one of his men. Was he one he would choose for tonight? As far as he knew, none of the bailiffs' men had used their bows outside of practicing at the butts, except for hunting game. The same with Jasper, and he was the better marksman. So, yes, he would have put him at the top of the list for tonight.

Though it was Owen who would top the list, had he the use of both eyes. He would enjoy going up against the archer he had known as Reynard. But no. Owen was also to blame for his own blinding. He had trusted the Breton jongleur. Had not seen the man's duplicity. He'd convinced his lord to have mercy on the man and release him. Because his music reminded him of home, and Owen had believed him a kindred spirit. Had he been wiser, he might yet be a soldier.

Never to meet Lucie, never to know this life he protected so fiercely. He would not have been here to take Jasper in when he was in danger after his mother died and he was orphaned. This precious son who'd had nothing of his father, John de Warrene, but a decorated bow. Which was why Owen had thought to teach him to use it. His son, who had used his bow so recklessly. He must allow him this chance at reparation.

Owen returned to the bench.

'You'll work with Ned. And Canter, most likely. He's a good runner. Hempe will choose our best bowman to stand on the roof of our house, watching St Helen's churchyard. You'll be on the roof of the York Tavern. Ned and Canter will keep circling, watching. Can you stay awake through the night?'

'Standing on a roof? I would not dare close my eyes.'

'You still want to do this?'

'I do.'

'May God watch over you.'

*   *   *

Lucie and Owen stood in the hall near the kitchen door while they talked so they might listen for signs of Trent waking. The confession had shocked her. *My Jasper?*

'I do not know what to think.' She hugged herself and whispered a prayer. 'What has happened to so change him? Is this all about Alisoun's betrayal? Or did I fail to see signs of a change?'

'You are not to blame, my love.'

'I thought his cruelty to Gwen a passing mood, but this— He might have killed one of them. And he meant it for Einar, who never harmed him.'

'In that moment he believed he had. He is not the first to want to kill a rival.'

'But to act on it.'

'I expect it will haunt him during his night on the watch.'

'Yes.' Her voice was soft with sorrow. 'I know Jasper. He will torment himself thinking how disappointed Brother Wulfstan would be.'

'He needs to face it.'

'He does, and your plan seems wise, yet I cannot help my worry. Nor can you. You will not sleep this night for listening for him.'

'I will be down here, watching over Trent,' said Owen.

'Will you tell Hempe or the sheriff what he did?'

'I cannot bring myself to do that. Nor will I tell Bess and Tom why he is doing this.'

'Are you certain they will agree to this?'

'I am captain of the city. But if they are adamantly against it, I will place him on the shop roof.'

Bess led them up the steps to Trent's room. Access to the flatter part of the roof was through the window. 'I cannot say I welcome the thought of you up there in the night, Jasper. Like a son to me, you are. I'll lie awake and worry.'

'That will make three of us,' said Owen, a hand on his son's shoulder.

Bow in hand, quiver of arrows slung over his shoulder, padded by a quilted tunic, Jasper tried to make light of it. 'Many my age go off to war,' he said.

Time for Jasper to understand what all the training at the butts is for – that was all Owen had told Bess. And that he needed a good marksman this night.

'Seeing you up there, they will think Trent is recovering in his room,' said Bess.

'They might,' Owen agreed. 'But Canter and Ned will be circling both our homes and the shop, watching for trouble.'

'And they will signal Jasper if they need him?'

'They will. But he is also to use his judgment about whether such force is needed.'

With a nod, Bess went to the window, instructing Jasper how to crawl out onto the ledge and over to where he might get a good footing. 'I know Tom's taken you out there from time to time to help him with a patch, but you've not done it at night.' She stood back, hands on hips, waiting for him to go out.

Owen saw the deep inhale before Jasper poked his head out the window. Doing precisely as Bess instructed, he was soon on the roof.

'Are the lanterns sufficient, or should I put out more?' Bess asked both of them.

'Any more and we reveal ourselves,' said Owen.

From the roof, Jasper agreed, though there was a hesitance in his voice.

'I will be leaving now,' said Owen. 'Anything you need, son?'

'No, Da. You prepared me well.'

'You are ready then.' Owen wanted to tell him to leave the watch if at any time he felt threatened, but that would undermine the lesson. *May God watch over him*, he silently prayed.

Bess took his place at the window, leaning out to see Jasper. 'I will leave a jug of water just inside the window for you. Don't mistake it for the pisspot, eh? Know that we are grateful you are watching over the York.'

Owen pressed her shoulder. 'Let him become accustomed to the dark.'

She stepped away from the window. 'I am not at ease with this,' she muttered as she led Owen back down the stairs.

'Nor I.'

At the bottom she turned to him, looking into his eye. 'I have not asked why you chose this night to train your son in courage. Not my place to ask. But you might trust me. I will not betray a confidence.'

'It's not for lack of trust, Bess, I assure you.'

She paused a moment longer, then said, 'We will be listening to help if he needs us.' Then continued on down the steps.

Hugh and Emma were asleep by the time Gwen heard her mother climb the stairs. Tiptoeing out, she met her on the landing.

'I remembered something that might be important,' Gwen whispered.

Her mother drew her into her bedchamber and closed the door. Sitting down on the bed, she patted the space beside her. 'What is it?' She smoothed Gwen's unruly curls back from her forehead, then kissed it.

'I saw Rhys arguing with a man in the market. When I asked him about it, he said a merchant thought he meant not to pay. But he was lying, I am sure of it. They knew each other and he didn't want me to know.'

'Why did you ask him about it?'

'He asked me about where Da was going – it was the morning he started out to Dom Jehannes's house and everything started happening, and I told him that he was going to see the Archdeacon of York. So he owed me an answer.'

Her mother looked uneasy. 'You must have a care with men you do not know well, Gwen. You are so young.'

'I thought we were friends. Now I'm not so sure.'

'There. You see the cause for my concern. We are puzzled why he disappeared as he did. He did not behave in a way to reward our trust in having him lodge with us.'

'But he helped with Jasper.'

'And his work was more than acceptable,' said her mother. 'But that says nothing about whether he can be trusted.'

She had the look that meant not to argue, but to hug her and promise to be more careful.

Hugging her back, her mother asked what the man looked like.

'Older than Rhys, but not so old as Alfred. He looked like he'd been on the road – not so clean and his clothes were torn in places. Like he was in a fight.'

'Had you ever seen him before? Or since?'

'No. *Is* it important?'

'I couldn't say. But I will tell your father.'

Gwen was glad she had spoken up, even though she knew her mother would watch her more closely for a while.

His daughter's boldness worried Owen, as it clearly did Lucie. 'How do we discourage this behavior without changing her, making her fearful?'

'We cannot,' said Lucie. 'It is her nature to be curious, to speak her thoughts – but she knows when to be silent, when it might be hurtful, or is not her tale to tell. Yet in this instance . . .'

'It could be important,' Owen admitted. 'She told us when she realized that.'

'Which is why I did not scold her, but warned her that the danger is in judging a stranger trustworthy when she knows little about him.' She sighed. 'At least she is not out on the roof of the York Tavern.'

'You did not tell her?'

'No.'

ELEVEN
Jasper's Penance, a Fox in the Fold

A t first Jasper did not believe he'd need to fight sleep while up on a roof and not easy about it, or about winning his father's trust. It worried him that whenever Ned passed beneath him in circling the tavern, he bobbed his head. A watcher would surely look round to see why, and eventually look up, find Jasper. Could he be seen? Ned should know better. The other one, Canter, slouched past without such acknowledgement, God be thanked. But Jasper wondered whether he was truly searching the darkness for trouble. His head hardly moved. Did he think intruders would come stand before him and announce themselves? He wondered about the other archer, the one standing on the roof of the house watching the cemetery. Did Ned nod up at him?

Jasper's hands felt stiff with cold. He'd not expected so much wind. Was a storm coming? He could step inside and warm up, take a drink from the jug of water, piss in the pot Bess had provided – a moment's grace now and then would keep him sharp, his father said. But he resisted, not wanting to be inside at the very moment trouble slipped into the garden. He needed to catch intruders at the garden gate, because once Ned or Canter were inside the garden they seemed to disappear, reappearing in the light spilling out from the kitchen and hall windows, then vanishing again as they moved on. Even worse, clouds skidded across the sky, occasionally blocking the moonlight.

But what if they entered the garden from Davygate? He needed to watch both the tavern yard and the part of the garden visible to him. He shifted from foot to foot, not realizing for a long while that he was doing it because he really needed to take a piss. Inside, all the while he used the pisspot and drank some water, he kept one eye on the yard from the window. The steps outside the room creaked. Bess checking on him?

The climb back out was better this time. For a while he had a sense of ease. He could do this. He could redeem himself. But it wasn't long before the tedium had him nodding. Once he woke with a start, and it terrified him. How would he aim if half asleep? How had he done so when drunk? He hadn't. He'd aimed for Rhys and managed to hit no one, according to Da. But that didn't absolve him. He'd been unforgivably reckless. What would Brother Wulfstan think of him? He prayed for forgiveness. But no, he must not close his eyes. Did he always close his eyes when praying? Why had he not noticed that before?

A movement down below. Canter, pissing against the garden fence.

The light in the hall winked out, though one still glowed soft in the kitchen where he imagined his father pacing. The tavern beneath him grew quiet. Again he startled awake. Perhaps he, too, should try pacing. Two, three steps and his foot began to slip. He reared back and almost stumbled sideways off the roof. Better to be still.

A sound down in the tavern, a man's voice, shouting a name, over and over. Someone shushed him. Nightmares. Jasper was no stranger to them. After his mother died he had been on the run, hunted by the murderer of Master Will Crounce, who would have married his mother. His mother. He could barely recall her face. But at the dying of the summer, a particular rose in the garden brought clear memories of her wrapping him in her arms to comfort him when he was small, especially after his father died, singing and gently rocking him, though he could hear only the tune, not the words. He had hummed it for Dame Marian, hoping she might know the tune, but she could not think of what it might be.

Lucie had insisted Owen lie down for a few hours while she sat with Trent. When he woke, she stood in the kitchen doorway, watching the garden, nodding to Ned, then Canter, as they passed.

Owen joined her. 'Can you see him?'

'Not from here, and I did not dare venture out. But all has been quiet. Trent as well.'

'Any sign of fever?'

'No, God be thanked.' She yawned. 'Did you sleep?'

'Long enough. Go now, rest.' He kissed her neck.

Once alone, he sat for a while beside Trent, bathing his face with a cloth moistened with lavender and hazel water, dripping some honey water in his mouth. When the warmth of the fire coaxed him into a doze, Owen went to stand in the doorway. He watched Canter pass once, then Ned – who reported all quiet, and when Canter returned he stepped into his path.

'Look round,' said Owen. 'An intruder will not appear at your feet.'

'I see well out of the corners of my eyes, Captain. Better at night.'

'Everyone does. But if you move your head, your range is wider. I'm not angry, Canter. Just helping you learn. Have you seen anything?'

'Rats in the churchyard. Night watch passing by. A lad sneaking out of a window down Davygate. Dropped his shoes when he saw me.'

Owen stepped away as Ned approached. Canter took off at a brisk pace.

A groan called Owen back into the kitchen.

Trent was trying to lift his head.

'Are you thirsty?'

The man licked his lips. 'I am.'

'Honey water or watered wine?'

'Wine. I . . . Where am I, Captain?'

Owen poured, then helped him sip. 'You're in my kitchen. You were brought here with an arrow in your side. I removed it, and my wife took care of the wound.'

'I remember being thrown to the ground. A man kicking me.'

'And then you were shot.' Owen told him what Alfred had witnessed. 'Was it Raymond who lured you into the alley?'

'Yes, God help me.'

'Who are the other men?'

'Don't know. But the one . . . building your wall . . . the young man . . . he was with them.' He pressed his side as he breathed.

'Slow and easy,' Owen said. 'I am in no hurry. Was that the first time you'd seen Raymond since the attack?'

'No. He came . . . to the York.' A few breaths. 'Few nights past. Told me to keep my mouth shut or I'd be dead.'

'He doesn't want you talking about what?'

'He . . .' a breath, 'and Beck . . .' another breath, 'knew you. Hated you.'

'How did he get into the tavern?'

'From roof. Through window.'

Jasper's access to the inn. By the rood, how had Owen not thought of that? He'd thrust his son into danger far beyond what was appropriate for a lesson. How could he forgive himself if . . . Giving Trent a little more wine, Owen told him he would be just outside the door. 'Sleep. You are well guarded.'

Jasper must have nodded off. One moment Ned had been passing beneath him, and now he was come again. Not good. It took him a while to pass again. How long had his eyes been closed? Now he watched Ned hesitate, cup an ear. Jasper held his breath, listening. Nothing. But something moved along the fence in the garden, heading from the midden toward the shop. Canter? He realized the dawn must be coming and he could see more. Or the moonlight was brighter. Ned still did not move. Canter came round from St Helen's churchyard. Ned signaled for him to stop. Then who was creeping from the midden? Crouching down, Jasper searched for something to toss at Ned, found a pebble, rose and tossed it. When Ned glanced up, Jasper motioned toward the garden, indicated direction. Ned crept that way, Canter following. Jasper readied an arrow. Ned entered the gate, which had been left open for silence. Canter stood in the gap, watching. A flurry of movement. Someone rushed into the kitchen light. Jasper aimed his arrow, ready to shoot to warn him to stop, choosing a spot ahead of him.

Just in front of the kitchen doorway. What if someone stepped out to see what was happening? He would never forgive himself if he shot Gwen, Kate, Da. Could he forgive himself for shooting anyone? What would Brother Wulfstan say? Is this what God intended for him? He was trained as a healer. He had taken a vow to heal.

As he fought with himself he heard Ned shout, 'Halt!' The runner obeyed, turning toward Ned just as the kitchen door opened, illuminating him. Rhys. And now his father was stepping out.

Lowering his bow Jasper froze, feeling someone's breath on the back of his neck. Glancing to one side he saw a gloved hand, the bow, the arrow.

'Down,' Jasper shouted. 'Down! Archer on the tavern roof!' He heard the arrow sing past him.

'Mewling pest. I might have finished him,' the archer hissed.

Jasper twisted round and sank his arrow into the man's middle. With a curse the man tore out the arrow and swung it at Jasper. He ducked, almost losing his balance. By the time he was ready to grab the man, he was already crawling up the roof. Slinging his bow over his shoulder, Jasper flattened himself and followed. The archer slithered over the summit and disappeared. The shingles were slippery, splintery, digging into his hands and knees. When he crested the roof he saw the man now crouched as he slid down toward the lower roof over the kitchen area. A lantern lit the ground, but not the roof. He still could not make out anything about the one he followed. He chose to continue crawling, letting himself slide, ignoring the pain, intent on reaching the man's legs. There. He grabbed an ankle.

'Bastard!' the man shouted as he tumbled forward, the force of his fall wresting his ankle out of Jasper's grip.

Down below, a thud, a cry, the sounds of a scuffle. As Jasper slid head-first toward the light, he saw the man, bow slung over his shoulder, scramble to his feet. 'Tell the captain the fox is in his fold,' he crowed, then took off running.

'No!' Jasper twisted himself around so he could slide feet forward toward the edge. Not nearly the fall he had feared. As he left the roof, he curled himself into a ball, landing hard. He was momentarily stunned. When he could think again, he cursed himself for a fool thinking he'd quickly untangle himself and chase after the archer. Instead, it was a slow process, stretching out one leg, and, when it worked, the other. Now an arm, and the other. Rolling over on his side, he discovered Tupper, the Merchet's nephew, lying on the ground beside him. Struggling to his knees, cursing as the splinters dug in, Jasper crawled over to him and gently rocked him.

'Tupper?'

A moan. He was alive. Rising to a crouch, Jasper felt around Tupper's head. Nothing sticky. That was a good sign. Felt his neck. Nothing strange about it. Gently he rolled him onto his back. Someone came running out of the tavern. Tom Merchet, barefoot and carrying a kitchen cleaver.

'It's me, Jasper,' he said. 'Tupper tried to grab the archer. He's not bleeding.'

'I thought *you* were the archer.' Bess stood in the doorway holding a lantern. 'Here now,' she hurried to Tupper, setting down the lantern, checking his eyes. 'He's coming to. Come, both of you, bring him inside.'

Jasper and Tom managed to lift Tupper to his feet and support him over the threshold and through the kitchen to a chair in Bess's quiet corner.

'You go on home,' she told Jasper. 'Let your father know. We'll see to him.'

Owen cursed himself as he rushed to the tavern with a dread deeper than anything he had ever felt, coming to an astonished halt as he saw Jasper walk out the door of the tavern. 'Praise God. I thought I might need to carry you home.'

'The bastard fell on Tupper and then got away.' Jasper hung his head. 'But I did jab him in the gut with my arrow.'

Owen was tempted to comfort his son but, remembering why he had been on guard, treated him as he would one of his men. 'You did well, calling out that warning, stabbing him.'

Wilfrid, the bowman who had watched from the roof of the house, came running over, asked Jasper which way the man had run and took off, pausing to toss back a hat.

Catching it, Owen called out his thanks. The hat was a soft wool, dark, smelling of the river.

'That's right, he was wearing that,' said Jasper.

'Tell me what happened.' As Owen listened he kept turning the hat round in his hands, a talisman, muttering a curse when Jasper finished with the message. *Tell the captain the fox is in his fold.* Reynard, the fox.

'Did he say anything else?'

'He called me a mewling pest for not shooting Rhys. "I might have finished him," he said. Why Rhys?'

'Did he say his name?'

'No. But surely—'

'You did the right thing, son, and I thank God that you survived the encounter and stand before me.' Jasper was clearly battered, his movements stiff, tentative, as if expecting pain. But he was whole. 'Injuries?'

'Bruises from a tumble off the roof – not too far, by the kitchen doorway, splinters and scrapes on hands and knees from crawling up there.'

Crawling on a shingled roof. Owen knew the pain. He poked his head into the tavern kitchen, ascertained that Tupper was now happily drinking brandywine and spinning quite a tale. Calling out his thanks, Owen put his arm round Jasper. 'Let's see to your injuries.'

In the kitchen, Kate nodded to them as she handed Rhys and Ned bowls of ale. 'And you two?' she asked as Owen helped Jasper with his boots.

'Brandywine for him,' said Owen. 'To dull the pain when I draw out the splinters.'

'Talk to Rhys,' said Jasper. 'I can see to myself in the hall.'

'I can help,' said Kate.

Before he went, Owen wanted to hear all Jasper noticed about the archer while it was fresh in his mind.

Jasper closed his eyes. 'Shorter than you, a rasp in his breath.' He was shaking his head when he leaned forward, excited. 'He wore a hat on the roof, but when he ran his head was bare. Light hair, couldn't tell the color. And he's nimble. Not fearful of heights.'

'I might say the same for you,' said Owen. 'Your jab might slow him down for a few days. Now go, take care of your injuries.'

As Jasper followed Kate to the hall door, Ned rose. 'A good night's work, Jasper. I was glad to have you up there.'

Jasper straightened and nodded to Ned before he disappeared into the next room.

'I *am* grateful he was up there,' Ned said to Owen as he moved toward the door. 'But this one . . . I'm curious what he was doing in the garden. No, wait – looking for a lost tool. Hah! Don't believe it, Captain.'

'Where are you headed?'

'To find Wilfrid.'

'Where's Canter?'

Ned stopped, shook his head. 'Haven't seen him since the arrow came flying. I'll keep an eye out for him, too.'

When he was gone, Rhys said, 'He's right to doubt me.'

'It would seem so. You were with the men who beat Gerald Trent.'

'I know how it looks, but I hoped I might convince them to leave the city. I failed. They want those tools you found in the cart.'

'Your brother David's tools.'

'You know?' He was silent a moment as tears pooled in his eyes, then bowed his head and crossed himself. 'May he rest in God's grace.' His voice broke on the last words.

'I am sorry you have suffered the loss of both your father and your brother. But the others – you do know they left your brother's body in a beck outside the city.'

Rhys flinched, but he met Owen's gaze. 'I came to warn you, Captain.'

'Were they here in the night?'

'I caught them coming over the back wall. Sent them off. But they'll be back.'

They were interrupted by a knock on the kitchen door. One hand on his knife, Owen crossed to it.

Ned, with Wilfrid and Bess's nephew Tupper behind him.

Owen motioned the first two into the kitchen. 'How are you?' Owen asked Tupper.

'I'm fine. Aunt Bess had me ready the donkey cart. I'm to take Master Gerald Trent to Brother Henry at the abbey. The cart's standing ready by your gate.'

How did Bess know where he'd meant to take him in the

morning? She was a wonder. 'Her advice is to take him there now?'

'She said best before dawn. And who would think I was carting him instead of my uncle's ale?'

'I will accompany them,' said Ned. 'In the shadows.'

Owen agreed. 'I will follow in the morning.' Perhaps Trent might revive enough to answer more questions. He noticed Wilfrid held a pair of bows. 'You brought two?'

'This one's not mine.' Wilfrid held one out to him. 'Found it on the riverbank. No sign of the man. Thought I'd heard a soft splash as I reached there, but it might've been a fish or a rat.'

'You watched to see if he surfaced?'

'As long as a man might breathe, Captain. He never came up.'

Owen and Wilfrid helped Ned move Trent to the cart, managing not to wake him. 'Tupper will let me know he's safely there, eh?' said Owen.

'I will, Captain.'

'Get some rest, Ned, Wilfrid. I will need you tomorrow.'

Nodding, the three strode off with the donkey cart.

Owen returned to Rhys, studying the young man, his pallor after a sleepless night accentuating the angry scar across his cheek. 'Who are those two men to you?'

'My uncle and cousin. I am sorry I pulled you into this, Captain. I never meant to cause you harm, or your family. You welcomed me.'

'We trusted you. As to my involvement, that was the sheriff's doing.'

'I did come to warn you last night.'

'Ned would think you say that now you were caught.'

'It's the truth.'

'I believe this all began when your father died in a fall at St Floribert's. Unfortunately for Gerald Trent, the two men accompanying him were the pair who ordered your father to climb up a scaffold knowing ice had made it a treacherous climb. Why did Beck and Raymond endanger him?'

'If you know so much about my family why did you—'

'I ask the questions,' said Owen. 'Why did they want to be rid of him?'

'I don't know. My father picked fights often enough. It might have been something between him and one of them.'

'Your mother was quick to accuse them of murder.'

'She did. Told everyone they were Bishop Wykeham's men. I don't know why. She knew they weren't. When the bishop's clerk came to offer us help she spat at him, said his master did it to save his name. But she took what he offered. More than we deserved.'

Owen searched for signs of deception. But he found none. 'You condemn it now, but from where I sit, you were part of the plan to attack Trent and his men.'

'Not willingly.' Said quickly, eyes hot. 'This scar . . .' Rhys touched his cheek. 'My mother sliced me for refusing to help my uncle avenge my father.'

David's carving. Was the Fury his mother? No wonder. 'Your brother was also with them,' said Owen.

'I *told* David people talked to you, that he was a fool to think you wouldn't learn about him.' He wiped his eyes. 'Down deep I think David agreed to help my uncle only because it meant he might talk to the masons here in York. Find work.'

'He paid dearly for the chance.'

'He was no more a fighter than I am. I heard that his body was taken to the castle. Could I see him?'

They had not yet buried David. 'I will take you to him in exchange for what you know about the attacks.'

'Like I said, I came to warn you. I never meant to hurt you or your family.'

'Is your mother often so violent?'

'She's like her brother, Uncle Walter. Angry at the world. But none of what they've done will bring back my father. I've no cause to protect Walter and Arn – he's my cousin. She set them on Gerald Trent and his men. But I don't think Trent had anything to do with it.'

'How did they know Trent and his men were coming to York?'

'I don't know. They never trusted that information with me. David just said they knew people.'

'Where are they hiding?'

'I don't know. I waited in the rooms where I'd taken them after Arn was hurt, off Coney Street, near the river, but they haven't returned. I just happened on them when I went to the man David had been working for. He said he told them to go away and stay away, that you were coming to talk to him. I can take you where they had been. I didn't see anything useful, but you might. I'd left Arn's bloody shirt and the arrow in the alley outside, but they're gone.'

'I have them.'

'You do? How?' He waved away the question. 'No matter. I'm glad you have them.'

'What else?'

'They say that Pete is lying, they never attacked Jonas Snicket. Went there once to see about lodgings and were sent away.'

Good that he'd set someone to watch Snicket's house, and Pete. 'Why would Pete lie?'

'I don't know.'

'Tell me about Arn and Walter.'

'Not much to tell. Ever in trouble with the law, thieving, setting fire to barns, brawling in taverns. My father would have nothing to do with them. But when he died, my mother sent for them. Asked them to help David and me avenge Father.'

'You said the bishop helped your family.'

'He provided us a home on one of his manors. Better than anything we'd had before. All we had to do was farm the land.'

'Your mother wanted more.'

'She said it was an insult to expect us to farm. She knew we both wanted to work with stone on a cathedral, David and I. He was gifted. He was meant to carve in stone.'

'He was. I have seen a head he sculpted.'

Rhys bowed his head. 'I should have been satisfied to work the land. I've no particular talent, not like David's. I might have persuaded Mother.' He wiped his eyes.

'Where is this manor?'

'North of Winchester. Not far.'

Not Llŷnfield then. Good. 'The attack on Alfred and Trent changed your mind about helping your uncle and cousin?'

'I told you, I never wanted anything to do with it. But after my brother . . .' He tried to hold back a sob, but it escaped him.

'What do they want with his tools?'

'To take to my mother, they said, so she might sell them. But they'll keep them to sell themselves. She's a fool to trust them.' Rhys wiped his eyes on his sleeve.

Owen handed him a bowl of ale and went into the hall to see whether Kate needed help with Jasper. He found Lucie tending him while Kate held Emma and watched that Gwen and Hugh did not interfere.

'I think we have found all the splinters,' said Lucie. 'He will be sore for a few days. And bruised.'

'I was lucky,' said Jasper.

'What have you learned about Rhys?' asked Lucie.

Owen glanced at the children.

'Hugh and Gwen know we are concerned about him,' said Lucie. 'The truth is likely less frightening than their imaginings.'

'The attackers were his brother, an uncle, and a cousin. It was his brother's body they found in the beck.'

'His kin?' Jasper said. 'And he lived with us?'

'He's attempting to make up for that by telling me everything he knows.' Owen glanced at Gwen as she crept closer.

'He meant to betray us all along?' Her eyes were filled with tears, her trust shattered.

He crouched down to her, held her close. 'He did not want to help with this vengeance. His scar is from his mother's anger when he refused.'

She pushed away, leveling her eyes on Owen, so like her mother. 'His mother cut him?'

'So he says.'

'Mother would never hurt us!' Hugh declared.

'I am glad you know that,' said Lucie.

Kissing all three of the young ones, pressing Jasper's shoulder and thanking him, promising they would talk in the evening, Owen headed for the kitchen. To his surprise, Lucie accompanied him.

'I will take Rhys out into the garden, return the kitchen to you,' said Owen.

'What will you do with him?' she asked.

'Take him to the castle to see his brother. And if the sheriff agrees, he will stay there until we have the archer, and Rhys's uncle and cousin, Walter and Arn.'

'What did Jasper tell you of the archer?'

Owen told her, including the message. 'Fox. He is Reynard.'

He watched as Lucie searched her memory, her eyes widening.

She touched his eye. '*That* archer,' she whispered. 'Holy Mother Mary. Why is he here?'

'To accomplish what he failed to do that night in the camp. Destroy me.'

'So that is who we face, the devil himself.' Lucie crossed herself, and then surprised him. 'We will not permit him to destroy you and all you have created out of your loss, will we?'

'I will do—'

She cupped his face in her hands and kissed him on the lips. 'I know. I have all faith in you. Your great heart will not be your undoing.'

He drank in the calm in her eyes. 'Where do you find your strength?'

She took his hand. 'In you.'

He wanted to believe in her certainty, but . . . 'Reynard came close to destroying me years ago.'

'He caught you by surprise. Not this time. You will be aware of him every second of every day until you bring him down.'

She was right. He kissed her hand.

'Now. Why don't we break our fast in the hall – you, Rhys, Jasper, and me – while Kate feeds the children in the kitchen? And then go find Reynard.'

'Why would you include Rhys?'

'You don't believe he wanted no part of this?'

'I do, but . . .'

'Take him to see his brother's corpse. Get a good sense of him. If you feel he's telling the truth, bring him back to stay with us.'

'But the danger, love.'

'Rhys is but a small part of it.'

He hesitated, thinking of all at stake, but her certainty calmed him. 'I'll bring him to the hall after I show him the arrow and bloody shirt. I am not sure about his lodging with us.'

They were indeed the items Rhys had removed from his cousin and tossed in the alley. Gwen might be slightly appeased to hear that she was the one Rhys most regretted betraying. But it was when he saw how badly his cousin was beating Alfred that he had given up any attempt to help his kin.

'Alfred's a good man,' said Rhys. 'He told me about his marriage, the children, his wife's father Old Bede. He didn't deserve what

Arn did to him. Seeing it, I hated myself. Felt unclean. I knew I could not be a part of it any more or no amount of penance could wash me clean.'

Gwen managed to sneak back into the hall while Owen, Lucie, Jasper, and Rhys broke their fast, peppering her brother with questions about his night on the roof of the tavern. He managed to respond with good-natured patience. When she turned to Rhys, Lucie signaled Owen it was time for him to depart.

Rhys was quiet as he led Owen to the rooms where he had stowed his things. His uncle and cousin had left nothing of interest. He shouldered his pack and they headed on to the castle.

'You didn't want Gwen talking to me?' he asked.

Owen chuckled. 'You heard how thoroughly she questioned her brother. I was sparing you a similar interrogation.'

'I would like the chance to ask her forgiveness.'

'Perhaps you will have it.'

Rhys glanced at him, but said nothing.

At the castle, Owen drew the guards aside. 'Give him time with his brother's corpse. I'll watch over him.'

Settling on a bench at a remove from Rhys – as much to avoid the stench of the ripening corpse as to give the man privacy, Owen tried to remember Magda Digby's lessons in using what she called his third eye to judge whether to trust Rhys. *Watch him with thy body, Bird-eye, not thine head. The body sees the truth long before the head understands.* Owen watched Rhys doubled over beside his brother's corpse, keening his grief, and felt the sadness in his bones. His mind told him that such emotion could lead either toward a hunger for revenge or a disgust with the waste of his brother's life. Rhys professed the latter, but now, seeing the corpse, he might feel differently. Yet Owen felt in his bones only the pain, remorse. *Thou seest?* He did.

And now he waited. While he sat there he considered why Wykeham wished to dine with him today, and why he'd included Lucie in the invitation. Dame Alice Perrers had recommended his wife, but Wykeham had already chosen this path of reparation with St Clement's. Did he think to convince Lucie to push Owen to argue Wykeham's case to Dame Marian? Lucie was not easily swayed, and would never interfere with a decision that would affect a person's

future. She would counsel that Marian must come to her own decision. He resented the interruption in his work. But Magda had
encouraged him to be kind to Wykeham.

Rhys rose and crossed himself, turning away from Owen to wipe
his eyes before approaching.

'Where will they bury him, Captain?'

'They spoke of the plague cemetery outside the city. It's used
for the poor and those with no kin to pay for a burial.'

'David in a plague pit? No. No! I have my wages. Would they
pay for a proper grave?'

'Yes. But that would leave you little for yourself.' There was
another source of money. 'You would get a good price for your
brother's tools at the minster stoneyard. But your mother—'

'She doesn't need them. Bishop Wykeham has provided her with
the means to live better than we did before. I'll return to work the
land and support her.'

'You would do that after what she did to your face?'

'She's my mother. And now she's alone.'

Owen put an arm round him. 'Come. We will talk to the bailiff
on duty here about your brother's burial, and then you can settle
back into the room above the shop while my wife and I dine with
Bishop Wykeham.'

'You would take me back? But I might draw trouble.'

'I don't believe your uncle and cousin have cause to attack you.
Nor does Raymond.' Not true, perhaps, but he trusted his sense that
he himself was the true target. 'I warn you, you will face my daughter
the interrogator.'

The hint of a smile. 'I will bear up.'

Remembering the carving, Owen drew it out of his scrip. 'The
mason David was working for gave me this – your brother's work.
I thought you might like it.'

As Rhys took the stone in hand he froze, staring, then burst into
laughter and tears. 'Our mother,' he said, laughing so hard that he
choked on the words. 'He caught her to the life.'

The Fury who had slashed her son's face for spite. As Owen had
guessed.

Hempe hailed them as they were leaving the castle. 'No sign of
the two attackers. Bolton says they did hide in David's old room
for a few days, but left when they heard him telling his wife about

talking to you. Hasn't seen them since. Heard about yesterday's trouble and thanked the Lord it hadn't happened near his home, with children at play.' He eyed Rhys. 'You're not keeping him here?'

'Come, walk with us,' said Owen. 'I'll tell you all he's told me.'

He waited until they reached the yard of the York Tavern and sent Rhys ahead to tell Lucie he was back, then told Hempe the rest.

'The archer betrayed you? That's how you lost the eye? This Reynard is a dead man.'

'He is the king's to punish.'

Hempe looked doubtful. 'I hear he disappeared in the river last night.'

'According to Wilfrid.'

'Snicket's house is near the river.'

'We have a guard on it.'

'Only now and then. We'll do better. Still dining with the bishop today?'

'I am.'

'I'll post some men there.'

'Good.'

On his return, Owen went to Bess Merchet to fetch Trent's things. He would take them to the abbey.

'Happy to be rid of them,' she said. 'Not for need of the room, but he's caused enough trouble. I warn you, though, someone's been there ahead of you. Must have been in the night.'

'What do you mean?'

'You'll see. I went up there this morning and found his things tossed about, the mattress turned over. Happened while Jasper was out on the roof, I would guess. I'd not thought to go check.'

Of course. Reynard accessed the roof from Trent's room. Owen headed up the steps, Bess behind him, asking about Jasper, Rhys, and, finally, Trent. 'Will he live?'

'Brother Henry will do his best to bring him back to health,' was all Owen could say for now. He stopped in the doorway, surveying the mess. It was as Bess had described. Picking through the items he found only a change of clothing, a cloak, boots, a comb.

'He had a fine leather travel pack,' said Bess. 'And a purse heavy with coin.'

Reynard would find that useful.

TWELVE
A Gift for the Bishop

Owen had not expected to find Jasper in the shop, hollow-eyed and limping as he tidied up after what must have been a large order. 'Couldn't sleep, so I thought I would be of some use.'

That was more like the thoughtful lad he had been before whatever had riled him of late, trying to emulate his mentor's selflessness. Owen hoped his news would not bring back the temper. 'Rhys will be lodging upstairs for now.'

'Ma warned me.' Said with no rancor. 'If you feel he's safe in the house, I have no objection. He helped me the other day when I made a fool of myself.' Raking back his fair hair, Jasper looked Owen in the eye. 'He's no longer protecting his uncle and cousin?'

'No. Thank you for accepting him back. And for keeping the shop open. Where is your mother?'

'She's dressing for the bishop. Gwen says she's wearing the blue dress you like so much.'

News to brighten his day. Owen debated about asking Jasper whether Reynard might have slipped in while he was on watch on the roof. He risked implying that sleep had overtaken Jasper. But he must know. He took the opportunity in between customers to tell him of the missing pack.

Jasper cursed. 'I heard a creak on the step when I went inside for a moment, but thought it was Bess. And back out on the roof I feared I might have fallen asleep for a moment. But it couldn't have been long or I would have fallen.'

A good point. Reynard was ever quick-fingered and quiet. Who knew how often the man had slipped past Owen before he caught on to what he was. 'You have saved me time trying to think of when else he might have found his way in by admitting to a lost moment. I'm grateful.'

'I let you down.'

'You chased him away before he could cause harm to innocent people. You did not let me down.'

'But Trent's pack is gone.'

'Reynard now has coin to find lodgings, it's true. But he might have stolen it elsewhere. We've saved others the grief, eh?'

A customer interrupted them.

'If you remember anything else of consequence, tell me. I am going to the abbey infirmary to see whether Trent has recovered sufficiently to talk,' Owen said quietly. 'I will check with you when I return.'

Brother Henry waved away Owen's apologies for foisting the man on him without warning. 'He is in Bishop Wykeham's company. I would not have turned him away. But you will get nothing out of him for a while. He is very weak with the loss of so much blood and sleeps the sleep of one on the ledge between this life and the next. God may choose to take him at any moment. He did seem to wake for a moment, thrashing about and crying that Bishop Ergham would be the death of him. He also seemed to curse his wife. Poor man.'

'You are certain he said Bishop Ergham, not Wykeham?'

'I am quite certain. Ergham, Bishop of Salisbury. I thought that might interest you.'

'It does.' Ergham, the Bishop of Salisbury, and also the Duke of Lancaster's chancellor. Did Reynard still serve Lancaster, or his chancellor? But why would either of them send him here?

'I see you have thought of something.'

'I have, but the meaning eludes me.'

'I warn you that Abbot William may not like that I am helping the Bishop of Winchester. He has spoken of how the former Lord Chancellor is out of favor with the king and his family.'

'He knows the bishop is in York?'

'It was thought a secret?'

'The bishop intended it to be. I confess I thought it unlikely he had succeeded. Thank you for this information, and especially for caring for Trent.'

'I follow my conscience, Captain, and this seems the clear path to the best resolution.'

*   *   *

The moment Owen stepped into the shop Jasper said, 'Canter walked with head forward, never looking to right or left. Seemed indifferent. And then he disappeared.'

'I noticed it as well.'

'How would Reynard know who would be watching?'

'I've no idea, except that Canter is the one we use as a runner, so he'd be quick to chase. And escape. Yet how Reynard would know that . . . A timely reminder. Thank you.'

At the door, Brother Michaelo asked about the incident during the night. He raised a brow at Owen's surprise. 'Word spreads quickly in York. You know that. I heard it in the minster yard early this morning. They sit around their fires at night trading news of the city.' Michaelo ministered to the poor who camped in the shadow of the minster. 'I pray Jasper is unharmed.'

'They heard of his part?' Lucie asked.

'The night watch stop and chat by their fires.'

'Minor injuries, and a job well done,' said Owen.

'I am glad of that. Some unexpected guests will be joining you for dinner.' Michaelo stepped aside to reveal Prioress Isobel, Dame Marian, and another Benedictine nun standing in the hall talking to Jehannes and Wykeham.

'They have news?' Owen asked.

'I believe Dame Marian wished to speak with His Grace once more before making her decision.'

'Will we be in the way?' asked Lucie.

'His Grace is keen for both of you to be part of the conversation.'

As soon as Lucie stepped through the door, Dame Marian excused herself and hurried over. '*Benedicite*, my friend.' She took Lucie's hand. 'I am so glad to see you. And you,' she said to Owen, smiling, it seemed to him, with her entire body. Her face glowed.

'Claire, come, meet Dame Lucie and her captain,' she said, waving the unfamiliar nun over.

The prioress pursed her lips, Wykeham bending to her to say something Owen could not hear. She seemed mollified by whatever he had said and relaxed a little.

'I have heard so much about you and your children, Dame Lucie, Captain Archer.' Dame Claire's smile was shy, but her eyes danced.

'I cannot think what might have happened to Marian had you not taken her in.'

'*Benedicite*, Lucie.' Prioress Isobel joined them. 'Captain Archer.'

Lucie and Isobel had been together at the convent as children, hardly friends, but since Isobel had become prioress she had reached out to Lucie for help, and had from time to time cooperated with Owen in his work.

Jehannes and Wykeham followed in her wake, and when the prioress began to say more, Jehannes interrupted to introduce the bishop to Lucie.

Owen noticed that Wykeham bowed to her and did not proffer his ring of office for her to kiss. Did he no longer feel he could claim such obeisance?

'*Benedicite*, Dame Lucie. I thank you for joining us,' said Wykeham.

Firmly taking control of the gathering, Jehannes escorted all to the table set up near the fire. Wykeham's two manservants stood ready to serve, coming round with wine as soon as everyone was seated. Owen found himself beside Wykeham, who sat at one head of the table, Lucie opposite him. Jehannes sat at the opposite end. The prioress sat between Lucie and Brother Michaelo, Dame Marian between Owen and Dame Claire.

During the fish course the conversation was about weather and news of the city. But by the time the meat course was served, Wykeham grew restless.

'Forgive me,' he said to the table at large, 'but I must know what the captain has learned.'

Lucie, such a contrast to the nuns, monk, and churchmen around the table in the deep blue gown that he so loved, gave Owen a small smile and a slight nod. Of course he must satisfy Wykeham, was that not the purpose of this dinner? But the nuns – he had not expected to take them into his confidence. Dame Marian he knew he could trust, but the other two?

Jehannes cleared his throat. 'We attempted to provide background for Mother Isobel and her companions so that they might be part of the discussion.'

'Ah.' Owen nodded, and without further hesitation he brought Wykeham up to date about everything, including the identity of 'Raymond', though only insofar as the man had once served under him, an angry, rebellious charge. He hoped Wykeham might provide some insight into his presence.

The bishop was uncommonly quiet while Owen spoke, Jehannes being the one asking for clarifications here and there. The man was the consummate host, a quality Thoresby had found most helpful.

Finishing with his visit to the abbey infirmary, Owen sat back with a refreshed mazer of wine.

'Ralph Ergham will be the death of a carter?' were the first comments from the bishop. 'How would Trent know the Bishop of Salisbury?' Wykeham's face seemed etched in chalk and shadows.

Owen recounted Trent's explanation of how the Bishop of Salisbury had introduced him to the men who called themselves Raymond and Beck. 'Coupled with the fact that they were not his choice for this journey but showed up at the moment of departure, it does make me wonder about Bishop Ergham's purpose. Then with last night's revelation . . . I'd begun to suspect, but now know for certain, as I said, that the men are in truth Reynard and his friend Bruin, former archers for Lancaster. Ergham being Lancaster's chancellor, somehow it must connect. But how and why I have yet to learn. Why they chose to travel with him—'

'Perhaps Reynard's goal was York,' said Michaelo, 'where he might confront you, Captain.'

The sisters all crossed themselves.

'This is most distressing,' said Mother Isobel.

'Perhaps once he was here that occurred to him,' said Wykeham, 'but what if it was mere felicity? As Archer says, Ergham is Lancaster's chancellor. His purpose was likely that they should spy on me once here.' Pressing his hands to his face, Wykeham did not move for a long while. When at last he looked up at Owen, he seemed at a loss. 'I thought this a small thing, nothing that anyone would take notice of.'

That was his mistake, Owen thought. It was often such small things that felled the wiliest schemers.

'I am out of favor at court,' said Wykeham. 'Anyone coming to my aid risks the same fate. I warn you all.'

'My uncle Sir Thomas warned me not to cooperate with you, Your Grace,' said Dame Marian. 'I am, as ever, a pawn being played by my ambitious kin. But I will base any decision on my own conscience.'

'I would not ask you to disobey your uncle,' said Wykeham.

'It was not an order.'

'Even so.'

The prioress cleared her throat to gain attention. 'If I might speak, this seems the time to tell you that a messenger arrived late yesterday – from Sir John Neville, telling me to expect a contingent sent to escort both the sisters of Wherwell and His Grace the Bishop of Winchester from York, seeing that they complete their journeys south in safety.'

That was a turn Owen had not anticipated.

Nor Wykeham. 'Sir John Neville is sending me an escort?' The bishop's hooded eyes were wide with surprise as he looked from Isobel to Marian to Owen. 'Why? What is his interest in us? And how had he learned of our company?'

Perhaps her aunt, Lady Maud Neville, was concerned, Owen thought. 'Did he mention Dame Marian?' he asked.

'No,' said Mother Isobel, 'no, he did not. But it was a brief message.'

'You think of my aunt,' said Marian, looking at Owen. 'And perhaps that is his purpose, that the company are safe, in case I choose to go. If he knows of the sisters from Wherwell, he doubtless knows their mission. As did my uncle. But who does he think might attack us?'

'My enemies,' said Wykeham. 'I have placed you in an uncomfortable and possibly dangerous position, Dame Marian. For that I am deeply sorry.'

Marian pressed hand to heart and bowed her head. 'I thank you, Your Grace. I came in the hope that what I heard would allow me to understand how best to move forward. I pray you, it would help me to know what is the root of the duke's complaint against you.'

'Dame Marian!' the prioress cried.

But Wykeham held up a hand to silence her. 'She is right to ask.' He told Marian about the plight of Lancaster's army in the Aquitaine, how the king's council and parliament had failed him. 'The duke must now tread with care, but I am the one man the king's councilors are at ease blaming and shunning. And so, being predisposed to dislike me, the duke makes use of me as an example.'

'Why have you so few champions?' asked Marian.

Wykeham again silenced Mother Isobel. 'There was a time when

King Edward entrusted to me building projects dear to him. An honor I will always treasure. But to my shame, as my power grew, so, too, did my arrogance. I was a nobody, a parvenue, yet I flaunted my favor, shed all humility. I acquired enemies who felt insulted by my incursion into their lofty heights, lowborn pretender. Then, when I became chancellor . . . Though that did not last, it was not forgotten. Some have waited a long while to enjoy the spectacle of my fall.'

'How unjust,' said Lucie. 'I have heard of the beauty of your building works. Prince Edward himself praised you.'

'You are kind.' Wykeham's smile was sad, weary. 'But I am keenly aware of my sinful pride.'

'A sin shared by most who accuse you,' Jehannes said in a soft voice.

The table grew quiet as a servant came forward with a flagon of wine. Owen welcomed more wine, but made certain to partake of the meat course before it was swept away. The younger sisters also took the opportunity to eat, as did Lucie, Jehannes, and Michaelo. The prioress sipped her wine and studied Wykeham's bowed head. When His Grace nodded for more wine and settled back to have some meat, she, too, partook. It was not until the servants came to clear the table for the savory that Mother Isobel spoke.

'As Dom Jehannes said, you are not alone in this sin,' she said. 'If only they could see the modesty with which you journeyed all this way to repair a wrong.'

Wykeham bowed to her.

Her eyes swept the table, settling on Owen. 'Might we count on your protection should Dame Marian choose to join the party returning to Wherwell?'

'Choose to join it?' Wykeham echoed.

'Of course. We will have men at the ready,' said Owen.

Hand to heart, the prioress thanked him.

'I would advise you delay the journey until Walter, Arn, and Reynard are safely in the castle,' said Owen.

'I will suggest that to the baron's men, Captain.'

Wykeham had leaned forward, his eyes on Dame Marian. 'You might return to Wherwell?' He looked to Mother Isobel. 'You would accept my protégée in her place?'

'No need,' said Isobel. 'Dame Claire has offered to remain. A pleasing solution.'

Claire was smiling. 'I was subcantrice of Wherwell before Dame Eloise replaced me with Dame Marian, whom I gladly assisted in her duties – she was far better suited to the role. Later I assisted Dame Prudence.' Wykeham's protégée. 'Since arriving at St Clement's, I've enjoyed my reunion with Dame Marian, working closely with her to learn all that she has set in place and helping her train the lower voices.'

Owen saw now that he had been wrong thinking Claire of an age with Marian. Subtle lines around her eyes suggested she was older, that it was the fullness of her face and an inner light that shone through in her eyes and complexion that gave her the dewy look of youth.

'To come together only to part once again is difficult,' said Marian, 'but we would both be blessed with our work.'

'And you would not be returning as Dame Prudence's assistant, surely,' said Wykeham. 'No matter Ergham's feeling, Dame Cecily will do what is best for Wherwell. I will make my intention clear to her and to Dame Prudence.'

Owen saw Marian's cleverness in this arrangement. Well done. He prayed it did not prove a dangerous gambit. Neville's interest troubled him.

THIRTEEN

A Test of Honesty

The bell above the shop door startled Jasper awake. He clutched the counter to catch his balance and winced, his hands stinging beneath the bandages and aching from his awkward movements while serving customers, several of whom had offered to help, or return when his mother was there. He was relieved to see that the newcomer was Ned, his father's man.

'I thought I would stop though I knew the captain and Dame Lucie were away,' said Ned. 'How are you coping?'

'Not so well. I've fumbled more than I've dispensed. In between customers I start nodding off, though when I tried sleeping earlier I couldn't.'

'I know the feeling. Can I leave you with some news for the captain?'

'Of course.'

Returning home from her lessons, Gwen stopped in the apothecary to see Jasper and noticed Rhys in the workshop, lingering by the doorway to the shop. She wanted to trust him, but he had sorely tested her faith in him. So she slipped in, silent as a cat, and crouched behind a table. Out in the shop she heard Ned telling Jasper that he'd been watching Jonas Snicket's house to see whether Rhys's kin returned, or whether anyone else ransacked the place. He'd learned that Pete, Snicket's elderly servant, had left with Laurence Gunnell, the sailmaker, the previous morning. As far as he could tell, Pete hadn't returned and he had a bad feeling about that. Nor had Gunnell opened his shop since then. This morning Ned had decided he needed to do more. Leaving someone else watching the house, he poked around to find out where Gunnell lived – with his mother in a house near the castle. When he went there, he saw Pete sitting outside the door talking to Laurence.

'It might be nothing,' said Ned, 'but I wanted the captain to know.'

All this while Gwen watched Rhys, his head bent, listening. Of course he was. Ned had mentioned his uncle and cousin. When he finally turned to leave, Gwen stayed hidden behind the table, then followed him out. She was almost to the bridge when the thought began to nag that Kate would be worried when she did not appear for lunch, and with her parents at Dom Jehannes's for the afternoon, there was no one to watch the children while Kate searched for her. But this was important. Rhys was once more lodging with them, and she needed to know whether they might trust him. Everyone else was busy. And no one else had seen him eavesdropping or knew what he'd heard. She might have told Jasper, but . . . well, it was too late for that.

Across the bridge, Rhys stopped at a tavern in an alley. Rundown, not respectable like the Merchets' tavern. As he stepped inside, Gwen pressed against the wall trying to stay in the shadow of the upper story and crept closer to the door. He was telling someone that he had a payment for Laurence Gunnell whose shop had been shut the past two days. A woman said something in a voice too soft for Gwen to understand. Rhys thanked her and hurried back out. Gwen ducked down, then followed him back over the bridge and up Castlegate, avoiding curious eyes – she kept her hood up, but she supposed people could still tell she was a child, though not a beggar, with her new boots and pretty green cloak. He moved so fast that she could not pause if she meant to keep up. She had not heard the directions to the house, so if she lost sight of him . . .

Why was he going there? What did he think it meant that Pete was talking to Laurence Gunnell?

She had to keep reminding herself why this was worth it. She must know if her family were safe. It's what her father would do, but he had so many people pulling him in all directions. She was helping him.

Castlegate was a wonder, large houses surrounded by gardens, so unlike the part of the city in which she lived. But they turned down a much more modest street running toward the river where a short row of houses ended at a large building. A warehouse? Rhys slowed his pace as he passed a house in the middle of the row, freshly painted white, a small tree in the yard. He slowed even more and she heard a man's voice. Pete? Or Laurence Gunnell? He walked on past the houses, slowing down by the large building, where he slipped into an alley between it and the last house.

Gwen hurried forward to press herself against the building and see where he was going. He had stopped at the end of the alley, looking down toward the back gardens of the houses. She was trying to think what to do, whether to stay to see what he did or hurry home, when someone grabbed her from behind, holding her close to him. She knew it was a man by his strength, how big the hands were that he put over her mouth and around her throat, pressing, pressing so hard she could not breathe. She was so afraid her whole body shook. She tried to pray for forgiveness but strange lights made her blink as the man uncovered her mouth. Just as she opened her mouth to scream, both hands pressed her throat. Choking her. Tiny red stars against the darkness. Her captor shouted something and then jerked her up and away. Again she opened her mouth to scream but her throat wouldn't work.

* * *

Lucie did not know what made her glance out the window when she did, but the sight of Kate rushing toward Jehannes's house had her running to open the door as her maidservant was lifting her hand to knock. Michaelo, who had followed on Lucie's heels, urged Kate inside.

'No time. We must search – Gwen is missing. She left the Ferriby schoolroom to come home for dinner, but she never arrived. No one has seen her. I have looked everywhere.'

'Come,' said Owen.

They hurried away, asking questions of Kate, learning that Rhys had also missed dinner, and Jasper had set off for a house near the castle. At least that's what she thought he'd said.

'Why there?' Owen asked.

'He said Ned came to tell him that Pete, Jonas Snicket's servant, went away with Laurence Gunnell, who lives with his mother near the castle.'

'And Jasper thinks Gwen went there?'

'I don't know what he was thinking, Captain. That's all I know.'

Lucie clutched his arm. 'Go. Find them. We will wait at the house in case she returns. Do you know where the widow lives?'

'I do.'

She had not noticed Brother Michaelo hurrying to keep up with them.

'Bless you,' Lucie cried. 'Go, my love. Find our Gwen.'

'You little—' a man at the head of the alley cried out. He held someone. A child by the size – God in heaven. Rhys recognized Gwen's green cloak. All he had was a small knife, the blade too short to do much harm. But it might turn the attention to him. Holding it high he rushed toward the man shouting, 'Release her!' as he lunged for the man's neck. He felt blood on his hand as his opponent staggered back and, with a shout of rage, threw Gwen against the wall. Her head hit hard and she slumped down, lifeless.

The man turned from Rhys toward Jasper, who had rushed up behind him. Rhys went to Gwen, lifting her head, calling her name. It was too dark beneath the eaves to see her eyes, but she was breathing. His hand came away from the side of her head with blood. Just a little, but still. Gently he propped her up against the wall and went to help Jasper, who struggled beneath the much larger man, bucking sufficiently that his opponent had to fight for balance. Lunging toward him, Rhys grabbed him and let himself fall backward, taking the man with him.

'There they are!' someone shouted.

The weight above him shifted as the man rolled off, then came down on him. Something sharp sank into his side, then released. He put his hand to the spot and felt the blood welling.

'I will follow him, Captain,' a man called.

Captain. God be thanked. Gwen's father was here. Another stab, then the weight lifted. Rhys closed his eyes and drifted down into darkness.

Nothing in all his years of soldiering had prepared Owen for the sight of two of his children on the ground, neither responsive. His first instinct was to chase after Reynard and hack him to pieces. For it must have been him. Who else would attack his children?

'I will chase him down,' said Ned. 'You two see to the injured.'

'Track him, but do not confront him on your own,' Owen growled. 'He is mine.'

He crouched beside Gwen, lifting her in his arms.

'Da.' She shaped the word, but he heard no sound.

'My sweetness, where are you hurt?'

She tried to lift her hand, but it fluttered and fell back as she went limp in his arms. Pressing her to him, he watched as Brother Michaelo knelt to Jasper. Not both of them, he prayed.

'He is bleeding a little, but aware, Captain.'

'Did you hear, Gwen? He is alive,' Owen whispered. She did not respond.

Jasper struggled to sit up. 'The man had his hands around Gwen's throat to stop her from screaming. He threw her at the wall when Rhys attacked him. Threw her.' His voice broke. 'I was trying to save her but I made it worse.'

'He was strangling her. You did save her, son.'

'I'm not badly injured, Brother Michaelo,' Jasper said. 'See to Rhys. He saved me.'

Rhys lay motionless, a knife in his hand smeared with blood. So, too, was his stomach. 'We need help moving Jasper and Rhys to my house,' said Owen.

Michaelo knelt down, pressing his ear to Rhys's chest. 'He is strong, and young,' he said, but his expression belied his words. He rose and moved away.

'Uncle,' Rhys whispered on an exhale. 'At Gunnell's. Heard him.' He coughed blood.

'We will send someone to catch them,' said Owen, gently rocking Gwen in his arms. 'Bless you for saving my children. We are taking you back to the house to see to your wounds.' He silently prayed the young man would live that long.

Looking round for Michaelo, he saw him disappearing into the warehouse. While he was gone, George Hempe appeared with several of his men.

'*Jesu*, what happened here?'

'Someone attacked the three of them. Ned has gone after him. I need a cart.'

They were interrupted by a rumble and squeak, and a man shouting. Brother Michaelo appeared around the far corner of the warehouse with a cart and donkey, followed by an irate warehouse worker. 'God placed it in my path,' said the monk as he came to a halt beside Rhys and Jasper.

'God help us,' the worker cried when he saw the bodies on the ground. 'I will tell my master you will return it, Captain Archer, Bailiff Hempe. Do you need help?'

'I brought sufficient men,' said Hempe, turning to bark orders for two of them to help Jasper and Rhys into the cart. 'Gently,' he cautioned. He held out his arms to Owen. 'I will take young Gwen while you climb up to the seat. I'll leave two with you and take the rest in search of Ned.'

'And Gunnell's house, the one with fresh white paint. Rhys says his uncle is there. I would think the cousin as well.'

'Leave it to us.'

Pacing the hall, Lucie hugged herself, grateful to hear Hugh and Emma shrieking with delight in the garden – Bess's nephew Tupper was playing pony, giving them gallops around the garden while Dame Marian clapped and sang with the one awaiting a turn. The prioress and Dame Claire were helping Kate prepare food, tisanes, gather blankets in case they were needed. Suddenly a calming presence entered the garden.

'Dame Magda!' Hugh shouted, rushing to the tiny healer swathed in colors that seemed to swirl in the pale October sunlight.

'Whoa, there, Mistress Emma,' the 'pony' cried as the toddler clumsily dismounted.

Magda kissed Hugh's forehead, then lifted Emma and chucked her in her arms.

'She does the heart good, doesn't she?' said Bess, rising from the corner where she had sat, keeping out of the way but ready if needed.

'Always,' breathed Lucie. 'But how did she know to come?' She hurried out into the garden. 'Magda. You heard about Gwen's disappearance?'

The healer held her with kind eyes as she rocked Emma. 'Magda senses she is in her father's arms, heading home. Come.' She set Emma down and led Lucie into the house. 'Build up a good fire in the hall. Evenings are chilly now.'

While Lucie worked on the fire, Magda pulled pallets out from underneath the stairs. Three of them.

A commotion drew her outside as Owen leaned from the seat of a donkey cart to hand Gwen down to Brother Michaelo.

Kate and Tupper fought to keep Emma and Hugh out of the way while the monk carried their sister through the gate and into the house. Lucie hurried beside him, telling him to lay her on the pallet closest to the fire.

Magda listened to Michaelo's account and then bent to Gwen, opening one eyelid, the other, feeling her pulse, listening to her heart, unbuttoning the top of her gown to examine her throat. 'Bring cushions to prop her up,' she said. 'She must sit up, her head as far above her heart as may be. Blood must not pool in her brain.'

Lucie knew how dangerous that might be. Propping up her daughter to an almost upright position, she perched beside her, rubbing her hands and whispering that she was home, she was safe. The bruises on her daughter's throat shocked her. How could a grown man do such a thing to a child?

She saw Owen's torment in the tightness of his jaw and the angry color of the scar around his eye patch as he entered the hall, helping Jasper to another pallet.

Owen felt Lucie's arm around his shoulders. 'Come, sit between Jasper and Gwen,' she said. 'I will bring brandywine.'

A part of him was still on the street, his entire body ablaze to see two of his children lying on the ground bleeding, victims of the devil Reynard. For it was, though Jasper said he could not be certain he was the one on the tavern roof the night before.

'Owen? My love.' Lucie was coaxing him to sit, placing a drinking bowl in his hands. 'Sip.'

He put the bowl to his lips but struggled to swallow for the bile in his throat. He could not see the room, could not feel the warmth of the fire, though he heard the crackle.

'One of them bloodied their attacker, Owen.' Brother Michaelo's voice, gentler than he had ever heard it. 'Reynard will hide a while to recover. You have time to be with your family.'

Someone pressed the middle of his forehead. 'Arrive, Bird-eye. Thou art needed here, as a healer. Thy nemesis must wait.'

Something within opened, and he saw his beloved bending to their daughter, Michaelo adding pillows beneath Rhys's head, Magda lifting one of Jasper's eyelids. Owen shook himself. All three glanced toward him with concern. No. This was not right. They must think only of the three who had fallen, not him. He finished the brandywine in a few swallows, feeling the warmth flow through him.

Magda felt around Jasper's torso. 'An elbow to the ribs?' she asked.

'Yes. And I hit my head when I went down. A little blood. But it's nothing. Will she wake?' His voice shook.

'Her heartbeat is strong.'

Lucie knelt beside Gwen, moistening her lips, then dripping brandywine into her sweet mouth.

Michaelo gingerly lifted Rhys's blood-soaked shirt and began to clean the wound in his side.

Bess had returned with one of her maids, both carrying stacks of pillows and bedding. She dropped some pillows onto Owen's lap. 'With that head bleed, Jasper needs propping up as well.'

Owen arranged them beneath Jasper.

'Rhys saved her, Da. Both of us.'

'For that he will be forever in my prayers. Now rest. I will come back.'

Owen knelt to his daughter. 'You are home now, Gwen. We are here.' He kissed her, held her hand for a few moments.

Lucie touched his cheek, her eyes glittering with tears. 'When the time comes, you will see that he answers for this.'

He kissed her forehead.

'How badly injured is Rhys?' she asked.

He had no idea. 'I'll see.'

Magda leaned close to the injury Michaelo had cleaned, murmuring words Owen could not understand. The gaping wound was up and to the side, not as deadly as it might have been. But bad enough. He had lost much blood.

'Has he spoken?' she asked Owen.

'A few words when he was lying on the ground, but nothing since, I think.' He looked to Michaelo, who had walked alongside the cart, observing Rhys and Jasper.

'Nothing more than a moan when we first lifted him, and a gasp as we helped him into the house.'

'Magda will see to him first.'

'I can help,' Jasper called.

'No, son. Lie back. Rest,' said Owen. 'We have sufficient to see to all three of you – the sisters, Magda, Michaelo, your mother, and me. I will pull your pallet close to Gwen's so you can hold her hand, eh?'

The sisters sat with Jasper and Gwen while Lucie and Owen assisted Magda in cleaning the wide wound in Rhys's side, Michaelo refreshing water, bringing more supplies as needed. Owen held Rhys still while Lucie mixed powders for Magda and helped pack the wound before Magda sewed him up. It looked as if Rhys had been stabbed twice, the skin between the wounds rupturing. He also bled from a gash in the back of his head, which they cleaned and bandaged.

Michaelo moved between the kitchen and the hall, keeping them supplied with clean cloths and water. Bess helped Kate prepare food for everyone. Tupper watched Hugh and Emma up in the nursery.

It reminded Owen of the hospital tents after a battle, when anyone sufficiently fit to assist took part. Not something he ever wanted to see in his home, involving his children. But he was grateful to all of them.

* * *

Night had fallen by the time Owen stepped into the kitchen for ale and food. The sisters were gone, the bargeman insisting on departing before sunset. Bess had gone home. Michaelo had left with Archdeacon Jehannes, who had come to say prayers over the injured. Now Kate sat by the fire, watching the flames as she sipped a cup of ale.

'Hugh and Emma fell asleep praying for Gwen, Jasper, and Rhys,' said Kate, brushing away tears. She nodded toward Hempe, who sat slumped by the fire, an ale forgotten beside him. 'He stayed to talk to you.'

Owen settled beside him. 'Did you find the bastard?' he asked.

Hempe snorted awake, sat up rubbing his scalp, then his eyes. 'Ned lost him somewhere near Ouse Bridge. A witness said he dived into the river and disappeared. Ned and several others watched the river but he didn't surface. God's blood, is the man the devil's own?'

Disappointing, but not unexpected. Wilfrid had also lost him at the river. The man was crafty. As someone with far more enemies than friends, he would not have survived in the ranks otherwise. But his mission incomplete, he would stay within reach of Owen. 'We'll deal with him soon enough.' He told Hempe about Neville's men expected at St Clement's, and Mother Isobel's request. 'He might choose that time to appear.'

'Neville's men? Sir John Neville's? What is his interest?'

'I will be keen to hear.'

'We'll be ready to assist at the priory,' Hempe assured him. 'How are Jasper and Gwen?'

'Jasper has a few bruised ribs – one might be broken. We bound him and he's managed to sit up and drink some ale, but by now I'd wager he's asleep. His head hit the ground when he fell. A bit of a lump, an abrasion. Last night, then today – he will sleep till morning or beyond. Gwen is awake at last, having difficulty swallowing, and dizzy.'

'That murderous monster,' Hempe growled. 'And Rhys?'

'He has not awakened.' Owen described the wound. 'So much blood loss, and it's difficult to tell what tore inside. We watch and wait. Jasper says he saved both of them.'

'After leading them into trouble.'

'I doubt he knew Gwen followed him.' But why? Her earlier

fascination betrayed by what she had learned of his purpose in coming to York? She had been angry. But why follow him?

'I am sorry to bring that up.'

'I don't know why she was there. What did you do with Walter and Arn?'

'Widow Gunnell was sweeping them out the door. She said that after witnessing the attack near the warehouse they spoke of vengeance for Rhys, and she wants no trouble in her house. They said the Gunnells had robbed them. We took the uncle and cousin to the castle.'

'Robbed them of what?'

'I paid them no heed. Men will say anything to wriggle away. My mind was set on two fewer to worry about.'

'You explained their crimes to them?'

'I did not want to spend the walk arguing with them. I told them I was taking them to the castle for their protection. But they must know they'll hang. Murdering a man in the bishop's service, on the sheriff's land, robbing an old man and inflicting mortal injuries, attacking an officer of the city – I cannot see it ending otherwise.'

Was it possible the Gunnells had robbed them? 'What if Laurence and Pete are behind the Snicket attack and theft?'

Hempe looked surprised. 'To be sure I have wondered how strangers guessed the old man had treasure hidden in that falling down house. Something doesn't feel right about it all. I'm glad I set two men to watch the house. We need to question the Gunnells and Pete, but I was busy with the other two, and then the sheriff wanting a report.'

'Tomorrow. You have good men on them?'

'Of course. I chose with care . . .'

Owen was only half listening, seeing again his firstborn lying limp on the ground, how lifeless she felt in his arms. He could not promise he would control himself when he found Reynard.

'Owen?'

He glanced up at Hempe's frowning face – not anger, but concern. 'Forgive me. Jasper's injuries are minor. But Gwen's – the swallowing, the dizziness . . .' Owen crossed himself. 'Magda is not smiling.'

'Leave everything to us. We will have men surrounding St

Clement's and escorting the travelers as far as need be –
though I would expect Sir John Neville to send adequate
protection.'

'If that is his purpose.'

'Ah. Of course.'

'Reynard is a skilled archer, battle-trained, and clever. I am the
one to stop him.'

'Your place is here at present, Owen. And, forgive me, but it
would be useful to capture him alive. We might learn of any others
involved. Could you trust yourself not to aim to kill him? I wouldn't
trust myself if Gwen and Jasper were mine. Can you truthfully say
you trust yourself not to snap?'

Not this night. 'I am too weary to argue. We will speak of this
again.' When Hempe began to rise, Owen caught his arm. 'Do not
underestimate him.'

Hempe placed a hand on Owen's. 'Rest assured we are all aware
of the danger.'

'I have a bad feeling about Laurence Gunnell.'

'As do I.'

'Good. Make sure our men do as well.'

'Of course,' said Hempe.

'Any word from Canter? He left without a word.'

'One of his mates said he hurt himself chasing after Reynard.
He's at home with his leg propped up.'

'I wonder whether he's to be trusted.'

'Canter? But—'

'When you told him he was on duty last night, how did he
behave?'

'Headed off to eat something.' Hempe nodded. 'If he shows up,
I will make some excuse not to use him. It occurs to me that he is
also one of our bowmen.'

'Doubly tempting for Reynard. Have his mate watch his house.'

'I will.' Hempe rose. 'And now I will take my leave. You need
to return to the children, and, I hope, sleep at some point.' At the
door he turned. 'I have men guarding St Clement's, and watching
the river, searching the area for a place Reynard might have slipped
in to hide.'

'Good. I want to question the Gunnells and Pete in the morning.'

'Would you like company?'

'I would appreciate that. You are a good friend, and I am grateful.'

With a nod, Hempe departed. Leaving Owen to his own darksome thoughts.

FOURTEEN
An Altogether Different Tale?

In the early hours Owen agreed to close his eyes, but he refused to climb to the bedchamber, instead stretching out on the bench beneath the garden window. Lucie understood. She sat wakeful and alert at Gwen's bedside. It was difficult enough to step away now and then to check Jasper's breathing or speak to Magda, who watched over Rhys. Something drove her to vigilance. She feared that if she were not there, awake, watching, one of her children would die. Even Magda could not ease her terror, could not dispel the awful sense of imminent loss.

Sometime before dawn, Lucie heard the latch click on the garden door, and felt a sharp breeze. Owen did not stir. Picking up scissors, she stood ready to defend her chicks.

'It's Alisoun. I did not wish to wake Kate.'

Lucie lowered the scissors with relief. 'Are you in the city for a birth? Is someone dying?'

'I am here to watch over Jasper and Gwen so that you might sleep awhile.'

'Accept her offer,' said Magda, joining them. 'Thy children will need thee in the days to come, all four of them. Rest is necessary so that thou canst hear and act from a clear mind. Magda says nothing thou dost not know.'

Her body found the temptation irresistible, but Lucie did not think her heart would allow her to rest. 'If something were to happen—'

'We will wake you and the captain at once.' Alisoun took her hands. 'You know that.'

She did. After giving Alisoun a thorough account of Gwen's and

Jasper's conditions, she woke Owen. Together they climbed to the bedchamber and lay down on the bed fully clothed, holding each other.

They slept but a few hours before returning to the little hospital in the hall, Owen with a burning question for Jasper. But his son still slept, a healing rest. While Owen waited for him to wake, he helped Magda, dripping a syrupy potion into Rhys's mouth, a tiring process he welcomed, allowing him time to gather his scattered thoughts into a plausible scenario.

He was so deep in thought that it took a nudge from Magda to realize he was holding an empty spoon to Rhys's lips. Her warm, light yet supportive touch drew him firmly into the present.

'Forgive me.'

'Nothing to forgive. Now that thou art truly here, Magda can trust thee to continue while she steps out into the garden.'

She departed with the grace of someone far younger.

Only when the cup of physick was empty did he move over to where Lucie sat beside Gwen, softly stroking her cheek and whispering a tale of a kitten with wings. Gwen's cat, Ariel, was curled up on her feet. Not wishing to interrupt the story, Owen half-listened, turning his thoughts to the sequence of events he had earlier strung together.

'Now, then, my love,' Lucie murmured at the end of the tale, 'think of all your Ariel might do if she sprouted wings.'

A rustle of covers as Gwen turned her head a little to look up at Lucie. 'Will Rhys live?' she asked in a tiny, breathy voice.

Owen snapped back to the present.

'Oh, my dear Gwen, we are determined that he will.' Lucie leaned down to kiss her forehead. 'It is so good to hear you speak. How do you feel?'

'Throat hurts. And I can't hear out of this ear.' She touched her left ear. 'I had to turn it away.'

Lucie glanced up at Owen. Her left ear had been the source of blood on her cheek, the swelling on that side of her head indicating that she had hit the wall hard.

Pushing down his anger, Owen bent to her, kissing her left cheek. 'Does it feel swollen?' he asked.

'Oh, swelling,' she said, wrapping her arms round his neck and pulling him down for another kiss. 'It's just stuffed then?'

'Could be.'

'My head aches, Da.'

He held her close, taking a deep breath before he could trust his voice. 'Do you know why? Because your body is busy healing you. It's hot, tiring work and makes it ache all over.'

Gwen's breath tickled his cheek. 'I feel their hammers.'

Beyond Lucie, Owen saw Jasper sit up. 'Do I hear Gwen?'

Lucie sat back so Jasper could see his sister.

'Your brother is glad to see you awake and talking,' Owen whispered.

Gwen let go with one arm and turned to smile at Jasper. 'I have carpenters hammering in my head,' she whispered.

'And that is enough excitement for now,' said Lucie, lifting her and settling her back onto the pillows. 'The more you sleep, the sooner the hammering will cease.' She held a cup to Gwen's lips. 'Are you ready to help?'

Gwen drank it down and lay back, closing her eyes.

Moving to Jasper's pallet, Owen reached for the cup of wine mixed with physick on a stool beside him. 'Are you thirsty?'

'I am.' Jasper drank a little. 'Is this to make me sleep as well?'

'I hope not, at least not at once. Could you tell me what you remember about the Gunnell house? When you passed it, did you hear anything?'

'Which one was it? People were coming out of all the houses in that row.'

'The white one. Did you see who stood there?'

Jasper took a moment. 'A woman and several men? But they might have been from the other houses. Why?'

'Trying to make sense of it. Enough of that. I am so proud of you, so thankful for your courage. You saved your sister's life.'

'Rhys would have—'

'You *did*. That is what happened.'

'I could never forgive myself if I hadn't tried.' He yawned.

'Rest now.'

'I heard that about her ear. Will it heal?'

'I don't know.'

'I wish I'd killed him.'

'I know. Sleep now.'

Owen went out to the kitchen to fetch some food for himself and

Lucie. Magda and Kate were talking softly on the settle before the fire. Seeing him, Kate rose.

'I have food ready for you and Dame Lucie.'

He gave them the good news about Gwen speaking. The two women hugged each other and laughed with tear-filled eyes.

When he had delivered food and drink to Lucie, Owen returned to the kitchen for his own. Kate handed him a platter with food and a bowl of ale. Magda invited him to join her. He felt her watching him as he did so.

He stretched out his legs and tried to calm his mind while he ate, but memories bombarded him. His early days as a captain of archers. At first he had been buoyed by the honor of the old duke's trust, the pride when a man improved under his tutelage. If one neglected his duties, Owen talked to him without anger, without punishment, giving him every chance to prove himself trustworthy. Gradually he had identified the difficult ones, those who took his generosity as a sign of weakness. With the help of the close circle he trusted implicitly, he watched them, learned how they functioned, those they held as comrades and those they used and cast aside. In the center of them was Reynard.

'Magda senses a great weight bearing down on thee.'

'Unwelcome memories long set aside as part of my old life, no longer needed. The past few days have stirred up all the misgivings and doubts, the anger and frustration.'

'Thou speakest of this Reynard, a man from thy past?'

'Him, and those he drew to him. One in particular, Madoc, is suddenly in my mind. Why? Could I have seen him and forgotten?'

'They served under thee when thou wert captain of archers?'

'They did. Every honor comes at a price, and Reynard's circle were my penance to bear. I spent many evenings seeking advice about how to control them from my peers and those immediately above me in rank. They all agreed that in every contingent there were those who devoted their waking hours to defying authority, telling themselves they were more deserving of the rank than their captains. It was part of the responsibility, handling the defiant. All advised strict discipline.'

'Magda sees how thy men respect and obey thee now. The defiant would have resented how loyal their fellows were to thee.'

'I wonder whether I might have done more to convince them never to cross my path in future.'

'Such men would take that as a challenge. Tell Magda more about Reynard.'

What to say? 'When he served the old Duke of Lancaster, he felt his skill with the bow earned him a place as my second in command. It would have done so had I trusted him.'

'Why didst thou not?'

'There was a darkness in him. He never met my eyes unless it was to challenge an order. He was slippery. Sly. His appetite for violence seemed to have no bounds. Any slight was sufficient cause to attack. To promote him – I did not trust what he would do if given authority over the men.'

He felt the healer's gaze boring through his eye to his soul. 'And thou dost believe he sees a way to punish thee by threatening the lives of thy children?'

'You said to heed my body's message. My gut tells me that was his purpose. To attack my daughter—' He stopped himself, feeling how quickly the spark ignited.

Magda nodded. 'Was it his appetite for violence, or for cruelty that alarmed thee?'

She was right. Many of his archers had a taste for violence. But Reynard was cruel. That's what made him the devil. 'Cruelty.'

'Thou art a careful and just judge of men.' She touched Owen's patch. 'Thy wounding. This was Reynard's work?'

'Yes. He studies others closely, finds their weaknesses, and uses them to his cruel purpose. That night he used what he had noticed about me and the jongleur, how I wanted to believe our connection and begged for mercy in his case. He had seen what I had not, that the jongleur would betray me. My commander had noticed that I did not use all my men in rotation for the duty of guarding the noble prisoners, and insisted I use even those I did not completely trust. He said they were all fighting against a common enemy, they could be trusted in this. Which is how Reynard came to be on duty that night. I believe he'd allowed the jongleur and his mistress to slip through.'

'No one warned thee?'

'I came upon the jongleur before my men were aware what had happened.'

Magda did not speak for a moment, gazing into the fire. 'What was his purpose in accompanying Gerald Trent?'

'In the beginning I thought Reynard had been sent to block Wykeham's attempt to make amends, but if that were so his attention would now be fixed on the priory, on Dame Marian. Yet last night he was at the tavern, and today he was watching Rhys's uncle and cousin – or following Gwen. Having failed to strike me last night, he may now mean to threaten me through my children.'

'Magda understands why thou wilt not rest until the fox is no longer a threat to the fold.'

'No, I will not.'

She put her hand over his and looked into his eye. 'Trust in thine own wisdom.'

'No one is right all the time.'

'It is wise to remember that. Caution is part of wisdom. But thou hast deep knowledge of thy nemesis. Trust what arises here.' She pressed the center of his forehead. 'And here.' She touched his stomach.

'How do I know?'

'Thou wilt know.'

When Hempe arrived shortly afterward, shedding wet cloak and boots, Kate was keeping Hugh and Emma engaged with a rainy-day activity, rehearsing a song for their brother and sister, and Rhys, if he woke. Owen sat alone by the kitchen fire, brooding over his conversation with Magda. He shook himself from his thoughts to greet Hempe, who settled down beside him, reporting a quiet night, no incidents, just wet, cold, grumpy men, eager to go home to dry off and sleep by their hearth fires. Most fortunate men, to Owen's mind.

'You look a bit more rested than when I left you,' Hempe observed.

'I slept a little,' said Owen. 'And I've had time to think it through. You'd set Ned to watch Gunnell's shop. But he showed up yesterday near the castle. Did you take him off that duty?'

'I did. He'd seen no activity. Why?'

'Where's Stephen?'

'Watching the river for signs of Reynard.'

'I want him watching the Gunnell shop. And two of our best men watching my home and the apothecary, front and back.'

'What are you thinking?'

'If he swam across the river, Gunnell's shop is close to the far bank.'

Hempe studied the floor for a moment. 'So you think Pete's biding at the widow Gunnell's house and Reynard in the shop.'

'I'm thinking a lot more than that, but it's a start.'

'Damned if I understand why you think Gunnell would risk so much. And what is his connection to Pete?'

Greed, that was the connection. But Owen could not be certain. 'Reynard counts on our confusion.'

'You believe this was his idea? I know you said he was sly, but how would he convince Gunnell?'

'Offer something worth the risk.' Hempe pulled a face that made Owen laugh. 'You may be right to think I'm mad. Time will tell. For now I want Stephen to watch the shop, and our men to take all who are in the Gunnell house to the castle, keep them under guard.'

'Not in the same chamber as Walter and Arn, I take it?'

'It might prove interesting, but let's keep them apart for now. Give the Gunnells a pleasant chamber.'

'What do I say to Laurence and the widow? They will demand to know why they're being taken to the castle.'

'Explain that they might be in danger and we can protect them at the castle. Same for Pete if he's still there.'

'They will argue.'

'Get them there.'

'You also think Reynard might attack your family?'

'He has, twice – the night he surprised Jasper on the roof of the York Tavern, and when he attacked my children.' The heat in Owen's head was building. He tried to breathe slowly, calming the storm. He had no cause to snap at Hempe.

'I should say,' said Hempe, as if oblivious to Owen's mood, 'though it will only encourage your flight of madness – when I asked Lotta whether Laurence Gunnell is a citizen of the city, she said he was fortunate he had any custom, always late with orders and the quality of his sails unreliable. Fabric and sewing both inferior to other sailmakers in the city. He has far to go to earn the support he would need to become a citizen.'

Hempe's wife was a reliable source. 'You asked because you wondered about his part in all this?'

'After finding Arn and Walter at the Gunnell house, yes, I did wonder. He has some explaining to do. And though he seems to live well, we've seen no customers at his shop. I'm wondering how he thrives, what his real business might be.'

'Let's question them together after I've searched the shop and the house.'

Hempe rose. 'Best begin. I will see you later, at the castle.'

'I will go first to Gunnell's shop.'

'I'll send Stephen there.'

After the prayers at terce the other sisters dispersed, but Marian had remained in the cloister, listening to the drumbeat of the rain on the lead roof, watching it bend the branches on the trees still laden with leaves, feeling the mist on her face. Though Sir John Neville's men had arrived eager to turn round and head south, there would be no traveling until the storm had passed. She had spent the hour before the others arrived for none kneeling before the Blessed Mother's altar praying for Gwen, Jasper, and Rhys. And, selfishly, for a sign. Her bag was packed, Dame Claire as ready to assume Marian's duties as she could be in so short a time, but she yearned for a clear sign to be certain she made this decision out of a true calling and not pride – to be the cantrice of Wherwell Abbey would be the greatest honor she could imagine. But did God mean this honor for her? Or had the abduction that had ripped her from there been His doing, to chasten her? Was she meant to stay here at St Clement's, a humbler establishment? Should she bend to the wishes of her family, who dared not antagonize the Duke of Lancaster in this delicate time, as all feared the death of the king and the accession of a child to the throne? A gust of wind sent a shiver through the tree just outside the part of the cloister where she stood, showering her with drops.

Alisoun had opened the apothecary mid-morning, handling the orders she could and making notes for Lucie and Jasper for more complicated compounds to be prepared later. During a lull she went to the house to see whether she was needed.

Jasper sat by the garden window watching the rain drip from the eaves.

'How is Gwen?' she asked.

He pulled his eyes away from the storm, settling on his sister. 'Quiet since she first spoke. Sleeping. It is a good sign that she can speak, isn't it?'

'Very good.'

'But her left ear.'

'I heard. Did Magda seem worried?'

'I would not know how to tell.'

Alisoun smiled. Magda rarely exhibited worry, and the signs were so subtle it had taken living with her and studying her closely to detect any. 'I know little about ear injuries. I will ask her. And you? How are your ribs? Do you have pain with deep breaths?'

'Some, but the binding helps. Do you need me in the apothecary?'

'Today is for rest. Tomorrow you might try a few hours.'

'It's only bruising.'

'I know how hard it is to be still, but if one or more ribs are broken, moving about too much will cause more damage. And you did hit your head.'

He reached up to take her hand. 'I have not had a chance to say how sorry I am for all I said.'

She stepped back, not ready to talk about his outburst. 'Not now. Not here. Too many ears.'

He turned away from her.

She joined Magda, who sat by Rhys's pallet. He lay so still it was no wonder Gwen had asked if he would recover.

'He has a long healing ahead of him,' said Magda. 'But no fever.'

'That bodes well. He hasn't awakened at all?'

'For a moment. Long enough to drink physick in a broth. He lost much blood from the stab wounds in his side, and the bloody knot on the back of his head suggests a rock on the ground where he fell.'

'Poor man.'

'Or fortunate to have been with members of this household when he fell.'

'And Gwen's ear?'

'Time will tell.' Magda nodded toward the pallet where Lucie sat beside her sleeping daughter. 'Reassure her that all is well in the shop.'

Lucie glanced up as Alisoun approached. 'Do you need me?'

'Today, no,' said Alisoun. 'And tomorrow Jasper means to return. He will easily fill the orders I could not in a short time, and then I will send him back here to rest.'

'How can I thank you?'

'You have done so by trusting me to see to the shop. Despite . . . everything.' She took a breath. 'And now I must eat and return for the late afternoon trade.' Kissing Lucie on the cheek, Alisoun escaped to the kitchen before the emotions in the room overwhelmed her. She felt their distress so keenly, all of them. In one way or another she had been part of the family ever since losing her own parents and siblings to the pestilence. And for a long while she had expected to marry Jasper and live among them. That she now saw no path to that future saddened her.

Before heading for Laurence Gunnell's shop, Owen talked with the already soaked and miserable men searching around the north end of the Ouse Bridge, as well as some of the workmen on the staithe. He was late to the game – all the hiding places they knew of had been searched, in vain.

The rain was penetrating Owen's cloak by the time he crossed the bridge. Stephen already stood in the shop doorway, arms folded, chin tucked, watching the neighbors watching him. With his considerable size and heft and his menacing frown, he was an intimidating presence.

Spotting Owen, he broke out in a wide grin. 'Come along in and dry off. Though I can't promise warmth.' He stepped back, shutting the door behind him as he followed Owen inside. 'You were right, Captain, someone's been biding here, in a room behind the shop. Meant to serve as an office, I reckon, but now a bedchamber. Pallet, blankets, cup and bowl on a table, warm coals in the brazier. Comfortable. One of the blankets is stained. Maybe blood.'

'That might prove helpful. Any clothing? A pack?' Owen asked as he pulled back his hood and shook the rain off his brows.

'Found none, but I've not yet searched this room. Thought I'd best block the doorway.'

'No lock?' He squinted back at the door as his eye adjusted to the dimness within.

'There's a lock, but the door is presently the only source of light. The window in here is boarded up.'

No wonder it was so dark. Put in place for Reynard? Or had this never been intended for regular trade? 'Help me tear off the boards.'

In the light from the open window, Owen found a few lamps. Once he lit them using the stoked coals in the brazier, he began a systematic search of the shop – Stephen had found all there was to find in the heated room behind it. Tallies and a list of clients spoke of a struggling business. Shelves held heavy fabric for sails as well as light fabric and straw, stuffing for cushions. A sniff confirmed his suspicion that mice had nested in the straw. Gone now, but they would return as winter set in. A long board on trestles served as a workspace on which lay a wooden box containing a few spools of heavy thread and large, sturdy needles. A pair of benches provided seating. No samples of goods, sketches of sails – Gunnell was either about to fail or he kept all of that at his mother's home. Not convenient. A third possibility came to mind – he was busy pursuing something else. Whatever supported him, Owen found no sign of it here.

Crossing over to the tavern, he ordered food to take over to Stephen, and some ale. While waiting he talked to the tavern maid.

'Much custom at the sailmaker's?'

She glanced round as if to be certain no one listened. 'I've seen few passing through those doors,' she said.

'How long has the window been boarded up?'

'A fortnight, maybe. Queer, isn't it? I expected to see a new tenant, but Master Laurence comes now and then, spends some time within.'

'Seen anyone else there since old Jonas died?'

'No. But I swear I smell smoke when I pass by of an evening – in the shop, not the house behind.'

The food arrived along with Dunn, the proprietor, ordering his informer off to clean tables.

Owen had heard enough, and was curious about the presence of Brother Michaelo at Laurence's shop, talking to Stephen. As he greeted Michaelo, a lad interrupted to say that Hempe needed him at once at the Gunnell house.

'What happened?'

The boy shook his head. 'He wouldn't let me in, but someone was crying.'

'I will accompany you,' said Michaelo. As they walked he

explained his presence. Two of Neville's men had called on Wykeham. 'As the prioress had heard, they are to escort him to Winchester, ensuring his safety on the road, and take the sisters to Wherwell. Sir Francis, who leads the small company, came with his page to discuss plans for the departure. The others are arranging their lodgings at St Mary's Abbey.'

'Another sign,' Owen muttered. He had wasted precious time in blaming Wykeham for all that had happened since his arrival.

'Whatever you mean by "sign", I doubt you are feeling the chill of this rain for the heat of your anger.'

'I have failed to hide it?'

'As much as I pride my skill in observing my fellow mortals, a blind man would sense the steam emanating from your person. Might I know the cause?'

'I have been so wrong,' Owen began . . .

Two women sat near the entrance to the modest hall of the widow Gunnell. By the clothing and age difference, Owen surmised it was the maidservant consoling the weeping widow, Dame Alys.

Brother Michaelo joined them on the bench, reaching for the widow's hand.

'He must have tumbled from the solar, the poor man,' she sobbed.

With a nod to him, Owen approached the body lying at the bottom of the ladder to the solar, which Hempe was descending. Even before he crouched down to see more clearly, Owen knew it was Pete, Jonas Snicket's servant. His neck was broken, as was likely when falling from the height of the solar. No doubt other bones broken as well, and the skull fractured. Not that it mattered. The dead felt no pain.

'Dame Alys and her servant returned from visiting a neighbor to find him so,' said Hempe as he joined Owen. '"Poor old man," she said, and blamed herself for not seeing that he was safely down in the hall before departing.' He sounded skeptical.

As was Owen. 'She sent for you?'

'No. We happened upon her standing over him, weeping loudly.'

'And Laurence?'

'Called away on business, she said. Left at first light, but I'm guessing he sneaked out in the night.'

As Owen rose, he glanced toward the widow who sat quietly

now, hands folded, as Brother Michaelo led her and her servant in a prayer. A man of many talents. 'How did our guards not see him depart?' He kept his voice low, despite Michaelo's attempt to distract Dame Alys.

'You might have a word with the men,' said Hempe. 'They don't like disappointing you.'

'They need experience, not my approval.'

Hempe winced at Owen's angry tone. 'Steady.'

'The trail of bodies does not disturb you?'

'Of course it does. And we're doing all we can to stop it.'

'And failing. Laurence's might be the next body discovered.'

'Gunnell? So he is not in league with Reynard?'

'Disappearing in the night is not the behavior of an innocent man, I grant you, though possibly a frightened one. Reynard trusts no one – uses them, then discards them. Laurence might talk if we could find him.'

'I've sent word to watch for Gunnell at all the gates. But if he killed Pete he will be long gone. You're right. I've failed you.'

'I am as much to blame, so ready to conclude that Wykeham brought trouble in his wake, looking no further. Have the body taken to the castle, and escort Dame Alys and her maidservant there. As planned, a comfortable chamber.'

'You think she is part of it?'

'I have yet to speak with her. But I smell a carefully staged drama. Let her stew at the castle. I'll return here to search after I've met with Sir John's men.'

'That's why the monk's with you?' Hempe nodded toward Michaelo. 'He has charmed the widow. Might be useful when we question her.'

Owen agreed. On his way out he paused to introduce himself to Dame Alys, offering his condolences regarding Pete. 'You knew him well?'

'I? No. Laurence believes it his Christian duty to take in strays.' A tight smile followed by much dabbing of the eyes.

'I am sorry I missed Laurence,' said Owen. 'When do you expect him to return?'

'I could not say.'

'Or do not care to incriminate him?' Even as he said it, he knew it a mistake.

Brother Michaelo sighed as Dame Alys reared up, her finger stabbing Owen as she demanded he apologize.

Too late for that. 'To convince me of your innocence, you've only to tell me all you know.'

'The mayor will hear of this!'

'He will indeed.' Owen bowed to her and departed.

Michaelo hurried after him. 'All my work calming her and you— What demon possessed you in there?'

'I thank you for distracting the women.'

'I make myself useful.'

'And I regret confronting the widow in such wise.'

'You have turned her against you when you need her.'

'I know, Michaelo,' Owen growled.

The monk raised a brow, but said no more about it. Glancing at the sky he proposed they hurry on. The rain had stopped, but the wind was rising and clouds scudded across a steel-gray sky.

Walking cleared Owen's head. By the time they reached the minster, near Jehannes's house, he was able to return to Michaelo's mission. 'Are Neville's men treating Wykeham with courtesy?'

'Most gracious, extending greetings from the baron himself, and his brother the archbishop.' Michaelo watched Owen's reaction.

'The Archbishop of York?'

'Insincere, to be sure. Elder brother smoothing over his sibling's shortcomings as the archbishop cannot be bothered with the affairs of York.'

'And ensuring that if such a prominent bishop as Wykeham is murdered in his brother's city, he will be able to claim having done all he could to protect him. They will find a way to put the blame on me and the bailiffs.'

'Indeed.'

'Do they know of Dame Marian's decision to return to Wherwell?' Even if this trouble had nothing to do with Wykeham, if from the beginning Reynard's purpose had been to destroy Owen, he had not expected Neville's men to approve of Dame Marian's return to Wherwell. After all, she had been warned away by her uncle, albeit a Percy.

'They do, and they say Lady Maud will be glad of it. I know this is an interruption in your day, but Dom Jehannes will be reassured by your presence.'

'I am glad to meet Neville's men. In return, I would have you accompany me as I talk to Walter, Arn, and the Gunnells at the castle.'

'I will honor that debt despite this not being my request.'

'Do not pretend you don't enjoy this.'

Michaelo raised a brow as he paused at the door. 'Think what you like.'

In the hall, Wykeham rose to greet them, the others following.

'Captain Archer. This is Sir John Neville's man, Sir Francis.'

'And my page, Phillip.' The knight was younger than Owen by several years, he guessed, but he was at ease with Owen's scarred face in the way only a man who had seen battle would be. 'I am glad to meet you. When I heard that you were captain of bailiffs in the city and seeing to His Grace's safety, I was reassured.'

'Come now, both of you, and sit by the fire,' said Dom Jehannes. 'Dry yourselves.'

As everyone settled, Jehannes steered the conversation to the coming storm, until Perkin and one of Wykeham's servants brought hot spiced wine for Owen and Michaelo. Sir Francis expressed his hope that they might depart as soon as the weather cleared. The bishop nodded in agreement, though the lines of weariness in his face spoke of his dread.

When the conversation turned to the reason for their visit, Owen listened with interest to Sir Francis's account of Sir John's orders. As he'd guessed, the baron was convinced it was in his and his brother's best interests to ensure that Wykeham was safely returned to Winchester, for if he or his party were injured or killed, people might blame the archbishop. When Wykeham asked why Sir John was concerned for his welfare, the knight grew quiet, glancing at Jehannes and Owen as if for help.

'Speak plainly,' said Wykeham.

'Your Grace, it is said that the Duke of Lancaster seeks to make an example of you as a warning to all who would see advantage in the king's illness and the royal family's mourning. My lord knows that his fellow bishops will be incensed by the treatment of one of their own, and if any ill should befall you in York, they would look to his brother the archbishop as responsible.'

'I should think we are most concerned about the potential source of trouble,' said Jehannes.

'Yes. If you might clarify, Sir Francis,' said Wykeham.

'My lord believes you have made enemies in the realm, Your Grace. As do all great men,' he said quickly with a strained smile. 'And he fears that once they learn you are being stripped of your temporalities, they will presume you have no protection, no allies, and they might' – he cleared his throat – 'use that to their advantage.'

Michaelo leaned close to Owen, saying quietly, 'Enemies who want him dead is what he cannot bring himself to say.'

'And therefore he is protecting me, and taking his place as my ally.' Wykeham raised a brow. 'I admit I did not anticipate such generosity from the Baron of Raby. I am grateful to Sir John.' A vein pulsed at his temple. He felt diminished. Which was Lancaster's purpose. And Neville's? Sir John could not risk Wykeham's death during a journey to York, but he could insult him.

Wykeham had risen and walked to the hearth. For a long while he stood facing it, his back to the company, gazing into the flame. His servant slipped into the hall to replenish cups, then withdrew. Owen noticed Perkin hovering in the doorway.

At last Wykeham turned, nodding to the gathering. 'I am grateful for the protection. We shall depart as soon as the weather permits. Now I should like to retire to the minster to pray.'

Sir Francis and his page rose, as did the others, as Wykeham departed. As soon as the door shut behind him, the knight asked whether someone should attend the bishop.

'One of my men will be following him,' said Owen.

'I am glad to hear it. Might we talk, Captain?'

Jehannes asked Brother Michaelo to accompany him to his parlor. 'If you should need anything, call Perkin,' he said, bowing out.

Sir Francis sat forward. 'It is said we are facing a formidable archer, one whom you trained. Is that true, Captain?'

'I would be curious to know who told you that.' Raby Castle was at the very least a two-day ride from York. How would Sir John have heard so quickly?

'I am not certain where I heard that.'

A lie. Owen noticed Perkin in the corridor leading to the kitchen, moving away from them now. 'You heard correctly.'

'Three of the men in my company are excellent bowmen, including my page. As you trained our opponent, I hoped you might work with them, prepare them. I should be grateful.'

Dredging up his memories of training Reynard was not something Owen welcomed, but he must do so in any case. 'You might ask Abbot William's permission to set up a butt in the abbey grounds. It would be best to work without an audience.'

'You mean this man Reynard?'

Even to the name. 'I doubt he is alone.'

'I will do my best with the abbot.'

'He is keen to please the Nevilles.' Owen rose. 'I cannot say when I will be free, but I will make the time before we engage with Reynard.' He nodded to Sir Francis and departed through the kitchen, where he found Perkin pretending to be busy by the door. Wykeham's serving man was tending a pot on the fire.

'Come with me to the kitchen garden,' he said in Perkin's ear.

The man shied from his nearness. 'Captain? But I have—'

Clutching his shoulder, hard, Owen looked into the man's frightened eyes. 'It is not a request.'

Perkin moved slowly toward the door, shaking his head when the one stirring the pot asked if he needed him. Outside, he glanced round the garden and up onto the roof before focusing on Owen.

'You've seen someone watching the house,' Owen guessed.

'What do you want of me, Captain?'

'To give you a piece of advice. When confiding in your superiors, impress upon them the importance of being discreet with the information. I saw you when Sir Francis mentioned Reynard.'

'I don't know what you mean.'

'You gather information well. But you have yet to learn whom you can trust. Still, Neville must have confidence in you.'

Perkin crossed his arms and tried to look stern, but his blush betrayed him.

'Why not help me help your master keep the peace for his brother?'

'I work for Dom Jehannes.'

And report to Sir John Neville, who placed you here, Owen thought, but did not say. Jehannes would deal with the man later. 'Tell me about the watcher.'

Another anxious glance round the garden. 'At first it was a boy.

When I caught him he said his mother sometimes cleaned for Dom Jehannes and he liked the garden. But the past several days it's been a man, large, not swift on his feet, but quiet. Withdraws into the shadows as soon as I'm aware of him.'

'Anything else you can tell me of his appearance?'

'A great bush of fair hair and thick brows.'

He might be describing Madoc. Except . . . 'Large, you said. Strong, or fat?'

'Muscle, but a belly, too. You know how old soldiers go to fat.'

As had Bruin. 'Has he spoken to you?'

'I think he started to last night, but the bishop's man came out and he slipped away.'

'This is helpful. Have a care, Perkin.'

'Will you tell Dom Jehannes?'

Nodding to him, Owen returned to the house, knocked on the door to the parlor where Jehannes was talking to Michaelo. He informed him of the spy in his household, asked if he would keep him on for now.

Jehannes closed his eyes. 'Until this is resolved. And then he goes.'

FIFTEEN
Half Truths and Accidental Gifts

Owen stood in front of a long window looking out on the back gardens in the widow's hall, watching water gathering in runnels from the roof and flowing toward the river. He was caught in a vivid memory of waking in the camp in excruciating pain and remembering the betrayal. Reynard had sworn innocence, confessing to a lesser sin, that of coercing another to take his watch. And though the substitute supported his claim, Owen knew it to be a lie.

'It is hardly a day to tramp about the city chasing criminals.'

Jolted back to the present, Owen took a moment to realize it was Brother Michaelo who had spoken, and that he was in the Gunnell house. 'Convenience is a luxury I cannot afford,' he finally said. 'He is here. Near. I can feel him.'

'Is this Dame Magda's training?'

The monk's unease was as clear as Owen's sense of Reynard. He himself could not explain how he knew, what it was that convinced him. Did this prove he had learned to use the extra sense Magda called his third eye, or clear seeing? It mattered not at present. He had much to do.

'Perhaps,' he said, donning his cloak and pulling up the hood, 'Hempe awaits us at the castle.' He led the way out into the storm.

Though it was not far, they were soaked by the time they joined Hempe, who paced at the door to the building where guests were lodged, those people either under protection or awaiting trial and able to pay for comfort.

'Have you questioned Dame Alys yet?' Owen asked.

'No. Letting her wonder whether I lied about why she is staying in the castle. She's furious with you, which made my job harder.'

'I will be all courtesy this time, I swear.'

'You'd best. The chamber is comfortable, but when she realized she's not free to go about the city, well, the woman has a sharp tongue.'

'All I want is information about her truant son.'

'Even if she gives him up, we cannot set her free just yet. Not without Reynard and Laurence in custody. Did you find anything in the house that might help us catch them?'

'Not yet. Scattered about the loft were what looked like Pete's clothes, castoffs from Snicket. Laurence and his mother appear to sleep in box beds behind a screen in the hall. In a chest there, and another in a space behind the kitchen, I found costly plate, a quantity of rare spices, bolts of silk, a pouch of assorted rings and brooches of quality. Have one of the men bring them here, for the sheriff's safekeeping.'

'So Laurence is a thief?'

'It will be interesting to hear Dame Alys's explanation.'

'What of the shop? Was it as you thought?'

'Yes.' Owen described the signs of habitation, the evidence of a failed enterprise, and the tavern maid's comments.

'But nothing pointing to Reynard. Besides your certainty.'

'It's the only arrangement that makes sense of it all.'

'Or Laurence takes his women to the bed behind the shop. An unwed man living with his widowed mother – I think it likely.'

'You might be right. It might be a woman with her courses who bloodied a blanket.'

'Ah.' Hempe nodded. 'Perhaps not. How does Wykeham fit in?'

'He afforded Reynard the opportunity to come north and confront me, nothing more. My prejudice against Wykeham blinded me.'

'Come north to confront you? Revenge? For what?'

'For not making him my second. For shaming him before his comrades in arms when I was new to leading men. Too late I saw what pride he took in his skill, expecting to become captain of archers in someone's guard. I became his barrier to what he felt he deserved. And now . . . it appears he's no longer part of Lancaster's archers but a common laborer. Perhaps he blames me. My successor, an old friend, knew I distrusted him and felt the same. He would be the first suspected of any trouble.'

'I can understand that. I hated you at first,' Hempe said with a fleeting grin. 'But he's not touched you.'

'He's done worse. He's touched my children. Shown me that – despite all my success – I cannot protect what I hold most dear.' Owen felt how he clenched his hands and forced himself to relax them. 'But you are right to doubt me. I count on you to correct me if I go off course. Let's hear what Arn and Walter have to say for themselves. Then we'll talk to Dame Alys.'

After a night in a chamber not much more comfortable than a dungeon, Walter and Arn huddled together, shielding their eyes from the glare of the lantern Owen carried with him as he entered. No wonder they were in such a state, considering the chamber: stone walls with a window far too high and small to provide anything but a bit of air, straw-stuffed pallets on the floor, a bucket for relieving themselves, weak light through the barred opening toward the top of their door from a lantern on the wall opposite. Worse than Owen had intended.

'Captain Archer himself,' said the older of the two, snarling. Rhys's uncle Walter – grizzled hair, lined face, a few teeth missing, paunch.

The younger one rose up, fists balled, grinning slyly – Arn, Walter's son. 'Which one first?' He feinted toward Owen, then Hempe. Light on his feet, with good form for a fist fight.

'Save your strength for the trial, you fool,' Hempe growled, stepping aside to let the guard push him back down to the pallet.

'I see you've brought us a priest,' said Walter.

'I am but a monk,' said Michaelo. 'Here to record your story for the sheriff.' He stood aside as guards brought a small table, a stool, and an oil lamp. 'Bless you,' he said, taking his seat.

Owen motioned the guards to leave and close the door, then leaned against it, arms folded.

'You're here to beat us for injuring your second, I'm guessing,' said Walter.

Arn turned to his father. 'Shut your mouth!'

'Our silence will not help,' Walter said in a weary voice. 'How is he?'

'He will mend,' said Owen. 'It's Trent you should worry about. He is the one who might not survive. That would be two of the bishop's men dead, one you murdered, one you attacked, giving Raymond the opportunity to kill him.'

Hempe crouched down near the uncle. 'So you're for hanging at best.'

'We kicked Trent, but the bishop's own man shot him. Our kicks aren't what will kill him,' said Walter. 'And the other – the carter's beast of a man was attacking our David. Not a fair fight, a bear attacking a lamb. We beat him off to save our lad and get away with our lives. We didn't hear until days later that he was dead. He was alive when we ran. I swear we never meant to kill anyone.'

Arn muttered something Owen could not quite hear, but he seemed to disagree.

'So you're saying Beck chose the weakest of you to fight?' Owen asked. That would be unlike the Bruin he had known. He always went for the challenge.

'If Beck's the big one, no, it was David threw himself at him, to avenge his father's death,' said Walter. 'We tried to pull him away. He wasn't the one, we kept saying. But the beast could not miss that David was no threat to him. I can't say I'm sorry the beast is dead. You know how it feels, Captain. You must want to kill his mate for what he did to your young daughter and your son.'

Hempe glanced at Owen, who took his time responding, fighting to keep his face passive and his body relaxed.

'I want him to answer to the king's justice,' said Owen. 'What do you mean that Beck wasn't the one?'

'The other, Raymond, him and another one killed David's father, not the one you call Beck. The other was not so big as this Beck, but large enough. Malcolm, I think.'

'Madoc,' said Arn.

'Right you are,' said Walter.

Madoc, too, had left Lancaster's service and was now a laborer. Was it possible he was the one Perkin saw watching Jehannes's house? 'Have you seen him here?'

'He's here,' said Arn. 'They're never apart, so folk said back home. Must have come up early to prepare for them.'

If so, this had been planned with care.

'If you did not set out to kill anyone, what was the purpose of your attack?' Hempe asked.

That silenced the man for a moment. Of course they'd come for blood.

'How is my cousin?' Arn asked.

'We are doing all we can for Rhys and pray it is enough,' said Owen.

'His family should be with him,' said Walter. 'Has he asked for us?'

'He has not awakened.'

Walter groaned and crossed himself. Arn muttered a string of curses, then hurriedly crossed himself as well.

'And your daughter? Your son?' Walter asked.

'They are mending much faster. Rhys may have saved both of them.'

'He's a good lad.'

'You attacked Jonas Snicket and stole a considerable amount of coin,' said Hempe. 'The man died from his injuries. That's another life you've taken.'

'We were nowhere near him that night,' Arn growled.

'Pete pointed to the two of you,' said Owen.

'Then he's lying,' said Arn.

'Might have guessed you would say that,' Hempe said.

'He described you as you would have looked that night,' said Owen, 'after the attack in the churchyard outside my home. Your injury, Arn.'

The younger man looked confused. 'How would he know? Bah! You're lying.'

Rhys, too, had said they'd not attacked Snicket, though he had only their word to go on. But he had believed them. Owen could think of another who could have described the wound, imagine how Arn would look afterward – the archer who had shot him. Reynard. It was time to see if some ale would loosen tongues. Owen knocked on the door, a signal for the guard to hand him a jug and bowls.

As he set them before the prisoners, Owen said, 'Why don't you tell us what happened the night you attacked the cart. Take your time. Tell us all you remember.'

Father and son filled their bowls, drinking greedily.

When Arn reached to refill his, Walter stayed him. 'Make it last.'

His son grumbled but sat back. 'Where do we begin?'

'How did you hear that Raymond and Beck were coming north with Trent?'

'We knew the two they paid off to stay behind,' said Walter. 'Bragging about it at the tavern. When we heard, we told my brother's widow. She gave us some coin to come with David and Rhys. Though in the end Rhys came later.'

'How did you know when they were approaching York?' asked Owen.

'David started working with one mason in the city, then heard of one whose brother was the priest at St Clement's. He had put out the word that they would be needing good stone workers soon. David went to him, showed him his work. He had the charm, our David. The mason took a liking to him. Said if they waited long enough he would recommend him. Told him when a carter named Trent was expecting to deliver the stones, the ones coming by cart, some fancy stones from an archway. The rest would come by barge. But we knew Raymond and Beck would be with the cart.'

'This was Marcus Bolton?'

Walter nodded. 'He took David on after the first job was complete.'

'Where were you lodging?' asked Hempe.

'That flea-ridden inn outside the walls,' said Walter. 'Green Man.'

Hempe laughed. 'You're better off here.'

'We were free to come and go,' said Walter.

'So you rode out to meet them,' said Owen. 'Crept up on their camp, and then?'

'We watched, saw where they tied up the carthorse,' said Arn. 'Waited until they ate, drank, and settled back. Then we charged, me first, then Da, then David.'

'That's when David locked arms with that beast Beck,' said Walter. 'Fool wasn't thinking.'

'Who thinks when the fight is on?' Arn muttered.

'The carter ran, probably pissing himself,' said Walter. 'And the other, the quick one, Raymond, he came for us. My son swatted him aside and went to pull the beast off David. Then Raymond came for me and I sliced him. He fell aside. And I went behind the beast, stabbed him in the back, a few times, until Raymond tossed me aside.'

'You said you'd sliced Raymond. Where?' Owen asked.

'Somewhere in his middle.'

'A long knife?'

'Long enough, I thought. Must not have gone deep enough. Didn't slow him down.'

If they were lucky, Jasper's arrow had reopened a wound just beginning to heal. Owen nodded. 'Go on. He'd tossed you aside.'

'When I got my wind, David was lying on the ground all bloodied and limp and the beast was slumped over him. It was too far from the fire to see if that one was breathing. But Arn moved right enough when Raymond came at him with a dagger, slashing and pouncing. I jumped him, caught him off balance, and as soon as he fell I grabbed Arn and we scrambled off. Don't know how we did it, my leg dragging some and Arn bleeding from his arm. We left our David there. God forgive us.'

'We didn't go far,' said Arn. 'Just down to a beck. Got water on our wounds, nice and cold. And hid, listening, watching. At first light we went back to the cart. No sign of the beast dead or alive. David was sitting up against a wheel. Could see he'd bled a lot. Clothes were soaked in it. But he was alive. Said he'd played dead until Raymond dragged the beast away. Then he tried to climb into the cart but couldn't manage. I say it like he was fine and chattering away but it came out in bits, him holding his middle and coughing up blood between the words. We carried him to the beck, thought the water . . .' His voice broke and he looked away.

Walter nodded. 'He was dying all the while. I hoped the cool water might revive him. But by the time we pulled him out he'd stopped breathing. We wanted to get him to the cart. We went for the horses – had two. Farther down the beck.'

'That's when the bastard Raymond came flying from a tree, knocking me down,' said Arn.

'I grabbed him and shoved his face in the water,' said Walter. 'The two of us held him down till he stopped struggling. How he's alive—'

'Can't kill the devil,' Arn spat. 'But we didn't know that then. He looked dead, limp and still.'

'Our horses weren't where we'd tethered them. We whistled and searched but they were nowhere, and we reckoned Raymond had hidden them for him and the beast. Arn's arm was useless, sliced open, and I was limping – so we couldn't carry poor David back to the cart. We thought Trent had likely taken the carthorse, but we found him right where he'd tethered him before we attacked. That was a bit of luck. I suppose Raymond preferred ours. We harnessed him and – God forgive us – by then Arn's arm was bleeding badly and he was having trouble sitting up on the cart. There was nothing we could do for David until we were fit to bury him. So I went on. Drove the cart to the Green Man. The cursed innkeeper handed us our packs. Had given our room to someone else. Greedy bastard. Said they'd offered more coin. We cleaned up as best we could and drove the cart into York. Who questions carters? We left the cart and went to Trinity Priory, got Arn's arm cleaned and bandaged, same with my leg. Didn't dare stay.'

'Should have checked there,' Hempe muttered to himself.

Owen ignored him, finding much of interest in the tale spun by father and son.

'We left the cart for the bishop,' said Arn with a laugh. 'He owes us.'

'But we should have checked it,' said Walter. 'Didn't know David had managed to tuck his scrip with his tools in there. Why did the lad bring them?' Walter's voice broke. He wiped his eyes and poured more ale for himself and his son.

'Those tools are our property,' said Arn, looking at Owen.

'Rhys's,' said Owen.

'It was his mother paid for them,' said Walter. 'My sister.'

'Did you know she sliced open Rhys's cheek when he refused to take part in your scheme?' Owen asked.

Michaelo made a sound, reminding Owen he was making notes.

'He's soft,' said Arn. 'Doesn't understand honor.'

'Robbing Jonas Snicket was honorable?' Hempe asked.

'We told you we had naught to do with that,' said Walter.

'You went to the Bell, the tavern across from Gunnell's shop,' said Hempe. 'You learned that Jonas Snicket might take lodgers.'

'That shriveled manservant shooed us off,' said Arn.

'Tell me about the night in the cemetery in front of my home,' said Owen. 'The night you were injured.'

Arn pressed his shoulder. 'The night you shot at us from the roof of your wife's shop?'

'That was not me. You saw someone up there?'

'Seemed to come from there,' said Walter. 'Both shots. We were easy targets, standing in the light from a lantern in the tavern yard.'

Two shots, Owen noted. Reynard's hit Arn. He salvaged Alisoun's for later. He must have been on the roof of the apothecary, just above Jasper. So close.

'Why were you there?' Hempe asked.

'For Rhys. Hoping he'd find out where his brother's tools were, and if you knew where Raymond was hiding,' said Walter.

'It wasn't you?' Arn did not look convinced.

'He wouldn't have missed,' said Hempe.

'Injuring you serves no purpose,' said Owen. 'I would have rounded you up. Did Rhys agree to aid you?'

'No. But when Arn was shot he helped us away, and I thought he might be having a change of heart.' Walter shrugged. 'But he left us.'

Lying? Rhys had told Owen it was the other way round. But it seemed a small matter.

'What were you doing at the Gunnell house yesterday?' Owen asked.

'Word was old Snicket's servant was hiding there, the bastard that blamed us for the old man's death. Yes, we'd heard. We went to talk to him,' said Walter.

'How were you received?'

'Bailiff saw,' said Arn. 'The widow treated us like stray dogs she could sweep from her door.'

'Did you see Pete?'

'He was sitting in front of the house with Gunnell when we came up,' said Arn. 'Ran into the house when he caught sight of us, the sailmaker following, and the woman came out to shoo us away.'

'We were arguing with her when we heard a commotion,' said Walter. 'Thought it was bailiff's men come for us so we hid.' He wiped his face. 'If Rhys dies I won't find it in me to forgive myself. I might have helped.'

Arn reached for his father's arm. 'Da, don't.'

Owen had heard enough for now. Nodding to Michaelo and Hempe, he moved to the door, gave the guard orders.

'You'll have blankets,' he said to father and son.

'How kind,' Arn muttered.

Walter poked him and thanked Owen for that and the ale.

'One more question. Was Beck fully clothed when you last saw him?'

Both men took a moment to react, then Arn burst out laughing while Walter, fighting a smile, said, 'Course he was wearing clothes. Why?'

'He was found naked.'

'And you think we stole his clothes? Would take three of me to fill out his tunic, two of Da,' said Arn, still grinning. 'The bastard Madoc could wear it. But it'd be tight round the middle.'

'You've no idea where they are hiding?' Owen asked.

'We wondered whether Gunnell's been hiding them,' said Walter. 'Seems to collect curs.'

Out in the corridor, Hempe shook his head. 'If Reynard carried Bruin away, why strip him? To see to his wounds? That's when he gave up and left him?'

'They mentioned Reynard's friend Madoc, that the clothes might fit him,' said Michaelo. 'But why would he want to wear clothes that would remind him of a friend's violent death?'

Owen was thinking about the brothers who had found the body, neither of them bulky like Bruin. 'Clothes well made could be valuable.'

'Not so easy to clean blood from them,' said Hempe. 'Would lower the value.' He shrugged. 'All in all they spun quite a tale. Might be helpful.'

'Will it save them from hanging?' asked Michaelo.

'If they're telling the truth about Jonas Snicket, it might,' said Owen. 'We need to find Gunnell.'

Hempe grunted. 'We're no closer to finding him or Reynard. And Dame Alys is not likely to tell you anything.'

'Let's give her time to consider her future.'

'She won't be happy,' said Hempe.

'None of us are,' said Owen.

'And who is Madoc? Another one of the archers who served under you?'

'He was. One of Reynard's group.' Owen told him what he suspected about the man watching Jehannes's house.

'God help us. Two archers.'

'Neville sent several.'

'A small blessing.'

'Have any of our men experience working with a smith?'

'Why? No, I see. You're thinking of the smithy by the Green Man. There's Frick. Strong but not clever.'

'Clever enough to watch for Laurence Gunnell and Reynard?'

'Reliable for watches, yes. You want to know why the taverner gave up Walter and Arn's room.'

'I want to know whether Reynard took it.'

'Do you think Gunnell joined him there?' Hempe looked doubtful. 'Why would Reynard risk your guessing that?'

'Arrogance?' Michaelo suggested. 'He may not have expected Walter and Arn to talk.'

'Or it might be a waste of time,' said Owen.

'I agree,' said Hempe, 'but we should check. Shall I send Frick up there in the morning? I can describe Gunnell. And Reynard's hair is fair, right? What else?'

'Thinning hair. Once red. Pale brows, dark eyes. About your height, broad shoulders.'

'What about Madoc?'

Owen described how he remembered the man, now with more padding round the middle.

'And we continue as we have begun in the city?'

'That's best. I'm for home.'

'I'll stay,' said Hempe. 'See that everyone is fed and has blankets for the night, hear what's been discovered so I can tell those on the night watch where to search, where to watch. I continue to pray for Gwen and Jasper. And Rhys.'

'We forget Trent,' said Michaelo.

It was true. 'I will speak with Brother Henry before I go home.' Reluctantly, but if Trent were stronger, he might have more to tell.

Though the rain had eased, the wind made talking impossible. Both Owen and Michaelo focused on dodging items blown in their path. Near the minster, Owen turned his back to the wind to thank the monk for attending him and agreeing to return in the morning.

'I do not understand why you would wait until tomorrow to speak with the widow Gunnell. Her anger will be all the hotter for the delay. Is it wise to give her more cause to refuse to cooperate?'

Owen had thought little of the woman, his mind turning on what he remembered of the men who clustered round Reynard. Michaelo brought him back to the matter at hand. Should he reconsider his treatment of Dame Alys? 'I cannot think out here. Come.' He led the way into the minster nave, choosing a quiet place away from the chantries. 'You believe I was too harsh.'

'Unless you wish to antagonize her.'

Was he allowing his frustration to lead him, rather than his wit? 'What do you suggest?'

'A brief visit this evening.'

No time. He had more urgent meetings this evening. But a visit from a man of the cloth might soften her. 'I agree.'

Michaelo took a step back. 'You do?'

'Once again you prove yourself indispensable. I will not forget this. You will attend her after your rounds in the minster yard?' It would fit with an idea pushing its way to the head of the plans he had been formulating.

'I will— No. That is not what I was suggesting.'

'If you would stay with her until I arrive, I will say a few words and we will return together. I caution you it might be quite late.'

'Captain, I am not the person she wishes to see.'

'Your presence will comfort her. When I arrive I will apologize for being delayed. You are inspired, Michaelo.'

'I will be in my tattered habit.'

'All the better. Tell her you came to her directly from your evening rounds. Well done, my friend.'

Michaelo stared down his nose at Owen for several heartbeats, then bowed. 'Do not make me wait too long, I pray you.' With another bow, he floated away down the nave toward the side door.

Already lost in planning, Owen pulled up his hood and headed back out into the wind toward Bootham Bar and on to the main gate of St Mary's Abbey.

When the infirmarian opened the door, Owen feared it was too late, he looked so spent.

'*Benedicite*, my friend,' said Brother Henry. 'You will be here about Master Gerald.'

'Is he dead?'

'I thought for a time last night that he was being called to God, but I watched over him, reciting psalms and assuring him that he was safe in the abbey grounds.' He stepped aside to allow Owen entry, shutting the door behind him. 'You look as if you might benefit from a taste of brandywine. Come. I will take you to Master Gerald while Brother Paul pours us both a swallow.' He gestured toward the young monk hovering nearby.

Lamplight glowed in sconces on the walls, warmth radiated from several braziers. Both welcome after Walter and Arn's castle cell followed by the wet, windy walk.

Trent lay on a pallet near a window overlooking the garden. Outside, wind lashed the trees, sending leaves in a wild dance over the beds piled with straw for the winter.

'Not that he has noticed his preferential placement,' Henry said softly. 'But Brother Wulfstan believed the soul was aware of such comfort.'

Owen took a seat by the pallet. The haughty carter had shrunk, the ruddiness of his skin from the long journey to York faded to a sickly pallor. At least his breathing was quiet and steady. 'Has he spoken?'

'A few words. He seems most concerned about meeting a barge at the staithe. As I prayed over him he asked me to thank you and your kind wife.'

'Anything else?'

'He asked us not to admit Raymond. When he spoke his name I could see his terror. I promised he would be refused. Bishop Wykeham's priests have taken turns sitting with him when His Grace gives them leave. Kindly men.'

'Has anyone come asking about him?'

'No one, God be thanked. He has had peace.' He leaned close to his patient, smelling his breath, then felt the pulse in his neck. Owen saw why Brother Henry's appearance had alarmed him – worry about his charges overrode self-care. 'I expect a slow recovery,' the infirmarian said as he straightened and settled opposite Owen, thanking the young monk who handed them cups of wine. He sipped his and closed his eyes with a sigh of pleasure.

Owen spoke softly to Trent, reassuring him that he was safe at the abbey. 'I would like to talk, if you have the strength.'

The carter opened his eyes, blinking at the light. 'Captain Archer,' he rasped, his eyelids closing.

'I came to check that you are comfortable, though I cannot think how you would not be. Brother Henry's infirmary is a sanctuary.'

Now the eyes fully opened. 'I am cared for, body and soul.' Trent rested a moment, his breath more labored. 'Worried about the shipment of stones. The barge. Should have arrived two days after I was attacked. I know not what day this is. Has it been met?'

That would be this day. 'The storm may have delayed it. I will speak with His Grace in the morning.'

'His Grace . . . He would not know whom to ask . . . Or did I tell him? I cannot recall.'

'You arranged the arrival with a merchant in York?'

'Gisburne. His factor.'

Gisburne was not one of Owen's favorite people, but perhaps his factor was reliable. 'I will speak with him.'

'Bless you. I do not deserve—'

'We want you to recover,' said Owen. 'If I might ask a few more questions. Had you ever before seen any of the men who attacked the cart?'

'I saw only shapes in the dark before I fled.'

'When Raymond worked for you, was another man, Madoc, in his company?'

Trent hissed. 'Another monster. Grateful he did not accompany us.'

'Have you seen him in York?'

'No.' He reached out a hand to clutch Owen's sleeve. 'Do not let him in here.'

'Madoc and Raymond will be refused,' said Brother Henry, taking

Trent's hand and tucking it beneath the covers. 'Rest now. You can
trust that the captain will ensure that all is as it should be.'

Owen bowed to the infirmarian and Trent and took his leave.

At a table brought close to the kitchen fire, Owen warmed his bones
while supping with Lucie and sharing the news of their days. Magda
sat with Gwen and Rhys. Jasper had gone to the apothecary to help
Alisoun.

'A difficult time for that pair to be thrown together,' said Owen.

'I know. But he is still recovering. He cannot do it all.'

Owen reported on Trent's condition, asking about Rhys.

'His injuries are visibly healing, the heat cooling, yet he does
not come fully awake.' Lucie was quiet a moment, her blue-gray
eyes seeking the solace of the fire.

'And Gwen?'

'She is eager to be up and about. The dizziness is fading. Her
ear no longer aches. How could it? We've used oil of thornapple,
bishopwort, henbane, and knotgrass on it, each time slowly dripping
the warm oil into her ear, me whispering prayers.' She began to
smile but shook her head. 'Yet the hearing doesn't return.'

'Time to try the dog's head?' Owen asked. 'Gaspar swore it
restored his father's hearing.' One of his archers, a good friend, had
suggested the remedy for a wounded soldier when Owen was
working with the camp physician. Burn a dog's head, spread the
ashes on the injured area. The physician had scoffed at the idea. It
was a treatment for headache, not loss of hearing. And he'd never
known it to work. Gaspar had argued that dogs hear far better than
humans do. It could not hurt to try. The physician had refused.
Behind his back, Gaspar had found the corpse of a dog, recent
enough that it still had some flesh and fur, burned it, and plastered
the ashes around the soldier's ear, wrapping it tightly. Within a few
days, the soldier said it was as if his ear had opened and he could
hear again.

'Magda did not advise against it,' said Lucie, 'but she doubted
it would work for Gwen. She thinks the thread of connection between
Gwen's ear and her mind snapped with the impact of the fall, and
that will take time to reconnect. Such a remedy is no substitution
for rest and patience.'

'She thinks the dog's head more a charm than a physick.'

Lucie sipped some wine, considering. 'Yes. So do I.' She gave him a teasing frown. 'I recall that the camp physician believed it was the good wrapping and the tinctures he gave the soldier to stir his blood that cleared his ear. You left that out this time.'

'So I did.' Owen reached for her hand. 'If only I could take on her suffering. I want our Gwen to be whole.'

Lucie leaned over to kiss his forehead. 'She is, my love, no matter whether she hears with one ear or two. Our part is to treat her as such. Do all we can to help her heal and forget the frightening experience, but encourage her to do all she would normally do once Magda judges her ready.'

'I count on you to guide me in this.'

'What of Laurence Gunnell and Reynard?'

She listened to his account with sad eyes, frowning at the news of Madoc, bowing her head at another death. 'Despite his apparent role in betraying his master, I am sorry to hear Pete met a violent end.'

'In truth, I feel nothing.'

'You feel too much. There is no room in which to fit pity for the old man.' She kissed his hand. 'Bruin's nakedness. Do you think it important?'

'It bothers me.'

'The sort of feeling that Magda would encourage you to notice?'

'I think it might be. A small detail, but it nags at me. Then again, it would be the sort of trick Reynard might play to confuse things. He delighted in his own cleverness.'

Lucie was watching him with concern. 'When you have him cornered, you will find it difficult to allow him to live.'

'Yes.'

'But I trust you will do your duty, delivering him up to the king's justice.'

'That is my intent.' He could not swear.

They were quiet for a few moments, staring at the fire, sharing some watered wine.

'This news of Madoc, that should make you more assured in your theory.'

'Yes. And adds another threat to the bishop. It's time to remove him from harm's way so that I might devote my attention to finding Reynard and his minions.'

'You will meet Crispin and George at the York this evening?'

Poole and Hempe. He grinned. 'You know me so well.' He took her hand. 'First let's visit the children.'

SIXTEEN

The Rift Widens, the Bishop's Men

In the late afternoon, Lucie had agreed that Jasper might spend time in the apothecary filling orders. Outside the apothecary workshop he found a handsome dog, young, yet with large paws, sitting by the door. He'd come alert as Jasper approached, as if on guard duty. Jasper crouched to let the pup smell his hand, then rubbed him behind his long, soft ears. The pup licked his hand.

'Good boy,' he murmured as he began to straighten. His ribs still protested against such movement and he had to press a hand to the wall to help himself rise.

From the workroom he heard Alisoun out in the shop with a customer. Speaking softly, both of them, so he could not decipher words. He found the wax tablets listing the unfilled orders, plenty to keep him busy for a while. As he set to work he relaxed, humming to himself, glad to be moving about and distracted from his remorse. He did not know how long she had been standing in the doorway watching him before he noticed her as he retrieved a jar of powdered mallow.

'Humming while you work.' She smiled. 'It is gladsome work, healing.'

'I feel worthwhile. I've not felt that of late.'

'You saved your sister.'

'Or did I cause her to risk her safety to prove herself?'

'Are you taking up the way of the flagellants? Calling your very life a sin?'

He felt himself blushing. 'I accused Gwen of betraying me and then lying about her innocence. I wouldn't even believe my father swearing she'd not told him. And then what I said about you . . .'

'I don't deny you've seemed intent on hurting the women who

care for you, but Reynard injured Gwen, not you. You chased after her to protect her.'

'You care for me? Even after what I said? And wouldn't listen to you?'

'I do. Maybe not the way—'

He reached for her hand. Held it against his heart. 'What I said . . . I had no cause. I apologize. What can I do to make amends?'

Gently she withdrew her hand. 'I accept your apology. It appears your friends managed to prevent everyone in the city from hearing. But there is more to this, Jasper, more than what you are willing to see, I think.' She turned at the sound of the shop-door bell. 'Wait here.'

'I'm not waiting, I'm working. But stay a moment. Who owns the dog sitting outside the door?'

'Magda, in trade for delivering a baby and setting a broken arm. Both in the same household.' She laughed. 'He's well trained, but a rock in the middle of the river is no place for a dog. We hope to find a home for him.'

'Handsome.'

'Yes.' Her mouth smiled, but her eyes were sad. 'I must see to the customer.'

As he returned to his work he no longer hummed, his mind abuzz with questions. What did she mean, more to this than he was willing to see? Did she think he'd meant what he said? Didn't she understand jealousy? Though he did blame her. Of course he did. And she knew she was to blame – why else did it take her a year to confess?

He growled when he realized he had lost track of what he'd measured. Wasteful. And dangerous. He sat down on a high stool and buried his head in his hands.

'Jasper?'

He glanced up.

Alisoun watched him, her large brown eyes dark with some emotion. Concern? Pity? 'I should not have started this when I knew we would be interrupted. But that was the last customer. I have shut the apothecary for the evening. Might I bring my companion inside?'

'As long as he behaves.'

He listened to her speak softly to the dog. When she returned, the pup padded along at her side. She pointed to the corner and he settled, his long face resting on his paws.

'What am I not willing to see?' he asked.

Alisoun drew a stool over to where he was working, repositioning it several times. Jasper watched with growing dread as she fussed and moved it about, guessing that she was about to tell him something she knew he would not like. More? There was more she'd held back? At last she settled not too far from him, where she might rest her feet on a bench, but not within reach. He heard the dog give a soft sigh.

'I am not accustomed to so much standing in place.' Alisoun winced. 'I sound like an old woman!'

'Never.'

'You are kind. And I know that is your way. Which is what made your recent behavior so unlike you. To punish Gwen as you did, and for no reason. I could not understand why you were doing it. And then to drink so much with your friends, aim your arrow – *my* arrow – at someone in the dark.'

'You heard about that?'

'Forgive me. I overheard your parents speaking of it.'

He frowned down at his hands. Did she expect him to explain what he himself did not understand?

'I was glad the captain offered you a way to test what you want – that night on the roof, and that you accepted the test.'

He glanced up, uncertain where she was headed. Her brow crinkled in concern. His heart leapt a little. She did care. 'I failed him,' he said.

She leaned toward him, her eyes fixed on his. 'But you learned something that night, didn't you?'

'I'm no soldier.'

Alisoun thrust her chin forward as if frustrated. 'Wasn't it that you don't care to be a soldier? That it is not why you enjoy practicing at the butts? You enjoy proving yourself, gaining strength, making your father proud. But you do not care to go further, to devote your life to it.'

'No. You're right.'

'Did you know that before?'

'I never thought to be a soldier.' He could tell his responses did not satisfy. 'What do you want? That's the truth.'

She looked away for a moment, then said, 'I ask because I hoped it might help you understand why I'm going away. Taking the routes that Magda takes in flood season, seeing to the people on the moors. That is, if Magda agrees.'

'Go away? Why? Why would you do that?'

'I need to try working alone, find my own path.'

'You're going to search for Einar.'

She reared back and he wished he had not spoken.

'Aren't you listening? Not like Einar. Magda sent him away to discover what he wants. My path is already clear to me. I'm called to be a healer. But what are my strengths? Do I still need to be near Magda, or can I spend months, even years, away from my teacher and continue to grow in my skill? Do I have something to learn from another teacher?'

'Years? What about us?'

'What about us?' She repeated it softly. It was almost a sigh. 'That is another reason to go. I don't know that we are meant to be together. I think the wife you dream of, always there to see to you, working beside you in the shop, in the garden, that is not what I want. When I've gone with Magda up on the moors my senses are keener, my thoughts clearer, and I feel – I think it's like Dame Marian's call to be a nun.'

He almost snarled about a whore becoming a nun, but he caught himself. He was hurt, as he'd been when he blamed Gwen. But he did want to understand. 'Did you feel that when you took Asa up on the moors?' *And lay with Einar*, he thought, but did not say.

'I did feel free. And I learned from that as well.'

'You want to wander, like Asa?'

'Not like her. Magda says her daughter is ever running from the trouble she causes. I want to find those who need a healer like me. Perhaps I will come upon people who need me as the people here needed Magda when she arrived.'

'It sounds like a long wandering.'

'I know.'

He waited for her to say something to soften it – that it would be hard to be away so long, that she would miss him. But she just studied his face with those big eyes. God help him, he loved those eyes, her slender face and neck holding up that crown of rich brown hair. He had thought she was his and he had been so proud to have won her love. How wrong he'd been.

'That's why you pulled away from me that night. It wasn't only that you hadn't told me about Einar, but that you were finished with me.'

Alisoun flinched. 'I didn't know. I thought it was my guilt about what I'd kept from you. Maybe I waited so long because I feared it might be so.'

'That makes it even worse that you didn't tell me. All this time I thought you loved me.'

'I do, Jasper. But not as a husband.' She held up a hand as he started to speak. 'Do not say what you will regret. What you said about me to your friends . . .'

'I was angry. Of course I was. You cuckolded me.'

'We are not wed.'

'No, but everyone expected that we would.'

'You are thinking only of *your* pain. You don't ask about mine.'

'Pain?' The word came out harsh, sneering. 'Forgive me. I didn't mean that. But what are you saying. That I hurt you?'

'It's not that. I've feared I wouldn't make you happy. And that hurt. All that dreaming, planning how we would live, all the while worrying what would happen when you began to understand what I wanted.'

'I love you as you are.'

'As you want to see me.'

Did she call him a fool? Blinded by love? 'The dog is for your wandering, isn't he?'

'What? No. I told you. He's Magda's.' Her eyes suddenly widened. 'Oh. Dame Lucie.'

The draft he'd felt from the garden door moments ago. Jasper looked over his shoulder. God help him, his mother stood in the doorway, looking from him to Alisoun and back with an apologetic expression.

'Forgive me for interrupting, but Alisoun is summoned to a birthing.'

Alisoun took a step toward him, her arms out, conciliatory. Why? She didn't want him. Did she think he could touch her and not care?

'Go,' he growled. 'And you don't need to return. I am sufficiently recovered to open the shop tomorrow.' He turned his back to her.

He heard her sigh, go to the shop for something. Returning, she asked his mother who summoned her, called softly to the dog, opened and shut the garden door. He did not look up until he was certain she had left.

But his mother remained.

'Jasper, I am sorry.'

'Don't be.' He moved a jar on the table, reached for another. 'Best I knew what she was before we wed.'

He heard her step closer. 'What do you mean, Jasper?' Her voice was the quiet one she used when on the verge of anger.

Judging him. Always judging him, all of them. He turned to her. 'Are you going to defend her? She slept with Einar. But she doesn't love him. Now she wants to go wandering. To taste more men? A whore, that's what she means to be.'

He expected a slap, but she just inhaled sharply and said, 'Your remorse for slandering her was short-lived. Have you heard anything she's said after telling you she lay with Einar?'

'She's told you I won't listen?'

'I am guessing you will not because of how you are now. To be honest, I always worried that she might not make you happy. When you spoke of your plans, I could not imagine her in them. They were your dreams, not hers. She has always wanted to be more like Magda than like me.'

'Now you say it?'

'I might have been wrong.'

'Please go. I don't want to talk now.'

'I will go when I've said what needs to be said. You are my apprentice as well as my son. I am responsible for ensuring that you are of good character and will respect the people you serve before I recommend you to the guild. If you slander a young woman because she will not bend to your will, I will report it.'

'What?'

'You are fortunate that your friends protected you.' She leaned close and kissed his cheek.

'You're on her side.'

'No sides, Jasper. What Alisoun did breaks my heart. But slandering her will not change it.' She touched his cheek, then departed.

He hated her. Hated all women. And he wished he were dead.

Wind drove an icy drizzle into his face as Owen crossed the garden and the tavern yard. He paused beneath the eaves of the York, shaking the rain off his hat and raking his hands through his hair. Warmth, light, and a cacophony of voices radiated from the tavern room as he opened the door.

'Business is good,' he said to Tom Merchet.

'When the weather closes in, aye. Saved your usual table back in the corner. Poole just arrived. And I see Hempe coming up behind you. How is Gwen?'

'Much better, God be thanked. Wanting to walk about, play with Hugh and Emma.'

'Is it true about her ear?'

Owen nodded, not trusting his voice despite the din. The mere mention knotted his stomach and brought on images of beating Reynard into a stupor from which he would never wake.

Seeming to sense Owen's mood shift, Tom said he would follow him to the table with a full jug.

Hempe tapped Owen's shoulder. 'A group of men were coming up behind me, talking about Gerald Trent. Neville's men?'

Owen glanced out in the yard. 'Sir Francis and his men, aye. Go on back to the table and warn Poole. Tom, might we shove a few more tables together to accommodate five more?'

With a nod and a wink, Tom called out for Tupper and the two went to work. Bess bustled behind them, listening to Tom's instructions, pausing near one of the tables already claimed, telling the men they'd have a round on the house if they would be so kind as to move to one nearer the door. Heads bobbed and the men rose.

'Captain Archer,' said Sir Francis. 'We came to join you for a round. On me, of course.'

Owen nodded. 'The Merchets are adding some room for you. How did you know to find me here?'

'Brother Oswald.' The hospitaller. 'I felt the men deserved some time away from the abbey.'

'Many a night I opened a barrel and invited all the men to indulge.'

Reaching the table, Owen introduced Francis to Poole and Hempe, and Francis, in turn, named his men. While they all settled at the now long table, Tom and Bess set tankards before them, filling them from jugs. As the Merchets disappeared into the crowd that watched the gang with curiosity, Owen lifted his tankard. 'To old mates and new.'

Settling in for a long evening, he drank little, though often lifting

the tankard to his mouth. He noticed several of the men watching
Crispin Poole, then whispering amongst themselves.

Poole must have noticed as well. 'I've met several of your men
in the field,' he noted to Sir Francis. 'Did you serve in France?'

'No. Up on the border with Scotland.' He glanced at his men.
'Hal and Mark are the archers, and Phillip, Carl, and I can handle
bows but are far more comfortable with sword and dagger. We'd
all appreciate training with you, Captain. Brother Oswald is organ-
izing a butt near the guest house.'

'I will come tomorrow. I cannot promise when.'

'Thank you. We will be there.'

Hempe proposed they talk about where everyone might be on
the day Wykeham departed, and they fell into a discussion, sorting
out posts for various routes. Owen did not mention the radically
different arrangement coming together in his mind, but the time was
not wasted, for all now had a sense of the others' strengths. By the
time they wandered off to other subjects, the four not involved in
the discussion were well and truly drunk.

'Tom Merchet's ale is potent,' said Poole.

'And the best I've tasted,' said Sir Francis. On his way out,
shepherding his men with care, he paused to loudly proclaim to
Tom his admiration.

'Well then,' said Bess, pausing by Owen, 'this has been a good
night for my Tom.' She hummed to herself as she and Tupper began
to move the tables back to their usual positions. Owen and Hempe
rose to help, but she shooed them away. 'I daresay you will have
much to discuss amongst yourselves. Be easy.'

She was right. High on Owen's list was finding out what Poole
knew about Hal and Mark.

Jasper stayed long in the workshop, but eventually his body ached
and his stomach growled. He found Magda sitting before the fire
in the kitchen, a bowl of ale beside her on the settle.

'Kate left the stew warming for thee. Bring thy food and ale here
and ease thy bones.'

Though he felt that if anyone might help him see what he wasn't
seeing, it was Dame Magda, he was tempted to take his food back
to the workshop, not knowing how ready he was to hear it. But
neither did he want to continue as he'd been. So he stayed, dishing

up stew, helping himself to bread and ale on the table, and joining Magda on the settle.

'I met the dog you received in trade,' he said. 'Seems well trained.'

'Tom Carver said his older dog wanted the hound pup gone. He's not a man will see an animal wasted and hoped Magda might find him a good home.'

'He seemed patient and obedient.' He noticed how Magda smiled, as if delighted with something. 'Do you mean for Alisoun to keep him?'

Still smiling, Magda tilted her head as if trying to understand his question. 'Dost thou think Magda's rock is a proper home for a spirited young dog?'

'No, but . . .' He usually enjoyed playing with Magda's riddling, but not tonight. 'No matter.' He tried to eat his stew, but the silence taunted him. 'You heard about my argument with Alisoun?'

'Magda saw thy mother's face after fetching Alisoun for the birthing. She guessed the rest.'

'You know about Alisoun and Einar?'

'Magda knows of their night together.'

'She betrayed me.'

Magda grunted. 'Dost thou believe she meant to wound thee?'

'She must have known that it would. I think that's why she waited so long to confess to me. How long have you known about it?'

'Since the day she told thee.' She raised a brow. 'Thou hast not answered the question. Dost thou believe she meant to wound thee?'

'I doubt she thought of me that night.'

Magda stared into the fire.

Jasper ate some stew, chewed on a piece of bread, glancing at Magda, wondering what she was thinking. 'No, I don't think she meant to hurt me. But she did.'

Magda nodded, then returned to her quiet study of the fire.

He gulped down his ale and rose.

She glanced up, meeting his gaze. 'Does Alisoun share thy pain?'

'How could she? I didn't betray her and wait a year to tell her.' But she had spoken of pain. 'How should I know?'

'Thou hast known her a long while.'

'I thought I did. And I thought you would give me advice, but you're just like all the rest, judging me.'

'Judging? No. That is not Magda's way.'

'Feels like it.'

'Magda sees a young man who is confused, uncertain what is in his heart. But pain and pride prevent him from seeing it. Magda cannot help what is unseen.'

Feeling the anger spark in him, he closed his mouth and sank down beside her. No more of that. 'I tried to apologize, but I can't seem to say the right thing.' He blew his hair off his forehead, hot from the fire and the warm food. 'Alisoun doesn't think she'd make me happy.' He thought about what she'd said and felt sick to his stomach. 'She told me what she thinks I want, and that it's not what she wants.' He made himself think about what else she'd said, all that he'd tried to push away. 'She wants to go away for awhile, be a traveling healer.'

While he was speaking, Magda fetched the jug of ale and replenished their bowls.

'Is there truth in what she says?' Magda asked as she handed him his bowl.

A lump in his throat kept his answer to a nod. He took a long drink, wiping his mouth with his sleeve.

'What didst thou say to that?'

'I called her a whore – said it to her and to my friends.' Deep breath. He needed to face it all. 'Seems my friends made sure no one else heard. I don't know how I'll face them again.'

'Friends forget such things,' said Magda.

He hoped that was true. 'But Alisoun . . .' Remembering all he'd said, he was shamed by her kindness. 'How can she forget? When she told me about going away, I accused her of doing it so she could keep whoring.' Tears stung his eyes and his face felt hot.

Magda put an arm round him, gently drawing his head to her shoulder. 'Hush now, breathe for a moment.'

She smelled of woodsmoke, herbs, and spice.

But he couldn't breathe easy. 'I can't stop thinking I'm to blame for what happened to my sister. Gwen wouldn't have gone after Rhys if I hadn't been mean to her.'

'Thou art not the cause of her decision. She thought Rhys a man she might love, but then it appeared he betrayed her family. She followed to know whether he might be trusted after all.'

'She's but a child.'

'To thee she is a child. But she likes to think herself a young woman.' Magda smoothed the hair from his forehead. 'Thou art half asleep. Might thou spend one more night on the pallet beside Gwen? It is a comfort to her. Tomorrow she will be ready to return to her chamber with Hugh and Emma.'

Jasper sat up, rubbing his eyes. He ached all over. 'And Rhys?'

'His will be a slow healing.'

'But he will live?'

'If he has the will.'

'The dog. Do you mean for him to be Alisoun's companion on her travels?'

'What did she tell thee?'

'The same thing you did.'

'Why dost thou not accept her answer?'

He frowned. His thoughts were getting jumbled. 'Is that what I do? Never take her at her word?'

'Is it?'

Upon rising, Jasper steadied himself with a hand on the back of the settle, breathless from the pain in his ribs. 'I think maybe that is what I do. Or don't do.'

Magda came round to take his elbow and guide him to the hall. His mother was sitting between Rhys and Gwen, telling a tale of a cobbler and an angel. One of his favorites when he was first living here and frightening dreams woke him in the night. He lay down beside Gwen and fell asleep to the telling. He dreamed of a tiny angel riding a pure white wolfhound.

Owen watched the room, curious what the Merchets' customers had thought of sharing their tavern with a knight and his men. Frowns and whispers, with furtive glances his way. The first deaths had at least been outside the city, but Jonas and his manservant had died within the walls, and Owen's own children had been attacked in the city, as well as a carter for the Bishop of Winchester. Now to see a knight and his men conferring with the captain of the city, one of his bailiffs, and the coroner of Galtres – of course they were uneasy. And until Owen ended Reynard's reign of terror, he could not reassure them. All were not safe.

He turned toward what he could do. 'Tell me about Mark and Hal,' he said to Poole. 'Who were they serving?'

'You mean who abandoned them in France? King Edward, Prince

Edward, Lancaster, it did not matter, the nobles left us there and we found each other. I met them on the road. They were seeking patronage from a wealthy Frenchman to protect property, earn enough to sail home. They wanted no part of my company. They knew we were robbing and pillaging our way through the land.'

Hempe listened, wide-eyed with disbelief.

'They saw my dark side,' Poole said. 'Angry, hungry for the power given me through violence.' He lifted the stump, all that was left of his right arm. 'I did not understand the justice of this until my beloved Muriel helped me see a different way to live. My own doing, drunk and still believing I controlled the world.'

'You had begun the change by returning to York,' Owen noted. 'But what you describe. You were much like Reynard, then, though I doubt he was ever part of such a company.'

'To my shame. Hearing about him, worrying about my family with him on the loose – it's a mirror held up to me. I have tried to think how I might help you. As your friend, as a citizen of the city, and as repentance.'

'I am listening.'

'Everything I did was to show that I was invincible, the rightful leader of the men. No one could touch me. I flaunted how easily I influenced men. I cared nothing about the quality of those followers. You understand why Hal and Mark eyed me with suspicion.'

'I did not realize,' said Hempe. 'You do sound like Reynard as Owen paints him.'

'So it is nothing you don't already know,' said Poole with a sigh.

'Tell me this,' said Owen. 'Considering everything you know, what would be your plan for Wykeham's departure?'

'My purpose would be to show you incapable of protecting the Bishop of Winchester. Now with the added advantage of humbling you in front of Sir John Neville's men.'

'So you would first go after the bishop,' said Owen.

'In a public way. And I would have my second attack your family.'

'God help us,' said Hempe. 'We should surround your home and the apothecary with men.'

'Madoc is likely his second,' said Owen. 'A good archer, though not as quick as Reynard, or as clever.' Though clever enough to have coerced the boy to watch the archdeacon's house. Unless that had been Reynard. Owen had been considering a plan that might fool Madoc. But it was not enough. He saw that now. 'I need archers on Wykeham and on my family on the day of departure, as well as the priory.'

'The priory,' said Poole, thoughtfully. 'My mother says Prioress Isobel has the lay workers walking a watch at night, armed with pitchforks.' His mother had retired to the nunnery. 'A precaution to be recommended. But I doubt they are in danger until Wykeham's party arrives to collect the sisters.'

Owen agreed. 'I will ask the sheriff to have his men stationed along the road between Micklegate Bar and the priory.'

'Archers on the bridge as well,' said Hempe. 'On the rooftops.'

Poole was not enthused. 'Why not go along the river? I walk that way once a week. A shorter distance, easier to defend, and the autumn rains have not yet filled what remains of the moat of the Old Baile. With no wagons, crossing is not difficult.'

'Still means crossing the bridge over the Ouse,' said Hempe.

Imagining arrows flying amidst the crowds on the Ouse Bridge brought home to Owen the flaw in the plans. 'Too much in a busy city.' He raked a hand through his hair. 'This is what Reynard wants, pushing me to endanger the people I am meant to protect.'

Poole agreed.

'We need to outwit him,' said Owen. 'Have our men ready, visibly deployed, to be used if all else fails, but, we hope, only to distract him from our purpose.'

Poole studied Owen. 'He will delight in imagining the chaos you inflict.'

'Still, we should be prepared to protect them with force,' said Hempe.

'Agreed. And it's important that only a few of us know the real plan. Not the men. Perhaps not even Sir Francis.'

Hempe thumped his tankard on the table. 'You're saying you don't trust our men, Owen?'

'Quiet,' Poole growled. 'Everyone is watching us.'

Owen leaned his head back and laughed loudly. 'Of course I knew they were having a bit of fun,' he said, grinning and slapping the table as he rose. 'And now for sleep. I have a long day ahead of me.'

Poole took a last gulp of ale, then followed. 'Muriel will be wondering where I fled.'

'I've men to see to before I head home,' Hempe muttered, the first to push out through the crowd.

Bess patted his shoulder as he passed. He put a hand on hers, nodding his appreciation.

'I'll have a word with him outside,' Owen told her as he followed. In a louder voice he expressed his gratitude to Bess for helping him impress Neville's men. 'And Tom's fine ale.'

'You bring us custom, we see that they leave smiling,' she said.

Tom met his eye as he stepped out the door. 'You carry a weight, my friend.'

SEVENTEEN
A Plot to Fool the Fox

Hempe stood by the gate to the apothecary garden. Owen led him through, Poole close behind. Though the storm had ceased, the surfaces were slick with the day's rain. They gathered in the center of the garden where they were least likely to be overheard.

Even so, Owen spoke quietly. 'You said yourself the men need more training.'

Hempe grunted.

'Watching their tongues when at home or with their fellows is not drilled into them. We cannot risk them slipping.'

'You're right. I'm just weary to the bone and don't see the end in sight.'

'We'll get him,' said Poole. He sounded confident. 'How do you plan to protect your house and the shop?'

'We will speak of that tomorrow. The matter to hand is tonight. We have work to do. If you would give me a moment.' Owen moved away from them to collect the strands of ideas that had come together in the tavern. Scudding clouds revealed the stars now and then. The rich scent of the rain-drenched garden refreshed his mind and spirit.

Sir Francis giving his men an evening in the tavern had revived memories of evenings with his own men when captain of archers.

He tried to see Reynard, Bruin, and Madoc in the crowd. They had not often stayed with the rest, filling their tankards and disappearing. But he did recall the night after he had begun training Madoc. He was a good archer, but a clumsy fighter with a sword or fist, wildly attacking without thought, easily duped. Owen had landed him on his rear over and over again, calling out suggestions that the man at first seemed unable to grasp. Gradually he'd caught on, and Owen had congratulated him. He'd rewarded all the men for a grueling day of training with extra ale, inviting Madoc to sit with him, tell him about himself. He was curious about such a large man having developed so little skill in fighting. But Madoc sulked, making it plain that he felt Owen had singled him out for public humiliation in the practice yard. Though Owen took pains to say it was all part of training, that he was coming along quickly, the man looked not to him but his fellows to see how he was regarded. Owen himself had been new to the role of captain of archers. Perhaps he had been too harsh. In the end, Madoc had limped off that night with Bruin. Poole was right. Madoc would be the one after his family.

Thinking of Bruin reminded him of the gap in the account of the original attack – the moving and stripping of his corpse. Even had Reynard wished someone to find the body, he could not imagine a reason for him to strip his friend and leave him unburied, unless they'd had such a falling out that it extended beyond death.

Someone else moved him from a protected spot and stripped Bruin? Had Reynard intended to return but did not want to risk it once the sheriff's men found the body? Was it important?

Returning to his friends, he shared what was on his mind. They put their heads together and devised a plan.

As Poole and Hempe dispersed to prepare for their parts, Owen sensed Lucie's approach. He drew her into his arms, kissing the top of her head. 'Everyone sleeping?'

'Even Jasper. Magda is sitting with Rhys. How was your meeting at the York?'

'Helpful. Perhaps.' He told her about it, and his memory of Madoc. 'I was inexperienced and made many mistakes.'

'Is that why you are out here pacing?'

'That. And wondering who stripped and moved Bruin's body. I can't see why Reynard would have exposed his corpse.'

Lucie did not respond at once, but considered it. He loved that about her. Never the quick response.

'Not the behavior of a friend. Perhaps Reynard callously used him all along and there never was a bond between them.'

His turn to pause and consider. 'I believe there was friendship. I noticed it because it was not what I had expected of Reynard. But that was long ago. What if I'm wrong about all of it?'

'Do you doubt that the one called Raymond is Reynard?'

'No.'

'Or that Laurence Gunnell is afraid of something?'

'No.'

'I have all confidence in you. And I hope . . . When Wykeham departs, might Reynard and Madoc follow?'

'I need to make certain of that. It is time to distract and confuse the fox.'

'Tonight?'

He heard her sigh and held her tighter, kissing her, whispering that he would do his best to put an end to this soon.

In the archdeacon's hall, Jehannes and Wykeham were sitting by the fire, drinking wine and quietly talking when Owen joined them.

Jehannes glanced toward the door, his usually smooth brow creased with worry. 'I hoped Brother Michaelo might be with you. He is never so late returning from his rounds.'

'He awaits me at the castle,' said Owen.

'I have caused more trouble,' said Wykeham.

'Brother Michaelo's presence at the castle is part of my plan to alleviate that concern, Your Grace. If I might explain.' Owen took the cup of wine Perkin offered him and settled down to describe what he had set in motion. Wykeham's initial resistance, indeed outrage, was expected, as was Jehannes's attempt to find a compromise. But as Owen pointed out the shortfalls of each suggestion, the bishop abruptly declared himself satisfied with the original proposal. Relieved, Owen bowed to him.

'I swear to you I will do everything in my power to protect you, Your Grace. Yet nothing is certain.'

'God's will be done.' Wykeham nodded to Owen and Jehannes before withdrawing to instruct his servants and dress in the required disguise.

When Jehannes rose to assist, Owen drew him back to discuss plans for two mornings hence, when Wykeham's party would depart for the priory and then south. He was answering Jehannes's many questions and concerns when the bishop rejoined them wearing the habit that had been a gift to Michaelo from Prince Edward and Princess Joan. Owen was pleased to see that it fit, though Wykeham filled it out more than Michaelo did.

The bishop stroked a sleeve. 'I did not expect silk. I doubt I wear it as well as the elegant monk.' He frowned out the window. 'Might I wear my own cloak?'

'Once we are past the minster gate.' Owen held up his hands at Wykeham's protest. 'The storm has passed. Remember, we will be hurrying along as I tell you of a prisoner ready to confess all he knows, and that I need you to record it all. You will be grumbling and fussing with this.' He held out the large scrip in which Brother Michaelo carried his wax tablets and stylus. 'Once out the gate, you can loudly complain of the cold and I'll hand you the cloak.'

His Grace paused for a heartbeat, then plucked the scrip from Owen's hands, hooking the long strap over his head, wearing it crossed over from shoulder to hip. Turning to Jehannes, he thanked him for his gracious hospitality.

'It has been my honor and privilege,' said Jehannes. 'May God watch over you, Your Grace.'

'Let us pray I am still in His favor.' Wykeham nodded brusquely to Owen. 'I am ready.'

Moving beneath the skimming clouds in the intermittent moonlight, Owen marveled at the zest with which the bishop played his role, softening his voice, taking on a good semblance of the tones of Michaelo's native Normandy, fussing with the scrip and sniffing with irritation. He had studied the monk. Trusting to the impetus that had set him on this path, Owen hurried along, opening his senses, aware of eyes in the shadows watching, then slipping out to follow. Out on Petergate, the false Michaelo let go his scrip and gasped at the cold. Owen draped the cloak over his shoulders.

A figure in a doorway withdrew into the dark. Owen sensed a friend, one of his men. He trusted Hempe had chosen with care. Wykeham walked faster than Owen had expected. They hastened through the darkened streets, making good time to the castle.

At the sheriff's chambers, a manservant answered Owen's knock, bowing his head for the message, then closing the door to deliver it to Sir Ralph. From the room they heard the sheriff saying something as he approached the door. As he stepped out, ready to protest, the bishop pushed back his hood.

'Sir Ralph,' he said.

The sheriff puzzled over the man he had thought to be Brother Michaelo. 'Do you never sleep, Archer? Who is this?'

'Your Grace, may I present Sir Ralph Hastings,' said Owen. 'His Grace the Bishop of Winchester requires your hospitality.'

Sir Ralph caught his breath, then bowed deeply. 'I pray you forgive me, Your Grace.'

'No need.' Wykeham smiled benevolently. 'I am delighted to see your confusion. It is what we hoped for in my borrowing Brother Michaelo's habit.'

'His Grace will be your guest for a few nights,' said Owen. 'I regret I could not risk sending a messenger to prepare you.'

'Of course, of course. I am most honored, Your Grace. Captain, if you would show His Grace to my bedchamber, I will say goodnight to my guests. My man will bring you some refreshment.'

'You trust your man not to talk?' Owen asked.

'I will make it plain to him that he must be silent, on pain of death, Captain.'

Owen escorted Wykeham to the sheriff's bedchamber, a spacious room already warmed with a fragrant fire. 'I will have your own clothes delivered tomorrow,' said Owen.

'You will not stay to talk?'

'I cannot, Your Grace. Brother Michaelo awaits me.'

'I pray this ruse accomplishes what you intended. A few nights here, you say?' Wykeham glanced round at the comfortably appointed chamber. 'I believe I will survive it.'

'I am grateful—'

Wykeham held up a hand to halt Owen's thanks. 'It is I who must thank you. I do not forget that. May God go with you.'

'And with you, Your Grace.'

Michaelo rose from the lamplit corner where he'd sat with Dame Alys.

She hissed her disgust with the lateness of the hour.

'I apologize for the delay,' said Owen. 'Matters took a turn. I have just now delivered someone to the castle.'

'My son? Is it Laurence?'

'No. Now I will leave you to your rest. Tomorrow we will talk. Do you have all you need?'

'I need my freedom. My own bed,' she snapped. But he could see her weariness in the droop of her shoulders.

'In good time, Dame Alys.' Owen bowed and departed.

In the corridor, Brother Michaelo hissed, 'You took your time.'

'I will explain. Come with me.'

Sir Ralph waited in the chamber in which he had received his guests, rising to peer closely at Michaelo. 'This time it is you.'

Brother Michaelo lifted a brow. 'This time?'

By the time they left the castle, Michaelo understood his part in the plan. He fussed with the scrip collected from the bishop – he had said nothing of the loan of his best habit, but Owen had noticed the slight wince. He would have Kate clean it with care. She was a wonder with cloth of all kinds.

'You rushed me to the castle after dark for so little?' Michaelo said, in character. 'In future you might ensure that you do not injure a potential witness to the point they can barely speak.'

'I am satisfied with the information,' said Owen, in a loud whisper, as if he did not wish to be overheard.

Just beyond the castle precinct, someone behind Owen and Michaelo dislodged a stone and stumbled, heavy-footed. They glanced at each other without breaking stride. Once again Michaelo complained of the late hour and being caught up in the city's business.

'Perhaps you should have returned to St Mary's Abbey,' said Owen.

A sniff. 'You forget. They would not have me. The fallen monk.'

'Of course.'

They fell into silence, punctuated now and again by Michaelo's complaints, parting at Owen's door on Davygate.

'Thank you, my friend. I will call on Jehannes tomorrow when I am finished at the castle.'

'I will tell him.' In a louder voice Michaelo said, 'Pray you do not arrive too early.' And walked off, muttering to himself.

At last Owen headed home for the night. In the kitchen the fire burned low, the house silent. As he poured himself a bowl of wine, he realized Lucie lay curled up on the settle by the fire, and bent to kiss her awake.

Blinking, she smiled and struggled to sit up as he settled beside her.

She leaned against him while coming fully awake. 'I feel I slept hours.'

'I did say I would be late.'

'Success?'

'I pray so.'

'Is that it for the night? Will you come up to bed now?'

'After I talk to Magda – she is still here?' He'd come through the garden to the kitchen, not wanting to wake the three sleeping in the hall.

Lucie nodded. 'I will sit with Rhys while you talk.' She began to rise.

He drew her back down. 'First we need to talk. I have a plan for protecting the apothecary and our home two mornings hence, when Wykeham's party leaves for Clementhorpe. I count on you to tell me if it is feasible, and if you agree. And if you think Jasper will agree.'

'It involves his participation?'

'His and Alisoun's.'

'Oh.' She looked at the fire, shaking her head but saying nothing. 'What is it?'

'Unfortunate timing. Alisoun made it plain to him this evening that they are no longer a couple. Jasper's heart is broken. To work together will require them to rise above their discomfort.'

'What was her mood?'

'Quiet. Collected. She was the one breaking it off. She cares for him, it's clear. But they do not want the same things. Magda says she is going up onto the moors as a traveling healer for a time.'

'And she told him all this tonight?'

'She did. What is it you need of them?'

'To be my bowmen, one on the roof of our house, one on the shop. So not together.'

'But they will depend on each other.'

'Yes. Would you be opposed to my talking to Jasper about it? And Alisoun, if Magda approves?'

'Of course not. But do not put too much hope in their cooperation.

Not only because of their parting, but Jasper found his previous experience harrowing. And this would be in daylight. Exposed.'

'There will be others, including a bowman on the roof of the tavern. But Jasper and Alisoun are two of the best archers in the city. And I believe it will be an archer – Madoc – who brings the trouble here.'

'That is why you were thinking about how you might have failed him.'

'Trying to understand him. Yes.'

She tilted her head once more, gazing at him. 'Time passes. Some move on, some cannot stop reliving every slight. He and Reynard are the latter. And jealous of you for creating a new life, a good life.' She curled her arm round his and kissed him. 'I will send Magda to you. Stay by the fire, warming yourself before sleep.'

The healer gazed deep into Owen's eye for several heartbeats. He held his breath.

'Breathe, Bird-eye. Magda is thy friend, not thine inquisitor.' She felt his wrist, his pulse. 'Thou are primed for battle. But thou needst a calm, steady mind to prepare and to see what is before thee on the day. Much can change in the moment. Thou must see clearly what is happening round thee.' She pressed her forehead to his.

Closing his eye and leaning toward her, he felt warmth spread from his head to his torso and limbs, his heartbeat steadying, slowing. When she sat back the feeling lingered.

'Thank you.'

She patted his arm. 'Now. What didst thou wish to ask of Magda?'

He told her his plan.

'Ah.' Magda sat quietly, her blue gaze unwavering.

The cat padded by and jumped up onto the bench beside Owen. Leaning against him, she began to groom.

'If thou art certain this is how to catch the fox, Magda will tell Alisoun in the morning.'

'You would advise me to find another way?'

'This is for thee to decide. It is thy reckoning, not Magda's. If Alisoun is able to help thee, she will. Magda will try to relieve her of other work on that day.'

'Bless you.'

She reached out and touched his scarred cheek. 'Magda will go to her at first light. And thou canst ask thy son in the morning. Now sleep. Thee and Lucie. Magda will stay in the hall, watching over all three who rest there.'

He poured himself another cup of wine, then thought to offer it to her.

She shook her head. 'Take that with thee.'

In the hall he gathered Lucie and headed up to their bedchamber, where they talked softly, sharing the wine, until sleep took them.

Bent over the table set up before the fire in the hall, Jasper shared breakfast with Gwen and his parents, listening to his father's proposal. He seemed to droop more with each word.

'Why me? I failed you last time.'

So that was the cause of his despondence. 'As a captain I am pleased with your performance on your first watch. More than pleased.'

Squinting at him, Jasper asked, 'Are you adding Alisoun in case I fail again?'

'No. I need at least one on each roof and hope to have one on the roof of the tavern. Who has impressed you lately at the butts in St George's Field?' Owen guided the men of the city in archery practice on Sunday afternoons, upholding an old royal order that would supply the king with sufficient experienced archers for war. Jasper assisted him.

'Ned Cooper has come along well.'

'Has he?' Owen nodded. 'That is good news, son. I can trust him to hear the plan beforehand and say nothing. Thank you. I will ask Hempe to talk to him.'

Jasper brightened. 'I am glad I can help. I will not disappoint you, Da.'

'What can I do?' asked Gwen, who had been listening intently.

Owen smiled on her, thanking God that the attack had not hurt her spirit. 'On that day, I would have you safe in the house.'

'But Da—'

'Today you might help out in the apothecary,' said Lucie.

The disappointed frown turned to a cautious smile. 'I can? You think me well enough?'

'I believe you are.' Lucie took her hand. 'There is much to do and I could use a helper.'

'But what about my lessons at the Ferribys'?'

'Until this is past I don't want you going so far,' said Owen. Seeing her disappointment he went to her, crouching beside where she sat. 'I am doing all I can to bring this to a close. If you are out and about, I will be distracted with worry. You do know how precious you are to me?'

Gwen flung her arms round him, kissing his scar. 'I do, Da. I will be good.'

'I propose that you spend time in the shop by my side on all days except the day the bishop departs,' said Lucie.

Gwen beamed.

Owen prayed she could keep that promise.

They were dispersing to their day's work when Brother Michaelo tapped on the garden window, motioning for Owen to join him.

'I am taking this to the castle.' He patted the leather scrip in which he usually carried his writing tools. 'A change of clothing for His Grace. But first, a woman who sleeps in the minster yard came to me this morning. She told me that she and several others saw a light in the palace last night, after I had departed. Only for a little while, flickering, moving along from the great hall toward the chapel.'

'Inside the palace?'

'Yes. They would see it as it passed the embrasures.'

'For a little while?'

'Yes. I thought it important. They swear none of them would dare to break into the archbishop's property. It is neglected, you know. Archbishop Neville should have men guarding it. The minster guards have their own responsibilities. They miss you.'

One of Owen's responsibilities in the former archbishop's household had been to ensure that both the palace in York and at Bishopthorpe were secure.

'I will have someone search it,' said Owen. 'You will spend some time with His Grace?'

'If he wishes. You are coming to speak with the widow Gunnell?'

'In a little while. I will see you there?'

'Of course.'

EIGHTEEN
Tracking a Fox

Alisoun arrived with the dog as Owen was talking to Hempe outside the apothecary workshop.

Hempe crouched down, scratching the pup's ears and being sniffed in return, then licked. 'A fine fellow. What have you named him?'

'Bard,' said Alisoun.

'Hah! A hound with a taste for a good tale.' Hempe laughed as he rose.

'Something like that.' She turned to Owen. 'Dame Magda came early this morning when I was breaking my fast with the new father. She was there but a moment, but time enough to tell me that you need me tomorrow morning. I said I would tell you before I went home to rest that I am glad to do it.'

'Good news. Did she say anything else?'

'Only that she will see to it I have the morning free. Though in our work we cannot always know what is ahead. Has Jasper agreed?'

'He has.' Owen could see the relief in her smile. Taking his turn to rub the dog's ears, he asked, 'Does Bard have a good nose?'

Hempe was nodding. 'You're thinking of the palace?'

Alisoun looked from one to the other. 'He does. Why?'

'I know you had a long night, but I wondered if I might beg a favor? Help me trace a fox to his den?'

Bard barked.

Alisoun laughed. 'He likes the sound of that.'

'I will explain what I need after Hempe and I settle the morning's plans.'

'We will await you in the kitchen. Might I introduce Bard to the children? I want him to know they are to be protected.'

Owen nodded. 'Gwen's in the shop, Emma and Hugh were telling Rhys a tale when I last saw them.'

'Magda said he'd awakened. I'm glad. Come, Bard, meet my
friends.' Alisoun and the pup moved as one.

'With Magda still here, how will those in need find either of
them?' asked Hempe.

'They're often both away. The children on the riverbank serve as
messengers.'

They finalized plans, Alfred going out to the smithy by the Green
Man to see what Frick had uncovered, Ned fetching the blood-stained
bedding from Gunnell's shop before joining Alisoun and Bard to
accompany them on the tracking. Owen would give them the hat
Reynard had dropped when Jasper chased him off the tavern roof.

Alisoun tucked the piece of bedding in her girdle, the hat in her
scrip. 'One at a time,' she said, 'in case one isn't the fox. Where
would it be best to enter the palace?'

'From the kitchen,' said Owen. 'Out of sight, and a place where
someone might check for food and drink.'

Ned nodded. 'I know the way.'

Bard barked.

Wykeham motioned Owen to the seat on his left, so that his sighted
side faced him. Again the small courtesy.

'I take it I am to depart on the morrow?'

'Yes. I doubt you wish to prolong this.'

'Indeed. I have been burden enough. But do you have time to
prepare?'

'I mean to make good use of the day.'

'I am grateful for all you have done, Archer.'

'After you are safely home, I would ask you to keep my family
in your prayers.'

'At the very least.' The bishop looked down at his hands, folded
in his lap. 'It was unwise to come, I see that now. I should have
entrusted the matter to my representatives. But what is done is done.'

'And you have the outcome you so desired. Which might not be
the case had you not been present to speak with Dame Marian.'

'Perhaps,' said Wykeham. 'It is kind of you to say so.'

'Trent worries about whether someone will see to the task of
receiving the stones when the barge arrives.'

'Assure him I have seen to it. He had mentioned John Gisburne.

I sent word that I counted on him to carry that out.' His tone was dismissive. Now that Dame Marian had agreed to return to Wherwell, did he not feel the need to follow through on the good deed?

'Have you spoken to Gisburne's factor?'

Wykeham waved the thought away. 'Trent said he had spoken with him.'

'Did you arrange for him to send word to you when the stones arrive?'

'They arrived yesterday and were sent downriver on a smaller barge to Clementhorpe. His messenger said all went well.'

'He will be glad to hear it. If I might ask, Your Grace, have you given any thought to assisting him in his return home? When he is sufficiently healed. The pack with his money was stolen.'

'You think me responsible for him? Or has he asked?'

'He is not yet thinking so far ahead. But it will fall to someone to see that he returns home to his family.'

'Very well. I will make arrangements.'

Sir Ralph began the meeting asking after Gwen. 'I regret that your work for me endangered your family, and that it keeps you from them at such a time.'

'No child ever had so many healing women surrounding her,' said Owen. 'My daughter is up and assisting my wife in the apothecary this morning.'

'That is happy news. You will be well compensated, but I know that will not make up for her suffering. Or your son's.'

Though Owen had explained his connection to the dead man and his partner, he had not mentioned the more personal reason Reynard might have had for attacking his family. He simply thanked the sheriff.

'You will be interested to hear that I dined with John Gisburne, Thomas Holmes, and the Graa brothers yesterday,' said Sir Ralph. 'They mentioned items disappearing at the staithes, asked if I might urge the mayor to investigate, as it hurts those within and without the city. I thought about the items we hold from the Gunnell house. Said nothing to them, but I hope to have news for them soon.'

'I do as well. Stealing directly from the ships?'

'They said the staithes, so perhaps as the goods are unloaded.'

Gunnell's shop was close enough to the staithes. 'Let's hope I have the opportunity to question him.'

'Indeed. Anything else?'

'What do you know of the brothers who found the body?'

'The brothers?' Sir Ralph paused. 'They live with their parents, are hard workers. Their father, Will Malton, a large, strong man in his day, until his knees gave way, hobbles about now, depends on his sons. Wife is a quiet woman. Ann, I believe.'

'I am curious whether they know why Bruin's corpse was stripped.'

Sir Ralph looked surprised. 'I had not thought to wonder why.' He paused, nodded. 'Now you mention it, the dead man was about their father's size. I will have one of my men ask them about it.'

'Thank you.' Owen had not expected that.

'I am keen to have you speak with Dame Alys. She complains about her treatment, particularly by you.'

'I regret that I addressed her harshly.'

'Understandable, but unhelpful. I trust you will find a way to coax her into cooperating. She did express gratitude for Brother Michaelo's visit in the evening.' A grin. 'That was a clever ruse. I do hope it works.'

'Brother Michaelo and I were followed home last night. Whether or not Reynard discovers the truth, it will at least distract him.'

Bard led Alisoun and Ned straight to the palace kitchen, whining and scratching at the door. When Alisoun pushed it wide, Bard raced inside, straight to a table near a window. Ned threw open the shutters. Oil and wax drippings on the table, fresh, not dusty.

'Look.' Ned crouched down and plucked several apple cores from the old rushes covering the floor, holding them out to her. 'Not been here long.'

She noticed bits of feathers fallen into the rushes and scooped up a handful. 'Someone has been fletching.'

Bard barked from a spot in the corner of the kitchen where the rushes had been mounded. He pawed it, then dragged out a long cloth. Alisoun retrieved it, scratching his ear in thanks.

'Stiff with dried blood,' she said. 'Looks like a bandage. Perhaps Reynard's injury from the first attack didn't heal.'

'If that's who's been here,' said Ned.

'The fletching suggests bowmen.' She held the bandage up to her nose. 'The wound has gone foul. Whoever it is, they're likely feverish.'

Ned crouched down where Bard still sniffled in the rushes. 'A lot of blood. Could he bleed for more than a week?'

'It depends on where he was injured, how deep the wound, and how well it was tended, though even a stitched wound can reopen if the patient continues to move about.'

'Jasper did say he'd stabbed Reynard in the gut with his arrow before the man tumbled off the tavern roof.'

'That would do it. We need to tell the captain.' She looked round for Bard. Called to him. When he did not appear she went still, listening, then headed out of the kitchen and up some steps.

'What is it?' Ned asked, close behind her.

'Bard. I heard a growl.' She put a finger to her lips and continued into a long passageway with rooms to the left and right. Bard's growls echoed up ahead. The way grew light and suddenly opened up into a great hall. The dog stood at a door on the far side that was slightly ajar. Seeing her, he ran back, circling her. 'Gone, are they?' Bard barked and wagged his tail. 'Good boy. Well done.' She crouched down, letting him sniff the blood-stained rag. Barking, he led her back to the door.

'We missed whoever it was,' said Ned, muttering a curse.

'No matter.' Alisoun gave Bard another good sniff of the piece of bedding. 'Where else was he?' The dog backtracked, taking them into a side corridor and down toward the chapel. That door was locked. But Bard was already returning to scratch at another door. Not locked. It opened onto steps leading down to an undercroft.

'The stonemasons will have a lantern,' said Ned, hurrying off.

'Come, Bard.' She led him out to the hall where she sat on a bench to wait.

Dame Alys stood at an embroidery frame near the one window, threaded needle in hand. Owen had not noticed much about the chamber the previous evening. Now he saw that it was well appointed, with fresh rushes on the floor, warmth radiating from a brazier, a small bed for Dame Alys and a pallet at the foot for her maidservant, a table, several stools and a bench, hooks for clothing, and the embroidery stand. Someone must have been sent to fetch it from the house. 'Again you make me wait, Captain.'

'I am a busy man.' Owen took a seat near the door.

With a sniff she proceeded to take a stitch.

'I had hoped to include your son Laurence in this conversation.'

She glanced up, betraying herself with a worried frown, fear in her pale eyes. 'You cannot find him? Or—?'

Owen realized she did not know where her son was and was frightened for him. 'No, we've not found him. Perhaps if you were to tell me the truth about his absence. The circumstances in which he departed. That would be to your advantage should he be in danger.'

'I told you. He was called away on business.'

'Where?'

'Why am I here?'

'As Bailiff Hempe explained, we brought you here to protect you. We do not believe Pete's death was an accident. Why don't you explain why you invited him to stay in your home?'

'He was grieving his master.'

A knock on the door. Owen bowed to the unhelpful widow and withdrew. It was Alfred, breathing hard. Remembering he had been sent out to check with Frick, Owen joined him in the corridor, closing the door behind him. 'What happened?'

'Frick and I were talking when who comes out of the Green Man but Laurence Gunnell. I followed him back into the city to John Gisburne's factor's office, that small shop in front of his manse on Micklegate. We have him down in the yard, waiting for your order.'

Gunnell had gone to the very man Wykeham had contracted to receive the stones. 'At last some good news. You managed to bring him all the way here alone?'

'The factor had one of his men assist me, and both accompanied me here. He said Gisburne wants no trouble with the sheriff. He's waiting in the yard to speak with you.'

'Gisburne's man of business?'

'Said he preferred that to having you seen coming to him. The struggle with Gunnell was bad enough for business.'

'Gunnell resisted?'

'Not as much as I'd expected, considering his bulk. Looks unwell, truth be told. But he did try to break away.' Alfred rubbed his shoulder.

'I'll come down to talk to the factor. Name?'

'Gordon.'

Owen tried the door next to Dame Alys's and found it unlocked, the room unoccupied. 'Get the keeper. Put Laurence Gunnell in this room beside his mother's.' Returning to Dame Alys, he said, 'You've no more need to worry. Your son is here at the castle.'

'God be— Why? Will he, too, be imprisoned?'

'You are the sheriff's guests, not prisoners,' said Owen. 'I will return after speaking with John Gisburne's factor.'

'What has he to do with this?'

'I will find out.' Owen bowed to her and departed.

Ned held high the lantern as he led the way down the steps. Alisoun ordered Bard to stay beside her as they descended. He might run free once she judged it safe.

'Empty but for those barrels,' said Ned.

Stacked high. Even from the steps she could smell the wine. Still she kept Bard at her side while Ned disappeared behind the stack of barrels.

'Someone sampled the wine. Aha! Another bandage.'

Alisoun joined him, now allowing Bard to explore. He sniffed the bandage, barked.

Alisoun remembered the hat in her scrip, drew it out. 'Bard.'

The floppy ears caressed the hat as Bard sniffed noisily.

'Track.'

He returned to the bandage.

'Reynard appears to be the one injured,' said Alisoun. 'Track, Bard.'

Nose to ground, he circled the empty barrel, once, twice, the circles growing wider, then moved to the steps.

'Wait,' Ned called. He'd rolled the barrel to one side and ran his hand over the stain, rubbed his fingers with his thumb, sniffed, then held out his hand to her. 'This isn't plain wine. Or blood. Oily.'

Alisoun smelled it. 'A salve for infection?' She crouched down, using a knife to dig up some of the wine-stained earth, examined it as she rose. 'Something added to the wine. I can't tell what it is, but I would guess to cleanse the blood. Or for pain.'

'A salve and something for pain. Fighting men might carry such things,' said Ned.

'Or someone is helping them.'

'Any way to know who by the ingredients?'

'That would take too much time. But it's something to tell the captain.' Alisoun called to Bard, let him smell the hat again, and followed him up the steps and out the hall door. The rain came down again. He spun in a circle, defeated. 'Rain washes it away, Bard. You've done well.' She thanked Ned. 'Tell the captain that it seems likely the bedding, bandages, and hat all carry the scent of the same man. And he might have consulted an apothecary. I'm off to sleep now.'

NINETEEN

Thieves and Soldiers

Owen found a quiet place out of the weather in which to talk to Gisburne's factor Gordon. Brother Michaelo sat near. He would listen, but not take notes. No need to risk silencing the man.

Gordon was watching Alfred and another guard escort Laurence Gunnell into the building in which his mother was lodged. Despite being safely inside the castle precinct, the man kept looking over his shoulder.

'Who is he expecting?' Owen wondered aloud.

Gordon chuckled. 'Unhappy customers?'

Gunnell stumbled as the door closed behind him.

'Sir Ralph will hear of your assistance in this,' Owen said. 'I know you are a busy man. If you could tell me what transpired.'

The factor brushed off his well-made tunic and nodded. He was of middle age, middle height and weight. Laugh lines suggested he was content with life. 'Laurence Gunnell presented himself as the man in charge of carting the stones to St Clement's for the bishop's man, who had been injured. I did not know what to make of that. They had already gone downriver to the landing at Clementhorpe.

Oversaw the loading myself yesterday. When I told him so, he shouted that I couldn't do that, he had his orders. Not from His Grace the Bishop of Winchester, I told him, and not from Gerald Trent, who had come to me shortly after he arrived in the city to arrange for the barge. He knew that to move so much stone a train of carts would be required, but it was easily done by river. He meant to be at Clementhorpe today to guide the lay brothers who would be moving them to the priory grounds. I had word to send one of my men along and did so. Heard Trent had been injured. Badly?'

'He will take time to heal.'

'At St Mary's, is he? I will pay him a visit when I've the time. He's far from home and friends.'

Working for Gisburne had not soured the man's disposition. 'That would be a kindness. Has Gunnell ever worked for you?'

Gordon looked puzzled. 'Never. He's a sailmaker, so he calls himself, though his work does not recommend him. I had not heard that he was trying his hand as a carter. He will fail at that as well if today's behavior is any sample. I heard that you were searching for him, so wasn't surprised to see your lieutenant.'

'We wanted Gunnell here for his own safety.'

'Oh?' The man looked keen to share something.

'Anything else about him you might tell me?'

'It's said he's making good money somewhere – some think on the staithes, where there have been reports of orders arriving incomplete. You know the sort of thing. Valuable items. We've suffered losses.'

'The guild knows the problem is here, not Hull?' Where most barges arriving in York were loaded.

'They have checked the shipping logs and found discrepancies between what was loaded there and unloaded here, and what makes it to the warehouses. Not to say the Hull merchants don't have their own problems.'

'What items have been short according to the logs?'

Gordon gave him a quizzical look. 'Sir Ralph asked for just such a list yesterday when he dined with my master and his colleagues. He has mentioned this?'

'He did. I had hoped that by today you might have a more complete list.'

'Happens I do, though not with me. But I have an excellent

memory.' He described much of the merchandise from the Gunnell cache now held in Sir Ralph's chamber, plus more.

'Any other names along with Gunnell's?'

'I take it from your interest that you will help end this thievery?'

'That would be to the benefit of all the city, would it not?'

'Answering questions with questions.' Gordon grinned. 'You are a sly one. I can name a pair of taverners. Barker, owns the Green Man outside Micklegate Bar, and Dunn, runs the Bell near the bridge.'

Reynard might be moving between the two taverns. 'How do they gain access?'

'That, Captain, is what we would all like to know.'

'You have been a great help. I'll walk you to the gate.'

'No need. I will find my way. You have work to do. I will give your regards to Master Gisburne.'

Seemed Gordon did not know of the bad blood between Owen and his boss. Owen watched the factor lift his hood and shrug down into his cloak as he hurried off. That he had come so far in this weather indicated how much it meant to his boss that the thieves were caught. But Owen did not expect gratitude. Not from Gisburne. He headed to the sheriff's chamber.

He found Sir Ralph complaining to Brother Michaelo about how long he had been away from his land and his family. 'My children will forget who I am. But it is my duty to stay until this is resolved. I am the one who set it in motion.' He nodded to Owen. 'Tell me this new arrival will reveal to us all we need to protect the bishop and sisters and bring the murderer to justice.'

'I cannot promise that, but with the bishop departing tomorrow, I believe Reynard will soon make his move. I would ask that you have your men watch the road between Micklegate Bar and the priory.'

'You won't go along the river? Or by river?'

'Those are my preferences, but I want to cover every possibility.'

'So many guarding against one man?'

'He is unpredictable. And it's likely he won't act alone.'

'How does a stranger gather supporters so quickly? In my experience the people of York eye newcomers with suspicion for a long, long while. Until they prove they might be trusted.'

'Reynard can be honey-tongued, very persuasive,' said Owen. 'Easily sniffs out those with something to hide from authority. Gisburne's factor said two taverners are suspected of working with Gunnell in robbing the staithes, from the Bell and the Green Man.'

A snort. 'Those two. I've never heard anything but complaints about either. Likely the source of more men, considering their clientele. But how would this Reynard find them in such short time?'

'Gunnell might know,' said Owen.

'He has much to lose by confessing,' said Michaelo.

'At the least he will lose a hand for the king, and his possessions,' said Sir Ralph, 'but if he cooperates he might live. By the sound of it he was headed for death outside the castle.'

That was true. But would Gunnell talk in the short time they had left? 'You will have your men watching the road tomorrow?'

'It will be done. You will be glad to see an end to this as well, I am sure.'

More than Sir Ralph could imagine.

'Do you have a watch on the Bell as well as the Green Man?'

Owen nodded. 'Might a few of your men go to the priory to ensure that no one is interfering with the delivery of the rocks?'

'Of course. You will talk to Laurence Gunnell next?'

'First Dame Alys. See what she might tell me.' Owen did not intend to linger if she continued to evade the truth. There was no time.

'Let's hope she's more forthcoming than she's been.' Sir Ralph nodded to Michaelo. 'Thank you for attending her last night.'

'I did it at the captain's request.'

'Then you both have my thanks.'

Once out in the corridor, Michaelo asked, 'Do you believe Gisburne's man?'

'In this, yes. He is protecting his employer's merchandise.'

'Captain!' Ned hurried towards them. 'Bard is a good tracker.'

'Alisoun thought he was. What did you find at the palace?' Owen leaned against the wall to listen to Ned's account. Interesting. Whoever wore those bandages would be weak with infection. The salve and whatever was in the wine would help, but once such inflammation set in, the body focused everything on fighting it. If Reynard was the one injured – and they had learned of two stabs to the gut – how had he managed to fight off Rhys and Jasper, then escape by foot and dive into the Ouse? He pushed off from the wall as Ned finished. 'What about the hat? Did Bard go elsewhere tracking that scent?'

'No. Not that we could tell. Once outside, the rain had washed away all scent.'

'So it was likely Reynard you just missed?'

'I believe so.'

'Good work, Ned.'

'It's Alisoun you should thank. And Bard,' he added with a blush. Still infatuated with Alisoun. 'I will.'

Michaelo cleared his throat. 'Dame Alys?'

'Of course. Ned, take a few others and search the rooms in the Bell. You've seen the bandages and the salve. I'd like to know whether Reynard's been hiding there.'

Ned nodded.

'One more thing. Jasper reminded me of your skill as an archer. I will need you in the morning, with your bow. You will be on the tavern roof, Alisoun and Jasper on the roofs of the apothecary and my house.'

'I will be there.'

Dame Alys looked up from her embroidery. 'Where is my son?'

'Resting nearby,' said Owen. 'I assure you he is safe.'

'Safe? You have taken him prisoner. He is not safe. Do you truly expect us to be grateful to be brought here against our will and left here to rot?'

Owen moved to the small window that looked out on the river, wondering how Reynard had fetched up in Gunnell's shop. Or had he first gone to the Bell?

'Are you listening to me?'

He turned to Dame Alys. 'I knew Raymond long ago. We called him Reynard, the wily fox. I watched how he set traps for the weak and used them for his purposes, let them take the blame. I am guessing that Laurence was already in trouble when Reynard trapped him.'

'You speak nonsense.'

'I know of his connection to the taverners who are stealing valuable goods on the staithes.'

'Laurence? You are mistaken.' Her tone was dismissive, but the hand holding the needle above the embroidery trembled. Noticing the direction of his gaze, she tucked the needle into the cloth and folded her hands together in her lap.

'John Gisburne is wise to him,' said Owen. 'Is that why Laurence planned to steal Snicket's hoard? To pay to transport the goods to London or some other port?'

'My son would never do such a thing.'

'I found a store of the goods in your home.'

'No.'

He chose a different tone, having little to gain by calling her a liar. 'I am not surprised he kept this from you. He would not want you to know that he was failing at his father's trade. But Reynard coaxed the information about Snicket's hoard from him, then nudged him toward the idea of blaming the theft on others, men already sought by us.' A guess, not a certainty, but she need not know. 'How clever that must have seemed.'

'I will not believe that of my son.' But her eyes flicked here and there, searching for surety.

'Were you in the house when Snicket's servant, Pete, was killed? Did Laurence push him from the solar?'

'Did my son murder the old man? How can you ask that?' Her voice broke and she sank back on the bench. 'No. It was not Laurence, I swear. Pete was walking about after my son departed.'

'As his mother you would say so.'

'I am certain of it! I went out for a time, to deliver food to a bedridden neighbor. You can ask him.' She pressed a hand to her forehead. 'Anyone who knows Laurence would never . . . But if you don't believe him, and John Gisburne suspects him . . .' She covered her face with her hands for a moment, seemingly whispering a prayer. When she was finished, she folded her hands in her lap. 'What will happen to him?' Her voice was softer, less confident.

'Reynard's plan is for Laurence to be tried for the deaths of Snicket and his servant, by which time the wily fox will be far from York with the old man's treasure.'

He watched that sink in.

'Unless you and Laurence help me stop him . . . I thought perhaps you might be able to convince your son to tell me all he knows.'

'Of course. If he is innocent, you will soon see your mistake.'

The 'if' spoke volumes.

*   *   *

Though he had dressed for business and slicked back his hair, Gunnell gave off a stench of too much ale, greasy food, and fear. Far different from the jovial shopkeeper he had seemed when Owen first met him outside Jonas Snicket's. While Dame Alys embraced him and drew him over to a bench by the brazier, the maidservant poured a bowl of warmed wine.

'What is a priest doing here? Is he meant to hear my confession?'

'I am making a record of the conversation,' said Michaelo.

'He kindly spent the evening with me,' said Dame Alys. 'I am grateful.'

'Pah.' Gunnell gulped the wine and wiped his mouth on his sleeve. 'Little better than piss,' he said, glaring at Owen.

'I doubt you've had better at the Green Man.'

'Is that where you've been, Laurence?' Eyes round with surprise, Dame Alys plucked at his sleeve, sniffed, made a face.

He jerked his arm from her. 'What lies has this one-eyed weasel told you? No. Do not bother to say. I am certain to learn in good time.'

Taking her son's hands, Alys bent low to look into his eyes. 'Now is the time to tell us the truth, then, Laurence. Show him his mistake. Make him understand that you have not been stealing from the staithes, that you did not covet Jonas Snicket's wealth, that the man you introduced to Pete is not this Reynard or Raymond wanted by the sheriff.'

Laurence watched his feet, not his mother, shaking his head long before she finished. 'They know nothing about my affairs.'

'John Gisburne believes he does.'

He went still at that, clearing his throat. 'What is Gisburne's part in this?'

'He and some other important merchants believe you to be responsible for the theft of their goods on the staithes.'

He met her gaze. 'Why? Because they see me on the riverbank? I am a sailmaker. As was my father.'

Dame Alys straightened, threw up her hands to Owen. 'I know this mood. He will not talk.'

Owen yanked Laurence up by his collar, ducking away from the man's half-hearted swing, and tossed him face down on the rush-strewn floor, catching his hands behind him and tying them.

His mother gasped. 'You are hurting him.'

Jerking him to an upright position, Owen held him up until he found his feet. 'We'll remove him from the comforts he might have enjoyed here. A few days in a windowless chamber down near the water might loosen his tongue.'

Brother Michaelo bowed to Dame Alys and opened the chamber door.

'Wait, I pray you.' She went to her son. 'Laurence, you must clear your name. Tell them all they need to know. This man, Reynard, he is not your friend. He cares nothing for your welfare. Pete is dead. Did you know? I found him crumpled and broken at the bottom of the ladder to the solar.'

'He could not live with what he'd done. Helping those men, the ones who attacked the bishop's men.'

'Is that what happened? He took his own life? In our home?' Dame Alys crossed herself and looked to Owen.

'Come along, then,' Owen said, pushing Laurence from the chamber.

Michaelo followed, closing the door behind him.

In the corridor, Owen pushed Gunnell at a guard. 'Throw him in one of the river cells.' Deep down, damp, without even the smallest opening for air.

'Is that necessary?' asked Michaelo.

'We will bring him up later today. When he's had time to think.'

As he walked down Castlegate, Owen felt pushed along by a rising wind that carried the scent of rain. Pray God it ended by morning. He sensed something building in Brother Michaelo, who walked beside him.

'What is it?'

'When I brought His Grace a change of clothes, he begged my forgiveness for wearing my finest robes, offering to have them replaced. He would consult Princess Joan, he began, and then went quiet. For he cannot at present, can he? I assured him that was unnecessary. He is beaten. They have diminished him. And to what end? I do not understand Lancaster.'

'The royal family is shaken by the death of Prince Edward, and the king's decline,' said Owen. 'Lancaster perhaps most of all, imagining enemies closing in round them.'

Michaelo glanced at him in surprise. 'Yes.'

At the minster gate, Brother Michaelo turned to Owen. 'May God watch over you, my friend. And may Sir Francis prove to have chosen his men wisely.'

'Ask Jehannes how I would arrange for a requiem service in the palace chapel. For tomorrow morning.'

'A requiem?'

'It is time we buried Rhys's brother David. I think the stone-masons will wish to attend.'

'I see. I will do all I can to assist him in arranging this,' said Michaelo. 'I should have it in hand by the hour of none.' He turned away, disappearing through the gates as a gentle rain began to fall.

In the abbey guest house, Owen found Sir Francis and his men already at the butts. Those watching stayed beneath the eaves of the building, keeping dry their bowstrings. Hal was up at the moment, aiming, unflustered by the sound of someone approaching, his stance excellent. He hit the center of the target.

'Well done, Hal!' Sir Francis was beaming as he turned to greet Owen. 'My best archer.'

'Let's see the others,' said Owen.

Mark took position next, his stance tight, tense.

Stepping up behind him, Owen put his hands on the man's shoulders. 'Shrug and release,' he said.

Once Mark had done that, his shoulders were more at ease.

'Now,' said Owen.

The arrow found a spot close to center.

'Good,' said Owen. 'Remember that.'

Phillip was next, the page glancing back at Sir Francis with uncertainty.

The knight smiled and nodded.

Turning back, Phillip notched the arrow and lifted the bow up, up.

'Too high,' said Owen.

Phillip lowered the bow, aimed, relaxed his shoulders, let the arrow fly. A hand's breadth from center.

'Are you better at a farther range? Is that why you aim high?' Owen asked.

'I don't usually stand so close,' Phillip admitted, as if he felt it a mistake.

'Choose your distance.'

Phillip moved back seven paces. This time his arrow hit center.

Owen looked back to Sir Francis. 'Station him farthest from where you believe the danger,' he said. He nodded to Phillip. 'A far shooter is a gift to a captain.'

Gathering them round in the entrance to the guest hall – no need to stand in the rain – he told them of Reynard's possible gut injury. 'Do not count on this. Be ready for him to be in good form.' They should watch him to see if he favored one side or the other. His other weakness was a tendency to favor his right when checking his surroundings. His power was in the speed with which he notched the next arrow and aimed. Madoc, on the other hand, was slow, and with age and additional weight he might be more so. But he'd had the farther range. They should be prepared for that.

They practiced a while longer, with Owen adjusting positions. Even Sir Francis and Carl took their turns, proving themselves less accurate than the others, but adequate in support, to keep arrows flying.

When the rain intensified, they retreated to the guest house to dry themselves by the fire with cups of ale.

'I will keep the men at the abbey tonight. They will be rested for tomorrow,' said Sir Francis. 'Pray God the storm passes by then.'

They talked strategy. Owen described the route from the minster close to the bridge and then down along the river. Crispin Poole would guide them from there. He talked them through watching the rooftops, and assured them he would have men along the way, especially in the Old Baile.

'The day will begin shortly after dawn with a mass in the chapel of the archbishop's palace,' said Owen. 'During the service I need you guarding the palace and the yard around it. Phillip will be an asset. After the mass, we will proceed to St Helen's churchyard for the burial. I will have archers on the roof of my house as well as the apothecary and the York Tavern. Place your men to complete the circle.'

'How will we recognize the enemy?'

'Look for unusual or furtive behavior, and watch the movements of the bailiff George Hempe and Crispin Poole. It will become clear. I will explain more in the morning.' He did not tell them that the bishop was already at the castle. Neville's men were likely trustworthy, but Owen preferred to tell them only as much as they needed to know.

TWENTY
Setting Up the Board

As he approached the palace kitchen, Owen half expected Maeve to open the door, beckoning him in. Archbishop Thoresby's cook had been devoted to keeping up Owen's strength, tempting him with meat pies, cheese, fine bread – he had enjoyed every morsel, the quality of her creations equal to that of Tom Merchet's ale. But today he found an echoing silence and the smell of old fires, damp, and the stench of rotting rushes and animal droppings. He found the corner with the blood-stained rushes, plucked some up to take out into the light. Perhaps a day old.

Pushing on through, he explored the rooms off the kitchen passage, up into the echoing hall. How bitter he had been when he first entered this place. Half-blinded and then robbed of the life he had made for himself in the old duke's service, sent on a mission to a land of snow and sleet, streets crowded, noisy, cursed with the bells of what seemed a hundred churches crammed inside the walls, he had hated everything about his new life. Most of all, he had hated Reynard.

Leaving the great hall, he continued to the more private chambers. He had spent many an hour in Thoresby's parlor. Day and night a fire had burned, a flask of brandywine and cups set near the archbishop's favorite high-backed chair. His throne, Owen had thought it. Gradually his bitterness had eased, or been diverted toward resentment of the time spent away from Lucie and his growing family. He had earned the respect of the people of York, finding friends in unexpected places – Dom Jehannes, once Thoresby's secretary; the Merchets; Dame Magda . . .

He found blood smeared on the windowsill. Still not proof it was Reynard who was weakened.

As he moved on toward the chapel, listening for sounds, tasting the sour air, Owen felt at peace with his new plan for the morning, and with his purpose in flushing out the fox and his cubs. At first he had sought revenge, but no longer. Reynard's attempt to destroy him had been the catalyst turning him away from the life of a captain of archers to something much more satisfying. The fox and his comrades must answer for their present crimes, not those of the past. Completing his circuit of the palace and finding no one lurking in the shadows, Owen headed home to dine with his family.

Dame Alys hissed as her son was half carried, half dragged into her chamber, his bare feet caked with dirt and blood.

Owen motioned toward a bench opposite where he sat with Michaelo so that the light would illuminate Gunnell's every expression.

The man slumped on the bench and demanded to know with what he was charged.

'Theft at the very least,' said Owen. 'We found in your house a quantity of stolen items. This is your opportunity to confess your part in the attack on Jonas Snicket. We are of the impression that you planned it and carried it out with the assistance of his servant Pete, whom you later silenced with a push from the solar of your home.'

'Pete? No.' Gunnell caught himself. 'I am saying nothing until I have food, drink, and shoes.'

'So be it,' said Owen, nodding to the guards. 'Take him back.'

The guards advanced on Gunnell, who looked to his mother. 'Tell them I am innocent.'

'No more, Laurence.' Her tone was sharp, not placating as before. 'As it is I must spend the remainder of my days atoning for my silence, praying that it is not too late to save my soul.'

'You will not abandon me!' he cried, the demand of a child stamping his foot in outrage.

Dame Alys turned to Owen. 'I will tell you all you want to know on the condition that you permit me to retire to my brother's house in Wakefield to live out my life in peace.'

'That is not for me to say. But if you help the sheriff in this, I believe he would accept your banishment from York.'

Gunnell squirmed as the guards lifted him from the seat. 'Mother!'

She looked away, turning back to Owen only when the door shut, muting his curses. 'Some wine,' she said to her maidservant, sitting with eyes closed until the bowl was put in her hands. Sipping it, she met Owen's gaze. 'I pray you are never so disappointed in your child,' she said. 'You were correct, of course, he failed at his father's trade. I watched and said nothing, believing he would pick himself up and start again. My fault he took to theft while pretending the shop was doing well?' She crossed herself. 'It might have gone on this way until Gisburne and the others tracked him down and had their way with him. But Reynard found him first, insinuating his way into the shop and taking up residence. My son foolishly believed he might offer the man a portion of the gain from the plan he and Pete had devised to steal old Snicket's treasure. They waited only for Laurence to find a trustworthy company of travelers with whom to go south to London. So he proposed the partnership. Stupid, stupid man. How could he not see the trap? From that moment Reynard had only to threaten taking the tale to the sheriff to get what he wanted from my son. The attack was his command. The money? Laurence has not seen it since handing it over to the man. But as I said, Laurence was gone before Pete's fall. The other one escorted him from the city. The large man. Madoc.'

'When did you learn all this?'

'He confessed all to me not long before Madoc took him away. Some I had guessed earlier – the chests of stolen items.'

'Who was it attacked Jonas Snicket?'

'Laurence and Pete. When I learned that Pete had gone to you pretending to be a victim, I lost all pity for him. Wicked old man. I left the house, my excuse my ailing neighbor. I could not trust what I would say when Pete woke, and I had promised Laurence I would say nothing.'

'Have you any idea where Reynard and Madoc are now?'

'None. In truth, I would not know Reynard if I passed him in the street. He has kept out of my sight.'

'Is he injured?'

'I know nothing about that. Madoc has a slight limp and a bandage on his neck.'

'Are there others with them?'

'I know only of my son's connection with the pair.'

'Has he spoken of the taverners of the Bell and the Green Man?'

'The Bell is so near the shop. Laurence mentioned it from time to time. But no names, and nothing beyond a place to retreat to in foul weather. I do not understand what he was doing at the Green Man.'

'Why did you not come to us?' Owen asked. 'Save him from himself?'

'I could not betray my son. I know the punishment for theft.' She eyed him coldly. 'You will see with your own.'

God grant Owen never knew the pain.

'What I know of Reynard is that he takes credit for blinding you,' she said. 'He boasts of it as proof of his prowess. Yet he hates you still. Madoc does as well. Is it true? Was it this Reynard who blinded you?'

'He failed in his duty the night I was injured, deserting his watch so that a spy could sneak into the camp. I fought the spy and his woman, not Reynard. But I am not surprised he changed the tale of his shame.'

'Do you hate him?'

'I did once. No longer – at least not for that.' For the threat to his family, yes. Owen rose. 'I am grateful for all you have told me.'

Brother Michaelo followed him from the room. 'She knew so much and said nothing all this time. Why now?'

'I imagine her son is wondering the same thing. Shall we see?' Owen saw the monk's reluctance. 'Perhaps you might tell Sir Ralph of tomorrow's burial. That Walter and Arn should be allowed to clean themselves for being released into my care tonight. Have them carted to Jehannes's garden shed with David's coffin. Under guard.'

Michaelo bowed. 'I will go to them after that? Tell them?'

'Yes. I will find you there.'

The lantern caught the sheen of damp on the stone walls, the dust rising from the foul rushes. The cell held the ghosts of former prisoners, their gut-emptying fear, the damp overlaying it. Gunnell had yet to make his mark. As the man struggled to sit up, Owen saw the blood-smeared face. He'd been wrong. Gunnell would leave his mark in this dark place.

'Come to gloat?'

Owen called for clean rags, water, a jug of ale and two bowls. He placed a bench near the door. 'No. I have seen my fill of men like you. I find no sport in kicking you.'

A guard returned with the rags and water.

'Clean your face, then wash out your mouth,' said Owen.

Gunnell made fast work of it. By the time he handed the bucket to the guard, another had come with the ale.

'Wash out the taste with this.' Owen poured a bowl and handed it to Gunnell.

'You have me treated like a cur, then show mercy. Why?'

Owen settled on the bench. While Gunnell drank, he began the tale of a captain of archers and his best marksman, through to the night of betrayal.

'What then?'

'My injuries were all that I knew for months. As the fog of pain lifted for me, my trusted men helped me remember who had the watch that night, who failed me. For a while I would not hear it, mired in my own failure. I was the fool to trust the jongleur. But I did consult with the old duke, who had already listened to Leif, my second, and sent a captain to investigate. Reynard expressed remorse, begged a chance to prove himself. "Trust that he will never see advancement in my ranks," said the old duke. "Look now to your own healing. I need my captain back."'

'You shrugged and moved on.' Gunnell spat into the rushes. 'And he was someone else's problem.'

Owen deserved that. Had he insisted on punishing Reynard, expelling him – how many victims might he have saved, not just those he knew of? 'In time, when my eye did not open to the light, the old duke found another use for me.'

'Reynard sounds no better, no worse than most.'

'The danger in him was his skill in turning good men into his toadies to punish others for resisting him, abandoning them when caught.'

Gunnell grunted. 'As he did me. Is that why you are here? To shame me?'

'The memories are snapping at my heels. To talk of them might release their hold. You are a captive audience.' Owen lifted the jug. 'More?'

Gunnell held out the bowl.

Owen settled back. 'We found a bloody rag in the kitchen of the archbishop's palace. Blood-stained rushes. The stench of sickness in the bandage. I see no such injury on you.'

'No.'

'Whoever it is will die without help.'

'You think I don't know that?' Gunnell turned away.

'That bothers you.' He had found Laurence's conscience.

'He was an innocent. One of the Malton brothers. Noah. Madoc slashed him for trying to run.'

'You saw this?'

'No. Madoc told me. Warned me.'

'Where is Noah now?'

'They tell me nothing. Saw the young man once. He and his brother helped search Snicket's house. Last I saw them.'

Tragic. If true. 'Where is Reynard hiding?'

'I told you, they tell me nothing. Haven't seen him since he took the chest we found in Snicket's house. He moves about by night, for the most part. At least that's how it was when he hid in my shop.'

'Anyone else sleep in the shop?' Gunnell shook his head. So it was almost certainly Reynard's scent on the bedding, the bandages, and the hat. 'Madoc, the Malton brothers, who else joined him?'

'Two taverners, but they're no threat to you. Provide food, drink, sometimes shelter. Reynard trusts only Madoc with weapons.'

'Not the brothers?'

'I don't know how he's using Abel. Sounds like Noah's of no use.'

'Where does Madoc hide?'

'Nowhere and everywhere. I'd say you trained them well, Captain.'

'You are quiet,' Michaelo noted as they crossed the city. 'Setting the pieces on the board?'

'Searching for the weakened king. Or the pawn.'

'Do you believe it is the Malton brother who is injured?'

In addition to Reynard, perhaps. Unless some dark angel watched over the fox. Alisoun and Ned had just missed whoever Bard was tracking. Could the dog have confused the scents? But why would Noah run from them? No. Even had the fox bandaged Noah, leaving his scent on the rag, there was the bedding and the hat. More likely someone asked about a bloody bandage and a tale was spun, pointing to one easily discarded. Where were the brothers now? Should Owen call off the search on the river? Or might Reynard choose the river over rotting in some hole?

'Owen?'

Startled by the monk's use of his given name, he met the worried gaze. 'It doesn't fit.'

'Care to tell me why?'

The monk nodded as he explained. 'I see.'

This monk, once his enemy, was now his partner. And Owen hated the favor he must ask him. But not out here. 'I will not rest easy until this is resolved. Not for my satisfaction, but for the safety of all taking risks to bring the two to justice.'

'We have a common purpose,' said Michaelo. He nodded ahead. 'We have been sighted.' One of Wykeham's servants stood in Jehannes's doorway.

With no time even to remove his cloak, Owen was set upon by Wykeham's priests and servants, clamoring for assurance that the bishop was comfortable, demanding to know when they might join him.

'His Grace is enjoying Sir Ralph's hospitality. He is quite comfortable. You will see him after the requiem and burial tomorrow morning.'

Dom Jehannes whisked Owen and Michaelo into his parlor, shutting the door. 'I cannot fault them. They feel responsible for His Grace, body and soul. But I have good news. When the dean opposed our using the chapel tomorrow, Dom Antoine sought Sir Francis's help, quite wisely. The knight informed the dean that Sir John Neville would approve, that they were sent to assist you, Captain, in any way necessary to protect Bishop Wykeham and rid York of the outlaws. The dean suggested St Helen's, offered to speak with the pastor, and all is arranged. Dom Sebastian has offered to preside over the mass and burial. Dom Antoine and I will assist. Now. Tell me how this came about, and what you hope to achieve.'

'First let me add the last detail to the ceremony,' said Owen, looking to Michaelo.

TWENTY-ONE
Requiem

Almost dawn, a hint of light to the east. Owen lay on the roof of Jehannes's house, watching, waiting, bow beside him, arrows ready. Word had gone out round the city of the unexpected honor being given the fallen David Wells: a mass in St Helen's, burial in the churchyard, by order of the Bishop of Winchester, a peace offering as he departed the city. Peace for whom, people would wonder. Not for those with reason to hate Wells and his kin for the murder that alerted Owen to their presence. And why? David had attacked the bishop's men. They would puzzle over it in the taverns for days to come.

Down below, a figure stood in the hall doorway, awaiting his cue. Behind the house, men guarded the coffin. David's body had been brought by cart from the castle to the archbishop's chapel after sunset, Walter and Arn lying pressed to either side of the coffin beneath the covering cloth. Dom Jehannes, Brother Michaelo, Dom Antoine, and Dom Sebastian had taken turns sitting the vigil, Owen's men on watch in the shadows. In the archbishop's palace beyond, Owen had moved among the rooms, listening. No sign of the fox, though nearby two men were pulled from the river, beaten, unconscious, but alive. The Malton brothers. Brother Henry made room for them in St Mary's infirmary. He found no old, festering wounds on either man. All were fresh.

After a fitful sleep in the early hours, Owen had broken his fast with Jasper, who was determined to greet the dawn on the roof.

Now, as light teased the darkness, Owen watched, listened. Though alert and ready, he was calm, the hour come at last. He thought only of Reynard's victims living and dead. He did not count himself among them.

Life stirred in the shacks of the poor in the shadow of the minster, making ready to disperse for the daylight hours. Owen waited.

At last, as dawn silvered the minster towers, he dropped a stone. Below him, the man stepped out from the archdeacon's doorway. He wore the dark, simple robes of a cleric, his modest appearance belied by a manservant rushing out with a fur-lined cloak. 'Your Grace, the chill,' he said, draping the cloak around his master's shoulders, the hood over his head. As His Grace walked slowly back and forth down below, prayer beads softly clinking, Owen watched the trees in the yard, the rooftops, listened for footsteps. All was quiet.

His Grace retired into the house as Sir Francis and his men arrived. Making his way down, Owen greeted them, taking the knight aside to inform him that the requiem had been moved to St Helen's across from his home, discuss the strategy.

'Abbot William wishes me to inform you that he disapproves,' said Francis. 'Though I guessed your purpose, I did not argue with him.' He took a deep breath. 'You have complicated the departure. Do you expect more than Reynard and Madoc?'

'I can't be certain. Tell your men to look to mine, notice who they're watching.'

'Of course. I wondered. The man in the bishop's cloak. It's not . . .' He stopped when Owen held up his hand. 'It is a risk,' said Francis.

'All who participate in the ceremony are at risk,' said Owen. 'I pray I can depend on you and your men to assist mine in protecting the crowd?'

'You may be sure of that, Captain.'

While Owen observed Neville's men taking their posts for the procession, the master mason from the minster works and Marcus Bolton, David's last employer, approached, leading a group of men who worked in the yard. Dom Jehannes stepped out to greet them, escorting them to the coffin waiting on the cart.

Owen moved on to the church, searching it with Alisoun and Bard before helping Rhys across the street and placing a stool for him beside where his brother's coffin would sit during the mass. Late the previous day, Owen had arrived home to discover him standing with one arm round Magda and the other round Kate, taking shuffling steps. Not only conscious and sitting up, but walking? 'What miracle is this?'

'He woke with a cramp in his leg. It will weary him more than Magda would like, but pain, too, is wearying.'

'Good,' Rhys gasped. 'It's gone.'

Owen helped them seat him on the settle by the fire, while Kate took his bedding outside for a good shake.

'If we help you cross to St Helen's Church, do you think you can sit through your brother's requiem in the morning?' Owen asked.

Rhys had looked at him in wonder. 'It is happening? Where will he be buried?'

'Outside in the churchyard. I warn you, there is danger. But you will be guarded, and your brother will be blessed and buried.'

The grieving brother sat quietly now, head bowed, praying, as the bells of St Helen's began to toll overhead.

Leaving him in the company of Tupper Merchet, Owen went out to watch as the coffin bearers and clerics processed through the minster gates and crossed into Stonegate. A few brave souls stood outside their doors watching. Owen signaled for all guarding the church and churchyard that the procession was near.

Still no move from Reynard and company.

Arn and Walter carried the coffin into the church, assisted by Marcus Bolton and the master mason. Then uncle and cousin supported Rhys to the coffin, all three bowing their heads to pray.

Throughout the service all the worshippers stood tense, heads turning at the smallest, unexpected sound. Owen had not expected such a sizable crowd, could not guess how many were there because the tale of the brothers touched their hearts, how many in defiance of those who wished to terrorize their city, how many merely curious.

Slipping from the church as the mass ended, Owen slowly walked past his home, the apothecary, the York Tavern, and down along the south end of the cemetery. He paused a moment at the south steps, watching the gravedigger tidy the hole for the coffin. Nodding to him when the digger glanced up, his eyes wary until they saw who stood there, Owen continued his circuit, moving up the far side toward Stonegate, closing his eye now and then to listen and reach for a sense of danger. A prickle of something, but faint. He saw no sign of what it might be. At the corner opposite the church he entered a goldsmith's shop as arranged earlier and up to the first floor, moving through a cluster of excited apprentices to take his place at the window. He warned them to back away, then readied his bow.

The procession flowed out of the church, Dom Antoine and Dom Sebastian followed by Dom Jehannes and His Grace, then the coffin, with Arn and Walter to the fore, the masons behind. After the coffin came Lucie and the children, quickly crossing the street and disappearing into the house. Owen breathed a little easier. Now came neighbors and men from the minster stoneyard, some hastening away, others walking solemnly up among the graves. Tupper Merchet and Rhys brought up the rear, going straight to Owen's house. The brother would have his moment at the grave later.

Sir Francis and his men closed in around the walled churchyard, watching the rooftops and windows as well as the crowd. As Dom Antoine intoned a prayer, Owen saw movement in a window to his right. An arrow flew out, striking His Grace, another arrow flying from the apothecary roof, over the people clustering around the fallen cleric, striking the shooter in the window. He jerked, then slumped over the windowsill, bow and arrow tumbling down into the street. Canter. *Well done, my son.*

In the midst of the chaos round the grave, a large man threw back his hood and rushed Arn, knocking him down. Marcus Bolton bent to help and was pulled away by one of his fellows as an arrow pierced the thigh or hip of the attacker. On the York roof, Ned reached for a replacement arrow. Bolton grabbed the wounded attacker and threw him off Arn. Walter helped his son to his feet, supporting him. Dom Jehannes tried to quiet the crowd, motioning for Antoine to continue as he bent to His Grace. Hempe pushed through the crowd, plucking up the one who had tackled Arn, dragging the flailing man away. As Owen had guessed, it was Madoc. Ned had shot him through the thigh.

Dom Antoine turned from the grave, blessing the crowd. Dom Jehannes helped His Grace to his feet, solicitous, helping remove the heavy cloak with the arrow, revealing Brother Michaelo, shaken, but uninjured.

They had Madoc and Canter. Where was Reynard?

Sir Francis and his men departed with Wykeham's servants and priests, and the bishop's cloak. They would meet His Grace at the castle, then cross the river to the priory by barge. Crispin Poole was in charge of the archers who would guard them from the Old Baile once they crossed out of the castle's protections. Brother Michaelo had withdrawn to Jehannes's to shed the chain mail, complaining of its weight. He'd been winded, and anticipated a painful bruise, but nothing serious. Magda and Lucie were caring for Arn in the house. The knife had gone deep. Owen had left Walter pacing in the garden, watched by two of the sheriff's men.

But Reynard was still out there.

Jasper stood near the garden gate, looking out toward where Madoc and Canter lay bound and under guard. 'He's the one who attacked us,' he said. 'Madoc, not Reynard.'

'And on the tavern roof?'

'No. Pale hair. So it *was* Reynard I stabbed with the arrow. I am glad. But where is he? Why wasn't he here?'

'He is here.' Owen felt it in his bones, and saw it in Madoc's eyes as he watched him, trying to look smug but faltering – he was in pain, the arrow through his thigh forcing him to lie with the leg bent. Reaching down, Owen gave the arrow a twist. Madoc clenched his teeth, barely daring to breathe. 'Where is the fox?'

'I see he has you worried. He is out there laughing. Three of us against so many. And still he's free.' Madoc coughed.

'I'll help you up.' Owen lifted him up by his collar, propped him against the coffin cart, then punched him in the face. And again. Blood flowed from his nose. 'That's for my children.' Punched him in the gut. 'And for Rhys.'

Doubled over, Madoc still could not resist peering up with a bloody leer. 'And the cousin?'

'I'll allow you that.' Owen nodded to Hempe. 'Toss him in the cart.'

He crouched down to Canter. 'What did he offer you?'

'Not enough,' the man mumbled, looking at the arrow in his shoulder. 'I'm ruined for the bow.'

'Some of Jonas Snicket's hoard?'

'And escaping the north. We're nothing here.'

Madoc chuckled. Owen reached out and fiddled with the arrow in his thigh. 'Quiet.' He studied Canter, took hold of his hands, examining the bruised and scabbed knuckles. 'Who helped you beat the Malton brothers and toss them in the river?'

'That bastard.' He nodded toward the cart.

'Toss him up,' he told the men. Canter was Hempe's to bloody, his recruit. Jasper had caught him in the shoulder, preventing him from taking another shot. He'd commended his son on his choice. *I thought it's what you would do.* He was right.

He called to Alisoun and Bard. 'Let's hunt a fox.'

Alisoun refreshed Bard on Reynard's smell with the bandage and the handful of blood-soaked straw, hoping the scent was still strong enough. They set out, circling the walled cemetery.

At first Bard meandered, unable to find a trail. But just past the house where Canter had positioned himself, the dog shot into a narrow alley and straight to a small cart tucked beneath the eaves. He circled it, then headed to the back of the house, spinning around, then running to a partially collapsed shed. Barking, he returned to Alisoun, sitting at her feet.

Owen crouched down and peered into the shed, saw the eyes, smelled the prey, the wounded fox, huddled in a corner.

Alisoun fetched the cart.

'Took you awhile . . . lordling Captain.' A weak chuckle. 'Ran you a . . . merry chase.' Reynard slurred his words, his breath rasping. Owen smelled wine on his breath. 'Saw it all. Outwitted us . . . in the end. Madoc missed the . . . switch. If I'd . . .' He closed his eyes, his breathing shallow.

Owen reached in to draw Reynard out by his feet, the stench of sweat, sickness, wine, and the festering wound stinging his nose. He helped him sit up. Fever wrapped Reynard in heat, yet he shivered. In the light, the visible signs of impending death, the mottling of the skin, the stain on the stomach blood mixed with pus.

'You crawled in there to die in peace?'

'Peace.' The attempt to spit left Reynard gasping for breath.

Alisoun helped lift the dying man into the cart, then crouched to Bard, rubbing his ears. 'Where shall we take him, Captain?'

'The tavern yard. We'll ask Magda what might ease his misery.' It might revive him sufficiently to answer for himself.

'Don't want your pity.'

'Nothing more than I would do for any suffering creature,' said Owen, picking up the cart handle and maneuvering out of the alley.

'Cut me down, damn you,' Reynard shrieked. 'End this.'

A woman hurrying by crossed herself.

'It was over for me long ago,' said Owen. 'You might have proved me wrong, gained a lord's trust. What did this festering hatred gain you?'

'Hell.' The fox closed his eyes and curled round his rotting flesh.

Late in the day, Owen sat by the fire in Sir Ralph's parlor in the castle.

'My men tell me Reynard curses when they apply the salve Dame Lucie prepared for him,' said the sheriff. 'Is it extending his life? Will he live to answer to the king's justice?'

'All that can be done is to make him more comfortable,' said Owen. 'With or without it, he has a few days left, at most a week, according to Dame Magda.'

'You took pity on your enemy?'

'I take no pleasure in his suffering. Madoc, on the other hand . . .' Owen sipped his wine.

'For attacking your children,' said Sir Ralph. 'I saw your handiwork. That I understand. And Canter – George Hempe instructed him with black eyes and a broken nose. I am sorry you suffered a betrayal. But you did say Reynard had a honeyed tongue.'

'Better men than Canter fell for it.'

'Still. Could he not see the man was ailing?'

'Madoc promised him Reynard's share.'

'A fool to believe such a man.' The sheriff shook his head, as if mystified. 'You might have heard that the Maltons have come for their sons. The father says Noah and Abel had dragged the corpse out into the field and stripped it. For him. Good cloth when cleaned and mended. Later that morning, Reynard and Madoc came accusing them of murdering their mate, threatening to kill them all unless the sons helped them. Father and mother were watched while the sons kept my men from the house. Later they took them away. Malton swears his sons are innocent. Should we believe him?'

'If for a moment either one saw gain in it, being beaten and tossed in the river sobered them,' said Owen. 'It seems sufficient punishment.'

'They have been talkative. Said Madoc arrived weeks before the others and struck up conversations in taverns, found friends in the taverners of the Green Man and the Bell. Barker and Dunn eventually offered him a share in their business with Gunnell, useful as a stranger, well-spoken.'

'I gave Madoc too little credit.' But in the end even Dunn and Barker had deserted him, taking off with Snicket's hoard on the day of reckoning. They'd been caught by the sheriff's men on the road south, recovering the old man's treasure for the king. Canter was the only one to hang on. And a few lads rounded up by Poole at the Old Baile.

'What of Walter and Arn Wells?' asked Owen.

'Bishop Wykeham wanted them sent to Winchester for trial, but I cannot permit that. Their crimes were committed on my land, and in the city of York.'

'They attacked the bishop's men. Murdered one of them.'

'And injured yours. They will be given a fair trial, I promise you. It was enough that I agreed to His Grace's wish that David Wells be buried with grace. What of young Rhys? Will he return to the land, or stay on here, to work in stone?'

'He says his place is with his mother, now alone.'

'Ah.' The sheriff raised his glass. 'It has been an honor to work with you.'

Owen raised his glass. 'And with you.'

'I am in your debt. I see why Prince Edward chose you.'

'You will sleep at home tonight?'

'Tomorrow. My men need rest before riding out.'

Owen drank deep, letting the fine wine warm him. Tonight he would sleep well.

TWENTY-TWO
Farewells

A Week Later

Cloaked against the early November chill, Rhys walked beside Gwen, taking his time. She felt grown up and responsible, escorting him to his brother's grave, and honored that he had asked her to gather some greenery from the garden to place there. She'd chosen rosemary for remembrance, and other herbs.

They had renewed their friendship as he grew stronger, sitting together after her lessons and her time in the apothecary. She had asked him for the truth about why he had come to York.

'I thought I might talk David out of helping Walter and Arn. And my mother wanted me gone. Called me a traitor to my father.'

'So why are you going back to her?'

'I'm all she has left. But now that Marcus Bolton has offered me employment, I am unsure. I have time to decide.'

He was not yet healed enough to travel. She saw that as he paused to catch his breath after climbing the few steps up into the cemetery. Magda had advised him not to travel for at least a few more weeks. By then, weather might prevent such a journey for months. She hoped he stayed.

As they made their way across to the fresh grave, Gwen tried not to think of the bones beneath her feet. It was a childish fear, and she knew better now. But her heart still raced. When they reached the grave, she said a prayer and then moved over to the wall to give Rhys time to talk to his brother.

Reynard lay in a small chamber, not unlike that in which the widow Gunnell had been lodged, warmed by a brazier. Fragrant herbs did little to mask the strong odor of dying flesh beneath the frequently changed blankets. It was a miracle he yet lived. Though his upper body was propped up with pillows, Reynard breathed with difficulty. Not yet a death rattle. He had refused the poppy drink Lucie had prepared for him. A friar wiped sweat from the man's face, then bowed to Owen and withdrew.

Feverish eyes watched as Owen took a seat beside the bed.

'Come to watch?' A labored breath. 'Make sure.' He sucked air. 'I die?'

'I trust the friar to tell me. And the guards.'

Reynard curled his lip. 'Saint Owen.'

An old taunt. Once it had cut. Long past. 'Why the complicated plan? Why not just slip into York and kill me?'

'Make you . . . martyr?' A weak, raspy cough. 'Not enough . . . wanted to watch . . . you . . . suffer . . .' A gasp. 'Ruin you.'

'Kill the bishop on my watch.'

A crooked leer. 'First . . . rape wife . . . slaughter child.'

Owen reared up and shoved the pallet, watching Reynard's eyes bulge as he gasped in pain. 'I would do far worse, but there's little sport in torturing a dying man.' He forced himself to return to his seat.

Reynard attempted a laugh, but choked. He fought to say, 'Pity. Plan ruined . . . when . . . bastards . . . attacked.'

Owen waited until he could trust his voice. 'You might have just buried Bruin. I would not have known of your presence until it was too late.'

'That was . . . plan.' Reynard closed his eyes, fought for a breath, managed to squeeze out, 'But Madoc said . . . you saw him.'

Madoc was wrong. Owen had not realized. It was only Reynard's presence that brought him to mind, made him wonder. 'I see.' He had his answer.

Still he sat, watching the struggle for breath. The anger had passed. He took no pleasure in the man's suffering.

Opening his eyes, Reynard rasped, 'End it.'

'I almost did once.' Owen had come upon Reynard sleeping in the shade at the edge of camp. He'd only that day been released to walk about, start to learn how to navigate with half his sight. He was furious, frustrated by the old duke's refusal to do more than chastise the traitor. Standing over him he felt again the hot pain as the blade sliced through his eye. He drew out his dagger, crept closer, reached out . . .

. . . Leif's large hand closed round his wrist. His second, and his closest friend. 'If you do you will regret it all your days.'

Owen had cursed him. And hated Reynard all the more.

Long ago. In another life.

'But for . . . son . . . had you . . . this time. But he . . . stabbed me . . . with arrow . . .' His body shook as he gulped air.

'Jasper reopened your wound.' Owen saw how it had gone. Falling from the roof, dirt in the freshly opened wound. Now the infection set in. 'But you were able to shoot Trent.'

The jaw tightened. 'Aimed for . . . your . . . second . . . not Trent.'

He'd meant to take Alfred, not the carter.

'Damn you . . . saint . . .' A rattling exhale, the eyes emptied. Silence.

'Be at peace.' Owen closed his lids.

*   *   *

While Jasper worked in the shop, basking in the praise of customers come to express their admiration and hoping to pick up a bit of gossip, Lucie and Gwen stood side by side in the workshop, stuffing small linen pillows with dried lavender, mugwort, rosemary, and chamomile for peaceful sleep.

'Why did you help Reynard?' Gwen asked.

'I hoped it might give your father time to talk to him.'

'Why?'

'So he might understand what happened. Then and now.'

'Then's when he betrayed Da the first time.'

'Yes.'

'Do you ever wish Da didn't have the scar?'

Lucie smiled. 'No. I love everything about your father just as he is. I wish he hadn't suffered the pain, and the doubt it caused him.'

'But without it, he would not have come to York and fallen in love with you. I wouldn't be here.'

'You see why I don't wish it happened differently.'

'Did you know you loved him the moment you saw him?'

'I . . .' How to explain to a child who had not yet felt the stirrings? 'Not at once, but there was something about him . . .' She smiled to herself, remembering the effect of his touch. 'I resisted it because I was still married.'

Gwen fiddled with the pillow in her hands. 'Like Alisoun should have resisted Einar if she truly loved Jasper?'

Ah, that's where she was leading this. 'Not just like it. They were not married. Or betrothed in the eyes of the Church. But your brother considered themselves pledged to each other. So to him, yes, it's very like that.'

Gwen sighed. 'I thought I loved Rhys. Now I don't know.'

For that, Lucie was grateful. But Gwen sounded so disheartened. Putting the work aside Lucie hugged her eldest to her heart. 'Enjoy dreaming of love, my sweet. When it comes . . .'

'It has thorns.'

Lucie laughed. 'Yes, my wise child. But so much joy and delight.'

'If he loves me back.'

'He is sure to love you, my sweet, my dearest.' Lucie held her close, silently praying that her child would find a love such as hers.

*   *   *

They sat on a fallen log by the river upstream from Magda's rock, beneath the trees. Late afternoon sunlight caught the gold of the falling leaves.

'I will miss you.' Alisoun slipped her hand in Jasper's and turned to look at him, the flaxen hair, the arched nose, strong, sharp chin, full lips, gentle eyes. So dear to her.

He tightened his hand round hers. 'Why not wait until spring?'

'You know why. Someone already needs me up on the moors.'

'They asked for Magda, didn't they?'

'She assured the man I have the skill to help his wife.'

'I don't doubt it. But are you ready?'

In truth she did not feel so. Yet Magda, her teacher, wished her to go. 'So she says.'

He frowned. 'What do you think?'

She dared say no more about it or she might reopen the wound, just as Jasper was finding his way forward. 'Wish me well.'

'I do.' He kissed her hand. 'I think I'll always love you.'

She touched his cheek, kissed it. 'And I you. But this is my life, going where I am needed. You would resent that.'

'If . . .' A lopsided grin. 'I would. I do.'

'Let's just sit here awhile.' She rested her head on his shoulder.

At the garden gate, Owen paused to take in the sight of his children chasing each other around the linden, laughing, shrieking as they were tagged. Behind them, Lucie bent to cut spikes of rosemary. As she straightened, she caught sight of him and smiled. He smiled back.

He was home, his enemy vanquished. All was well.